THE MARK TWAIN PAPERS

To Napier Wilt

"Tu se' lo mio maestro, e il mio autore. . . ."

Acknowledgments

M Y THANKS are due to graduate students enrolled in seminars dealing with Mark Twain at the University of Chicago for discoveries that they made when studying the following three works: Mary Jane Daicoff, Jessie C. Cunningham, and Allen D. Goldhamer—"Huck Finn and Tom Sawyer among the Indians"; Kerry Anne Reidy, Richard Eliel, and Robert Solotaroff—"Tom Sawyer's Conspiracy"; Claude Hubbard, Gordon L. Harper, and Robert W. Gladish—"Tom Sawyer: A Play."

Henry Nash Smith of the University of California several years ago very kindly arranged for the Mark Twain Company to grant me permission to edit these materials, and over the years he has helped me solve many baffling problems. Claude M. Simpson, Jr., of Stanford University scrutinized the manuscript as a representative of the Center for Editions of American Authors of the Modern Language Association and made useful suggestions for its improvement.

The Center for Editions of American Authors was generous in providing funds to support research. I am grateful to the Rare Book Department of the Detroit Public Library for making available for publication the manuscript of "Huck Finn and Tom Sawyer among the Indians"; and to the Doheny Collection at St. John's Seminary, Camarillo, California, for providing photocopy of some working notes for "Tom Sawyer: A Play."

Frederick Anderson, Editor of the Mark Twain Papers, not only gave much invaluable aid himself, he also efficiently directed the activities of a gifted group of young assistants at the University of California in Berkeley: Victor Fischer, Theodore Guberman, Bruce T. Hamilton, Mariam Kagan, Mark Miller, and Jill Newman served as typists and proofreaders. Michael Frank, Alan D. Gribben, Robin N. Haeseler, Robert Hirst, and Bernard L. Stein proofread and checked both texts and editorial matter. The number of errors which this group prevented me from making was incredible—or at least so I hope. So large was their contribution that I place their names here with regret: I would have preferred to place them on the title page along with mine.

WALTER BLAIR

February 1968

Contents

Abbreviations

MS	Manuscript
MT	Mark Twain
MTP	The Mark Twain Papers, University of California, Berkeley
SLC	Samuel L. Clemens
TS	Typescript
WDH	William Dean Howells

A1911	Anderson Auction Company, catalog no. 892—1911 ("The Library and Manuscripts of Samuel L. Clemens")
IE	Albert E. Stone, *The Innocent Eye* (New Haven, 1961)
LLMT	*The Love Letters of Mark Twain*, ed. Dixon Wecter (New York, 1949)
MMT	William Dean Howells, *My Mark Twain* (New York, 1910)
MTA	*Mark Twain's Autobiography*, ed. Albert Bigelow Paine (New York, 1924)
MTAm	Bernard DeVoto, *Mark Twain's America* (Boston, 1932)
MTB	Albert Bigelow Paine, *Mark Twain: A Biography* (New York, 1912)
MTBus	*Mark Twain, Business Man*, ed. Samuel C. Webster (Boston, 1946)

MTDW	Henry Nash Smith, *Mark Twain: The Development of a Writer* (Cambridge, Mass., 1962)
MTE	*Mark Twain in Eruption,* ed. Bernard DeVoto (New York, 1940)
MT&EB	Hamlin Hill, *Mark Twain and Elisha Bliss* (Columbia, Mo., 1964)
MT&HF	Walter Blair, *Mark Twain & Huck Finn* (Berkeley, 1960)
MTHL	*Mark Twain-Howells Letters,* ed. Henry Nash Smith and William M. Gibson (Cambridge, Mass., 1960)
MTL	*Mark Twain's Letters,* ed. Albert Bigelow Paine (New York, 1917)
MTN	*Mark Twain's Notebook,* ed. Albert Bigelow Paine (New York, 1935)
MTSatan	John S. Tuckey, *Mark Twain and Little Satan* (West Lafayette, Ind., 1963)
MTW	Bernard DeVoto, *Mark Twain at Work* (Cambridge, Mass., 1942)
NF	Kenneth R. Andrews, *Nook Farm: Mark Twain's Hartford Circle* (Cambridge, Mass., 1950)
SCH	Dixon Wecter, *Sam Clemens of Hannibal* (Boston, 1952)
WWD	*Mark Twain's Which Was the Dream?,* ed. John S. Tuckey (Berkeley, 1966)

Introduction

I

THREE OF Mark Twain's literary executors have noticed that, "imprisoned in his boyhood," he apparently was compelled to relate its story "repeatedly, in fiction, semi-fiction, and purported fact," drawing from it "images he would use in *Tom Sawyer* and *Huckleberry Finn,* and all his later writings of major importance."[1] In a letter of 1890 the author himself noticed that although his greatly varied careers had given him a wealth of literary capital, "I confined myself to the boy-life out on the Mississippi because that had a peculiar charm for me . . ." In a postscript he explained that he could not "go away from the boyhood period & write novels" about later epochs in his life because personal experience "is not sufficient by itself & I lack the other essential: interest . . ."[2]

The terms "boyhood" and "boy-life" are a bit too restrictive to indicate Mark Twain's favorite era unless they are stretched to include a youthful period beyond boyhood when the writer was an

---

[1] *MTW,* p. 49; *SCH,* p. 65; *MTDW,* p. 72. For a list of abbreviations, see pp. x–xi.

[2] *The Portable Mark Twain,* ed. Bernard DeVoto (New York, 1946), pp. 773–774, p. 9. The postscript was crossed out. As usual, Clemens exaggerated. He did not confine himself in the fashion indicated here in at least five novels and in many shorter fictional works.

1

apprentice and licensed pilot. Proof of the great personal appeal
that this period had for Mark Twain is offered by vast numbers of
notebook entries, letters, and writings, both published and unpublished, written during more than half a century. After early fragmentary and tentative uses of this material, in the seventies and
eighties Mark Twain made it the substance of his finest books—
Tom Sawyer (1876), the best parts of *Life on the Mississippi*
(1883), and *Huckleberry Finn* (1884). Thereafter, although he
tried again and again to evoke the magic of these works, he succeeded only in short passages—many of them stretches of his autobiography.

The writings in this collection attempt in various ways to mine
this vein. A significant part of only one of them, "Jane Lampton
Clemens," has been published; it was inserted unjustifiably in
Twain's *Autobiography*.[3] Written soon after the death of Clemens's
mother on 27 October 1890, it arranges and assesses a son's recollections of a vibrant personality important in shaping his life. At the
start the author turns to the time when he, a six-year-old, knelt with
his mother by the bed on which his dead brother lay—a harassing
experience that understandably seared the boy's memory. The
sketch moves on to a host of details about antebellum Hannibal, its
society and its attitudes towards slavery, and to vivid memories
about the child, his mother, and his father in the 1840's and 1850's.
The movement from a single remembered episode to a series of
loosely associated recollections was a typical performance in
Clemens's "autobiography" and his fiction.

The other pieces were concentrated in two periods, (1) between
1876 and 1884: "Tupperville-Dobbsville," "Huck Finn and Tom
Sawyer among the Indians," "Clairvoyant," and "Tom Sawyer: A
Play"; and (2) in the years 1897 to 1899: "Villagers of 1840–3,"
"A Human Bloodhound," "Doughface," "Tom's Gang Plans a

---

[3] There is no evidence that the author wrote this for the *Autobiography*; and
there is conclusive evidence that Paine juggled it out of its proper chronological
place. It first appeared among "Unpublished Chapters from the Autobiography of
Mark Twain," *Harper's Magazine*, CXLIV (February 1922), 277–280, dated in
accordance with internal evidence "1890–91." Later, in *MTA*, I, 115–125,
however, Paine included it in the section headed "Written 1897–8."

Naval Battle" (the date for these last two pieces cannot be established absolutely), and "Tom Sawyer's Conspiracy." [4] All these writings, particularly "Villagers," have biographical interest, and almost all have flashes of excellence; but all are brief compositions, fragments or failures. Factual pieces and autobiographical sketches have been placed at the start of this volume under the heading "Hannibal." The second section, "Huck & Tom," draws together fictional fragments, and the collection ends with a play based upon *Tom Sawyer*. Each is preceded by an introductory comment upon its composition, its sources in life, in books, or in both, and its literary qualities. A full description of the editorial procedures followed in this volume appears in the Textual Apparatus, after the Appendixes. The concern of this general introduction is with the author's life and work during the two periods when all passages, except the essay on Jane Clemens, probably were written and with a lost fragment concerning Tom and Huck which was written in 1902.

II

The years bounding the first period, 1876 and 1884, are landmarks in the literary career of Mark Twain because two of the most admired works utilizing the Matter of Hannibal appeared in those two years, respectively—*The Adventures of Tom Sawyer* and *Adventures of Huckleberry Finn*. During the years between, the author and his family lived in Hartford. Their home was the oversize, opulent mansion which he and his wife painstakingly planned and carefully furnished, partly in the hope of proving that a man still often called a vulgar Funny Fellow not only had impeccable taste but also could move gracefully in polite society. The family's hospitality rivaled that of Southern aristocrats whom the author had glimpsed or read about during his impoverished childhood. Open house was perpetual, with neighbors wandering

---

[4] The dates of these are discussed in Appendix B.

through unlocked doors at all hours; house guests came for long visits; elaborate formal dinners were served frequently.[5]

Although Clemens gloried in the mansion and its hospitality, he was irked by them too. The vision of married life that he had when he was courting his future wife, of "peace, & quiet—rest, & seclusion from the rush & roar & discord of the world," [6] had not been realized. More and more often he wrote wistfully of escaping to "a life of don't-care-a-damn in a boarding house," [7] to the South Seas, to Europe. Physically he escaped at intervals to a summer retreat near Elmira, New York, where he did much of his writing, and for about seventeen months in 1878/79 he escaped to Europe. In imagination and in his writings, with the cub pilot of *Life on the Mississippi* and with Tom and Huck, Mark Twain revisited pre-Civil War Hannibal or its more glamorous fictional counterpart, St. Petersburg, the nearby woods and islands and the Mississippi as he viewed them through the mists of memory. Like many contemporaneous American authors, he longingly looked back from a world transformed by industry and commerce to a world where nature was unspoiled and life untrammeled. Published as well as unpublished works of these years—especially, in this volume, the play based upon *Tom Sawyer*—show such nostalgia.

Another concern of the author between 1876 and 1884 helped cultivate this feeling and stimulate its expression: a preoccupation with financial matters. As Kenneth Andrews remarks, "he lived in an expensive neighborhood with Hartford standards to spur him to make money . . . He engaged in business enterprises that devoured money faster than his books could supply it. The more money he made, the more he needed." [8] So, like his literary neighbors in the prosperous Hartford community, Nook Farm, he definitely wrote for money.[9]

---

[5] Most statements about Clemens's life during this period here and in paragraphs that follow are elaborated and documented in *MT&HF*.

[6] *LLMT*, p. 70.

[7] *MTHL*, I, 389.

[8] *NF*, p. 157.

[9] "The writing of books was a profession in Hartford, recognized by the community as such . . . [The Hartford authors] looked longer at the commercial

Initially the building and furnishing of his large house in 1873/74 cost $122,000. In 1878/79 the family lavished money on new paintings and bric-a-brac which they imported from Europe. When the mansion was only seven years old, Clemens and his wife spent more than $30,000 on remodeling and redecorating. They kept six, seven, or eight servants. They spent large sums for entertaining. In addition, Clemens engaged in a host of costly commercial enterprises. Statistics for the year 1881 show him spending more than $54,000—almost the entire return from books and investments—on household expenses. He drew on capital to sink $46,000 in business ventures, most of them so unsound that they would bring no returns. Although he eventually hired a hard-working financial manager, he found that business was devouring a large share of his energy and time. Increasingly, therefore, he pined to escape the pressures of frenetic business activity. And again his escape took the form of an imaginary return to the "easier" life of the past.

The play based upon *Tom Sawyer,* like the novel itself, fondly visited childhood scenes. The author described the costumes and ways of living in antebellum St. Petersburg in affectionate detail, and it was clear that he even delighted in setting down children's chatter at length. But he was not solely interested in evoking nostalgic remembrances; he had a very practical aim as well. Like every dramatic work that Twain wrote, this one was a blatant bid for success in the highly commercialized theater of the era. The one successful drama in whose writing Mark Twain had a hand—*Colonel Sellers* (1874)—delighted him by making a great deal of money. His friend William Dean Howells told of witnessing

> the high joy of Clemens in the prodigious triumph of . . . *Colonel Sellers* . . . an agent . . . counted out the author's share of the gate money, and sent him a note of the amount every day by postal card. The postals used to come about dinner-time, and Clemens would read them aloud to us in wild triumph. One hundred and fifty dollars—

than at the artistic possibilities of each book they contemplated" (*NF,* pp. 149–150). A complete account of Clemens's relationship with his chief publisher through 1880 is given in *MT&EB.*

two hundred dollars—three hundred dollars were the gay figures which they bore, and which he flaunted in the air before he sat down at table, or rose from it to brandish, and then, flinging his napkin into his chair, walked up and down to exult in.[10]

Such success caused him to try playwriting again and again during many years that followed, sometimes with a collaborator, more often on his own. The letters to his business agent about the play "Tom Sawyer" and another drama that he was trying to peddle simultaneously show that a constant spur was the tremendous return that a successful dramatic work could bring.[11]

Like the "Tom Sawyer" play, "Tupperville-Dobbsville" (so designated because the village portrayed is given both names) caresses details in a remembered scene. The village here described in 1877 has many of the aspects that Twain recalled during the same year when he wrote "Early Years in Florida, Missouri" for his autobiography.[12] Florida, the writer's birthplace, was the site of Uncle John Quarles's farm, which he visited every summer until he was twelve or so. The house described in the fourth and fifth paragraphs of "Tupperville-Dobbsville" is the Quarles house, and Twain would also recall many aspects of it soon after in *Huck* and many years later in his autobiography.[13] The dilapidated houses insecurely perched along the riverbank until floods swept them into the stream, the muddy roads, and the sleepy villagers also would recur in the description of Bricksville in *Huck*.

"Clairvoyant," written during the year when *Huck* was published, is so brief a fragment that one can only guess where it was heading. Its chief interest is its amalgamation of the author's recollections of Hannibal characters with his long-term interest in what he called "mental telegraphy." Even more fragmentary are several notations which show that between 1883 and 1885 Twain occasion-

---

[10] *MMT*, pp. 22–23.

[11] *MTBus*, pp. 227–237. The other play was a sequel to *Colonel Sellers*, written in collaboration with Howells.

[12] *MTA*, I, 7–8.

[13] Both the Grangerford house and the Phelps plantation in the novel are described in terms applicable to the Quarles farm; the farm is described in *MTA*, I, 96, 102–103.

ally pondered ways of using Huck as a narrator in a sequel to his masterpiece. In a notebook kept between May 1883 and September 1884, for instance, he pasted a newspaper clipping:

> A Montana belle, says the Bismarck *Tribune*, being asked by a Bismarck man if they possessed any culture out her way, replied: "Culture? You bet your variegated sock we do! We kin sling more culture to the square foot in Helena than they kin in any camp in America. Culture? Oh, loosen my corsets till I smile!"

This he followed with a query:

> Put her in a Tom Sawyer book and let Huck tell her story? Hunts bears and things with a rifle, breaks horses, etc. Has some eastern folk visit her?—or she goes east to study? Tom's far-western cousin? Or she's a Pike-Co Californian for Swinton? [14]

His next notebook has several notations made in 1884 and 1885:

> Continue Tom and Huck. Put more of Sid the mean boy in.
> Immense sensation of Huck and Tom and the village when some aged liar comes there and says he has been in the Holy Land etc!—spins long sea yarns and yarns of travl—been a sailor! misuses sea phrases and naval technicalities.
>
> Make a kind of Huck Finn narrative on a boat—let him ship as Cabin boy and another boy as cub pilot—and so put the great river and its bygone ways into history in form of a story.
>
> The garrulous woman—or man—talk, talk, talk—never lets anybody get in more than a word—dreaded by everybody—make her or him a chief character in a (Tom Sawyer?) book.
>
> Put Huck and Tom and Jim through my Mo. campaign and give a chapter to the Century.
> Union officer accosts Tom and says his name is U S Grant. [15]

Noteworthy are the characteristic tendencies to make use of personal experiences as the basic ingredients of these narratives—the

[14] Notebook 17, TS p. 20.
[15] Notebook 18, TS pp. 19, 21, 22, 31. The last entry deals with the wartime experiences which Twain recounted in the first person in "The Private History of a Campaign That Failed," published in *Century Magazine* in December 1885.

trip to the Holy Land, life on a steamboat, the author's brief military career—and to identify a possible buyer, *Century Magazine,* immediately.

"Huck Finn and Tom Sawyer among the Indians" is the longest fragment of this period. In its opening chapter Twain again revisits the Quarles place. Soon, however, he has the three most famous inhabitants of St. Petersburg—Huck, Tom, and the Negro, Jim—start "to light out for the Territory" for adventures among the red men, on the trip about which Huck had written at the end of his novel. Twain's idea was to confront Tom, who cherishes notions derived from Cooper's novels and similar romanticizations, with the disillusioning reality, and in the course of the narrative to provide interesting pictures of life on the plains.

The Far West, of course, had long fascinated Americans. Shortly before *Roughing It* appeared in 1872, its author had worried whether its subject matter, the West, was too "hackneyed." [16] It did appear in the midst of a flood of books about that area—Bret Harte's, John Hay's, Joaquin Miller's, and such subscription books as Mrs. Frances Victor's *The River of the West,* Fanny Kelly's *Narrative of My Captivity Among the Sioux Indians,* [17] Buffalo Bill's autobiography, and Captain Dodge's *Our Wild Indians.* Nevertheless *Roughing It* sold briskly—96,000 copies by the end of 1879. The Custer massacre of 1876 attracted nationwide attention, and myths began to cluster about it. In 1883 Buffalo Bill Cody started touring the country with his Wild West Show; and within a year the show was thriving, and the Clemens daughters had honored the showman by naming a favorite cat after him. Hordes of stock Indians were biting the dust in dime novels. Edward L. Wheeler, who between 1877 and 1884 wrote twenty-nine stories about the prodigiously popular Deadwood Dick for Beadle & Adams, in the latter year informed a friend that he was still "engaged in the old business of 'sending boys out west to kill injuns' as the unco' good newspaper editors have it." Wheeler would kill his

---

[16] *LLMT,* p. 166.
[17] Hamlin Hill, "Mark Twain: Audience and Artistry," *American Quarterly,* XV (Spring 1963), 35.

hero and die himself in 1885, but other writers would trace the exploits of Deadwood Dick, Jr., in nearly a hundred cheap thrillers.[18] Helen Hunt Jackson's novel about California's Indians, *Ramona*, in 1884 went through the first of more than three hundred printings. Writing about Indians and the Far West at the precise time when he was engineering grandiose schemes to peddle *Huckleberry Finn* to legions of buyers, the author-entrepreneur no doubt hoped to make the new book equally successful. Here, as elsewhere during the period, therefore, Mark Twain combined the urge to write about Hannibal characters with the urge to make his writings pay well.

III

In *Tom Sawyer Abroad* (1893/94) and "Tom Sawyer, Detective" (1896), Twain again told stories about his boyish heroes. The former novella has Tom, Huck, and Jim start from St. Louis and drift in a mysteriously powered balloon over Africa, Egypt, and the Holy Land, observing and discussing them and a host of other engrossing subjects along the way. As Bernard DeVoto noticed, the arguments among the "errornorts," differentiating as they do the knowledge and ways of thinking of the trio, exhaustively explore the Hannibal mind—"its prejudices, ignorances, assumptions, wisdoms, cunning." [19]

In the later work, Twain recalled four settings associated with his youth: St. Petersburg-Hannibal, a sternwheeler steamboat, the Phelps-Quarles farm, and the rural countryside. Except in occasional paragraphs, though, settings and characterizations are sketchy, in part because the author is preoccupied with his complicated detective story. Although several critics have spoken kindly about *Tom Sawyer Abroad*, DeVoto is a rather lonely advocate for

---

[18] Albert Johannsen, *The House of Beadle & Adams* (Norman, Oklahoma, 1950), II, 294–295.

[19] *The Portable Mark Twain*, p. 20; *MTAm*, pp. 302–303.

this narrative. He hails it for showing Tom in the act of "utilizing the shrewdness which proceeds from the woodscraft that the frontier found necessary for survival. . . . a shrewdness peculiarly and indigenously American." [20] But many readers may be puzzled by the claim that Tom's shrewdness, adapted in this instance from a story about detection in Sweden, is particularly American. Shortly before the narrative was published, the author implied that he had a low opinion of it,[21] and one is inclined, on the whole, to share his estimate.

The next surviving attempts to utilize the Matter of Hannibal were made between 1897 and 1899. Earning money, an imperative aim between 1893 and 1896, was no longer a pressing consideration. By 1897 the humorist had sighted the end of the financial difficulties which had forced him into bankruptcy in 1894, and by February 1898 he had overcome them. But between 1894 and 1897 calamity had been heaped upon calamity—bankruptcy, the discovery in 1895 that his investment of more than $100,000 in the Paige typesetting machine was a total loss, the diagnosis of his daughter Jean's illness as epilepsy and the death of his favorite daughter Susy in 1896, and the perilous health of his always frail wife in 1897.

During the months that followed Susy's death, writing was an anodyne. Clemens wrote Howells on 23 February 1897 from London that he found himself "indifferent to nearly everything but work. I like that; I enjoy it, & stick to it. I do it without purpose & without ambition; merely for the love of it. . . . I am a mud image, & it puzzles me to know what it is in me that writes, & that has comedy-fancies & finds pleasure in phrasing them." [22] Eleven months later he indicated that his attitude was unchanged:

> I couldn't get along without work now. I bury myself in it up to the ears. Long hours—8 & 9 on a stretch, sometimes. And all the days, Sundays included. It isn't all for print, by any means, for much

---

[20] *MTAm*, p. 301.

[21] In June 1896, he made a notebook entry: "What a curious thing a 'detective' story is. And was there ever one that the author needn't be ashamed of, except 'The Murders in the Rue Morgue'?" (Notebook 30, TS p. 32.) Twain's detective story was serialized in *Harper's* during the following August and September.

[22] *MTHL*, II, 664.

of it fails to suit me; 50,000 words of it in the past year. It was because of the deadness which invaded me when Susy died.[23]

This was in January 1898. Late in the following summer he calculated that after finishing proofs for *Following the Equator* he had started three books and thirteen magazine articles, and practically all of them were "wrong." [24]

Although they obviously were written for therapy—perhaps because they were—the works of this period are interesting. "Villagers of 1840–3" is particularly fascinating; probably it is the most piquant item in this collection. Precisely what Twain had in mind when he wrote this series of notations concerning the Hannibal of his boyhood and its folk cannot be guessed. The notes may have been made for use in the autobiography, for which he wrote a number of extremely good pages only a bit later,[25] they may have been for use in writing one of the fictional works pondered or attempted at this time,[26] or they may have represented an exercise in memory. In any case, they are remarkable. Since the writer was in Europe when he composed them, almost certainly he had few or no relevant documents that he might use for reminders. Except for a few brief visits, he had been away from the town for four and a half decades. Yet he set down in detail facts about a hundred and sixty-eight inhabitants of Hannibal in his day—some of them quite surprising for a youth to have learned between the ages of four and seventeen. As accounts of all the people mentioned show, most of his memories can be independently verified (see Appendix A). And his few deviations from fact, whether accidental or deliberate, are as interesting as is his painstaking accuracy.

---

[23] *MTHL*, II, 670.
[24] *MTHL*, II, 675.
[25] *MTA*, I, 81–115.
[26] Notebook 32a, kept between 2 June 1897 and 24 July 1897, has pages of notes about the folk of antebellum Hannibal, many of whom are mentioned in "Villagers." An entry on TS p. 39 repeats the idea of the 1884/85 notebook about the old liar who comes to Hannibal and misuses sea terms. Later in the same notebook an entry lists several happenings and labels them, "For New Huck Finn" (TS pp. 56–57). Notebook 32b contains fewer Hannibal items; but it mentions Clemens's starting a story, "Hellfire Hotchkiss," which uses many characters mentioned in "Villagers" (TS p. 24).

Several characters mentioned in "Villagers" also figure in "A Human Bloodhound." This, and the fact that the latter sketch makes preliminary use of a character type and a plot device which are important in Twain's later writings, provide the latter's chief interest. Although "Villagers" purports to be autobiographical, "Doughface," which does not, is actually Huck's telling of a story associated with Roberta Jones in "Villagers" and often recalled by the author between 1883 in *Life on the Mississippi* and a notebook entry in 1902. "Tom Sawyer's Gang Plans a Naval Battle" was foreshadowed by an entry in a notebook kept in the autumn and the winter of 1896:

> Huck and Tom. Gen. Putnam swam out to the Eng. war vessel at anchor—in the night—with a mallet and wedge, and drove the wedge in between the rudder and the rudder-post. When they got up the anchor in the morn she drifted ashore and was captured.[27]

In the "Naval Battle" fragment, Tom supervises the building of two fleets of rafts to be used in a naval battle on the Mississippi and prepares to be, not General Putnam, but Lord Nelson. Even if this narrative may not be, as DeVoto has claimed, "actually painful," it is lacking in distinction.

The longest fragment of the 1897 to 1899 period is "Tom Sawyer's Conspiracy," a ratiocinative story that Twain nearly completed in a manuscript running to more than 30,000 words. Again he trotted out a favorite detective-story plot, which he linked, this time, to the slavery question and the frenzied activities of abolitionists and pro-slavery villagers. As far back as 1884, the author had recalled Hannibal's vigilantes of the 1850's, "the pater-rollers" of the streets, on guard against any abolitionists who might try to help slaves escape.[28] Another entry of 1896 outlined an early version of the plot. The narrator is Huck; the scene, St. Petersburg and nearby Jackson's Island. Characters adapted from "Villagers" play

---

[27] Notebook 31, TS p. 22.
[28] The introductory note preceding this fragment cites this and the second notebook entry. Joel Chandler Harris, whose stories Clemens greatly enjoyed, had Uncle Remus recall "the patter-rollers" in "How Mr. Rabbit Saved His Meat," *Uncle Remus His Songs and His Sayings* (New York, 1880), pp. 92–93.

roles related to Clemens's early associates, and some episodes derive from his experiences as a printer. The murderers, exposed in a typical courtroom scene dominated by Tom Sawyer, turn out to be the confidence men who call themselves the King and the Duke, last seen in *Huck*. Although it eventually disappears, one theme recurs through much of the manuscript—the unreasonableness of man's attitudes toward Providence. Albert Stone has made the best possible critical case for this narrative:

> Though morally incoherent, "Tom Sawyer's Conspiracy" is the most interesting boyhood story Mark Twain never finished. It tries to combine the Bad Boy manner of *Tom Sawyer*, the detective plot of *Pudd'nhead Wilson* and "Tom Sawyer, Detective," and the narrative technique and some of the moral atmosphere of *Huckleberry Finn*. As fiction, it is disjointed, incomplete . . . nevertheless the social situation it portrays is highly promising as a source for dramatic action.[29]

At least momentarily, in the summer of 1898 Twain thought of putting Tom and Huck, as well as his prince and pauper, into a fanciful story. A notebook entry headed "Creatures of Fiction" ran:

> Hans Brinker, ⟨Lau⟩rence [30] Hutton, Tom Bailey, ⟨Bob Sawyer⟩ Uncle Remus's Little Boy, George Washington (with hat check), Sanford and Merton, Rollo and Jonas, Mary and little lamb, Tom and Huck, Prince and Pauper, Casabianca. Last comes Mogli on elephant with his menagerie and they all rode away with him.
> It is a hot day. The place a grassy meadow with scattering shade trees, a ⟨small⟩ prairie hid away in the forest—very still and sad, buzzing insects. They appear one or two at a time, and get acquainted, and talk. Climb trees when the menagerie appears. . . . Add: burial of Babes in Wood and of Cock Robin. The Midshipmate. Make Casabianca sing "All in the Downs the Ship lay moored" and dance hornpipe. Introduce Mother Goose and her people.[31]

---

[29] *IE*, pp. 198–199.

[30] Angle brackets appearing in quotations in editorial material enclose matter which Mark Twain canceled in the original.

[31] Notebook 32, TS pp. 26–27. Laurence Hutton was the current editor of *Harper's Monthly*; why he was included is a puzzle.

Luckily this coy narrative was either allowed to die in this form or was destroyed.

What the humorist next planned and actually started to write is indicated in another notebook passage of the same year: he would tell how Satan, Jr., came to Hannibal, went to school, and performed feats of magic. The resulting manuscript of about 15,000 words written in November and December 1898 was the "Schoolhouse Hill" version of "The Mysterious Stranger." In it the author again conjured up ancient scenes and some of the citizens of Hannibal–St. Petersburg who had been recalled in "Villagers." Although this version of the story is comic, the bitter remarks that young Satan makes about the Moral Sense resemble those in the more somber versions that preceded and followed it.[32]

IV

On 15 October 1900 when Clemens returned to America after a long stay abroad, he was interviewed by a New York *Herald* reporter who asked:

> "Will you have any more [books] like 'Huckleberry Finn' and 'Tom Sawyer'?"
>
> "Perhaps," and Mr. Clemens smiled as he thought of these creations. "Yes, I shall have to do something of that kind, I suppose. But one can't talk about an unwritten book. It may grow into quite a different thing from what one thinks it may be."

And a notebook paragraph of 1900 shows that during that year he thought of having Huck narrate another story for him:

> Huck tells of those heros the 2 Irish youths who painted ships on Goodwin's walls and ran away. They told sea-adventures which made all the boys sick with envy and resolve to run away and go to

---

[32] Notebook 32, TS p. 50. "Schoolhouse Hill" is included in the volume in this series, *Mark Twain's Mysterious Stranger Manuscripts*, edited by William M. Gibson (Berkeley, 1969).

sea—then later a man comes hunting for them for a small crime—
laughs at their sailor-talk (Get it from my "Glossary of Sea Terms")
Put the Spanish Grandee barber into Huck's mouth.[33]

Again the folk of "Villagers" and misused sea terms are involved in
this sketch of what might have been a detective story involving
Huck.

There is evidence that in 1902 the author did try once more to
tell a story about his boyish heroes in a manuscript of some length
and some merit. An idea which he had pondered at intervals for
years finally was to be developed. In 1873 or 1874 on the first page
of a manuscript of *Tom Sawyer*, he scribbled an outline that he
apparently planned to follow:

> 1, Boyhood & youth; 2 y & early manh; 3 the Battle of Life in many
> lands; 4 (age 37 to 40[?],) return & meet grown babies & toothless
> old drivelers who were the grandees of his boyhood. The Adored
> Unknown a [illegible] faded old maid & full of rasping, puritanical
> vinegar piety.[34]

The idea of having the boys return as mature men to the village of
their childhood persisted in the synopsis of *Tom Sawyer: A Drama*
that was deposited for copyright on 21 July 1875. Here the return
would take the form of a comic parade at the end: "FIFTY YEARS
LATER.—Ovation to General Sawyer, Rear-Admiral Harper,
Bishop Finn, and Inspector Sid Sawyer, the celebrated
detective."

An 1891 notebook entry is closer in tone to the outline for the
end of the novel; indeed it may be even more lugubrious. It
specifies that Huck, now sixty years old and insane, would return to
St. Petersburg and piteously search everywhere for familiar childhood faces, then "Tom comes at last from sixty years' wandering in
the world, and attends Huck and together they talk of old times;

---

[33] Notebook 33, TS p. 6.
[34] Quoted in *MT&EB*, p. 102, from the manuscript in the Riggs Memorial
Library, Georgetown University. Correspondence between the humorist and
Howells shows that Clemens still was considering extending Tom's story "beyond
boyhood," when the novel as we now have it was completed (*MTHL*, I, 91–92).

both are desolate, life has been a failure, all that was lovable, all that was beautiful is under the mold. They die together." [35]

The motif recurs in three pages of notes on identical paper and in handwriting which, with external and other internal evidence, places them in 1902. One note is rather cryptic: "Notes. 50 yr after. Tom hears the laughing martin after 50 years! talks martin-box, gourd, blue-bird etc. How judge pistoled the pirate blue-birds Yet martin considered brave." A 1902 entry may refer to this, but since it simply reads "Martins and bluebirds," it does not disclose the meaning. [36] The second page of rough notes is headed "HUCK" and reads:

> The time John Briggs's nigger-boy woke his anger and got a cuffing (which wounded the lad's heart, because of his love and animal-like devotion to John (it is two or 3 years gone by—a life-time to a boy, yet John still grieves and speaks to Huck and Tom about it and they even meditate a flight south to find him)—John went, hearing his father coming, for he had done something so shameful that he could never bring himself to confess to the boys what it was; no one knew but the negro lad, John's father is in a fury, and accuses the lad, who doesn't deny it; (Beebe comes along) no corporeal punishment is half severe enough—he sells him down the river. John aghast when he sneaks home next day and learns it. "What did you sell him for, father?" Tells him. John is speechless,—can't confess.
>
>   The lad, very old, comes back in '02 and he and John meet, with the others left alive.

Again a 1902 notebook entry seems relevant: "Draw a fine character of John Briggs. Good and true and brave, and robbed orchards tore down the stable stole the skiff." [37] A few lines later in the same notebook, the author told himself, "Name all the sweethearts." The third page of notes seems to do so: "Laura Hawkins Becky Pavey Mary Miller Artemissa Briggs Jane Robards Sarah Robards

---

[35] *MTN*, p. 212. The author's tone was similar in a letter to his wife dated 17 May 1882, which tells of a recent visit to Hannibal (*MTL*, I, 419); and in chapter fifty-five of *Life on the Mississippi*.

[36] Notebook 35, TS p. 22.

[37] Notebook 35, TS p. 13. The page is in DV20a, MTP.

Nanny Ousley Becky Thatcher Cornelia Thompson Jenny Brady Jenny Craig." [38]

The likelihood is that the pages and the notebook entries were written shortly before or soon after Clemens himself carried out the action that he thought of assigning to his fictional characters. In the spring of 1902, slightly under fifty years after he had left Hannibal, he went back to the town and reminisced before audiences and former playmates. The visit apparently triggered the definite planning of a narrative, for not only did he write several notes, he also clipped a report of the visit from the *Ralls County Record,* headed it, "Hannibal. Texts for the final Huck Finn book. 1902. . . ." and preserved it.[39] The report describes some very emotional moments: before the Labinnah Club the sixty-six-year-old author gave "a very humorous and touchingly pathetic" speech, "breaking down in tears at its conclusion." "Commenting on his boyhood days and referring to his mother," says the report, "was too much for the great humorist, and he melted down in tears." Later, wandering around the town, Clemens and his boyhood friend John Briggs kept up "a rambling chat about old times, of the people who were living fifty years ago, of those who died and the few left among the living."

Notebook entries show him pondering a story based upon this visit:

Huck: "they eat 'em guts and all!" Work it in. . . . "50 Years Later."
. . . Walk streets at midnight reminiscing. Manufacture a retribution after 50 years. . . . Dough-face—old lady now, still in asylum—a bride then. What went with *him?* Shall we visit her? And shall she be expecting him in her faded bridal robes and flowers? . . . Call the roll of the boys and girls at midnight on Holidays hill. Old Jim answers for them—where we rolled the rock down. The Cold Spring —Jim has gone home—they can't find it—all railway tracks. . . . The lost playmate found by the lost boys in the Cave—McDowell's

---

[38] This page was sent to the Mark Twain Papers by Harper & Brothers on 29 August 1955. Another entry, in Notebook 35, TS p. 21, lists five of these names with those of other Hannibal girls and boys.

[39] Document file, MTP. Paine gives details from the clipping in *MTB,* pp. 1167–1170.

child—no, found by them 50 years after. Good! This is a place which only they know. . . . "The Last Leaf" quoted: The mossy marbles rest—and again after 50 years. At first by old man? . . . Get the remnants together and play school.—girls, too. . . . The gang's meeting-sign, its badge (skull, &c) stuck up (TS. G.) around. This must be the summons (with date and nothing more) 50 yrs hence.[40]

Between these items are others that refer to boyhood memories, a number of which are recorded in "Villagers." The nature of the story that Twain was planning can be inferred from the notes and from this entry:

Moonlight night parting on the hill—the entire gang. "Say, let's all come back in 50 years and talk over old times." "I bet we'd be back in 50 weeks." [41]

The narrative evidently was to be in two divisions. The first part would be set in antebellum St. Petersburg, would involve Tom's gang, and would make use of recollected events and characters that Twain often had considered using, plus a few such newly recalled or invented incidents as: "Tearing down the stable. Marbles. Kites —sleds—skates. Swings—picnics . . . Doughnut party. Horse-hair snakes . . . serenades. The piano and singing. On the barge, at night. . . . Shumake berries, end of September—eat them." [42] Somehow a reunion of the gang was to be arranged to take place after fifty years. The second part of the story would recount this meeting. (Several notes are concerned with ways of interrelating the two divisions.)

The summer of 1902 the Clemenses spent in York Harbor,

---

[40] Notebook 35, TS pp. 2, 12, 13, 14, 15, 19. This notebook is an engagement book containing dates for 1902. Some entries record engagements at appropriate points. Others, however, are working notes that could have been written at any time in 1902. The plan to recount a mock school session, however, probably was suggested by correspondence in January and February 1902 between the author and his friend H. H. Rogers about a reunion of Rogers's old classmates in Fairhaven. There, a similar session was staged, which Rogers evidently had described. See Clemens's letter of 31 January 1902 in which he mentions a plan to "transfer your school-jubilee to the banks of the Mississippi" (*Mark Twain's Correspondence with Henry Huttleston Rogers*, ed. Lewis Leary [Berkeley, 1969]).
[41] Notebook 35, TS p. 14.
[42] Notebook 35, TS pp. 12, 17, 22.

MARK TWAIN'S

HANNIBAL,

HUCK & TOM

Edited with an Introduction by
Walter Blair

Mark Twain

UNIVERSITY OF CALIFORNIA PRESS
Berkeley, Los Angeles, London

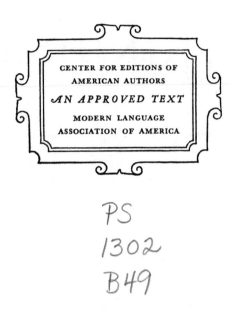

CENTER FOR EDITIONS OF
AMERICAN AUTHORS

AN APPROVED TEXT

MODERN LANGUAGE
ASSOCIATION OF AMERICA

UNIVERSITY OF CALIFORNIA PRESS
Berkeley and Los Angeles, California

UNIVERSITY OF CALIFORNIA PRESS, LTD.
London, England

© 1969 The Mark Twain Company
Second Printing, 1974
ISBN: 0–520–01501–0
Library of Congress Catalog Card Number: 69–10575

Designed by Adrian Wilson
in collaboration with James Mennick

Manufactured in the United States of America

Maine. The Howells family was vacationing at Kittery Point, forty minutes away. Howells often made the brief trip to visit his friend, and the two read manuscripts to one another. Eight years later Howells recalled a particular manuscript:

> . . . and there, unless my memory has played me one of those constructive tricks that people's memories indulge in, he read me the first chapters of an admirable story. The scene was laid in a Missouri town, and the characters such as he had known in boyhood . . .[43]

Clemens later denied having read such a manuscript, and Paine believed that Howells misremembered. There is evidence, though, that Howells's memory was correct. The humorist in a letter to Howells dated 3 October 1902 regrets "making Huck Finn tell things that are imperfectly true [in a stretch of writing done during] this last week or two. . . ." "He exaggerates," Clemens continues. Then he justifies the procedure: "Still, I have to keep him as he was, & he was an exaggerator from the beginning." On 20 October, Howells clearly indicated in a letter that he had been reading a manuscript about Huckleberry Finn:

> I have got Huck Finn safe, and will keep it till I come down, or will send it by express, as you say. It is a great layout; what I shall enjoy most will be the return of the old fellows to the scene, and their tall lying. There is a matchless chance there. I suppose you will put plenty of pegs in, in this prefatory part.[44]

Since the manuscript obviously is to fall into the two divisions described in the notes and since "tall lying" of the sort mentioned in the humorist's letter of 3 October is also mentioned here, the reference is apparently to a manuscript containing part of the projected narrative.

Mark Twain seems to have uttered his last word on this uncompleted story about Tom and Huck in a passage for his autobiography dated 30 August 1906. In 1902, he says, he half-finished a story told by Huck which had Tom and Jim as its heroes. He "carried it as far as thirty-eight thousand words," but, believing that his char-

---

[43] *MMT*, p. 90.
[44] *MTHL*, II, 746, 747.

acters "had done work enough in this world and were entitled to a permanent rest," he destroyed the manuscript "for fear I might some day finish it." [45] It is true that the author at times claimed that he had destroyed manuscripts when in fact he had not. Yet, inasmuch as not a single page of this one has been found, the likelihood is that he did destroy it.

At any rate, he did not publish it. Nor did he complete, publish, or attempt to publish any of the fictional works in this collection except the play.[46] Inasmuch as he could have finished all of his narratives in some way or another, and inasmuch as he indubitably could have found a publisher for them or could have published them himself (in all likelihood profitably), the frequently drawn picture of Mark Twain as a writer more interested in sales than in artistic integrity is rather effectively discredited. And it suggests one of the interesting problems about each fragment—why he did not complete and publish it. The answers to this question vary greatly and illuminate both the fascinating personality of the man and the highly individual methods of the author. In the end the illumination will prove to be the chief value of the flawed pieces which follow.

---

[45] *MTE*, p. 199.

[46] He did try to sell the finished play. Like many writers of that era, including Howells and James, he justifiably thought most of the dramas being produced were more commercial than literary.

HANNIBAL

Villagers of 1840–3

THE FOLLOWING notes concerning the inhabitants of Hannibal, Missouri, and their lives in the days before the Civil War were written by Mark Twain in 1897.[1] The title is his. The manuscript survives as a fragment inasmuch as the last entry breaks off in the middle of a sentence at the bottom of a page. A possible explanation is that the remainder of the piece dealt in a derogatory manner with the author's brother Orion, for Twain wrote much that was highly critical of his erratic sibling. If so, he may have destroyed the rest of the manuscript upon hearing of Orion's death on 11 December 1897.

Fragment though this is, it represents a remarkable feat of memory. The author was taken by his parents to Hannibal in 1839, when he was less than four years old. He left the town, never to live there again, in 1853 when he was seventeen. Whatever he learned about the community and its people thereafter, before writing "Villagers," he learned by revisiting it briefly in 1861, 1867, 1882, 1885, and 1890, by talking or corresponding with former and continuing residents, and by reading news stories and histories.[2] Writing in Switzerland, he almost certainly had little or no opportunity to check his accuracy. He was sixty-one years old.

---

[1] For evidence about the date, see Appendix B.

[2] In his library when he died was a copy of Return Ira Holcombe, *History of Marion County, Missouri* (St. Louis, 1884), to which his brother Orion had contributed.

23

Bearing these facts in mind, one must, I believe, find this document impressive. Perhaps it was no great feat for him to recall titles of songs played and sung by antebellum beaux and belles—"Last Link Is Broken," "Oh, on Long Island's Sea-girt Shore," "For the Lady I Love Will Soon Be a Bride," "Bonny Doon," and others. Perhaps it was no more striking an achievement to name the popular authors of the day and to generalize about the literature of that "intensely sentimental age." It may be that others in their sixties could recall equally well details about costumes of the era—"Cloak of the time, flung back, lined with bright plaid. Worn with a swagger. . . . Slouch hat. . . . Hoop-skirts coming in." Yet taken together such evocations demonstrate Clemens's enduring power of recall. So does this outline of rituals observed in the celebration of a holiday:

> *4th July.* Banners. Declaration and Spreadeagle speech in public square. Procession—Sunday schools, Masons, Odd Fellows, Temperance Society, Cadets of Temperance, the Co of St P Greys, the Fantastics (oh, so funny!) and of course the Fire Co and Sam R. Maybe in the woods. Collation in the cool shade of a tent. Gingerbread in slabs; lemonade; ice cream. Opened with prayer—closed with a blessing.

And surely readers will be impressed by the author's extensive recollections of the lives of so many townsfolk—a hundred and sixty-eight of them. These are all the more interesting when one realizes that he must have acquired most of the facts used in the descriptions between the ages of three and seventeen and that he was setting them down after four and a half decades or more had intervened. To be sure, fifteen of those who are not named and thirty-three who are named I was unable to identify outside the document. But the accuracy of the biographies which I was able to check suggests that Clemens may well have made few errors concerning this untraced group of forty-eight. The remaining one hundred and twenty villagers mentioned—ninety-seven named, twelve not named, and eleven given fictional names—are identifiable in documents other than this one, and with remarkably few exceptions his statements about them prove to be entirely correct.[3]

One may speculate on the reasons for Twain's ordering this parade of old acquaintances as he did. A good guess may be that he starts with Judge Draper because the judge was the oldest inhabitant of the town

---

[3] See Appendix A, where ascertainable facts about persons mentioned have been indicated.

as the boy knew it. He may proceed to the Carpenter family because Judge Carpenter (under another name) was a close associate of Draper. He next recalls the Carpenters' doctor, Meredith, and Meredith's family, and then two other doctors. Why Lawyer Lakenan is recalled next it is hard to say, but it is possible to guess why the next group considered is the Robards family: one of the Robards boys courted Mary Moss, who eventually married Lakenan. It is not surprising to find that the notes on the Robards family are followed by notes on the Moss family, which include the grim story of the marriage between Mary Moss and Lakenan.

This is typical of the luck one has when trying to see what associations in Twain's mind account for the arrangement of the biographies: some names seem to come together unaccountably, but a number have clear associations. Dana Breed, Lot Southard, and Jesse Armstrong logically cluster because all three were clerks, and the mention of a printer is followed by notes on several printers. Writing about the Briggs family, the author mentions three teachers of the Briggs children and then treats Hannibal's schoolmarms in more detail in the following paragraphs. His writing about Owsley (which he spells "Ouseley"), the merchant who shot old Smarr, evidently suggests memories of several other villagers involved in violence—the slave who raped and murdered a thirteen-year-old girl, the unidentified California emigrant who was stabbed, Judge Carpenter who knocked down MacDonald with a mallet, and MacDonald who tried to shoot Colonel Elgin.

These last entries stress aspects of Hannibal that will surprise any readers who have been persuaded by Mark Twain's fictional representations of the town that his memories of it were wholly idyllic. Some entries, of course, are in this mode—the one about the town's being nonmaterialistic, for instance, and the astonishing and internally contradicted generalization about the good repute of all the young women. But a number of entries suggest resemblances not between the folk of Hannibal and those of Arcady but between them and the inhabitants of Spoon River, Winesburg, and Peyton Place. The account of the Lakenan–Moss marriage places in the Missouri village a situation and a disastrous sleigh ride which foreshadow those in Edith Wharton's *Ethan Frome.* Sam Bowen's marriage and subsequent degradation are the stuff of tragedy. The bitterly ironic outcome of Roberta Jones's playful prank is a lifetime of horror. The Ratcliff family, with its persistent strain of madness, is presented as both frightening and pitiable. And unaccented, quite incidental details about other townsfolk show that, far from being sweetly serene, this was a community with its full share of grisly secrets.[4]

One interest that these reminiscences have derives from the fact that they show something important about Mark Twain's writing: they prove beyond any doubt that, as a rule, when he pictured Hannibal either in fiction about children or in purportedly factual reminiscences, he greatly modified and even deleted the more sordid aspects. They also prove that fictionizing must have been compulsive for him. For the form —or the formlessness—of these notes makes it evident that they were meant for the author's eye alone, that he set them down as mere notations to be developed in one of his many current works utilizing antebellum Hannibal scenes and townspeople: parts of his *Autobiography*,[5] the "Schoolhouse Hill" version of "The Mysterious Stranger," "Hellfire Hotchkiss," and "Tom Sawyer's Conspiracy." But even in these private notes, the author is highly inventive.

Although he gives several other towns and cities their actual names in the notes, when he refers to the village of Hannibal he calls it "St P," an abbreviation for St. Petersburg, its fictional name in stories about Tom and Huck. Furthermore, he must have deliberately made the dates in his title inaccurate, for he surely knew that few of his memories dated back to the period beginning with his fourth year and ending with his seventh. There are a few significant changes in the names: the Carpenters actually are his own family, the Clemenses, and their Christian names, although they begin with appropriate initials, are also fictitious. Mother Jane Clemens becomes Joanna Carpenter, brother Orion becomes Oscar, and so forth. The young man who, according to family legend, jilted Jane before she married John Marshall Clemens on

---

[4] Documentation for the claim that some of the citizens of Hannibal carried on in an unseemly fashion is provided by a pamphlet, *The Case of C. O. Godfrey,* which was in Clemens's library when he died. This records a trial held in 1879 by a committee of the Congregational church in Hannibal. Godfrey confessed to fondling a Mrs. M. E. Cruikshank at every opportunity during the course of a year, although he claimed that their affair had been one of "familiarity," and "never intercourse." Charges against the pair were made by a Mrs. C. P. Heywood after Mrs. Cruikshank learned that John Cruikshank, her husband, had been intimate with Mrs. Heywood. Clemens's signed note on the cover reads: "Both of these 'ladies' are wealthy, and move in the first society of their city. I knew them as little girls. The guilt of neither of them is doubted" (MTP).

[5] "Early Days," "Playing 'Bear,'" and "Jim Wolf and the Cats," MTA, I, 81–115, 125–143, utilize much of the matter of "Villagers."

the rebound is called Dr. Ray, although a decade earlier Clemens had known that in fact his name was Barrett.[6] Histories of Hannibal contain no reference to the picturesque unbeliever, Blennerhasset, and if there was such a person, he almost certainly bore another name. The melodramatic quality of the account of the man's death makes one suspect that he is largely if not wholly an imaginary character.

The most extraordinary invention occurs in the entry concerning Jesse Armstrong and his wife. It states that after the wife (given name unspecified) began to have an affair with her physician, someone entered the house one night and chopped Armstrong to pieces with an ax picked up from the woodpile. The widow and her lover, so the note says, were tried but were freed because evidence was lacking. Within a year they married. Now, there was a Jesse Armstrong who was a distant cousin of Clemens. But nothing like this ever happened to him, his wife, or her doctor. In this note, meant for his eye alone, the author attributed to the Armstrongs actions which actually involved a different trio of citizens and occurred in Hannibal in 1888, long after he had left the town.[7]

"Villagers of 1840–3" thus is interesting for its remarkable accuracies as well as its deliberate and its unintentional inaccuracies. It provides a striking verification for Dixon Wecter's assertion that "All his days he wrote fiction under the cloak of autobiography, and autobiography with the trappings of fiction." [8]

---

[6] He so called him in a letter to Howells dated 19 May 1886—*MTHL*, II, 567–568. In his autobiographical dictation of 29 December 1906, Clemens gave him another name, Gwynn (MTP).

[7] See Minnie T. Dawson, *The Stillwell Murder, or A Society Crime* (Hannibal, 1908). The husband was Amos J. Stillwell; the wife was the former Fannie C. Anderson; the doctor was Joseph C. Hearne. In the 1850's Stillwell was a partner in St. Louis of Clemens's brother-in-law, William A. Moffett, and probably was known by the author. Hearne did not settle in Hannibal until 1874.

[8] *SCH*, p. 65.

Villagers of 1840–3

J UDGE *Draper,* dead without issue.

Judge Carpenter. Wife, Joanna. Sons: Oscar, Burton, Hartley, Simon. Daughter, Priscella.

Dr. Meredith. Sons, Charley and John. Two old-maid sisters. He had been a sailor, and had a deep voice. Charley went to California and thence to hell; John, a meek and bashful boy, became the cruelest of bushwhacker-leaders in the war-time.

Dr. Fife. Dr. Peake.

Lawyer Lakenan.

Captain Robards. Flour mill. Called rich. George (flame, Mary Moss,) an elder pupil at Dawson's, long hair, Latin, grammar, etc. Disappointed, wandered out into the world, and not heard of again for certain. Floating rumors at long intervals that he had been seen in South America (Lima) and other far places. Family apparently not disturbed by his absence. But it was known that Mary Moss was.

John Robards. When 12, went to California across the plains with his father. Gone a year. Returned around Cape Horn. Rode in the Plains manner, his long yellow hair flapping. He said he was appointed to West Point and couldn't pass because of a defect in his eye. Probably a lie. There was always a noticeable defect in his veracity. Was a punctual boy at the Meth. Sunday school, and at Dawson's; a good natured fellow, but not much *to* him. Became a lawyer. Married a Hurst—new family. Prominent and valued citizen, and well-to-do. Procreated a cloud of children. Superintendent of the Old Ship of Zion Sunday school.

Clay Robards. A good and daring rebel soldier. Disappeared from view.

Sally Robards. Pupil at Dawson's. Married Bart Bowen, pilot and captain. Young widow.

Russell Moss. Pork-house. Rich. Mary, very sweet and pretty at 16 and 17. Wanted to marry George Robards. Lawyer Lakenan the rising stranger, held to be the better match by the parents, who were looking higher than commerce. They made her engage herself to L. L. made her study hard a year to fit herself to be his intellectual company; then married her, shut her up, the docile and heart-hurt young beauty, and continued her education rigorously. When he was ready to trot her out in society 2 years later and exhibit her, she had become wedded to her seclusion and her melancholy broodings, and begged to be left alone. He compelled her—that is, commanded. She obeyed. Her first exit was her last. The sleigh was overturned, her thigh was broken; it was badly set. She got well with a terrible limp, and forever after stayed in the house and produced children. Saw no company, not even the mates of her girlhood.

Neil Moss. The envied rich boy of the Meth. S. S. Spoiled and of small account. Dawson's. Was sent to Yale—a mighty journey and an incomparable distinction. Came back in swell eastern clothes, and the young men dressed up the warped negro bell ringer in a travesty of him—which made him descend to village fashions. At 30 he was a graceless tramp in Nevada, living by mendicancy and borrowed money. Disappeared. The parents died after the war. Mary Lakenan's husband got the property.

Dana Breed. From Maine. Clerk for old T. R. Selmes, an Englishman. Married Letititia Richmond. Collins and Breed—merchants.—This lot all dead now.

Lot Southard. Clerk. Married Lucy Lockwood. Dead.

Jesse Armstrong. Clerk for Selmes. Married ─────. After many years she fell in love with her physician. One night somebody entered the back door—A. jumped out of bed to see about it and was chopped to pieces with an axe brought from his own woodpile. The widow and the physician tried for the murder. Evidence insufficient. Acquitted, but Judge, jury and all the town believed them guilty. Before the year was out they married, and were at once and rigorously ostracised. The physician's practice shrunk to nothing, but Armstrong left wealth, so it was no matter.

Bill Briggs. Drifted to California in '50, and in '65 was a handsome bachelor and had a woman. Kept a faro-table.

John Briggs. (Miss Torrey and Miss Newcomb and Mrs. Horr.) Worked as stemmer in Garth's factory. Became a 6-footer and a capable rebel private.

Artemissa Briggs. (Miss Torrey, N. and Mrs. H.) Married Richmond the mason, Miss Torrey's widower.

Miss Newcomb—old maid and thin. Married Davis, a day laborer.

Miss Lucy Davis. Schoolmarm.

Mrs. Hawkins. Widow about 1840. 'Lige—became rich merchant in St Louis and New York.

Ben. City marshal. Shot his thumb off, hunting. Fire marshal of Big 6 Company.

Jeff. Little boy. Died. Buried in the old graveyard on the hill.

Sophia. Married ──── the prosperous tinner.

Laura. Pretty little creature of 5 at Miss Torrey's. At the Hill street school she and Jenny Brady wrote on the slate that day at the noon recess. Another time Laura fell out of her chair and Jenny made that vicious remark. Laura lived to be the mother of six 6-foot sons. Died.

Little Margaret Striker.

──── *Striker the blacksmith.*

McDonald the desperado (plasterer.)

Mrs. Holiday. Was a MacDonald, born Scotch. Wore her father's ivory miniature—a British General in the Revolution. Lived on Holiday's Hill. Well off. Hospitable. Fond of having parties of young people. Widow. Old, but anxious to marry. Always consulting fortune-tellers; always managed to make them understand that she had been promised 3 by the first fraud. They always confirmed the prophecy. She finally died before the prophecies had a full chance.

Old Stevens, jeweler. Dick, Upper Miss. pilot. Ed, neat as a new pin. Miss Newcomb's. Tore down Dick Hardy's stable. Insurrection-leader. Brought before Miss N., brickbats fell out of his pockets and J. Meredith's. Ed was out with the rebel company sworn in by Col. Ralls of the Mexican war.

Ed. Hyde, Dick Hyde. Tough and dissipated. Ed. held his uncle down while Dick tried to kill him with a pistol which refused fire.

Eliza Hyde. "Last Link is Broken." Married a stranger. Thought drifted to Texas. Died.

Old Selmes and his Wildcat store. Widower. His daughter married well—St Louis.

'Gyle Buchanan. Robert, proprietor of Journal. Shouting methodists. Young Bob and Little Joe, printers. Big Joe a fighter and steamboat engineer after apprenticeship as a moulder. Somebody hit young Bob over the head with a fire-shovel.

Sam Raymond—fire company, and editor of (Journal?) St Louis swell. Always affected fine city language, and said "Toosday." Married Mary Nash?

Tom Nash. Went deaf and dumb from breaking through ice. Became a house-painter; and at Jacksonville was taught to talk, after a fashion. His 2 young sisters went deaf and dumb from scarlet fever.

Old Nash. Postmaster. His aged mother was Irish, had family jewels, and claimed to be aristocracy.

Blankenships. The parents paupers and drunkards; the girls charged with prostitution—not proven. Tom, a kindly young heathen. Bence, a fisherman. These children were never sent to school or church. Played out and disappeared.

Captain S. A. Bowen. Died about 1850. His wife later.

John, steamboat agent in St Louis; army contractor, later—rich.

Bart. Pilot and Captain. Good fellow. Consumptive. Gave $20, time of Pennsylvania disaster. Young McManus got it. Left young widow.

Mary. Married lawyer Green, who was Union man.

Eliza—stammered badly, and was a kind of a fool.

Will. Pilot. Diseased. Mrs. Horr and all the rest (including Cross?) Had the measles that time. Baptist family. Put cards in minister's baptising robe. Trouble in consequence. Helped roll rock down that jumped over Simon's dray and smashed into coopershop. He died in Texas. Family.

Sam. Pilot. Slept with the rich baker's daughter, telling the adoptive parents they were married. The baker died and left all his wealth to "Mr. and Mrs. S. Bowen." They rushed off to a Carondolet magistrate, got married, and bribed him to antedate the marriage. Heirs from Germany proved the fraud and took the wealth. Sam no account and a pauper. Neglected his wife; she took up with another man. Sam a drinker. Dropped pretty low. Died of yellow fever and whisky on a little boat with Bill Kribben the defaulting secretary. Both buried at the head of 82. In 5 years 82 got washed away.

Rev. Mr. Rice. Presbyterian. Died.

Rev. Tucker. Went east.

Roberta Jones. Scared old Miss ————— into the insane asylum with a skull and a doughface. Married Jackson. "Oh, on Long Island's Sea-girt Shore."

Jim Quarles. Tinner. Set up in business by his father—$3,000 —a fortune, then. Popular young beau—dancer—flutist—serenader—envied—a great catch. Married a child of 14. Two babies the result. Father highly disapproved the marriage. Dissipation—often drunk. Neglected the business—and the child-wife and babies. Left them and went to California. The little family went to Jim's father. Jim became a drunken loafer in California, and so died.

Jim Lampton. A popular beau, like the other. Good fellow, very handsome, full of life. Young doctor without practice, poor, but good family and considered a good catch. Captured by the arts of Ella Hunter, a loud vulgar beauty from a neighboring town—one of the earliest chipper and self-satisfied and idiotic correspondents of the back-country newspapers—an early Kate Field. Moved to St Louis. Steamboat agent. Young Dr. John McDowell boarded with them; followed them from house to house; an arrant scandal to everybody with eyes—but Jim hadn't any, and believed in the loyalty of both of them. God took him at last, the only good luck he ever had after he met Ella. Left a red-headed daughter, Kate. Doctor John and Ella continued together.

In sixty years that town has not turned out a solitary preacher; not a U.S. Senator, only 2 congressmen, and in no instance a name known across the river. But one college-man.

Wales McCormick. J––s H. C.

Dick Rutter.

Pet McMurry. His medicine bottle—greasy auburn hair—Cuba sixes. Quincy. Family. Stove store.

Bill League. Married the gravestone-cutter's daughter. "Courier." Became its proprietor. Made it a daily and prosperous. Children. Died.

The two young sailors—Irish.

Urban E. Hicks. Saw Jenny Lind. Went to Oregon; served in Indian war.

Jim Wolf. The practical jokes. Died.

Letitia Honeyman. School. Married a showy stranger. Turned out to be a thief and swindler. She and her baby waited while he served a long term. At the end of it her youth was gone, and her cheery ways.

Sam. Lost an arm in the war. Became a policeman.

Pavey. "Pigtail done." A lazy, vile-tempered old hellion. His wife and daughters did all the work and were atrociously treated. Pole —went to St Louis. Gone six months—came back a striker, with wages, the envy of everybody. Drove his girl Sunday in buggy from Shoot's stable, $1.50 a day. Introduced poker—cent ante. Became second engineer. Married a pretty little fat child in St. Louis. Got drowned.

Becky. Came up from St Louis a sweet and pretty young thing —caused many heart-breaks. Silver pencil—$1.50—she didn't care for it. Davis a widower, married her sister Josephine, and Becky married Davis's son. They went to Texas. Disappeared. The "long dog."

The other sisters married—Mrs. Strong went to Peoria. One of them was Mrs. Shoot—married at 13, daughter (Mrs. Hayward) born at 14. Mrs. Hayward's daughter tried the stage at home, then at Daly's, didn't succeed. Finally a pushing and troublesome London newspaper correspondent.

Jim Foreman. Clerk. Pomeroy Benton & Co. Handkerchief.

Mrs. Sexton (*she* pronounced it *Saxton* to make it finer, the nice, kind-hearted, smirky, smily dear Christian creature—Methodist.)

Margaret. Pretty child of 14. Boarders in 1844 house. Simon and Hartley, rivals. Mrs. S. talked much of N-Yorliuns; and hints and sighs of better days there, departed never to return. Sunday-school.

Cloak of the time, flung back, lined with bright plaid. Worn with a swagger. Most rational garment that ever was.

Slouch hat, worn gallusly.

Hoop-skirts coming in.

Literature. Byron, Scott, Cooper, Marryatt, Boz. Pirates and Knights preferred to other society. Songs tended to regrets for bygone days and vanished joys: Oft in the Stilly Night; Last Rose of Summer; The Last Link; Bonny Doon; Old Dog Tray; for the lady I love will soon be a bride; Gaily the Troubadour; Bright Alforata.

Negro Melodies the same trend: Old Kentucky Home; (de day goes by like a shadow on de wall, wid sorrow where all was delight;) Massa's in de Cold Ground; Swanee River.

The gushing Crusaders admired; the serenade was a survival or a result of this literature.

Any young person would have been proud of a "strain" of Indian blood. Bright Alforata of the blue Juniata got her strain from "a far distant fount."

All that sentimentality and romance among young folk seem puerile, now, but when one examines it and compares it with the ideals of to-day, it was the preferable thing. It was soft, sappy, melancholy; but money had no place in it. To get rich was no one's ambition—it was not in any young person's thoughts. The heroes of these young people—even the pirates—were moved by lofty impulses: they waded in blood, in the distant fields of war and adventure and upon the pirate deck, to rescue the helpless, not to make money; they spent their blood and made their self-sacrifices for "honor's" sake, not to capture a giant fortune; they married for love, not for money and position. It was an intensely sentimental age, but it took no sordid form. The Californian rush for wealth in '49 introduced the change and begot the lust for money which is the rule of life to-day, and the hardness and cynicism which is the spirit of to-day.

The three "rich" men were not worshiped, and not envied. They were not arrogant, nor assertive, nor tyrannical, nor exigent. It was California that changed the spirit of the people and lowered their ideals to the plane of to-day.

Unbeliever. There was but one—Blennerhasset, the young Kentucky lawyer, a fascinating cuss—and they shuddered to hear him talk. They expected a judgment to fall upon him at any moment. They believed the devil would come for him in person some stormy night.

He was very profane, and blasphemous. He was vain of being prayed for in the revivals; vain of being singled out for this honor always by every new revivalist; vain of the competition between these people for his capture; vain that it was the ambition of each in his turn to hang this notable scalp at his belt. The young ladies were ambitious to convert him.

Chastity. There was the utmost liberty among young people— but no young girl was ever insulted, or seduced, or even scandalously gossiped about. Such things were not even dreamed of in that society, much less spoken of and referred to as possibilities.

Two or three times, in the lapse of years, married women were whispered about, but never an unmarried one.

Ouseley. Prosperous merchant. Smoked fragrant cigars—regalias
—5 apiece. Killed old Smar. Acquitted. His party brought him
huzzaing in from Palmyra at midnight. But there was a cloud upon
him—a social chill—and he presently moved away.

The Hanged Nigger. He raped and murdered a girl of 13 in the
woods. He confessed to forcing 3 young women in Va, and was
brought away in a feather bed to save his life—which was a
valuable property.

The Stabbed Cal. Emigrant. Saw him.

Judge Carpenter knocked MacDonald down with a mallet and
saved Charley Schneider. Mac in return came near shooting Col.
Elgin in the back of the head.

Clint Levering drowned. His less fortunate brother lived to have
a family and be rich and respected.

Garth. Presbyterians. Tobacco. Eventually rich. David, teacher
in S. school. Later, Supt.

John. Mrs. Horr and the others. He removed to New York and
became a broker, and prosperous. Returned, and brought Helen
Kercheval to Brooklyn in '68. Presently went back to St P. and
remained. Banker, rich. Raised 2 beautiful daughters and a son.

Old Kercheval the tailor. Helen did not like his trade to be
referred to.

His apprentice saved Simon Carpenter's life—aged 9—from
drowning, and was cursed for it by Simon for 50 years.

Daily Packet Service to Keokuk. The merchants—envied by all
the untraveled town—made trips to the great city (of 30,000
souls). St. L papers had pictures of Planters House, and sometimes
an engraved letter-head had a picture of the city front, with the
boats sardined at the wharf and the modest spire of the little Cath
Cathedral showing prominently; and at last when a minor citizen
realized the dream of his life and traveled to St. Louis, he was
thrilled to the marrow when he recognized the rank of boats and
the spire and the Planters, and was amazed at the accuracy of the
pictures and at the fact that the things were realities and not
inventions of the imagination. He talked St Louis, and nothing but
S L and its wonders for months and months afterward. "Call *that* a

fire-uniform! you ought to see a turn-out in St L.—blocks and blocks and blocks of red shirts and helmets, and more engines and hosecarts and hook and ladder Co's—my!"

4th July. Banners. Declaration and Spreadeagle speech in public square. Procession—Sunday schools, Masons, Odd Fellows, Temperance Society, Cadets of Temperance, the Co of St P Greys, the Fantastics (oh, so funny!) and of course the Fire Co and Sam R. Maybe in the woods. Collation in the cool shade of a tent. Gingerbread in slabs; lemonade; ice cream. Opened with prayer—closed with a blessing.

Circus.

Mesmerizer.

Nigger Show. (the swell pet tenor) Prendergast

Bell-Ringers (Swiss)

Debating Society.

National Intelligencer. Dr. Peake.

St. L. Republican.

Old Pitts, the saddler. Always rushed wildly down street putting on coat as he went—rushed aboard—nothing for him, of course.

John Hannicks, with the laugh. See black smoke rising beyond point—"Steeammmm*boat* a coming!" Laugh. Rattle his dray.

Bill Pitts, saddler, succeeded his father.

Ben Coontz—sent a son to W. Point.

Glover (protégé of old T. K. Collins) really did become a famous lawyer in St L., but St P always said he was a fool and nothing *to* him.

The Mock Duel.

Lavinia Honeyman captured "celebrated" circus-rider—envied for the unexampled brilliancy of the match—but he got into the penitentiary at Jefferson City and the romance was spoiled.

Ratcliffes. One son lived in a bark hut up at the still house branch and at intervals came home at night and emptied the larder. Back door left open purposely; if notice was taken of him he would not come.

Another son had to be locked into a small house in corner of the yard—and chained. Fed through a hole. Would not wear clothes, winter or summer. Could not have fire. Religious mania. Believed his left hand had committed a mortal sin and must be sacrificed. Got hold of a hatchet, nobody knows how, and chopped it off. Escaped and chased his stepmother all over the house with carving knife. The father arrived and rescued her. He seemed to be afraid of his father, and could be cowed by him, but by no one else. He died in that small house.

One son became a fine physician and in California ventured to marry; but went mad and finished his days in the asylum. The old Dr., dying, said, "Don't cry; rejoice—shout. This is the only valuable day I have known in my 65 years." His grandfather's generation had been madmen—then the disease skipped to his. He said Nature laid a trap for him: slyly allowed all his children to be born before exposing the taint.

Blennerhasset enlarged upon it and said Nature was *always* treacherous—did not single *him* out, but spared nobody.

B. went to K. to get married. All present at the wedding but himself. Shame and grief of the bride; indignation of the rest. A year later he would be found—bridally clad—shut into the family vault in the graveyard—spring lock and the key on the outside. His mother had but one pet and he was the one—because he was an infidel and the target of bitter public opinion. He always visited her tomb when at home, but the others didn't. So the judgment hit him at last. He was found when they came to bury a sister. There had been a theft of money in the town, and people managed to suspect him; but it was not found on him.

Judge Carpenter. Married in Lexington in '23; he 24, his wife 20. She married him to spite young Dr. Ray, to whom she was engaged, and who wouldn't go to a neighboring town, 9 miles, in the short hours of the night, to bring her home from a ball.

He was a small storekeeper. Removed to Jamestown and kept a store. Entered 75,000 acres of land (oil land, later). Three children born there. The stray calf.

Removed to village of Florida. M. born there—died at 10. Small storekeeper. Then to St P middle of 1838. Rest of the family born there—Han and B. died there. The mother made the children feel the cheek of the dead boy, and tried to make them understand the calamity that had befallen. The case of memorable treachery.

Still a small storekeeper—but progressing. Then Ira Stout, who got him to go security for a large sum, "took the benefit of the bankrupt law" and ruined him—in fact made a pauper of him.

Became justice of the peace and lived on its meagre pickings.

Stern, unsmiling, never demonstrated affection for wife or child. Had found out he had been married to spite another man. Silent, austere, of perfect probity and high principle; ungentle of manner toward his children, but always a gentleman in his phrasing—and never punished them—a look was enough, and more than enough.

Had but one slave—she wanted to be sold to Beebe, and was. He sold her down the river. Was seen, years later, ch. on steamboat. Cried and lamented. Judge whipped her once, for impudence to his wife—whipped her with a bridle.

It was remembered that he went to church—once; never again. His family were abandoned Presbyterians. What his notions about religion were, no one ever knew. He never mentioned the matter; offered no remarks when others discussed it. Whoever tried to drag a remark out of him failed; got a courteous answer or a look which discouraged further effort, and that person understood, and never approached the matter again.

If he had intimates at all, it was Peake and Draper. Peake was very old in the 40s, and wore high stock, pigtail and up *to* '40, still wore kneebreeches and buckle-shoes. A courtly gentleman of the old School—a Virginian, like Judge C.

Judge C. was elected County Judge by a great majority in '49, and at last saw great prosperity before him. But of course caught his death the first day he opened court. He went home with pneumonia, 12 miles, horseback, winter—and in a fortnight was dead. First instance of affection: discovering that he was dying, chose his daughter from among the weepers, who were kneeling about the room and crying—and motioned her to come to him. Drew her down to him, with his arms about her neck, kissed her (for the first time, no doubt,) and said "Let me die"—and sunk back and the death rattle came. Ten minutes before, the Pres. preacher had said, "Do you believe on the Lord Jesus Christ, and that through his blood only you can be saved?" "I do." Then the preacher prayed over him and recommended him. He did not say good-bye to his wife, or to any but his daughter.

The autopsy.

Jimmy Reagan, from St Louis.

Carey Briggs, from Galena and also from Bayou Lafourche.

Priscella. Old maid at 25, married W. Moffett, mouldy old bachelor of 35—a St L commission merchant and well off. He died 1865, rich ($20,000) leaving little boy and girl.

Oscar. Born Jamestown, 1825. About 1842, aged 17, went to St. L to learn to be a printer, in Ustick's job office.

At 18, wrote home to his mother, that he was studying the life of Franklin and closely imitating him; that in his boarding house he was confining himself to bread and water; and was trying

Jane Lampton Clemens

ALTHOUGH Albert Bigelow Paine included this essay in the author's *Autobiography* without Mark Twain's authority, it is ordered much as that work is. As early as 1876, Twain had told Mrs. James T. Fields that he would write the story of his life "fully and simply . . . as truly as I can tell it . . . and at whatever age I am writing about, even if I am an infant, and an idea comes to me about myself when I was forty, I shall put that in."[1] Eventually he wrote and dictated his personal reminiscences so as to bring together events by association. Here, he says, he will merely talk about his mother, "not give her formal history, but . . . furnish flash-light glimpses of her character . . ."

In this brief essay, the result is less chaotic than it is in the longer work, probably because, as luck has it, there are no capricious digressions. The essay begins with the author's earliest recollection of his mother, a vivid one—no doubt, because it is associated with what must have been a harrowing experience for a six-year-old: kneeling with her at the bedside of his dead brother Ben.[2] His memory of the way Jane startled him by weeping and moaning introduces a major point that he wants to make about her, that she had "a large heart; a heart so large

---

[1] M. A. DeWolfe Howe, *Memories of a Hostess* (Boston, 1922), p. 251.
[2] He mentions the experience in "Villagers" and several miscellaneous autobiographical notes, and as late as 1902 he set down among other childhood memories, "I saw Ben in shroud" (Notebook 35, TS p. 21).

41

that everybody's griefs and everybody's joys found welcome in it and hospitable accommodation"—"people," as he puts it, "and the other animals."

He next offers several instances: her defense of Satan, her courageous defiance of "a vicious devil of a Corsican" who was chasing his grown daughter with a rope, her exploitation by pathetic cats, her consideration even of slaves. Because the last illustration cannot be seen as climactic until the reader knows how the residents of Hannibal felt about slaves, Mark Twain contrasts at some length his "humane" father's compassion for a slave with his compassion for a white man.[3]

In a final long paragraph, the author turns to Mrs. Clemens's sunny disposition as evinced by her dancing (described also by Orion in a sketch printed in Appendix C) and her humor. His praise of her "ability to say a humorous thing with the perfect air of not knowing it to be humorous" has particular interest. For Twain held in "How to Tell a Story" (1895) that such a deadpan narrator was an essential for the most effective telling of an American humorous story: "The humorous story is told gravely; the teller does his best to conceal the fact that he even dimly suspects that there is anything funny about it." Mark Twain used the humorless narrator in his finest tall tales and in *Huckleberry Finn*.

---

[3] After reading Mark Twain's characterizations of John Marshall Clemens in "Villagers" and elsewhere, one suspects that here the author overemphasized his humanity in order to make a point.

Jane Lampton Clemens

THIS was my mother. When she died, in October, 1890, she was well along in her eighty-eighth year; a mighty age, a well contested fight for life for one who at forty was so delicate of body as to be accounted a confirmed invalid and destined to pass soon away. I knew her well during the first twenty-five years of my life; but after that I saw her only at wide intervals, for we lived many days' journey apart. I am not proposing to write about her, but merely to talk about her; not give her formal history, but merely make illustrative extracts from it, so to speak; furnish flash-light glimpses of her character, not a processional view of her career. Technically speaking, she had no career; but she had a character, and it was of a fine and striking and lovable sort.

What becomes of the multitudinous photographs which one's mind takes of people? Out of the million which my mental camera must have taken of this first and closest friend, only one clear and strongly defined one of early date remains. It dates back forty-seven years; she was forty years old, then, and I was eight. She held me by the hand, and we were kneeling by the bedside of my brother, two years older than I, who lay dead, and the tears were flowing down her cheeks unchecked. And she was moaning. That dumb sign of anguish was perhaps new to me, since it made upon me a very strong impression—an impression which holds its place still with the picture which it helped to intensify and make memorable.

She had a slender small body, but a large heart; a heart so large that everybody's griefs and everybody's joys found welcome in it and hospitable accommodation. The greatest difference which I find between her and the rest of the people whom I have known, is this, and it is a remarkable one: those others felt a strong interest in a few things, whereas to the very day of her death she felt a strong interest in the whole world and everything and everybody in it. In all her life she never knew such a thing as a half-hearted interest in affairs and people, or an interest which drew a line and left out certain affairs and was indifferent to certain people. The invalid who takes a strenuous and indestructible interest in everything and everybody but himself, and to whom a dull moment is an unknown thing and an impossibility, is a formidable adversary for disease and a hard invalid to vanquish. I am certain it was this feature of my mother's make-up that carried her so far toward ninety.

Her interest in people and the other animals was warm, personal, friendly. She always found something to excuse, and as a rule to love, in the toughest of them—even if she had to put it there herself. She was the natural ally and friend of the friendless. It was believed that, Presbyterian as she was, she could be beguiled into saying a soft word for the devil himself; and so the experiment was tried. The abuse of Satan began; one conspirator after another added his bitter word, his malign reproach, his pitiless censure, till at last, sure enough, the unsuspecting subject of the trick walked into the trap. She admitted that the indictment was sound; that Satan was utterly wicked and abandoned, just as these people had said; *but,* would any claim that he had been treated fairly? A sinner was but a sinner; Satan was just that, like the rest. What saves the rest?—their own efforts alone? No—or none might ever be saved. To their feeble efforts is added the mighty help of pathetic, appealing, imploring prayers that go up daily out of all the churches in Christendom and out of myriads upon myriads of pitying hearts. But who prays for Satan? Who, in eighteen centuries, has had the common humanity to pray for the one sinner that needed it most, our one fellow and brother who most needed a friend yet had not a single one, the one sinner among us all who had the highest and clearest *right* to every Christian's daily and nightly prayers for the plain and unassailable reason that his was the first and greatest need, he being among sinners the supremest?

This Friend of Satan was a most gentle spirit, and an unstudied and unconscious pathos was her native speech. When her pity or her indignation was stirred by hurt or shame inflicted upon some defenceless person or creature, she was the most eloquent person I have heard speak. It was seldom eloquence of a fiery or violent sort, but gentle, pitying, persuasive, appealing; and so genuine and so nobly and simply worded and so touchingly uttered, that many times I have seen it win the reluctant and splendid applause of tears. Whenever anybody or any creature was being oppressed, the fears that belonged to her sex and her small stature retired to the rear, and her soldierly qualities came promptly to the front. One day in our village I saw a vicious devil of a Corsican, a common terror in the town, chasing his grown daughter past cautious male citizens with a heavy rope in his hand, and declaring he would wear it out on her. My mother spread her door wide to the refugee, and then instead of closing and locking it after her, stood in it and stretched her arms across it, barring the way. The man swore, cursed, threatened her with his rope; but she did not flinch or show any sign of fear; she only stood straight and fine, and lashed him, shamed him, derided him, defied him, in tones not audible to the middle of the street, but audible to the man's conscience and dormant manhood; and he asked her pardon, and gave her his rope, and said with a most great and blasphemous oath that she was the bravest woman he ever saw; and so went his way without other word, and troubled her no more. He and she were always good friends after that, for in her he had found a long felt want—somebody who was not afraid of him.

One day in St. Louis she walked out into the street and greatly surprised a burly cartman who was beating his horse over the head with the butt of his heavy whip; for she took the whip away from him and then made such a persuasive appeal in behalf of the ignorantly offending horse that he was tripped into saying he was to blame; and also into volunteering a promise which of course he couldn't keep, for he was not built in that way—a promise that he wouldn't ever abuse a horse again.

That sort of interference in behalf of abused animals was a common thing with her all her life; and her manner must have been without offence and her good intent transparent, for she always carried her point, and also won the courtesy, and often the friendly applause, of the adversary. All the race of dumb animals had a friend in her. By some subtle sign the homeless, hunted, bedraggled and disreputable cat recognized her at a glance as the born refuge and champion of his sort—and followed her home. His instinct was right, he was as welcome as the prodigal son. We had nineteen cats at one time, in 1845. And there wasn't one in the lot that had any character; not one that had a merit, except the cheap and tawdry merit of being unfortunate. They were a vast burden to us all—including my mother—but they were out of luck, and that was enough; they had to stay. However, better these than no pets at all; children must have pets, and we were not allowed to have caged ones. An imprisoned creature was out of the question—my mother would not have allowed a rat to be restrained of its liberty.

In the small town of Hannibal, Missouri, when I was a boy, everybody was poor but didn't know it; and everybody was comfortable, and did know it. And there were grades of society; people of good family, people of unclassified family, people of no family. Everybody knew everybody, and was affable to everybody, and nobody put on any visible airs; yet the class lines were quite clearly drawn, and the familiar social life of each class was restricted to that class. It was a little democracy which was full of Liberty, Equality and Fourth of July; and sincerely so, too, yet you perceive that the aristocratic taint was there. It was there, and nobody found fault with the fact, or ever stopped to reflect that its presence was an inconsistency.

I suppose that this state of things was mainly due to the circumstance that the town's population had come from slave States and still had the institution of slavery with them in their new home. My mother, with her large nature and liberal sympathies, was not intended for an aristocrat, yet through her breeding she was one. Few people knew it, perhaps, for it was an instinct, I think, rather than a principle. So its outward manifestation was likely to be accidental, not intentional; and also not frequent. But I knew of that weak spot. I knew that privately she was proud that the Lambtons, now Earls of Durham, had occupied the family lands for nine hundred years; that they were feudal lords of Lambton Castle and holding the high position of ancestors of hers when the Norman Conqueror came over to divert the Englishry. I argued—cautiously, and with mollifying circumlocutions, for one had to be careful when he was on that holy ground, and mustn't cavort—that there was no particular merit in occupying a piece of land for nine hundred years, with the friendly assistance of an entail; anybody could do it, with intellect or without; therefore, the entail was the thing to be proud of, just the entail and nothing else; consequently, she was merely descended from an entail, and she might as well be proud of being descended from a mortgage. Whereas my own ancestry was quite a different and superior thing, because it had the addition of an ancestor—one Clement—who *did* something; something which was very creditable to him and satisfactory to me, in that he was a member of the court that tried Charles I and delivered him over to the executioner. Ostensibly this was chaff, but at bottom it was not. I had a very real respect for that ancestor, and this respect has increased with the years, not diminished. He did what he could toward reducing the list of crowned shams of his day. However, I can say this for my mother, that I never heard her refer in any way to her gilded ancestry when any person not a member of the family was present, for she had good American sense. But with other Lamptons whom I have known, it was different. "Col. Sellers" was a Lampton, and a tolerably near relative of my mother's; and when he was alive, poor old airy soul, one of the earliest things a stranger was likely to hear from his lips was some reference to the "head of our line," flung off with a painful casualness that was wholly beneath criticism as a work of art. It com-

pulpit, but had heard it defended and sanctified in a thousand; her ears were familiar with Bible texts that approved it, but if there were any that disapproved it they had not been quoted by her pastors; as far as her experience went, the wise and the good and the holy were unanimous in the conviction that slavery was right, righteous, sacred, the peculiar pet of the Deity, and a condition which the slave himself ought to be daily and nightly thankful for. Manifestly, training and association can accomplish strange miracles. As a rule our slaves were convinced and content. So, doubtless, are the far more intelligent slaves of a monarchy; they revere and approve their masters the monarch and the noble, and recognize no degradation in the fact that they are slaves; slaves with the name blinked; and less respect-worthy than were our black ones, if to be a slave by meek consent is baser than to be a slave by compulsion— and doubtless it is.

However, there was nothing about the slavery of the Hannibal region to rouse one's dozing humane instincts to activity. It was the mild domestic slavery, not the brutal plantation article. Cruelties were very rare, and exceedingly and wholesomely unpopular. To separate and sell the members of a slave family to different masters was a thing not well liked by the people, and so it was not often done, except in the settling of estates. I have no recollection of ever seeing a slave auction in that town; but I am suspicious that that is because the thing was a common and commonplace spectacle, not an uncommon and impressive one. I vividly remember seeing a dozen black men and women chained to each other, once, and lying in a group on the pavement, awaiting shipment to the southern slave market. Those were the saddest faces I ever saw. Chained slaves could not have been a common sight, or this picture would not have taken so strong and lasting a hold upon me.

The "nigger trader" was loathed by everybody. He was regarded as a sort of human devil who bought and conveyed poor helpless creatures to hell—for to our whites and blacks alike the southern plantation was simply hell; no milder name could describe it. If the threat to sell an incorrigible slave "down the river" would not reform him, nothing would—his case was past cure.

My mother was quite able to pity a slave who was in trouble; but not *because* he was a slave—that would not have emphasized the case any, perhaps. I recal an incident in point. For a time we had as a house servant a little slave boy who belonged to a master back in the country, and I used to want to kill him on account of the noise he made; and I think yet, it would have been a good idea to kill him. The noise was music—singing. He sang the whole day long, at the top of his voice; it was intolerable, it was unendurable. At last I went to my mother in a rage about it. But she said—

"Think; he is sold away from his mother; she is in Maryland, a thousand miles from here, and he will never see her again, poor thing. When he is singing it is a sign that he is not grieving; the noise of it drives me almost distracted, but I am always listening, and always thankful; it would break my heart if Sandy should stop singing."

And she was able to accommodate a slave—even accommodate the whim of a slave, against her own personal interest and desire. A woman who had been "mammy"—that is, nurse—to several of us children, took a notion that she would like to change masters. She wanted to be sold to a Mr. B., of our town. That was a sore trial, for the woman was almost like one of the family; but she pleaded hard —for that man had been beguiling her with all sorts of fine and alluring promises—and my mother yielded, and also persuaded my father.

It is commonly believed that an infallible effect of slavery was to make such as lived in its midst hard-hearted. I think it had no such effect—speaking in general terms. I think it stupefied everybody's humanity, as regarded the slave, but stopped there. There were no hard-hearted people in our town—I mean there were no more than would be found in any other town of the same size in any other country; and in my experience hard-hearted people are very rare everywhere. Yet I remember that once when a white man killed a negro man for a trifling little offence everybody seemed indifferent about it—as regarded the slave—though considerable sympathy was felt for the slave's owner, who had been bereft of valuable property by a worthless person who was not able to pay for it.

My father was a humane man; all will grant this who knew him. Still, proof is better than assertion, and I have it at hand. Before me is a letter, near half a century old, dated January 5, 1842, and written by my father to my mother. He is on a steamboat, ascending the Mississippi, and is approaching Memphis. He has made a hard and tedious journey, in mid winter, to hunt up a man in the far south who has been owing him $470 for twenty years. He has found his man, has also found that his man is solvent and able to pay, but—

—"it seemed so very hard upon him these hard times to pay such a sum, that I could not have the conscience to hold him to it. On the whole I consented to take his note, payable 1st March next, for $250 and let him off at that. I believe I was quite too lenient, and ought to have had at least that amount down."

Is not this a humane, a soft-hearted man? If even the gentlest of us had been plowing through ice and snow, horseback and per steamboat, for six weeks to collect that little antiquity, wouldn't we have collected it, and the man's scalp along with it? I trust so. Now, lower down on the same page, my father—proven to be a humane man—writes this:

"I still have Charley; the highest price I was offered for him in New Orleans was $50, and in Vicksburg $40. After performing the journey to Tennessee I expect to sell him for whatever he will bring when I take water again, viz., at Louisville or Nashville."

And goes right on, then, about some indifferent matter, poor Charley's approaching eternal exile from his home, and his mother, and his friends, and all things and creatures that make life dear and the heart to sing for joy, affecting him no more than if this humble comrade of his long pilgrimage had been an ox—and somebody else's ox. It makes a body homesick for Charley, even after fifty years. Thank God I have no recollection of him as house servant of ours; that is to say, playmate of mine; for I was playmate to all the niggers, preferring their society to that of the elect, I being a person of low-down tastes from the start, notwithstanding my high birth, and ever ready to forsake the communion of high souls if I could strike anything nearer my grade.

She was of a sunshiny disposition, and her long life was mainly a holiday to her. She was a dancer, from childhood to the end, and as capable a one as the Presbyterian church could show among its communicants. At eighty-seven she would trip through the lively and graceful figures that had been familiar to her more than seventy years before. She was very bright, and was fond of banter and playful duels of wit; and she had a sort of ability which is rare in men and hardly existent in women—the ability to say a humorous thing with the perfect air of not knowing it to be humorous. Whenever I was in her presence, after I was grown, a battle of chaff was going on all the time, but under the guise of serious conversation. Once, under pretence of fishing for tender and sentimental reminiscences of my childhood—a sufficiently annoying childhood for other folk to recal, since I was sick the first seven years of it and lived altogether on expensive allopathic medicines— I asked her how she used to feel about me in those days. With an almost pathetic earnestness she said, "All along at first I was afraid you would die"—a slight, reflective pause, then this addition, spoken as if talking to herself—"and after that I was afraid you wouldn't." After eighty her memory failed, and she lived almost entirely in a world peopled by carefree mates of her young girlhood whose voices had fallen silent and whose forms had mouldered to dust many and many a year gone by; and in this gracious companionship she walked pleasantly down to the grave unconscious of her gray head and her vanished youth. Only her memory was stricken; otherwise her intellect remained unimpaired. When I arrived, late at night, in the earliest part of her last illness, she had been without sleep long enough to have worn a strong young person out, but she was as ready to talk, as ready to give and take, as ever. She knew me perfectly, but to her disordered fancy I was not a gray-headed man, but a school-boy, and had just arrived from the east on vacation. There was a deal of chaff, a deal of firing back and forth, and then she began to inquire about the school and what sort of reputation I had in it—and with a rather frankly doubtful tone about the questions, too. I said that my reputation was really a wonder; that there was not another boy there whose morals were anywhere near up to mine; that whenever I passed by, the citizens stood in reverent admiration, and said: "There goes the model boy." She was silent a while, then she said, musingly: "Well, I wonder what the rest are like."

She was married at twenty; she always had the heart of a young girl; and in the sweetness and serenity of death she seemed somehow young again. She was always beautiful.

Tupperville-Dobbsville

ALBERT BIGELOW PAINE noted that this manuscript was "Two unfinished sketches. Unfinished and unusable." However, the manuscript in MTP is clearly a single piece. Apparently Paine was confused because Mark Twain assigned to the town both the names here given as the title. Despite their fragmentary nature, these paragraphs written in the late 1870's (see Appendix B) are of interest because so many of the author's favorite motifs cluster in them. The loafing river-town villagers who can be aroused from somnolence by nothing less than a dog-fight had appeared in early chapters of *The Gilded Age* (1873) and "Old Times on the Mississippi" (1875) and would soon reappear in chapter twenty-one of *Huckleberry Finn*. The dusty and mud-filled streets and the ramshackle houses occur in a passage in the *Autobiography* written in 1877 (I, 7) and also would be described in the chapter of *Huck*. Widow Bennett's house has features that soon would distinguish the Grangerford residence and the Phelps house in chapters seventeen and thirty-two, respectively, of *Huck*. As Mark Twain indicates in a passage written for his *Autobiography* in 1897/98 (I, 96), the prototype of the dwelling was his Uncle John A. Quarles's farm near Florida, Missouri, where the author spent his boyhood summers. Quarles is referred to in "Villagers" and in Appendix A. In the margin of the final paragraph of this fragment Twain wrote " 'Lige," indicating that he may have planned to use 'Lige Hawkins, junior or senior, also recalled in "Villagers."

Tupperville-Dobbsville

Chapter 1

THE SCENE of this history is an Arkansas village, on the bank of the Mississippi; the time, a great many years ago. The houses were small and unpretentious; some few were of frame, the others of logs; a very few were whitewashed, but none were painted; nearly all the fences leaned outward or inward and were more or less dilapidated. The whole village had a lazy, tired, neglected look. The river bank was high and steep, and here and there an aged, crazy building stood on the edge with a quarter or a half of itself overhanging the water, waiting forlorn and tenantless for the next freshet to eat the rest of the ground from under it and let the stream swallow it. This was a town that was always moving westward. Twice a year, regularly, in the dead of winter and in the dead of summer, the great river called for the front row of the village's possessions, and always got it. It took the front farms, the front orchards, the front gardens; those front houses that were worth hauling away, were moved to the rear by ox-power when the danger-season approached; those that were not worth this trouble were timely deserted and left to cave into the river. If a man lived obscurely in a back street and chafed under this fate, he only needed to have patience; his back street would be the front street by and by.

55

Above and below the town, dense forests came flush to the bank; and twice a year they delivered their front belt of timber into the river. The village site, and the corn and cotton fields in the rear had been formerly occupied by trees as thick as they could stand, and the stumps remained in streets, yards and fields as a memento of the fact. All the houses stood upon "underpinning," which raised them two or three feet above the ground, and under each house was usually a colony of hogs, dogs, cats and other creatures, mostly of a noisy kind. The village stood on a dead level, and the houses were propped above ground to keep the main floors from being flooded by the semi-annual overflow of the river.

There were no sidewalks, no pavements, no stepping stones; therefore, on a spring day the streets were either several inches deep with dust or as many inches deep with thick black mud. People slopped through this mud on foot or horseback, the hogs wallowed in it without fear of molestation, wagons got stuck fast in it, and while the drivers lashed away with their long whips and swore with power, coatless, jeans-clad loafers stood by with hands in pockets and sleepily enjoyed this blessed interruption of the customary monotony until a dog-fight called them to higher pleasure. When the dog-fight ended they adjourned to the empty dry-goods boxes in front of the poor little stores and whittled and expectorated and discussed the fight and the merits of the dogs that had taken part in it.

One of the largest dwellings in this village of Tupperville was the home of the widow Bennett and her family. It was built of logs, and stood in the back part of the town next to the corn and cotton-fields. In the common sitting room was a mighty fire place, paved with slabs of stone shaped by nature and worn smooth by use.—The oaken floor in front of it was thickly freckled, as far as the middle of the room, with black spots burned in it by coals popped out from the hickory fire-wood. There was no carpeting anywhere; but there was a spinning wheel in one corner, a bed in another, with a white counterpane, a dinner table with leaves, in another, a tall eight-day clock in the fourth corner, a dozen splint-bottom chairs scattered around, several guns resting upon deer-horns over the mantel piece, and generally a cat or a hound or two curled up on the hearth-stones asleep. This was the family sitting room; it was also the dining room and the widow Bennett's bed-chamber. The rest of the house was devoted to sleeping apartments for the other members of the household. A planked passage-way, twenty feet wide, open at the sides but roofed above, extended from the back sitting room door to the log kitchen; and beyond the kitchen stood the smoke-house and three or four little dismal log cabins, otherwise the "negro quarter."

Since this house was in all ways much superior to the average of the Dobbsville residences, it will be easily perceived that the average residence was necessarily a very marvel of rudeness, nakedness, and simplicity.

Clairvoyant

In *Sam Clemens of Hannibal* Dixon Wecter discusses the "strain of primitive folk belief in dreams and second sight—gained perhaps from Quarleses' slaves, perhaps from . . . backwoods mysticism" (p. 197) which Clemens acquired early in life. The Clemenses claimed that when he was less than four years old, Sam walked in his sleep to his sister Margaret's bedside and plucked at her cover, thus warning of her death a few days later. The family also believed that several weeks earlier a shoemaker, who was a neighbor, had a vision in which he watched Margaret's funeral. A few years later, Sam was said to have foreseen the death of a schoolmate; and on the river in 1858, so he held, he had a dream prophetic of his brother Henry's death in a steamboat explosion. Traditions perpetuated by the author himself concerned uncannily accurate foretellings of his future by palmists.

On 2 March 1874, Clemens had the idea that he should urge an old Western friend, William H. Wright, to prepare a book about Virginia City, Nevada, and its Comstock lode. He wrote a letter to this effect, outlining an organization, but pigeonholed it. On 9 March he received a letter sent by Wright from Nevada, and before he opened it Clemens successfully predicted that it would concern the writing of just such a book and would repeat his own suggestions about the organization.

This and several similar experiences Twain recounted in the article "Mental Telegraphy," written in 1878, augmented in 1891, and pub-

58

lished in *Harper's Magazine* for December of that year. "Mental Telegraphy Again" in *Harper's* for September 1895 continued the discussion, as did an unpublished article of seven hundred words, written in November 1907 and now in the Mark Twain Papers (DV254). Had Clemens heard that an Englishman, F. W. Meyers, coined the word "telepathy" while Clemens was collecting examples of what he termed "mental telegraphy," this coincidence would doubtless have been cited as yet another example of the phenomenon.

The author, however, distinguished between the mental telegraphy which made possible his communication with Wright and clairvoyance: "I think the clairvoyant professes to actually *see* concealed writing, and read it off word for word. This was not my case." Again, "I have never seen any mesmeric or clairvoyant performances or spiritual manifestations which were in the least degree convincing . . . but I am forced to believe that one human mind (still inhabiting the flesh) can communicate with another, over any sort of a distance. . . ." [1]

Despite this assertion of disbelief, the author in this fragment, apparently written early in the 1880's,[2] pictures a character, John H. Day, who evidently can see the unseeable—the intimate thoughts and feelings of his fellow townsmen. After seeing and talking with a person, and (for reasons never clarified) after peering into that person's ears, Day at a distance could watch that person's deeds and fathom his inmost thoughts. This incomplete narrative shows him doing so on three occasions.

Fact and fiction are interestingly blended. The setting is Hannibal, not the fictional St. Petersburg. The Sny which is mentioned is Sny Island, actually across the river from Hannibal and a palpable part of Pike County, Illinois. Stevens, the jeweler; young Ratcliff and his mother; Selmes, the merchant; and Brittingham (a druggist) were flesh-and-blood citizens of Hannibal.[3] Whether the characters designated as G——, B——, and E—— were factual or not, and whether their actions were real or invented, it is impossible to say; but the use of initials suggests their reality. Although "Old printer Day and the spirits" occurs among Hannibal notes in Notebook 33, TS p. 3 (1900),

---

[1] "Mental Telegraphy," *Literary Essays* (Definitive Edition, New York, 1923), XXII, 118, 122.

[2] See Appendix B.

[3] The author recalled three of them in "Villagers"; see pp. 31, 37.

the name of the character John H. Day has not been found elsewhere in the annals of Hannibal. Day's eyes, "which, when in repose, suggested smouldering fires, and, when the man was stirred, surprised one by their exceeding brilliancy," seem to have moved inexplicably into this fact-laden narrative from a romance by Hawthorne. There is no indication that young Clemens was apprenticed to a jeweler, so it is likely that this is fictional substitution for the factual printer's apprenticeship. And even Mark Twain would have considered Day's clairvoyant feats highly improbable.

It is not difficult to think of reasons why the author may have abandoned this fragment. Although the story about the Ratcliff boy is sufficiently chilling as melodrama, nothing else in the narrative is anything like as bloodcurdling. Certainly the accounts of G——'s hidden remorse and of E——'s plan to forge a check are anticlimactic. From the outset, the narrative does not seem to move with any discernible purpose. And throughout, Mark Twain's writing lacks the gusto which can make even dull happenings attractive.

Even such a plodding performance still has some elements of interest. One is the evidence of the author's abiding interest in supernatural communications. Another is the peculiar combination of fact and fiction here. And a third is in finding here a rehearsal—this early—for the uncanny clairvoyant feats which long after would be performed by young Satan in versions of "The Mysterious Stranger."

Clairvoyant

WHEN I was a boy, there came to our village of Hannibal, on the Mississippi, a young Englishman named John H. Day, and went to work in the shop of old Mr. Stevens the jeweler, in Main street. He excited the usual two or three days' curiosity due to a new comer in such a place; and after that, as he seemed to prefer to keep to himself, the people bothered themselves no more about him, and he was left to his own devices. It was not difficult to give him his way in this, for he was taciturn, absorbed, and therefore uncompanionable and unattractive. As for looks, he was well enough, though there was nothing striking about him except his eyes, which, when in repose, suggested smouldering fires, and, when the man was stirred, surprised one by their exceeding brilliancy.

Mr. Day slept, cooked for himself, and ate, in the back part of the jewelry shop, and he was not seen outside the place oftener than once in twenty-four hours. He seemed to be nearly always at work, days, nights and Sundays. By and by, one noted this curious thing: he would accost a citizen, go to his house once, apparently study him an hour, then drop the acquaintanceship. You must understand that there were no castes in our society, and the jeweler's journeyman was as good as anybody and could go anywhere. At the end of a year he had in this way made and discarded the acquaintanceship of pretty much everybody. So here was a man who might be said to know all the town; and yet if any one were spoken to about him, the reply would have to be, "Well, I have met him—once—but I am not acquainted with him; I don't know him." It was odd—Mr. Day really knew everybody, after a fashion, and yet had wrought so quietly and gradually, that the town's impression was that he didn't know anybody and didn't wish to.

He seemed to have but one object in view in contriving his brief acquaintanceships; and that was, to get an opportunity to examine people's ears to see if they were threatened with deafness. He did not claim that he could cure deafness, or do anything for it at all; he only claimed that if a person had the seeds of future deafness in him he could discover the fact. The physicians said that this was nonsense; nevertheless, as Mr. Day did not charge anything for his examinations, the people were all willing to let him inspect their ears. He had no disposition to keep his theory a secret; but while his explanations of it sounded plausible to the general public, they only confirmed the physicians in their conviction that there was nothing in it. In time the irreverent came to speak of Day as the "Earbug," and he of course got the reputation of being a monomaniac—if "reputation" is not too large a word to apply to a person who was so little talked about.

By and by, I was apprenticed to the jeweler, and was placed under the tuition of his journeyman. Day was kind to me, and gentle; but during the first week or two he did not speak to me, except in the way of business, although I was with him all day and slept in the same room with him every night. I quickly grew to be fond of my silent comrade, and often staid about him, evenings, when I could have been out at play. He would work diligently at something or other until I went to bed at ten. Then, as the stillness of the night came on and I seemed to be sleeping, (which I wasn't,) he would presently tilt himself back in his chair and close his eyes —and then the strong interest of the evening began, for me. Smiles would flash across his face; then the signs of sharp mental pain;

then furies of passion. This stirring panorama of emotions would continue for hours, sometimes, and move me, excite me, exhaust me like a stage-play. Now and then he would glance at the clock, mutter the time and the day of the month, and say something like this: "People who think they know him would say the thing is incredible." Then he would take a fat note-book out of his breast pocket and write something in it. I marveled at these things, but took it out in marveling; I believed that the observing them clandestinely was dishonorable enough without gossiping about them.

One summer night, about midnight, I was watching him through my half closed lids, waiting for him to begin—for he had been reading all the evening, to my disappointment and discontent. Now he put down his book, and for a moment appeared to be doing something with his hands, I could not see what; then he settled himself back in his chair, closed his eyes peacefully, and the next moment sprang out of his seat with his face lit with horror and snatched me from the bed, stood me on my feet, and said:

"Run! don't stop to dress! young Ratcliff, the crazy one, is going to murder his mother. Don't tell anybody I said it."

Before I knew what I was about, I was flying up the deserted street in my shirt; and before I had had time to come to myself and realize what a fool I was to rush after one lunatic at the say-so of another, I had covered the two hundred yards that lay between our shop and the Ratcliff homestead, and was thundering at the ancient knocker of the side door with all my might. Then I came to myself, and felt foolish enough; I turned and looked toward the hut in a corner of the yard where young Ratcliff was kept in confinement; and sure enough, here came young Ratcliff flying across the yard in the moonlight, as naked as I was, and I saw the flash of a butcher knife which he was flourishing in his hand. I shouted "Help!" and "Murder!" and then fled away, still shouting these cries. When I got back to the shop, Day was not there; but in the course of half an hour he came in, and for the first time was talkative. He said a crowd gathered and captured the lunatic after he was inside the house and climbing the stairs toward his mother's room. He said Mrs. Ratcliff ought to know that I had saved her life, but he would take it as a great favor if I would keep carefully secret the fact of his own connection with the matter. I said I would, and it seemed to please him; and from that time forward he began to talk with me more or less every day, and I became his one intimate friend. We talked a good deal, that night, and at last I asked him why he hadn't gone to give the alarm himself instead of sending me, but he did not reply; and by and by when I ventured to ask him how he had divined that a man two hundred yards away was about to murder his mother, he was silent again; so I made up my mind that I would not push him too closely with questions thenceforward, at least until his manner should invite the venture.

Almost every day, now, my curiosity was laid on the rack. For instance, we would be sitting at work, and I would chance to mention some man or woman; whereupon Day would take up the person as a preacher would a text, and proceed in the placidest way to delineate his character in the most elaborate, searching and detailed way—and in nine cases out of ten his delineation would contain one and sometimes a couple of most absurd blunders, though otherwise perfect. I would point these out to him, but it never made any difference, he said he was right, and stuck calmly to his position. Then I would say, "Do you know this man personally?" And he would answer, in all cases, "No, not what you would call personally; I have met him once, for an hour." And when I retorted, "Why, I've known him all my life," he would simply say, as sufficient answer, "No matter; I know him as he is, you merely know him as he seems to be." On one occasion something brought up the name of G——, who had killed B——, over on the Sny, four years before, in a quarrel over some birds—the gentlemen being out shooting together at the time. Straightway Mr. Day began to paint G——'s character, according to his custom; and it was beautiful to hear him; you couldn't help saying to yourself all the time, "How true that is; how well he does it; how perfectly he knows this man, inside and out." But all at once, as usual, he spoilt it all, by remarking upon G——'s remorse on account of the homicide.

"Remorse!" I said. "What an idea that is. Why, the thing that

G—— is mainly hated for, in this town, is that he can be so perpetually and unchangeably cheerful, day in and day out, with that thing in his memory."

Day looked at me gravely and said:

"I tell you the man has never had one good, full, restful, peaceful hour in all these four years. He thinks of that crime with every breath he draws, and all his days are days of torture."

I said I didn't believe it and couldn't believe it. Day said:

"He has wanted to commit suicide, this long time."

I said that that statement would make the public laugh if they could hear it.

"No matter. He is his mother's idol, and is resolved to live while she lives; but he is also resolved to release himself when she dies. You will see; he will kill himself when she is taken away, and people will think grief for her loss moved him to it. She has been very sick for a week or two, now. If she should die, then you will see."

She did die, two or three days after that; and G—— killed himself the same night.

My days were full of interest, passed, as they were, in the presence of this fascinating and awful power. Now and then came an incident which one could smile at. One day old Mr. E——, a miserly person but of honorable reputation came into the shop and said to Mr. Day:

"Here is a bill on a broken Indiana bank which you gave me last Thursday in change. I ought to have brought it back sooner, but I was called away to Palmyra."

Day gave him a good bill for it, and E—— thanked him and went away. Then Day stood there with the bad bill in his hand, thinking, and presently said, as if to himself:

"There must be some mistake; I couldn't pay out a ten dollar bill and not remember it."

Then he did a thing which I had often seen him do before. He took a metal box out of his pocket, searched in it, put it back, and the next moment he said, in a surprised voice:

"Why, the man is a pitiful rascal."

"What has he done?" I asked.

"He has brought me a bad bill which he knew he did not get here."

I wanted to ask how he knew; but I restrained that impulse, and merely said it was a pity the shop had to lose all that money.

"It isn't lost," said Day; "he is on his way back, now, to get his bad bill again."

A minute or two later Mr. E—— bustled in, and said he had been mistaken about getting that bill in our shop, and he couldn't see how he happened to make such a—and there he stopped. Day was looking him placidly in the face, and just there E—— looked up, caught his eye, stopped speaking, turned red, re-exchanged the bills, and went away without another word, looking very crest-fallen.

I was prodigiously surprised, and said so; but Day said that if he had thought a moment he would have suspected E—— in the first place.

"He was the first man in whose parlor I sat in this town. I spent an hour or two there, talking; and he had it in his mind to forge T. R. Selmes's name to a check, for he was in money difficulties at the time."

"He—forge a check! Impossible. Did he say he was going to?"

"Nonsense—of course he didn't. But he had it in his mind to do it. I made a memorandum of it at the time."

He got out his note-book, and said:

"No, it wasn't Selmes—it was Brittingham he was going to forge it on."

A Human Bloodhound

(*From my Abandoned Autobiography.*)

PAGE NUMBERINGS indicate that "A Human Bloodhound" was first written as a continuous, self-contained narrative which Twain deliberately disguised as an excerpt by using the subhead, "From my Abandoned Autobiography" and by preceding the first sentence with three dots.

At some time while he was writing the abortive story "Indiantown," Twain decided to endow one of its characters, Orrin Lloyd Godkin, with a bloodhound-like sense of smell. He therefore decided to insert the matter of "A Human Bloodhound" at an appropriate point in "Indiantown." [1] So he rewrote some of the story originally told about Harbison, using Godkin's name,[2] and at other points in the original manuscript he merely substituted Godkin's name for Harbison's. Eventually, however, he decided against including the insertion.[3]

Although this fragment was written a decade or so after

---

[1] "Indiantown" is included in *WWD*, pp. 153–176. The insertion was to follow the words "in the dark," p. 166, line 3.

[2] This fragment is printed here as the "Godkin Fragment" immediately following the text of "A Human Bloodhound."

[3] On MS p. 46 of "Indiantown" he wrote a notation of the sort he often used for inserts, "Run to A &c," but later canceled it.

"Clairvoyant," [4] it has affiliations with the earlier composition. Both purport to be autobiographical, and the chief character in each has an unusual skill that brings him knowledge unavailable to other villagers. Both narrators are enabled to watch their heroes at close range and tell of the character's use, on several occasions, of his extraordinary powers. In both cases, as Paul Baender has noticed in writing about other works of the same period, "a character from outside a normal society is introduced to impart wisdom the society badly needs but cannot discover." [5] During the period when this fragment was being written, Mark Twain used the device most notably in successive versions of "The Mysterious Stranger," in which Philip Traum and "44" became just such figures. [6] These may well have seemed more satisfactory vehicles for such a character, since they enabled Clemens to develop some themes which were very important to him. Nevertheless in his burlesque on detective fiction, "A Double-Barrelled Detective Story," finished shortly before 8 September 1901 [7] and published in 1902, Twain gave Harbison-Godkin's bloodhound scent to Archy Stillman and made extensive use of it. The new story managed to be slightly better than the uncompleted "A Human Bloodhound."

---

[4] For the date, see Appendix B.
[5] "Alias MacFarlane: A Revision of Mark Twain Biography," *AL*, XXXVIII (May 1966), 192–193.
[6] See *MTSatan*.
[7] See Clemens's letter to Joseph Twichell dated 8 September 1901 in MTP.

A Human Bloodhound

(From my Abandoned Autobiography.)

. . . B<small>UT</small> as I have shown, the account of him which
my father left behind, deals with only one aspect of him, and
merely broadly generalizes that, without going much into particulars. That was like my father. He was always more interested in
reasoning out the origin of a curious thing than he was in playing
and fussing with the thing itself. But to others the particulars in
Harbison's case were the most interesting part. It was so with me,
and that was natural, I being only a boy and not a philosopher; and
it was so with the Corpse and also with his brother the lawyer—his
elder brother, I mean—Edward; for Alfred, the other one, as I have
already indicated, was too sick a man in those days to care for
earthly things of any kind. If any one in the village could be said to
be intimate with Harbison, it was the Corpse; and next to him,
Johnson. These two knew all about Harbison from his own lips; he
talked with them pretty freely, although he was so reserved with
the rest of the community. In turn they talked freely together about
Harbison almost every day; and of course, situated as I was, I heard
it all. And so in the course of time I came to know as much about

that human freak as there was to know. It gave him a tremendous interest in my eyes, and I used to stare at him with a fascinated gaze and an imagination surcharged with uncanny fancies as he passed by. The bigness of him, his breadth of shoulder, his slow and stately tread, his head bent in thought, his gloomy mien, the absence of the usual signs of age,—these things, assisted by his story, made him an impressive figure, and the three purple birthmark stripes across his face gave him the air of looking through a grating and supplied a touch of weirdness to the general effect which properly rounded it out and perfected it.

He was five or six years old before he found out that he was not as other children were. He was playing near a deserted house in a deserted field one day with some small comrades, in the summer gloaming, when a small creature raced past them and ran into the house. The startled children wondered what it was. He said it was a little cat. They said no, it might be a little dog, and it might be a little rabbit, it was too dark to tell. He said they were stupid—come, and he would show them the cat. So they entered the house and stood within the ruined door, but would venture no further, for the place was dark. He said, "I told you so—there she is, over there."

"Where?"

"In the corner."

"Do you see her?"

"No."

"Then how do you know?"

"Why, can't I smell her? Can't you?"

They laughed, and said he was a little fool; and they made so much fun of him that he was ashamed, and went and brought the cat, to establish his case. The children told the wonderful thing at home, and everybody came and tested him, and he was soon a much sought lion. This was pleasant enough for a time, but it presently became a distress and a bother; not to himself alone, but to his mother as well. He grew ashamed of being different from other children, and of being called a "dog-boy," and the matter was a distress to his mother because she lived a secluded life and neither paid nor received visits, and did not wish to know any one. Exhibitions of the boy's strange gift were stopped entirely, and by and by they ceased from being called for. After that, the young widow's peace was not disturbed again, and in time the lad's specialty dropped out of the people's talk and became a forgotten thing.

In his age Harbison did not make a secret of his gift, but it was not easy to get him to make idle exhibitions of it for the satisfaction of curiosity-mongers. He allowed Johnson and the Corpse to test him whenever they chose, in private, and so of course I had plenty of chances to be a witness. There was a strong feeling in the town against the Corpse on account of the new religion which he pretended to be getting up, and when the manuscript of his extravagant "Account of the Creation" was stolen it was Harbison who hunted the thief down and got it back. I was to blame for the theft, and was well scared when I missed the MS., for I had been often warned to put it away when I was called from my copying, but this time I didn't do it because I was only going across the street and expected to be back in a moment. But there was a street fight, and it lasted as much as ten minutes, and that was what made the trouble. I had left Johnson and the Corpse chatting in the front room, and of course they were a sufficient protection for the back one. Would have been, but for the fight. I was back from the fight a little before they were, and when I found the place empty and both doors standing open I was frightened. And cause enough, too. A glance into the back room realized that to me. My superiors arrived just then, and I told them what had happened, and I was almost crying. Of course the Corpse comforted me and said it wasn't any great matter, he could write it again and do it better this time—which was a lie, it made him sick and pale to think of that vast loss, but he was a good heart and couldn't bear to see anybody suffer if a lie could help him out any.

To make matters as bad as possible, Harbison was out of town and not expected back for a week, otherwise the thing would not have been so serious. But at this moment, when I was feeling my worst, Harbison stepped in. It was a great relief to us all. Harbison named the fifteen or twenty citizens who had been in the front room in the course of the day, then he went into the back room and said only one person had been in there besides me. He named poor old deacon West! That was a thunder-clap out of a clear sky, for if there was a man in the town with a more honorable record than the deacon, he had not been discovered yet. I went along with Harbison, but Johnson and the Corpse didn't wish to go, and stayed behind.

The deacon was confused, and ostensibly indignant, but Harbison walked by him and into a bedroom, and went to the bed and said "it's about this bed somewhere; will you search, deacon, or must I? Spare me that."

So the deacon apologised, and got it out from between the ticks. He said he had done wrong, but not from a selfish motive; he had heard that it was a wicked book and would do harm if published, and he wanted to save the people from moral injury by destroying it; but he was willing to confess that he had done wrong, and he begged that for the sake of his previous good name we would not tell his sin. We promised, and that was the end of it.

When Harbison was tracking anything you would not know it by the look of him, for he walked erect and did not need to stoop down to get the scent. He knew the scent of every person in the town, and could go along the empty streets at midnight and name all the people who had gone about them during the day. Also, he not only knew an old scent from a new one, but he could name the age in hours. He would say "Mr. Black passed here about four hours ago, and stepped on the track made by Mr. White about twenty hours ago;" and if you went and inquired you would find he was right. He couldn't ever be alone! the streets were crowded with the scent-spectres of men and women and dogs and cats and children, for him, when they were empty for you and you couldn't see a living thing. It was like crowding your way through swarms of ghosts when you walked by night with him, and although it was dead still you seemed to hear them rustle. It was very interesting and unpleasant, and I always liked it. When he found that I didn't talk and he could trust me, he took me along for company many a time—particularly after I had the luck to do him the good turn mentioned in a previous chapter. He mainly walked at night, and late; he liked to know who had been around during the day, but he didn't want their physical company.

He could keep secrets himself. The time that Jack Collins disappeared and everybody thought he was drowned, Harbison knew he was hiding in the town all the while; for he came out disguised and took exercise on dark nights and Harbison ran across his scent and we followed it to his hiding place and had a talk with him. We went there more than once, but didn't betray him. Harbison could go and walk through the church on a Sunday afternoon and name every person who had attended church and Sunday school there in the morning. No dog had any advantage of him; with the wind in his favor he could detect a stranger or any animal a measured distance of—I don't remember how many yards, but I know he could beat any of our hunting dogs on distance. He couldn't name the stranger, but he could name the animal without seeing it. I saw him stand the leeward of a decaying and offensive dead horse and "point" a covey of partridges that were behind some bushes twenty yards to windward of it. I smelt the horse myself, but not the birds. Our hunters had doubts about the birds, but Harbison was right, as it turned out. He said that there were five hundred smells present —of earth, grass, water, bees, bugs, butterflies, snakes, toads, numberless wild flowers and all manner of things, including the strenuous horse—but that each had its own peculiar and individual scent and projected it through the horse's fragrance distinct, undefiled, and easily recognizable. His sense of smell may be likened to the visual capacity of the most powerful microscope. Such a microscope makes large and clear a myriad of things that are wholly invisible to the naked eye, and Harbison's gift made smellable to him a myriad of things which to us are destitute of smell. To him rocks, sand, bricks—in fact everything—had a smell; a smell of its own; and he could go in the dark into a room which he had never been in before and by his nose locate every object in it and come out and name each of them and its place—always pretending to do it by sight. He could go on naming and locating the things until the listener was tired—which would happen before he could name all of them, of course, if there happened to be a thousand. He said that no two cats smelt alike, nor no two bricks, nor no two nails, nor apples, nor pieces of paper, nor men, nor elephants, nor fleas, nor flies, nor coins, nor anything you could mention in the universe. He said no two faces, nor hands, nor apples, nor peas, nor grains of sand, nor any other two things were ever of exactly the same form and dimensions, and that this law of nature was rigidly carried out in the matter of smells. He said that all the air was thick with smells, and that none of them was to him or to the finest dog unpleasant; and that it was the foolish prejudice of our training that made carrion unpleasant to us—it was not unpleasant to any savage.

His sense of smell would have been eyes for him if he had lost his sight. Wherever he was—even in the densest fog—he knew where every big and little object around about him was located, and the nature of it; and could name it and go straight to it and lay his hand upon it. By his talent he could tell when it was going to rain or snow, without having to go outside and consult the wind or the clouds.

His smell-memory was miraculous, and enduring. He said he did not think it possible for him to ever forget the smell of a friend; certainly not of an enemy. He said Ulysses' aged dog did not recognize his long-exiled master by his face and form, but by his smell. You could blindfold Harbison and bring fifty books from a library and deliver them to him one at a time as fast as he could take them and lay them down; and then you could carry them back and make a list of them as a help to your memory, scatter them here and there and yonder among the shelves, and send for him to come and find them. He would make his way through the house, easily following your track with his bandage on, and pass along the shelves and touch the fifty chosen books and no others. All done by niceness of sight, he pretended.

Lost children were a specialty with Harbison. A child of his acquaintance could not lose itself, winter or summer, on ice or sand or rocks or ground, where he couldn't find it. He was nonplussed only once. That was the time that Clark's little boy wandered away. Harbison walked the whole circuit of the yard, and said little Billy was in the house somewhere—he hadn't left the yard. The parents knew better, and were frightened; they believed Harbison had lost his discriminating sight. They said they had *seen* Billy playing outside the fence. Harbison went the rounds again, and said Billy was still on the premises; he said he knew the track that Billy's shoe would leave, and it wasn't there; there was no small track but a stranger's.

"Show me where he was playing, outside."

They took him to the place, but Harbison said—

"Billy hasn't been here—it's the stranger." Then he had an idea, and said, "How thoughtless you are—he has new shoes on, hasn't he? why didn't you say so?"

That was what had made the trouble. They swiftly followed the new shoes into the woods, and tracked them around a wide and erratic course; and when night came on, papa and the others retired from the hunt and sat down in the deeps of the forest to wait—for they had confidence in Harbison's capacities—but mamma held Harbison's hand and plowed through the briers and over the tree-roots and dead logs with him, for mothers can't wait; and toward midnight she had her desire and her reward, for they found the child curled up asleep on the ground, with his hands and face stained with the purple blood of blackberries, these signs being clearly visible to Harbison's nose.

It was Harbison that saved Henry Blake once, when he was in a bad scrape. He was a loafer and a thief, but that was believed to be the worst of him; but one winter's night screams were heard in the widow Aldrich's house, and Blake came flying out at the door and was caught. The widow was found lying on the floor of her bed-room up stairs covered with wounds and gasping her last. She died without speaking. Blake declared that he was not guilty of the murder. He said he had often robbed the widow's cellar of eatables, and that he was down there on the like errand when he heard the screams and tried to make his escape undetected. He had taken a few potatoes, and they were still in his overcoat pockets—they could search. Which they did, and found nothing else; nothing else except sixteen dollars in paper money. That was a bad detail, for two reasons: in the first place it was too much money for Blake to honestly possess at one time, and in the second place he had concealed it in the lining of his hat. He explained that he had stolen it from a stranger, but as he confessed that he couldn't produce the stranger, the explanation went for nothing.

By this time all the town had gathered, and the cry "lynch him, lynch him!" went up in a general chorus. A rope was brought and an end of it thrown over the limb of a tree; a tar-barrel was fired, and as the flame and smoke rose and the glare lit up the angry faces of the people and the cringing form of the noosed and beseeching poor outcast, Harbison came bursting through the crowd and seized Blake's end of the rope just as the executioners had begun to haul down upon the other. He said—

"This man didn't do it; I'll find you the right one."

The statement was doubted.

"Come with me," Harbison said, "and bring him along, if you like; you needn't let him out of your hands till I've shown you."

The crowd followed him to the house and up stairs, with lights, and he said—

"There—lift the blind, and you will see that the window is up."

They found it was true, but said—

"What of it?"

"Well, the man came in there, over the shed, and he went out that way, again."

"But how can you prove it?"

"By finding the man. Come with me and I will do it."

"Is it your smell that you are depending on?"

"Yes."

"All right, then. That is satisfactory. Who is the man?"

"I don't know; it's a stranger."

There were murmurs, and something was said about a bird in the hand being worth several in the bush, and Blake began to plead again; but Harbison said—

"You shall come with me, Blake, I will take care of you."

He was able to do it; that was recognised. The procession moved. Harbison walked around the house, picked up the track, and started off at a brisk pace, down the lane, into the road, over a rail fence, through a stubble-field, and onward to the river, then out on the ice and straight toward the further shore through a thaw-mist which was rapidly thickening into a fog.

[GODKIN FRAGMENT]

Godkin possessed one marvelous gift. Sight, *he* called it. It wasn't; but he made everybody believe it was sight, and no one ever knew any better until he disclosed his secret late in life when near his death. He claimed that all godkins had his wonderful vision, and that it was a part of their divine inheritance; that no genuine godkin was without it; that it was one of their trade-marks, and a sure identifier; that a pretender was certain to lack it, and the lack of it was proof absolute that he was no godkin.

When he finally revealed his secret it turned out that his specialty was not sight at all, but a bloodhound's sense of smell—and enlarged and improved, at that! A man with his gift might get along very well without sight, in fact. Godkin was probably right in hiding his gift from the people; no doubt he had more liberty to exercise it than he could have had if the nature of it had been known. He pretended that he could see through a blindfold, a wall, a board, through the pitch dark, through the thickest fog—through anything and everything you might mention. And he said that no two objects, big or little were exactly alike in shape or color, and that he could detect the differences by sight, howsoever slight they might be. He had to pretend all this, otherwise he could not have accounted for the bulk of the curious things which he ostensibly did with his eyes.

When he was tracking anything it was not suspected that he was not doing it with his eyes, for he walked erect and did not need to stoop down to get the scent. He knew the scent of every person in the town, and could go along the empty streets at midnight and smell out the day's history of every one's comings and goings. This all came out when he told his secret by and by and went into details. He not only knew an old scent from a new one, but he knew the age of a scent in hours. He would say to himself, "Mr. Black passed here about four hours ago and crossed the track made by Mr. White about twenty hours ago." He couldn't ever be alone! the streets were crowded with the scent-spectres of men and women and dogs and cats and children, for him, when they were empty and lonesome for other men and they couldn't see a living thing. It was like crowding and jostling his way through swarms of ghosts, and although the stillness might be perfect he always imagined he heard them rustle. He found it interesting and unpleasant, and always liked it.

He could walk through the church Sunday afternoon and name to himself every person who had attended Sunday school and the morning service. With the wind in his favor he could detect a stranger a mile. Once he stood to leeward of a decaying dead horse and "pointed" a covey of partridges that were behind some bushes thirty yards to windward of it. Of course he said he had seen them run in there, and the hunters believed him; whereas he had only smelt them. He spoke of this incident in his post-secret days, and said that when the thing happened there were five hundred smells present—of earth,

[Here Mark Twain meant to insert revised pages of the "Human Bloodhound" manuscript—pp. 73.21–75.22 in the present text.]

the purple blood of blackberries, these signs being clearly visible to Godkin's nose.

HUCK & TOM

Huck Finn and Tom Sawyer
among the Indians

I

EMERGING when most respected dramas and novels were romantic, nineteenth-century American humorists often won laughter by attacking such fictions. They did this indirectly in narratives full of realistic (and hence for the time incongruous) details and directly in essays, burlesques, and parodies. When Mark Twain comically contrasted the romantic portrayals of Europe or of the Far West or of the chivalrous South with the reality—in, respectively, *The Innocents Abroad, Roughing It,* and *Life on the Mississippi*—he was following a well established tradition.

Often Twain used specific authors as targets. In the third of these books he attacked Walter Scott, and in *Huckleberry Finn* he had a fine time lampooning unduly complex accounts of prison escapes. He was reading proofs of the "evasion" chapters during the summer of 1884. And he may well have decided then to write a book (vaguely predicted at the end of Huck's novel) that overtly attacked the romanticized Indians of Cooper and others.

His grudge against such idealized Indians was voiced at least as far

back as 1867 in a letter to the San Francisco *Alta California* in which
he deplored Eastern misapprehensions about the red men, and continued, "The Cooper Indians . . . died with their creator. The kind
that are left are of altogether a different breed." Passages written in
1869, 1870, 1872, and 1879 continued to contrast comically the Indian
of romantic fiction—physically impressive, noble, bold, truthful, mag-
nanimous, grateful, and modest—with what the author thought was the
Indian of reality. The latter he described as puny and dirty, ignoble,
cowardly, "a cesspool of falsehood," treacherous, sadistic, ungrateful,
and boastful.[1]

The relevance of these contrasts becomes clear when one realizes that
in the fragment, "Huck Finn and Tom Sawyer among the Indians"
(probably written in the summer of 1884),[2] Mark Twain traces a
development like those which gave several of his earlier books a unify-
ing theme—a change from romantic belief to disillusionment. Shortly
after the final events recorded in *Huckleberry Finn*, Tom Sawyer, Jim,
and Huck find themselves on a hemp farm in western Missouri. Tom,
always eager for adventure, revives the plan mentioned at the end of
Huckleberry Finn to "light out for the Territory." When Jim objects
that Indians are "a powful ornery lot," Tom represents them in the
conventional romantic fashion as physically magnificent and morally
admirable in every way. The trio goes West, eventually joining the
Mills family, which also is traveling westward. In time, the party
encounters and befriends five Indians. The Indians' later treacherous
attack upon the Mills family, their killing of several members, and their
kidnapping of the two Mills daughters and Jim lead Huck to ask:

> "Tom, where did you learn about Injuns—how noble they was, and
> all that?"

---

[1] The 1867 passage is in *Mark Twain's Travels with Mr. Brown*, ed. Franklin
Walker and G. Ezra Dane (New York, 1940), p. 266; in 1869 on 21 August "A
Day at Niagara" appeared in the Buffalo *Express* (it was reprinted in *Sketches,
New and Old* six years later); in September 1870 "The Noble Red Man" was
published in *The Galaxy*; in 1872 chapter nineteen of *Roughing It* carried on the
attack; in 1879 a chapter written for *A Tramp Abroad* but not included in the
book said stern things about the Comanche Indians (published in *Letters from
the Earth*, ed. Bernard DeVoto, [New York, 1962]). In *Roughing It* the author
mentioned novelist Emerson Bennett and playwrights for the Bowery Theatre, as
well as Cooper, as false portrayers of the Indian. In *The Galaxy* he claimed that
"all history and honest observation" verified his less romantic view and cited
specific evidence in De Benneville Randolph Keim, *Sheridan's Troopers on the
Borders* (Philadelphia, 1870).

[2] For a discussion of the dating, see Appendix B.

He give me a look [Huck reports] that showed me I had hit him hard, very hard, and so I wished I hadn't said the words. He turned away his head, and after about a minute he said "Cooper's novels," and didn't say anything more, and I didn't say anything more, and so that changed the subject.

The conversation comes slightly more than a third of the way through the fragment. In the remaining portion the boys and Brace Johnson, a seasoned plainsman and the fiancé of Peggy Mills, the older daughter, follow the kidnappers' trail and see even more devastating evidence of Indian cruelty. Brace has just donned a disguise which he believes will protect him from Indian hostilities when the narrative breaks off at the end of chapter nine.

II

In this narrative, as in others, Clemens drew upon his personal experiences and his reading. Tom, Huck, and Jim, as has been indicated many times, had prototypes in the Hannibal of their creator's boyhood. The living on the hemp farm where the action starts is as easy and opulent as it had been on the Quarles farm, pictured by John Quarles's nephew Samuel Clemens in factual and fictional works. As eighty or more Hannibal folk did in the 'forties—and as Mark Twain recalled some of them had done in "Villagers"—the boys set out for the West. When he wrote, the humorist probably recalled some of the news that had filtered back to Hannibal about the brushes of such migrants with Indians. Jim cites Widow Douglas's claim that "Ef dey [the Indians] ketches a body out, dey'll take en skin him same as dey would a dog," a belief that her prototype Mrs. Holliday of "Villagers" may have acquired when she heard about her husband's death in the West. Jim also cites "Gin'l Gaines," one of Hannibal's town drunkards, as an authority who has "been amongst" the Indians.

The location of the story is part of the Oregon Trail from western Missouri to the Platte River and along the Platte to its north fork. The fragment ends in Sioux territory near Fort Laramie. In 1861 the author had followed the same route on his way to Nevada Territory; Clemens (with assistance from his brother Orion, who also made the trip) had told the story in *Roughing It*. Huck's shocked reaction to the demon-

strative love of the Mills family recalls the author's comparison of his
family's refusal to show affection with his wife Olivia's greater warmth.
Huck's infatuation with the much older Peggy Mills recalls the boy
Sam Clemens's unrequited love for two girls several years older than he
was. Indian massacres like the one in which several members of the
Mills family died were part of Jane Clemens's family tradition.

Finally, the author was convinced that he had seen enough of
Indians during his years in Nevada to have become an authority on
them. He so stated in a *Galaxy* article in September 1870, and in the
summer of 1886 he complimented Buffalo Bill Cody on the authenticity
of his Wild West Show, which he had seen on two successive days:

> [It] brought back to me the breezy, wild life of the Rocky Mountains . . .
> Down to its smallest details, the show is genuine—cowboys, vaqueros,
> Indians, stage coach, costumes and all; it is wholly free from sham and
> insincerity and the effects it produced upon me by its spectacles were
> identical with those wrought upon me a long time ago by the same
> spectacles on the frontier.[3]

Despite familiarity with some aspects of Western life, Clemens did
much reading about others' Western experiences, and he made a great
deal of use of literary sources. This may have become a habitual
procedure: he had drawn upon many books in writing *The Prince and
the Pauper* (1881) and *Life on the Mississippi* (1883); in the winter of
1883 and 1884 he had collected in his billiard room great piles of books
and notes for a projected story on the Sandwich Islands; and soon he
would embark upon *A Connecticut Yankee,* based upon much research
concerning the Middle Ages. Moreover, regardless of his claims, he had
not had enough experiences of the right sort to provide many details for
his narrative; the fact that he could draw so little on experience for this
narrative probably accounted for serious weaknesses in it.

In addition to the romantic portrayals of Indians by Cooper, Emerson
Bennett, and Robert Montgomery Bird which he had encountered as a
boy, Clemens had read several factual books about Indians before
1884. The *Galaxy* article mentions evidence that Indians are treacherous and cruel from Keim's *Sheridan's Troopers on the Borders* (1870).
In *Roughing It* and *Life on the Mississippi* Clemens quotes Parkman's
The Oregon Trail, a copy of which was in his library when he died. In a

---

[3] New York *Dispatch,* 18 July 1886, as cited in Don Russell, *The Lives and
Legends of Buffalo Bill* (Norman, Oklahoma, 1960), p. 321. In 1906, Cody
would figure in Mark Twain's story, "A Horse's Tale."

letter of 22 February 1877 he told William Dean Howells of his hope that President Rutherford B. Hayes would make Richard Irving Dodge head of the Indian Department, identifying his nominee as an army officer "who knows all about Indians and yet has some humanity in him." Late in life the author gave to the library in Redding, Connecticut, a copy of Dodge's *The Plains of the Great West and Their Inhabitants, Being a Description of the Plains, Game, Indians, &c. of the Great North American Desert* (New York, 1877) containing some of his annotations. In July 1884, at Clemens's request, the author's business agent secured copies of this book (presumably a second copy) and Dodge's *Our Wild Indians: Thirty-three Years' Personal Experience Among the Red Men of the Great West* (Hartford, 1883). Although the latter book merely repeats and expands a part of the first, Clemens wrote three hundred and seventy-five notes in its margins and also annotated the earlier book. At the same time he asked for "several other *personal narratives* of life & adventure out yonder on the Plains & in the Mountains . . . especially life *among the Indians*." "I mean," he added, "to take Huck Finn out there." The agent jotted down the name, "Gen G. A. Custer USA," author of *My Life on the Plains*, serialized in *The Galaxy* from 1872 to 1874 and published as a book in 1874; he may have sent Clemens a copy. The agent did send a copy of "Buffalo Bill's book"—a purported autobiography issued in 1879, and on 17 July the author told him, "Don't need any more Injun books." [4]

Mark Twain made some use of Keim, Parkman, and Cody as sources; he constantly—it may well be too constantly—used both of Dodge's books. He drew upon these authorities for character portrayals of both whites and Indians, for descriptions, for incidents, and for details developing themes. The Explanatory Notes will indicate his borrowings in detail, but I will mention a few instances here:

The names of two characters mentioned in Twain's narrative come from Parkman's book—old Vaskiss, the trader, and Roubidou, the blacksmith of Fort Laramie. The full portrait of Brace Johnson, a typical plainsman, includes physical aspects found in many narratives, including Mrs. Custer's description of her husband in her introduction to *My Life on the Plains*, and Buffalo Bill's picture of Horace Billings.

---

[4] *A1911*, p. 56; Albert Stone's catalog of Clemens's books in the Redding (Connecticut) library; *MTHL*, I, 172; *MTBus*, pp. 264–265, 267, 270; a letter from Charles Webster to Clemens dated 9 July 1884 and a letter from Clemens to Charles Webster dated "Thursday" [10 July 1884], (TS in MTP).

Custer's description of Wild Bill Hickok is strikingly similar in the
details and their ordering, and it may be significant that Clemens could
have seen the passage in any of three places—in Custer's narrative
either in *The Galaxy* or in book form, or in William F. Cody's autobiography, *The Life of the Hon. William F. Cody, Known as Buffalo Bill,
the Famous Hunter, Scout and Guide* (Hartford, 1879). Here are two
passages for comparison:

MARK TWAIN	CUSTER
Brace Johnson was . . . more than six foot tall . . . and had broad shoulders, and he was as straight as a jackstaff . . . He had the steadiest eye you ever see, and a handsome face, and his hair hung all down his back, and how he ever could keep his outfit so clean and nice, I never could tell . . . His buckskin suit looked always like it was new, and it was all hung with fringes, and had a star as big as a plate between the shoulders of his coat, made of beads . . . and had beads on his moccasins, and a hat as broad as a barrel-head, and he never looked so fine and grand as he did a-horseback . . . And as for strength, I never see a man that was any more than half as strong . . . and a most lightning marksman with a gun or a bow or a pistol. . . .	In person he [Wild Bill] was about six feet and one inch in height, straight as the straightest of the warriors whose implacable foe he was. He had broad shoulders, well-formed chest and limbs, and a face strikingly handsome; a sharp, clear blue eye, which stared you straight in the face when in conversation; . . . His hair and complexion were those of the perfect blonde. The former was worn in uncut ringlets, falling carelessly over his powerfully formed shoulders. Add to this figure a costume blending the immaculate neatness of the dandy with the extravagant taste and style of the frontiersman, and you have Wild Bill. . . . Whether on foot or on horseback, he was one of the most perfect types of physical manhood I ever saw. . . . His skill in the use of the pistol and rifle was unerring . . . He seldom spoke himself unless requested to do so.[5]
He didn't talk very much . . .	

Mark Twain might have found details for his characterizations of
Indians in the works of many writers, for the contrast he drew between

---

[5] Custer, as quoted in *The Life of the Hon. William F. Cody*, p. 70. The
resemblance between Brace Johnson and Horace Billings, as described by Cody, is
striking. Billings "was about six feet two inches tall, was well built, and had a
light, springy and wiry step. He wore a broad-brimmed California hat, and was
dressed in a complete suit of buckskin, beautifully trimmed and beaded" (p. 30).
Cody's book, incidentally, was published in 1879 by Frank Bliss, who in that year
was selected by the humorist to publish *A Tramp Abroad*. Clemens later changed
his plans.

Cooper's romantic characters and real Indians was commonplace. But since he considered Dodge an authority, the humorist chiefly depended upon Dodge's books for such information. In fact, he took more from Dodge than from all his other authorities combined. The religious beliefs which Brace adopted from the Indians, for example, are exactly those which Dodge discusses at length. These include faith in two gods, one good and one bad, and the belief that only the bad god has to be propitiated. We know that Clemens (as one would expect) was interested in the passages concerning religion, because he made notes on them in his copy of *Our Wild Indians*.

However, traces of other sources are clear. The massacre of the Mills family, for instance, closely resembles that of the Germaine family as described by William Blackmore in an Introduction to Dodge's *The Plains of the Great West* (pp. l–li). Like the Millses, the Germaines travel alone; in both accounts, Indians shoot the father, tomahawk the mother, kill all the children except the daughters, burn the wagon, and carry the girls away tied on horses. One Germaine girl, like Huck, helplessly watches the massacre and later describes it. For reasons which Dodge indicates, Brace knows that the child Flaxy and the Negro Jim are safe when the Indians capture them. He also knows that when the Indians kidnap Peggy, by contrast, they intend to torture and rape her (in a manner described by Dodge). But Brace is relieved to recall that Peggy can use a dirk that he has given her to kill herself. Blackmore says that "the western man . . . makes arrangement to kill himself, wife, and children, rather than any of them should fall into the hands of Indians on the war path" (Introduction to *The Plains of the Great West*, p. xlix). Huck has no heart to tell Brace, therefore, that Peggy no longer has her dirk. Her defenselessness adds horror to Brace's discovery in a deserted Indian camp of four pegs driven into the ground and Huck's discovery of a bloody scrap of the girl's dress. For Dodge reports that the woman captive who resists has her clothes torn off, and then is roped to four such pegs and is raped by her captors.

Dodge provides other material developed at length in Twain's fragment—the fog in which Tom and the stranger are lost, their panic, Huck's vigil over the stranger, and details about the waterspout. As the narrative breaks off, Brace has disguised himself as a crazy man by sewing dried insects and lizards on his clothing, hopeful that this expedient will protect him. In *Our Wild Indians*, Dodge recounts the story of "a prominent scientist" who is considered insane and is therefore not harmed by the Indians who have found his pack "loaded with insects, bugs and loathsome reptiles." Twain took several less important characterizations, descriptions, details, and incidents from Dodge as well.

III

In a discussion of "Indians" which accompanies the fragment in the Mark Twain Papers, Bernard DeVoto weighed its faults and its merits. Some details he found improbable: "worst of all the initial one that so small a party should be traveling alone in the Plains," the propitiation of the Indians' bad god by fasting, the fog on the plains, the details about the waterspout. Since all these are based upon Dodge and at least two (the fog and the waterspout) are also described by Custer, his criticism hardly holds. Other details drawn from Dodge were commended by DeVoto as authentic; for example, Brace's adoption of Indian beliefs, the motivation for the massacre, and Brace's plan to persuade the Indians that he is mad. When one considers these and other such authentic touches, one sees that, as DeVoto pointed out, Twain's plan was characteristic—"to get in all typical plains experiences and sights." As Albert E. Stone has said, "As far as the narrative is carried, it is an honest portrayal of life on the plains." [6] Such a depiction, typical for this period of thriving local-color writing, gives historical interest to the narrative. The author showed his customary tendency to develop subject matter which was very popular at the moment: in 1884, Deadwood Dick was still going strong in Half-Dime Library paperbacks; Helen Hunt Jackson's novel portraying West Coast Indians, *Ramona,* was a best-seller; and Buffalo Bill's Wild West Show was making its second triumphant tour of the country. To his credit, Twain refused merely to shovel his subject matter into his narrative; he managed to dramatize it, relate it to the narrative, and integrate it.

DeVoto was unhappy about the style of the fragment, and with some reason. Brace Johnson talks as Clemens later would scold Natty Bumppo for talking—at times in highfalutin phrases, at times quite colloquially. Even Huck now and then sounds unlike his vernacular

---

[6] *IE,* p. 180.

self, for example, "so I let it just rest there, not ever having any disposition to fret or worry any person." But despite unevenness, Huck's language occasionally recovers the merits it had in *Huckleberry Finn*. While remaining in character, it vividly describes scenes and events—the vast stretches of the prairie, thunderstorms, the striking presence of Brace Johnson, the ravaged face of the starving man lost in the fog, the fog itself, the waterspout, and the massacre. Now and then it provides welcome touches of humor. A grammatical invention may amuse momentarily, as when Huck, having urged Peggy to talk about her sweetheart, says with alarm, "It looked like the mainest trouble was going to be to stop her again." A malapropism may make a point accidentally, as when Huck paraphrases Brace's comment on the bad god: "He said a body had got to perpetuate him in all kinds of ways." A figure of speech may be at the same time incongruous and highly appropriate, as in Huck's account of Brace's action when he forces the boy to dismount from his mule: "he . . . snaked me off like I was a doll, and set me on the ground." Another figure exaggerates the boy's fear and speed as he runs away after a lightning flash has revealed a dead man in the tent with him: "I was out in the public wilderness before the flash got done quivering . . ." Or the phrasing may comically underline Huck's traits. His combination of parochial intolerance and genial tolerance becomes evident in his remark about the unrestrained way the Mills family displays affection: "it took me two or three days to get so I could keep from blushing, I was so ashamed for them, though I knowed it warn't the least harm, because they was right out of the woods and didn't know no better." His practical way of evaluating religion even when it helps a "wicked" activity is shown as he tells the aftermath of Peggy's giving a Bible and religious instruction to Blue Fox: "it didn't do him no particular good—that is, it didn't just then, but it did after a little, because when the Injuns got to gambling . . . he put up his Bible against a tomahawk and won it."

If these were typical passages, at least one element in the fragment might be fairly good—its style. For the most part, however, compared with Huck's best passages, the style is flat and undistinguished. One reason, one suspects, is that the events invented for this narrative were not so truly felt as events in narratives based upon Twain's own experiences. A second reason, surely, is that, instead of consistently utilizing Huck's peculiar qualities as a first-person narrator, the author uses them only occasionally. Much of the impact of *Huckleberry Finn* comes from the boy's unconscious revelation throughout the novel of important matters of which he is unaware, for instance, the conflict between false social codes and true morality and the inferiority of living by conventions to living by instinct. No such revelations can run through the Indian narrative, since Huck's creator never hits upon a theme which such an unconscious revelation can develop.

One may go further and say that Twain never hits upon *any* significant theme. The humorist's belief that Cooper's Indians are falsely drawn and that actual Indians are scoundrels is hardly a fitting theme for a long narrative. As soon as the Indians have been shown being treacherous and cruel part way through chapter three, the theme has been developed, and further instances of treachery and cruelty are superfluous. The theme is developed, moreover, by the author's representing the Indians as wholly malicious and evil—as "Bad Guys," more appropriate for cheap melodrama than for memorable fiction. Perhaps because they find themselves in such impossible company, the whites of the story tend to become impossible too. Not only the feminine characters, who often are unbelievably angelic when Twain pictures them, but also the men—the rebellious Huck and Tom and even the tough plainsman Brace Johnson—become paragons of virtue.[7] At one point Huck (of all people!) even confesses himself incapable of thinking up a convincing lie, and he is never allowed to display his ingratiating human frailties.

A more promising theme than Indian depravity was the contrast between Christian and Indian beliefs, a contrast allowing satire since it favored the non-Christian religion. The author's awareness of this theme is shown by two notes in the margin of his copy of *Our Wild Indians*: "Our illogical God is all-powerful in name, but impotent in fact; the Great Spirit is not all-powerful, but does the very best he can for his injun and does it free of charge." And: "We have to keep our God placated with prayers, and even then we are never sure of him— how much higher and finer is the Indian's God."[8] In chapter six, Twain has Brace state that in dealing with their two gods the Indians disregard the good one and placate the bad one. The Indians' two gods thus provide a logical solution for what the humorist saw as two unsolved dilemmas in Christian belief—the inexplicable combination in the

---

[7] Jim is given so small a role that one wonders why Mark Twain did not make the slight effort needed to remove him from his first draft.

[8] *A1911*, p. 24. The marginalia occur on pp. 108 and 112 of Dodge's book.

Christian deity of superhuman benevolence with ferocity and the puzzling fact that men were required to fear and placate a God who purportedly loved them. Huck's practical vision underlines the incongruity when he says that among the Indians "there warn't any occasion to be bothering him [the good god] with prayers and things" and when he pictures the bad god "setting up nights to think up ways to bring them bad luck and bust up all their plans, and never fooled away a chance to do them all the harm he could." Huck might have achieved satire quite typical of him at his best had he consistently assumed that the Indian religion was as degraded as the Indians were, all the while unwittingly proving that Indian doctrines were logically superior to the Christian. But somehow, in this version Twain failed to develop that inherent incongruity.

He might have done better in a rewriting, but no revised version has been found. Paine says that "at the end of Chapter IX Huck and Tom had got themselves into a predicament from which it seemed impossible to extricate them, and the plot was suspended for further inspiration, which apparently never came." [9] In his notes on the fragment, DeVoto defines the predicament—and it was Twain's rather than his characters'. The humorist, always prudish in his writings, had to deal with the fearful signs that Peggy Mills had been staked to the ground and then raped. Twain might have achieved a happy ending, to be sure, by having his characters discover that the stakes had been used for another purpose—for the torture of male captives or for the torture of a female captive by a squaw. But even so, Huck would have had to talk less ambiguously about rape than he does in the fragment—and Mark Twain probably decided that this was impossible in a novel by him. True, he might have avoided this impasse by having the Indians capture only Flaxy and Jim (whom they had reasons to spare). Then Peggy might have joined the boys and Brace in the pursuit. But one suspects the author would have been unhappy about being unable to reveal what for him was the Indians' most horrible iniquity. When the problem of the ending loomed up, along with problems of weak characterization, plotting, thematic development, and handling of fictional point of view, Mark Twain may well have concluded that completion of the narrative was impossible.

---

[9] *MTB*, p. 899.

Huck Finn and Tom Sawyer among the Indians

Chapter 1

THAT OTHER book which I made before, was named "Adventures of Huckleberry Finn." Maybe you remember about it. But if you don't, it don't make no difference, because it ain't got nothing to do with this one. The way it ended up, was this. Me and Tom Sawyer and the nigger Jim, that used to belong to old Miss Watson, was away down in Arkansaw at Tom's aunt Sally's and uncle Silas's. Jim warn't a slave no more, but free; because—but never mind about that: how he become to get free, and who done it, and what a power of work and danger it was, is all told about in that other book.

Well then, pretty soon it got dull there on that little plantation, and Tom he got pisoned with a notion of going amongst the Injuns for a while, to see how it would be; but about that time aunt Sally took us off up home to Missouri; and then right away after that she went away across the State, nearly to the west border, to stay a month or two months with some of her relations on a hemp farm out there, and took Tom and Sid and Mary; and I went along because Tom wanted me to, and Jim went too, because there was white men around our little town that was plenty mean enough and ornery enough to steal Jim's papers from him and sell him down the river again; but they couldn't come that if he staid with us.

Well, there's liver places than a hemp farm, there ain't no use to deny it, and some people don't take to them. Pretty soon, sure enough, just as I expected, Tom he begun to get in a sweat to have something going on. Somehow, Tom Sawyer couldn't ever stand much lazying around; though as for me, betwixt lazying around and pie, I hadn't no choice, and wouldn't know which to take, and just as soon have them both as not, and druther. So he rousted out his Injun notion again, and was dead set on having us run off, some night, and cut for the Injun country and go for adventures. He said it was getting too dull on the hemp farm, it give him the fan-tods.

But me and Jim kind of hung fire. Plenty to eat and nothing to do. We was very well satisfied. We hadn't ever had such comfortable times before, and we reckoned we better let it alone as long as Providence warn't noticing; it would get busted up soon enough, likely, without our putting in and helping. But Tom he stuck to the thing, and pegged at us every day. Jim says:

"I doan' see de use, Mars Tom. Fur as I k'n see, people dat has Injuns on dey han's ain' no better off den people dat ain' got no Injuns. *Well* den: we ain' got no Injuns, we doan' need no Injuns, en what does we want to go en hunt 'em up f'r? We's gitt'n along jes' as well as if we had a million un um. Dey's a powful ornery lot, anyway."

"*Who* is?"

"Why, de Injuns."

"Who says so?"

"Why, I says so."

"What do *you* know about it?"

"What does *I* know 'bout it? I knows dis much. Ef dey ketches a body out, dey'll take en skin him same as dey would a dog. *Dat's* what I knows 'bout 'em."

"All fol-de-rol. Who told you that?"

"Why, I hear ole Missus say so."

"Ole Missus! The widow Douglas! Much she knows about it. Has *she* ever been skinned?"

"Course not."

"Just as I expected. She don't know what she's talking about. Has she ever been amongst the Injuns?"

"No."

"Well, then, what right has she got to be blackguarding them and telling what ain't so about them?"

"Well, anyway, ole Gin'l Gaines, *he's* ben amongst 'm, anyway."

"All right, so he has. Been with them lots of times, hasn't he?"

"Yes—lots of times."

"Been with them *years,* hasn't he?"

"Yes, *sir!* Why, Mars Tom, he—"

"Very well, then. Has *he* been skinned? You answer me that."

Jim see Tom had him. He couldn't say a word. Tom Sawyer *was* the keenest boy for laying for a person and just leading him along by the nose without ever seeming to do it till he got him where he couldn't budge and then bust his arguments all to flinders *I* ever see. It warn't no use to argue with Tom Sawyer—a body never stood any show.

Jim he hem'd and haw'd, but all he could say was, that he had somehow got the notion that Injuns was powerful ornery, but he reckoned maybe—then Tom shut him off.

"You reckon maybe you've been mistaken. Well, you have. *Injuns* ornery! It's the most ignorant idea that ever—why, Jim, they're the noblest human beings that's ever been in the world. If a white man tells you a thing, do you know it's true? No, you don't; because generally it's a lie. But if an Injun tells you a thing, you can bet on it every time for the petrified fact; because you can't get an Injun to lie, he would cut his tongue out first. If you trust to a white man's honor, you better look out; but you trust to an Injun's honor, and nothing in the world can make him betray you—he would die first, and be glad to. An Injun is *all* honor. It's what they're *made* of. You ask a white man to divide his property with you—will he do it? I think I *see* him at it; but you go to an Injun, and he'll give you everything he's got in the world. It's just the difference between an

Injun and a white man. They're just all generousness and unstin-
geableness. And brave? Why, they ain't afraid of anything. If there
was just one Injun, and a whole regiment of white men against
him, they wouldn't stand the least show in the world,—not the
least. You'd see that splendid gigantic Injun come war-whooping
down on his wild charger all over paint and feathers waving his
tomahawk and letting drive with his bow faster than anybody could
count the arrows and hitting a soldier in any part of his body he
wanted to, every time, any distance, and in two minutes you'd see
him santering off with a wheelbarrow-load of scalps and the rest of
them stampeding for the United States the same as if the menag-
erie was after them. Death?—an Injun don't care shucks for death.
They prefer it. They *sing* when they're dying—sing their death-
song. You take an Injun and stick him full of arrows and splinters,
and hack him up with a hatchet, and skin him, and start a slow fire
under him, and do you reckon he minds it? No sir; he will just set
there in the hot ashes, perfectly comfortable, and *sing,* same as if he
was on salary. Would a white man? *You* know he wouldn't. And
they're the most gigantic magnificent creatures in the whole world,
and can knock a man down with a barrel of flour as far as they can
see him. They're awful strong, and fiery, and eloquent, and wear
beautiful blankets, and war paint, and moccasins, and buckskin
clothes, all over beads, and go fighting and scalping every day in the
year but Sundays, and have a noble good time, and they love
friendly white men, and just dote on them, and can't do too much
for them, and would ruther die than let any harm come to them,
and they think just as much of niggers as they do of anybody, and
the young squaws are the most beautiful be-utiful maidens that was
ever in the whole world, and they love a white hunter the minute
their eye falls on him, and from that minute nothing can ever shake
their love loose again, and they're always on the watch-out to
protect him from danger and get themselves killed in the place of
him—look at Pocahontas!—and an Injun can see as far as a tele-
scope with the naked eye, and an enemy can't slip around anywhere, even in the dark, but he knows it; and if he sees one single
blade of grass bent down, it's all he wants, he knows which way to

and not showing fire or a light; and just before dawn we crept up pretty close and then sprung out, whooping and yelling, and took it by surprise, and never lost a man, Tom said, and was awful proud of it, though I couldn't see no sense in all that trouble and bother, because we could a took it in the day time just as well, there warn't nobody there. Tom called the place a cavern, though it warn't a cavern at all, it was a house, and a mighty ornery house at that.

Every day we went up to the little town that was two mile from the farm, and bought things for the outfit and to barter with the Injuns—skillets and coffee pots and tin cups, and blankets, and three sacks of flour, and bacon and sugar and coffee, and fish hooks, and pipes and tobacco, and ammunition, and pistols, and three guns, and glass beads, and all such things. And we hid them in the woods; and nights we clumb out of the window and slid down the lightning rod, and went and got the things and took them to the cavern. There was an old Mexican on the next farm below ours, and we got him to learn us how to pack a pack-mule so we could do it first rate.

And last of all, we went down fifteen or twenty mile further and bought five good mules, and saddles, because we didn't want to raise no suspicions around home, and took the mules to the cavern in the night and picketed them in the grass. There warn't no better mules in the State of Missouri, Tom said, and so did Jim.

Our idea was to have a time amongst the Injuns for a couple of months or so, but we had stuff enough to last longer than that, I reckon, because Tom allowed we ought to be fixed for accidents. Tom bought a considerable lot of little odds and ends of one kind and another which it ain't worth while to name, which he said they would come good with the Injuns.

Well, the last day that we went up to town, we laid in an almanac, and a flask or two of liquor, and struck a stranger that had a curiosity and was peddling it. It was little sticks about as long as my finger with some stuff like yellow wax on the ends, and all you had to do was to rake the yellow end on something, and the stick would catch fire and smell like all possessed, on account of part of it being brimstone. We hadn't ever heard of anything like that,

before. They were the convenientest things in the world, and just
the trick for us to have; so Tom bought a lot of them. The man
called them lucifer matches, and said anybody could make them
that had brimstone and phosphorus to do it with. So he sold Tom a
passel of brimstone and phosphorus, and we allowed to make some
for ourselves some time or other.

We was all ready, now. So we waited for full moon, which
would be in two or three days. Tom wrote a letter to his aunt Polly
to leave behind, telling her good bye, and saying rest easy and not
worry, because we would be back in two or three weeks, but not
telling her anything about where we was going.

And then Thursday night, when it was about eleven and everything still, we got up and dressed, and slid down the lightning rod,
and shoved the letter under the front door, and slid by the nigger-
quarter and give a low whistle, and Jim come gliding out and we
struck for the cavern, and packed everything onto two of the mules,
and put on our belts and pistols and bowie knives, and saddled up
the three other mules and rode out into the big moonlight and
started west.

By and by we struck level country, and a pretty smooth path, and
not so much woods, and the moonlight was perfectly splendid, and
so was the stillness. You couldn't hear nothing but the skreaking of
the saddles. After a while there was that cool and fresh feeling that
tells you day is coming; and then the sun come up behind us, and
made the leaves and grass and flowers shine and sparkle, on account
of the dew, and the birds let go and begun to sing like everything.

So then we took to the woods, and made camp, and picketed the
mules, and laid off and slept a good deal of the day. Three more
nights we traveled that way, and laid up daytimes, and everything
was mighty pleasant. We never run across anybody, and hardly
ever see a light. After that, we judged we was so far from home that
we was safe; so then we begun to travel by daylight.

The second day after that, when we was hoping to begin to see
Injun signs, we struck a wagon road, and at the same time we
struck an emigrant wagon with a family aboard, and it was near
sundown, and they asked us to camp with them, and we done it.

There was a man about fifty-five and his wife, named Mills, and three big sons, Buck and Bill and Sam, and a girl that said she was seventeen, named Peggy, and her little sister Flaxy, seven year old. They was from down in the lower end of Missouri, and said they was bound for Oregon—going to settle there. We said we was bound for the Injun country, and they said they was going to pass through it and we could join company with them if we would like to.

They was the simple-heartedest good-naturedest country folks in the world, and didn't know anything hardly—I mean what you call "learning." Except Peggy. She had read considerable many books, and knowed as much as most any girl, and was just as pretty as ever she could be, and live. But she warn't no prettier than she was good, and all the tribe doted on her. Why they took as much care of her as if she was made out of sugar or gold or something. When she'd come to the camp fire, any of her brothers would get up in a minute and give her the best place. I reckon you don't see that kind of brothers pretty often. She didn't have to saddle her own mule, the way she'd have to do in most society, they always done it for her. Her and her mother never had anything to do but cook, that is all; the brothers got the wood, they built the fires, they skinned the game; and whenever they had time they helped her wash up the things. It ain't often you see a brother kiss his own sister; fact is, I don't know as I'd ever seen such a thing before; but they done it. I know, because I see them do it myself; and not just once, but plenty of times. Tom see it, too, and so did Jim. And they never said a cross word to her, not one. They called her "dear." Plenty of times they called her that; and right before company, too; they didn't care; they never thought nothing of it. And she didn't, either. They'd say "Peggy dear," to her, just in the naturalest off-handedest way, it didn't make no difference who was around; and it took me two or three days to get so I could keep from blushing, I was so ashamed for them, though I knowed it warn't the least harm, because they was right out of the woods and didn't know no better. But I don't wish to seem to be picking flaws in them, and abusing them, because I don't. They was the splendidest people in the world; and

after you got that fact stowed in your mind solid, you was very well
satisfied, and perfectly willing to overlook their manners; because
nobody can't be perfect, anyway.

We all got to be uncommon friendly together; it warn't any
trouble at all. We traveled with them, and camped with them every
night. Buck and Bill and Sam was wonderful with a lasso, or a gun,
or a pistol, or horseback riding, and they learned us all these things
so that we got to be powerful good at them, specially Tom; and
though he couldn't throw a lasso as far as a man could, he could
throw it about as true. And he could cave in a squirrel's or a wild
turkey's or a prairie chicken's head any fair distance; and could send
both loads from his pistol through your hat on a full gallop, at
twenty yards, if you wanted him to. There warn't ever any better
people than the Millses; but Peggy she was the cap-sheaf of the lot,
of course; so gentle, she was, and so sweet, and whenever you'd
done any little thing for her it made you feel so kind of all over
comfortable and blessed to see her smile. If you ever felt cut, about
anything, she never asked about the rights of it, or who done it, but
just went to work and never rested till she had coaxed the smart all
out and made you forget all about it. And she was that kind of a girl
that if you ever made a mistake and happened to say something that
hurt her, the minute you saw by her face what you had done, you
wanted to get down on your knees in the dirt, you felt so mean and
sorry. You couldn't ever get tired looking at her, all day long, she
was so dear and pretty; and mornings it warn't ever sun-up to me
till she come out.

One day, about a couple of weeks after we had left the United
States behind, and was ever so far away out on the Great Plains, we
struck the Platte river and went into camp in a nice grassy place a
couple of hours before sun-down, and there we run across a camp of
Injuns, the first ones we had been close enough to, yet, to get
acquainted with. Tom was powerful glad.

Chapter 3

IT WAS just the place for a camp; the likeliest we had found yet. Big stream of water, and considerable many trees along it. The rest of the country, as far as you could see, any which-way you looked, clear to where the sky touched the earth, was just long levels and low waves—like what I reckon the ocean would be, if the ocean was made out of grass. Away off, miles and miles, was one tree standing by itself, and away off the other way was another, and here and yonder another and another scattered around; and the air was so clear you would think they was close by, but it warn't so, most of them was miles away.

Old Mills said he would stop there and rest up the animals. I happened to be looking at Peggy, just then, because I mostly always happened to be looking at her when she was around, and her cheeks turned faint red and beautiful, like a nigger's does when he puts a candle in his mouth to surprise a child; she never said nothing, but pretty soon she got to singing low to herself and looking happy. I didn't let on; but next morning when I see her slip off to the top of one of them grass-waves and stand shading her eyes with her hand and looking away off over the country, I went there and got it all out of her. And it warn't no trouble, either, after she got started. It looked like the mainest trouble was going to be to stop her again.

She had a sweetheart—that was what was the matter of her. He had staid behind, to finish up things, and would be along when he got done. His name was Brace Johnson; big, and fine, and brave, and good, and splendid, and all that, as near as I could make out; twenty-six years old; been amongst the Injuns ever since he was a boy, trapping, hunting, scouting, fighting; knowed all about Injuns, knowed some of the languages, knowed the plains and the mountains, and all the whole country, from Texas to Oregon; and now he was done with all that kind of life, and her and him was going to

settle down in Oregon, and get married, and go to farming it. I
reckon she thought she only loved him; but I see by her talk it was
upwards of that, she worshiped him. She said we was to stay where
we was till he come, which might be in a week, and then we would
stay as much longer as her pap thought the horses needed to.

There was five of the Injuns, and they had spry little ponies, and
was camped tolerable close by. They was big, strong, grand looking
fellows, and had on buckskin leggings and moccasins, and red
feathers in their hair, and knives and tomahawks, and bows and
arrows, and one of them had an old gun and could talk a little
English, but it warn't any use to him, he couldn't kill anything with
it because it hadn't any flint—I mean the gun. They was naked
from the waist up, when they hadn't on their blankets.

They set around our fire till bedtime, the first night, and took
supper with us, and passed around the pipe, and was very friendly,
and made signs to us, and grunted back, when we signed anything
they understood, and pretty much everything they see that they
liked, they wanted it. So they got coffee, and sugar, and tobacco,
and a lot of little things.

They was there to breakfast, next morning, and then me and
Tom went over to their camp with them, and we all shot at a mark
with their bows and arrows, and they could outshoot anything I
ever see with a bow and arrow, and could stand off a good ways and
hit a tree with a tomahawk every time.

They come back with us at noon and eat dinner, and the one
with the gun showed it to Peggy, and made signs would she give
him a flint, and she got one from her father, and put it in the
gunlock and fixed it herself, and the Injun was very thankful, and
called her good squaw and pretty squaw, and she was ever so
pleased; and another one named Hog Face that had a bad old hurt
on his shin, she bandaged it up and put salve on it, and he was very
thankful too.

Tom he was just wild over the Injuns, and said there warn't no
white men so noble; and he warn't by himself in it, because me and
Jim, and all the rest of us got right down fond of them; and Peggy
said she did wish Brace was here, he would change his notions

about Injuns, which he was down on, and hated them like snakes, and always said he wouldn't trust one any how or any where, in peace time or war time or any other time. She showed me a little dirk-knife which she got out of her bosom, and asked me what I reckoned it was for, and who give it to her.

"I don't know," says I. "Who did give it to you?"

"Brace." Then she laughed, gay and happy, and says, "You'll never guess what it's for."

"Well, what is it for?" says I.

"To kill myself with!"

"O, good land!" says I, "how you talk."

"Yes," she says, "it's the truth. Brace told me that if I ever fell into the hands of the savages, I mustn't stop to think about him, or the family, or anything, or wait an hour to see if I mightn't be rescued; I mustn't waste *any* time, I mustn't take any chances, I must kill myself right away."

"Goodness," I says, "and for why?"

"I don't know."

"Didn't you ask him why?"

"Of course; and teased him to tell me, but he wouldn't. He kept trying to get me to promise, but I laughed him off, every time, and told him if he was so anxious to get rid of me he must tell me *why* I must kill myself, and then maybe I would promise. At last he said he *couldn't* tell me. So I said, very well, then, I wouldn't promise; and laughed again, but he didn't laugh. By and by he said, very serious and troubled, 'You know I wouldn't ask you to do that or any other thing that wasn't the best for you—you can trust me for that, can't you?' That made me serious, too, because that was true; but I couldn't promise *such* a thing, you know, it made me just shudder to think of it. So then he asked me if I would keep the dirk, as his gift and keepsake; and when I said I would, he said that would do, it was all he wanted."

One of the Injuns, named Blue Fox, come up, just then, and the minute he see the dirk he begun to beg for it; it was their style— they begged for everything that come in their way. But Peggy wouldn't let him have it. Next day and the next he come teasing

around her, wanting to take it to his camp and make a nice new
sheath and a belt for her to wear it in, and so she got tired at last
and he took it away. But she never let him have it till he promised
he would take good care of it and never let it get out of his hands.
He was that pleased, that he up and give her a necklace made out
of bears' claws; and as she had to give him something back, of
course, she give him a Bible, and tried to learn him some religion,
but he couldn't understand, and so it didn't do him no particular
good—that is, it didn't just then, but it did after a little, because
when the Injuns got to gambling, same as they done every day, he
put up his Bible against a tomahawk and won it.

They was a sociable lot. They wrastled with Buck and Bill and
Sam, and learned them some new holts and throws that they didn't
know before; and we all run foot races and horse races with them,
and it was prime to see the way their ornery little ponies would split
along when their pluck was up.

And they danced dances for us. Two or three times they put on
all their fuss and feathers and war paint and danced the war dance,
and whooped and jumped and howled and yelled, and it was lovely
and horrible. But the one with the gun, named Man-afraid-of-his-
Mother-in-law, didn't ever put on any paint and finery, and didn't
dance in the war dances, and mostly he didn't come around when
they had them, and when he did he looked sour and glum and
didn't stay.

Yes, we was all stuck after the Injuns, kind of in love with them,
as you may say, and I reckon I never had better times than I had
then. Peggy was as good to them as if she was their sister or their
child, and they was very fond of her. She was sorry for the one with
the gun, and tried to encourage him to put on his war paint and
dance the war dance with the others and be happy and not glum;
and it pleased him to have her be so friendly, but he never done it.
But pretty soon it struck her what maybe the matter was, and she
says to me:

"He's in mourning—that's what it is; he has lost a friend. And to
think, here I have been hurting him, and making him remember

his sorrows, when I wouldn't have done such a thing for the whole world if I had known."

So after that, she couldn't do too much for him, nor be sorry enough for him. And she wished more than ever that Brace was here, so he could see that Injuns was just like other people, after all, and had their sorrows and troubles, and knowed how to love a friend and grieve for him when he was gone.

Tom he was set on having the Injuns take me and him and Jim into their band and let us travel to their country and live in their tribe a week or two; and so, the fourth day, we went over to their camp, me and Tom did, to ask them. But they was fixing for a buffalo hunt next morning, to be gone all day, and maybe longer, and that filled Tom so full of excitement, he couldn't think about anything else, for we hadn't ever seen a buffalo yet. They had a plan for me and Jim and Tom to start before daylight with one Injun and go in one direction, and Buck in another with another Injun, and Bill with another and Sam with another, and leave the other Injun in their camp because he was so lame with his sore leg, and whichever gang found the buffaloes first was to signal the others. So it was all fixed.

Then we see Peggy off there on one of them grass-waves, with Flaxy, looking out over the country with her hand over her eyes, and all the Injuns noticed her at once and asked us what she was looking for. I said she was expecting a lot of friends. The Injun that spoke a little English asked me how many. It's always my disposition to stretch, so I said seven. Tom he kind of smiled, but let it go at that. Man-afraid-of-his-Mother-in-law says:

"Little child (meaning Flaxy, you know,) say only *one*."

I see I was ketched, but in my opinion a body don't ever gain anything by weakening, in them circumstances, so I says:

"*Seven*," and said it firm, and stuck to it.

The Injuns talked amongst themselves a while, then they told us to go over and ask Bill and Buck and Sam to come and talk about the hunt. We done it, and they went over, and we all set down to wait supper till they come back; they said they reckoned they would

be back inside of a half an hour. In a little while four of the Injuns
come and said the boys was staying behind to eat supper with Hog
Face in their camp. So then we asked the Injuns to eat supper with
us, and Peggy she passed around the tin plates and things, and
dished out the vittles, and we all begun. They had put their
war paint and feathers and fixings on since we left their camp,—all
but the one with the gun—so I judged we would have another
good time. We eat, and eat, and talked, and laughed, till by and by
we was all done, and then still we set there talking.

By and by Tom shoved his elbow into my side, soft and easy, and
then got up and took a bucket and said he would fetch some water
for Peggy, and went santering off. I said I would help; so I took a
bucket and followed along. As soon as we was behind some trees,
Tom says:

"Somehow everything don't seem right, Huck. They don't
smoke; they've always smoked, before. There's only one gun outside
the wagon, and a minute or two ago one of them was meddling
with it. I never thought anything of it at the time, but I do now,
because I happened to notice it just a minute ago, and by George
the flint's gone! There's something up, Huck—I'm going to fetch
the boys."

Away he went, and what to do I didn't know. I started back,
keeping behind the trees, and when I got pretty close, I judged I
would watch what was going on, and wait for Tom and the boys.
The Injuns was up, and sidling around, the rest was chatting, same
as before, and Peggy was gathering up the plates and things. I
heard a trampling like a lot of horses, and when it got pretty near, I
see that other Injun coming on a pony, and driving the other ponies
and all our mules and horses ahead of him, and he let off a long
wild whoop, and the minute he done that, the Injun that had a
gun, the one that Peggy fixed, shot her father through the head
with it and scalped him, another one tomahawked her mother and
scalped her, and then these two grabbed Jim and tied his hands
together, and the other two grabbed Peggy, who was screaming and
crying, and all of them rushed off with her and Jim and Flaxy, and

as fast as I run, and as far as I run, I could still hear her, till I was a long, long ways off.

Soon it got dark, and I had to stop, I was so tired. It was an awful long night, and I didn't sleep, but was watching and listening all the time, and scared at every little sound, and miserable. I never see such a night for hanging on, and stringing out, and dismalness.

When daylight come, I didn't dast to stir, at first, being afraid; but I got so hungry I had to. And besides, I wanted to find out about Tom; so I went sneaking for the camp, which was away off across the country, I could tell it by the trees. I struck the line of trees as far up as I could, and slipped along down behind them. There was a smoke, but by and by I see it warn't the camp fire, it was the wagon; the Injuns had robbed it and burnt it. When I got down pretty close, I see Tom there, walking around and looking. I was desperate glad; for I didn't know but the other Injun had got him.

We scratched around for something to eat, but didn't find it, everything being burnt; then we set down and I told Tom everything, and he told me everything. He said when he got to the Injun camp, the first thing he see was Buck and Sam and Bill laying dead —tomahawked and scalped, and stripped; and each of them had as much as twenty-five arrows sticking in him. And he told me how else they had served the bodies, which was horrible, but it would not do to put it in a book. Of course the boys' knives and pistols was gone.

Then Tom and me set there a considerable time, with our jaws in our hands, thinking, and not saying anything. At last I says:

"Well?"

He didn't answer right off, but pretty soon he says:

"I've thought it out, and my mind's made up; but I'll give you the first say, if you want it."

I says:

"No, I don't want it. I've tried, but I can't seem to strike any plan. We're here, and that's all there is to it. We're here, as much as a million miles from any place, I reckon; and we haven't got anything to eat, nor anything to get it with, and no way to get anywhere but just to hoof it, and I reckon we'd play out and die before we got there that way. We're in a fix. That's all I know about it; we're just in a fix, and you can't call it by no lighter name. Whatever your plan is, it'll suit me; I'll do whatever you say. Go on. Talk."

Chapter 4

So HE says:

"Well, this is my idea, Huck. I got Jim into this scrape, and so of course I ain't going to turn back towards home till I've got him out of it again, or found out he's dead; but you ain't in fault, like me, and so if we can run across any trappers bound for the States—"

"Never mind about that, Tom," I says, "I'm agoing with you. I want to help save Jim, if I can, and I want to help save Peggy, too. She was good to us, and I couldn't rest easy if I didn't. I'll go with you, Tom."

"All right," he says, "I hoped you would, and I was certain you would; but I didn't want to cramp you or influence you."

"But how are we going?" says I, "walk?"

"No," he says, "have you forgot about Brace Johnson?"

I had. And it made the cold misery go through me to hear his name; for it was going to be sorrowful times for him when he come.

So we was to wait there for him. And maybe two or three days, without anything to eat; because the folks warn't expecting him for about a week from the time we camped. We went off a half a mile to the highest of them grass-waves, where there was a small tree, and took a long look over the country, to see if we could see Brace or anybody coming, but there wasn't a living thing stirring, anywhere. It was the biggest, widest, levelest world—and all dead; dead and still; not a sound. The lonesomest place that ever was; enough to break a body's heart, just to listen to the awful stillness of it. We talked a little sometimes—once an hour, maybe; but mostly we took up the time thinking, and looking, because it was hard to talk against such solemness. Once I said:

"Tom, where did you learn about Injuns—how noble they was, and all that?"

He give me a look that showed me I had hit him hard, very hard, and so I wished I hadn't said the words. He turned away his head, and after about a minute he said "Cooper's novels," and didn't say anything more, and I didn't say anything more, and so that changed the subject. I see he didn't want to talk about it, and was feeling bad, so I let it just rest there, not ever having any disposition to fret or worry any person.

We had started a camp fire in a new place further along down the stream, with fire from the burnt wagon, because the Injuns had burnt the bodies of old Mr. Mills and his wife along with the wagon, and so that place seemed a kind of graveyard, you know, and we didn't like to stay about it. We went to the new fire once in a while and kept it going, and we slept there that night, most starved.

We turned out at dawn, and I jumped up brash and gay, for I had been dreaming I was at home; but I just looked around once over that million miles of gray dead level, and my soul sucked back that brashness and gayness again with just one suck, like a sponge, and then all the miserableness come back and was worse than yesterday.

Just as it got to be light, we see some creatures away off on the prairie, going like the wind; and reckoned they was antelopes or Injuns, or both, but didn't know; but it was good to see some life again, anyway; it didn't seem so lonesome after that, for a while.

We was so hungry we couldn't stay still; so we went loafing off, and run across a prairie-dog village—little low mounds with holes in them, and a sentinel, which was a prairie dog, and looked like a Norway rat, standing guard. We had long cottonwood sticks along, which we had cut off of the trees and was eating the bark for breakfast; and we dug into the village, and rousted out an owl or two and a couple of hatfuls of rattlesnakes, and hoped we was going to get a dog, but didn't, nor an owl, either; but we hived as bully a rattlesnake as ever I see, and took him to camp and cut his head off and skinned him and roasted him in the hot embers, and he was prime; but Tom was afraid, and wouldn't eat any, at first, but I knowed they was all right, because I had seen hogs and niggers eat them, and it warn't no time to be proud when you are starving to death, I reckoned. Well, it made us feel a powerful sight better, and nearly cheerful again; and when we got done we had snake enough left for a Sunday School blowout, for he was a noble big one. He was middling dry, but if we'd a had some gravy or butter or something, it wouldn't a been any slouch of a picnic.

We put in the third day that we was alone talking, and laying around, and wandering about, and snaking, and found it more and more lonesomer and drearier than ever. Often, as we come to a high grass-wave, we went up and looked out over the country, but all we ever saw was buzzards or ravens or something wheeling round and round over where the Injun camp was—and knowed what brought them there. We hadn't been there; and hadn't even been near there.

When we was coming home towards evening, with a pretty likely snake, we stopped and took another long look across country, and didn't see anything at first, but pretty soon we thought we did; but it was away off yonder against the sky, ever so far, and so we warn't certain. You can see an awful distance there, the air is so clear; so we calculated to have to wait a good while. And we did. In about a half an hour, I reckon, we could make out that it was horses or men or something, and coming our way. Then we laid down and kept close, because it might be Injuns, and we didn't want no more Injun then, far from it. At last Tom says:

"There's three horses, sure."

And pretty soon he says:

"There's a man riding one. I don't make out any more men."

And presently he says:

"There's only one man; he's driving three pack mules ahead of him; and coming along mighty brisk. He's got a wide slouch hat on, and I reckon he's white. It's Brace Johnson, I guess; I reckon he's the only person expected this year. Come—let's creep along behind the grass-waves and get nearer. If it's him, we want to stop him before he gets to the old camp, and break it to him easy."

But we couldn't. He was too fast for us. There he set, on his horse, staring. The minute we showed ourselves he had his gun leveled on us; then he noticed we warn't Injuns, and dropped it, and told us to come on, and we did.

"Boys," he says, "by the odds and ends that's left, I see that this was the Mills's camp. Was you with them?"

"Yes."

"What's happened?"

I never said nothing; and Tom he didn't, at first; then he said: "Injuns."

"Yes," he says, "I see that, myself, by the signs; but the folks got away, didn't they?—along with you?—didn't they?"

We didn't answer. He jumped off of his horse, and come up to us quick, looking anxious, and says:

"Where are they?—quick, where are they? Where's Peggy?"

Well, we had to tell him—there warn't no other way. And it was all he could do to stand it; just all he could do. And when we come to tell about Peggy, he *couldn't* stand it; his face turned as white as milk, and the tears run down his cheeks, and he kept saying "Oh, my God, oh my God." It was so dreadful to see him, that I wanted to get him away from that part of it, and so I worked around and got back onto the other details, and says:

"The one with the gun, that didn't have no war paint, he shot Mr. Mills, and scalped him; and he bloodied his hands, then, and made blood stripes across his face with his fingers, like war paint, and then begun to howl war-whoops like the Injuns does in the circus. And poor old Mrs. Mills, she was down on her knees, begging so pitiful when the tomahawk—"

"I shall never never see her again—never never any more—my poor little darling, so young and sweet and beautiful—but thank God, she's dead!"

He warn't listening to me.

"Dead?" I says; "if you mean Peggy, *she's* not dead."

He whirls on me like a wild-cat, and shouts:

"Not dead! Take it back, take it back, or I'll strangle you! How do *you* know?"

His fingers was working, and so I stepped back a little out of reach, and then says:

"I know she ain't, because I see the Injuns drag her away; and they didn't strike her nor offer to hurt her."

Well, he only just groaned; and waved out his hands, and fetched them together on top of his head. Then he says:

"You staggered me, and for a minute I believed you, and it made me most a lunatic. But it's all right—she had the dirk. Poor child, poor thing—if I had only been here!"

I just had it on my tongue's end to tell him she let Blue Fox have the dirk for a while and I didn't know whether he give it back to her or not—but I didn't say it. Some kind of instinct told me to keep it to myself, I didn't know why. But this fellow was the quickest devil you ever see. He see me hesitate, and he darted a look at me and bored into me like he was trying to see what it was I was keeping back in my mind. But I held my face quiet, and never let on. So then he looked considerable easier, but not entirely easy, and says:

"She had a dirk—didn't you see her have a dirk?"

"Yes," I says.

"Well, then, it's all right. She didn't lose it, nor give it away, nor anything, did she? She had it with her when they carried her away, didn't she?"

Of course I didn't know whether she did or not, but I said yes, because it seemed the thing to say.

"You are sure?" he says.

"Yes, perfectly sure," I says, "I ain't guessing, I *know* she had it with her."

He looked very grateful, then, and drawed a long sigh, and says:

"Ah, the poor child, poor friendless little thing—thank God she's dead."

I couldn't make out why he wanted her to be dead, nor how he could seem to be so thankful for it. As for me, I hoped she wasn't, and I hoped we would find her, yet, and get her and Flaxy away

from the Injuns alive and well, too, and I warn't going to let myself
be discouraged out of that thought, either. We started for the Injun
camp; and when Tom was on ahead a piece, I up and asked Brace if
he actually hoped Peggy *was* dead; and if he did, *why* he did. He
explained it to me, and then it was all clear.

When we got to the camp, we looked at the bodies a minute, and
then Brace said we would bury them presently, but he wanted to
look around and make some inquiries, first. So he turned over the
ashes of the fire, examining them careful, and examining any little
thing he found amongst them, and the tracks, and any little rag or
such like matter that was laying around, and pulled out one of the
arrows, and examined that, and talked to himself all the time,
saying "Sioux—yes, Sioux, that's plain"—and other remarks like
that. I got to wandering around, too, and once when I was a step or
two away from him, lo and behold, I found Peggy's little dirk-knife
on the ground! It just took my breath, and I reckon I made a kind
of a start, for it attracted his attention, and he asked me if I had
found something, and I said yes, and dropped on my knees so that
the knife was under my leg; and when he was coming, I let some
moccasin beads drop on the ground that I had found before, and
pretended to be looking at them; and he come and took them up,
and whilst he was turning them over in his hand examining them, I
slipped the dirk into my pocket; and presently, as soon as it was
dark, I slipped out of our camp and carried it away off about a
quarter of a mile and throwed it amongst the grass. But I warn't
satisfied; it seemed to me that it would be just like that fellow to
stumble on it and find it, he was so sharp. I didn't even dast to bury
it, I was so afraid he'd find it. So at last I took and cut a little hole
and shoved it in betwixt the linings of my jacket, and then I was
satisfied. I was glad I thought of that, for it was like having a
keepsake from Peggy, and something to remember her by, always as
long as I lived.

Chapter 5

THAT NIGHT, in camp, after we had buried the bodies, we set
around and talked, and me and Tom told Brace all about how we
come to be there, on account of Tom wanting us to go with him
and hunt up some Injuns and live with them a while, and Brace
said it was just like boys the world over, and just the same way it
was with him when he was a boy; and as we talked along, you could
see he warmed to us because we thought so much of Peggy and told
him so many things she done and said, and how she looked. And
now and then, as we spoke of the Injuns, a most wicked look would
settle into his face, but at these times he never said nothing.

There was some things which he was a good deal puzzled about;
and now and then he would bust into the middle of the talk with a
remark that showed us his mind had been wandering to them
things. Once he says:

"I wonder what the nation put 'em on the war path. It was
perfectly peaceable on the Plains a little while back, or I wouldn't a
had the folks start, of course. And I wonder if it's *general* war, or
only some little private thing."

Of course we couldn't tell him, and so had to let him puzzle
along. Another time, he busted in and says:

"It's the puzzlingest thing!—there's features about it that I can't
seem to make head nor tail of, no way. I can understand why they
fooled around here three or four days, because there warn't no
hurry; they knowed they had from here to Oregon to do the job in,
and besides, an Injun is patient; he'd ruther wait a month till he
can make sure of his game without any risk to his own skin than
attempt it sooner where there's the least risk. I can understand why
they planned a buffalo hunt that would separate all the whites from
each other and make the mastering of them easy and certain,
because five warriors, nor yet fifteen, won't tackle five men and two
boys, even by surprise when they're asleep at dawn, when there's a

safer way. Yes, I can understand all that—it's Injun, and easy. But the thing that gits me, is, what made them throw over the buffalo plan and act in such a hurry at last—for they did act in a hurry. You see, an Injun don't kill a whole gang, that way, right out and out, unless he is mighty mad or in a desperate hurry. After they had got the young men safe out of the way, they would have saved at least the old man for the torture. It clear beats me, I can't understand it."

For the minute, I couldn't help him out any; I couldn't think of anything to make them in a hurry. But Tom he remembered about me telling the Injuns the Millses was expecting seven friends, and they looked off and see Peggy and Flaxy on the watch-out for them. So Brace says:

"That's all right, then; I understand it, now. *That's* Injun—that would make 'em drop the buffalo business and hurry up things. I know why they didn't kill the nigger, and why they haven't killed him yet, and ain't going to, nor hurt him; and now if I only knowed whether this is general war or only a little private spurt, I would be satisfied and not bother any more. But—well, hang it, let it go, there ain't any way to find out."

So we dropped back on the details again, and by and by I was telling how Man-afraid-of-his-Mother-in-law streaked his face all over with blood after he killed Mr. Mills, and then—

"Why, he done that for war paint!" says Brace Johnson, excited; "warn't he in war-outfit before?—warn't they all painted?"

"All but him," I says. "He never wore paint nor danced with the rest in the war dance."

"Why didn't you tell me that before; it explains everything."

"I did tell you," I says, "but you warn't listening."

"It's all right, now, boys," he says, "and I'm glad it's the way it is, for I wasn't feeling willing to let you go along with me, because I didn't know but all the Injuns was after the whites, and it was a general war, and so it would be bad business to let you get into it, and we couldn't dare to travel except by night, anyway. But you are all right, now, and can shove out with me in the morning, for this is nothing but a little private grudge, and like as not this is the end of

it. You see, some white man has killed a relation of that Injun, and
so he has hunted up some whites to retaliate on. It wouldn't be the
proper thing for him to ever appear in war fixings again till he had
killed a white man and wiped out that score. He was in disgrace till
he had done that; so he didn't lose any time about piling on
something that would answer for war paint; and I reckon he got off
a few war-whoops, too, as soon as he could, to exercise his throat
and get the taste of it in his mouth again. They're probably satisfied, now, and there won't be any more trouble."

So poor Peggy guessed right; that Injun was "in mourning;" he
had "lost a friend;" but it turns out that he knowed better how to
comfort himself than she could do it for him.

We had breakfast just at dawn in the morning, and then rushed
our arrangements through. We took provisions and such like things
as we couldn't get along without, and packed them on one of the
mules, and *cachéd* the rest of Brace's truck—that is, buried it—and
then Brace struck the Injun trail and we all rode away, westward.
Me and Tom couldn't have kept it; we would have lost it every
little while; but it warn't any trouble to Brace, he dashed right
along like it was painted on the ground before him, or paved.

He was so sure Peggy had killed herself, that I reckoned he
would be looking out for her body, but he never seemed to. It was
so strange that by and by I got into a regular sweat to find out why;
and so at last I hinted something about it. But he said no, the
Injuns would travel the first twenty-four hours without stopping,
and then they would think they was far enough ahead of the
Millses' seven friends to be safe for a while—so then they would go
into camp; and there's where we'd find the body. I asked him how
far they would go in that time, and he says:

"The whole outfit was fresh and well fed up, and they had the
extra horses and mules besides. They'd go as much as eighty miles
—maybe a hundred."

He seemed to be thinking about Peggy *all* the time, and never
about anything else or anybody else. So I chanced a question, and
says:

"What'll the Injuns do with Flaxy?"

"Poor little chap, she's all right, they won't hurt her. No hurry about her—we'll get her from them by and by. They're fond of children, and so they'll keep her or sell her; but whatever band gets her, she'll be the pet of that whole band, and they'll dress her fine and take good care of her. She'll be the only white child the most of the band ever saw, and the biggest curiosity they ever struck in their lives. But they'll see 'em oftener, by and by, if the whites ever get started to emigrating to Oregon, and I reckon they will."

It didn't ever seem to strike him that Peggy wouldn't kill herself whilst Flaxy was a prisoner, but it did me. I had my doubts; sometimes I believed she would, sometimes I reckoned she wouldn't.

We nooned an hour, and then went on, and about the middle of the afternoon Brace seen some Injuns away off, but we couldn't see them. We could see some little specks, that was all; but he said he could see them well enough, and it was Injuns; but they warn't going our way, and didn't make us any bother, and pretty soon they was out of sight. We made about forty or fifty miles that day, and went into camp.

Well, late the next day, the trail pointed for a creek and some bushes on its bank about a quarter of a mile away or more, and Brace stopped his horse and told us to ride on and see if it was the camp; and said if it was, to look around and find the body; and told us to bury it, and be tender with it, and do it as good as we could, and then come to him a mile further down the creek, where he would make camp—just come there, and only tell him his orders was obeyed, and stop at that, and not tell him how she looked, nor what the camp was like, nor anything; and then he rode off on a walk, with his head down on his bosom, and took the pack mule with him.

It was the Injun camp, and the body warn't there, nor any sign of it, just as I expected. Tom was for running and telling him, and cheering him up. But I knowed better. I says:

"No, the thing has turned out just right. We'll stay here about long enough to dig a grave with bowie knives, and then we'll go and tell him we buried her."

Tom says:

"That's mysterious, and crooked, and good, and I like that much about it; but hang it there ain't any sense in it, nor any advantage to anybody in it, and I ain't willing to do it."

So it looked like I'd got to tell him why I reckoned it would be better, all around, for Brace to think we found her and buried her, and at last I come out with it, and then Tom was satisfied; and when we had staid there three or four hours, and all through the long twilight till it was plumb dark, we rode down to Brace's camp, and he was setting by his fire with his head down, again, and we only just said, "It's all over—and done right," and laid down like we wanted to rest; and he only says, in that deep voice of his'n, "God be good to you, boys, for your kindness," and kind of stroked us on the head with his hand, and that was all that anybody said.

Chapter 6

AFTER ABOUT four days, we begun to catch up on the Injuns. The trail got fresher and fresher. They warn't afraid, now, and warn't traveling fast, but we had kept up a pretty good lick all the time. At last one day we struck a camp of theirs where they had been only a few hours before, for the embers was still hot. Brace said we would go very careful, now, and not get in sight of them but keep them just a safe distance ahead. Tom said maybe we might slip up on them in the night, now, and steal Jim and Flaxy away; but he said no, he had other fish to fry, first, and besides it wouldn't win, anyway.

Me and Tom wondered what his other fish was; and pretty soon we dropped behind and got to talking about it. We couldn't make nothing out of it for certain, but we reckoned he was meaning to get even with the Injuns and kill some of them before he took any risks about other things. I remembered he said we would get Flaxy "by and by," and said there warn't no hurry about it. But then for all he talked so bitter about Injuns, it didn't look as if he could actually kill one, for he was the gentlest, kindest-heartedest grown person I ever see.

We killed considerable game, these days; and about this time here comes an antelope scampering towards us. He was a real pretty little creature. He stops, about thirty yards off, and sets up his head, and arches up his neck, and goes to gazing at us out of his bright eyes as innocent as a baby. Brace fetches his gun up to his shoulder, but waited and waited, and so the antelope capered off, zig-zagging first to one side and then t'other, awful graceful, and then stretches straight away across the prairie swift as the wind, and Brace took his gun down. In a little while here comes the antelope back again, and stopped a hundred yards off, and stood still, gazing at us same as before, and wondering who we was and if we was friendly, I reckon. Brace fetches up his gun twice, and then the third time; and this time he fired, and the little fellow tumbled. Me and Tom was starting for him, seeing Brace didn't. But Brace says:

"Better wait a minute, boys, you don't know the antelope. Let him die, first. Because if that little trusting, harmless thing looks up in your face with its grieved eyes when it's dying, you'll never forget it. When I'm out of meat, I kill them, but I don't go around them till they're dead, since the first one."

Tom give me a look, and I give Tom a look, as much as to say, "his fish ain't revenge, that's certain, and so what the mischief is it?"

According to my notions, Brace Johnson was a beautiful man. He was more than six foot tall, I reckon, and had broad shoulders, and he was as straight as a jackstaff, and built as trim as a racehorse. He had the steadiest eye you ever see, and a handsome face, and his hair hung all down his back, and how he ever could keep his outfit so clean and nice, I never could tell, but he did. His buckskin suit looked always like it was new, and it was all hung with fringes, and had a star as big as a plate between the shoulders of his coat, made of beads of all kinds of colors, and had beads on his moccasins, and a hat as broad as a barrel-head, and he never looked so fine and grand as he did a-horseback; and a horse couldn't any more throw him than he could throw the saddle, for when it come to riding, he could lay over anything outside the circus. And as for strength, I never see a man that was any more than half as strong as what he was, and a most lightning marksman with a gun or a bow or a pistol. He had two long-barreled ones in his holsters, and could shoot a pipe out of your mouth, most any distance, every time, if you wanted him to. It didn't seem as if he ever got tired, though he stood most of the watch every night himself, and let me and Tom sleep. We was always glad, for his sake, when a very dark night come, because then we all slept all night and didn't stand any watch; for Brace said Injuns ain't likely to try to steal your horses on such nights, because if you woke up and managed to kill them and they died in the dark, it was their notion and belief that it would always be dark to them in the Happy Hunting Grounds all through eternity, and so you don't often hear of Indians attacking in the night, they do it just at dawn; and when they do ever chance it in the night, it's only moonlight ones, not dark ones.

He didn't talk very much; and when he talked about Injuns, he talked the same as if he was talking about animals; he didn't seem to have much idea that they was men. But he had some of their ways, himself, on account of being so long amongst them; and moreover he had their religion. And one of the things that puzzled him was how such animals ever struck such a sensible religion. He said the Injuns hadn't only but two Gods, a good one and a bad one, and they never paid no attention to the good one, nor ever prayed to him or worried about him at all, but only tried their level best to flatter up the bad god and keep on the good side of him; because the good one loved them and wouldn't ever think of doing them any harm, and so there warn't any occasion to be bothering him with prayers and things, because he was always doing the very best he could for them, anyway, and prayers couldn't better it; but all the trouble come from the bad god, who was setting up nights to think up ways to bring them bad luck and bust up all their plans, and never fooled away a chance to do them all the harm he could; and so the sensible thing was to keep praying and fussing around him all the time, and get him to let up. Brace thought more of the Great Spirit than he did of his own mother, but he never fretted

about him. He said his mother wouldn't hurt him, would she?—
well then, the Great Spirit wouldn't, that was sure.

Now as to that antelope, it brought us some pretty bad luck.
When we was done supper, that day, and was setting around
talking and smoking, Brace begun to make some calculations about
where we might be by next Saturday, as if he thought this day was
a Saturday, too—which it wasn't. So Tom he interrupted him and
told him it was Friday. They argued over it, but Tom turned out to
be right. Brace set there a while thinking, and looking kind of
troubled; then he says:

"It's my mistake, boys, and all my fault, for my carelessness.
We're in for some bad luck, and we can't get around it; so the best
way is to keep a sharp look-out for it and beat it if we can—I mean
make it come as light as we can, for of course we can't beat it
altogether."

Tom asked him why he reckoned we would have bad luck, and it
come out that the Bad God was going to fix it for us. He didn't *say*
Bad God, out and out; didn't mention his name, seemed to be afraid
to; said "he" and "him," but we understood. He said a body had got
to perpetuate him in all kinds of ways. Tom allowed he said
propitiate, but I heard him as well as Tom, and he said perpetuate.
He said the commonest way and the best way to perpetuate him
was to deny yourself something and make yourself uncomfortable,
same as you do in any religion. So one of his plans was to try to
perpetuate him by vowing to never allow himself to eat meat on
Fridays and Sundays, even if he was starving; and now he had
gone and eat it on a Friday, and he'd druther have cut his hand off
than done it if he had knowed. He said "he" has got the advantage
of us, now, and you could bet he would make the most of it. We
would have a run of bad luck, now, and no knowing when it would
begin or when it would stop.

We had been pretty cheerful, before that, galloping over them
beautiful Plains, and popping at Jack rabbits and prairie dogs and
all sorts of things, and snuffing the fresh air of the early mornings,
and all that, and having a general good time; but it was all busted
up, now, and we quit talking and got terrible blue and uneasy and

scared; and Brace he was the bluest of all, and kept getting up, all night, and looking around, when it wasn't his watch; and he put out the camp fire, too, and several times he went out and took a wide turn around the camp to see if everything was right. And every now and then he would say:

"Well, it hain't come yet, but it's coming."

It come the next morning. We started out from camp, just at early dawn, in a light mist, Brace and the pack mule ahead, I next, and Tom last. Pretty soon the mist begun to thicken, and Brace told us to keep the procession closed well up. In about a half an hour it was a regular fog. After a while Brace sings out:

"Are you all right?"

"All right," I says.

By and by he sings out again:

"All right, boys?"

"All right," I says, and looked over my shoulder and see Tom's mule's ears through the fog.

By and by Brace sings out again, and I sings out, and he says:

"Answer up, Tom," but Tom didn't answer up. So he said it again, and Tom didn't answer up again; and come to look, there warn't anything there but the mule—Tom was gone.

"It's come," says Brace, "I knowed it would," and we faced around and started back, shouting for Tom. But he didn't answer.

Chapter 7

WHEN we had got back a little ways we struck wood and water, and Brace got down and begun to unsaddle. Says I:

"What you going to do?"

"Going to camp."

"Camp!" says I, "why what a notion. I ain't going to camp, I'm going for Tom."

"Going for Tom! Why, you fool, Tom's lost," he says, lifting off his saddle.

"Of course he is," I says, "and you may camp as much as you want to, but I ain't going to desert him, I'm going for him."

"Huck, you don't know what you're talking about. Get off of that mule."

But I didn't. I fetched the mule a whack, and started; but he grabbed him and snaked me off like I was a doll, and set me on the ground. Then he says:

"Keep your shirt on, and maybe we'll find him, but not in the fog. Don't you reckon I know what's best to do?" He fetched a yell, and listened, but didn't get any answer. "We couldn't find him in the fog; we'd get lost ourselves. The thing for us to do is to stick right here till the fog blows off. Then we'll begin the hunt, with some chance."

I reckoned he was right, but I most wanted to kill him for eating that antelope meat and never stopping to think up what day it was and he knowing so perfectly well what consounded luck it would fetch us. A body can't be too careful about such things.

We unpacked, and picketed the mules, and then set down and begun to talk, and every now and then fetched a yell, but never got any answer. I says:

"When the fog blows off, how long will it take us to find him, Brace?"

"If he was an old hand on the Plains, we'd find him pretty easy; because as soon as he found he was lost he would set down and not budge till we come. But he's green, and he won't do that. The minute a greeny finds he's lost, he can't keep still to save his life—tries to find himself, and gets lost worse than ever. Loses his head; wears himself out, fretting and worrying and tramping in all kinds of directions; and what with starving, and going without water, and being so scared, and getting to mooning and imagining more and more, it don't take him but two or three days to go crazy, and then—"

"My land, is Tom going to be lost as long as that?" I says; "it makes the cold shudders run over me to think of it."

"Keep up your pluck," he says, "it ain't going to do any good to lose that. I judge Tom ain't hurt; I reckon he got down to cinch up, or something, and his mule got away from him, and he trotted after it, thinking he could keep the direction where the fog swallowed it up, easy enough; and in about a half a minute he was turned around and trotting the other way, and didn't doubt he was right, and so didn't holler till it was too late—it's the way they always do, consound it. And so, if he ain't hurt—"

He stopped; and as he didn't go on, I says:

"Well? If he ain't hurt, what then?"

He didn't say anything, right away; but at last he says:

"No, I reckon he ain't hurt, and that's just the worst of it; because there ain't no power on earth can keep him still, now. If he'd a broken his leg—but of course he couldn't, with this kind of luck against him."

We whooped, now and then, but I couldn't whoop much, my heart was most broke. The fog hung on, and on, and on, till it seemed a year, and there we set and waited; but it was only a few hours, though it seemed so everlasting. But the sun busted through it at last, and it begun to swing off in big patches, and then Brace saddled up and took a lot of provisions with him, and told me to stick close to camp and not budge, and then he cleared out and begun to ride around camp in a circle, and then in bigger circles, watching the ground for signs all the time; and so he circled wider and wider, till he was far away, and then I couldn't see him any more. Then I freshened up the fire, which he told me to do, and throwed armfuls of green grass on it to make a big smoke; it went up tall and straight to the sky, and if Tom was ten mile off he would see it and come.

I set down, blue enough, to wait. The time dragged heavy. In about an hour I see a speck away off across country, and begun to watch it; and when it got bigger, it was a horseman, and pretty soon I see it was Brace, and he had something across the horse, and I reckoned it was Tom, and he was hurt. But it wasn't; it was a man. Brace laid him down, and says:

"Found him out yonder. He's been lost, nobody knows how long —two or three weeks, I judge. He's pretty far gone. Give him a spoonful of soup every little while, but not much, or it will kill him.

He's as crazy as a loon, and tried to get away from me, but he's all used up, and he couldn't. I found Tom's trail in a sandy place, but I lost it again in the grass."

So away he started again, across country, and left me and this fellow there, and I went to making soup. He laid there with his eyes shut, breathing kind of heavy, and muttering and mumbling. He was just skin and bones and rags, that's all he was. His hands was all scratched up and bloody, and his feet the same and all swelled up and wore out, and a sight to look at. His face—well, I never see anything so horrible. It was baked with the sun, and was splotchy and purple, and the skin was flaked loose and curled, like old wall paper that's rotted on a damp wall. His lips was cracked and dry, and didn't cover his teeth, so he grinned very disagreeable, like a steel-trap. I judged he had walked till his feet give out on him, and then crawled around them deserts on his hands and knees; for his knees hadn't any flesh or skin on them.

When I got the soup done, I touched him, and he started up scared, and stared at me a second, and then tried to scramble away; but I catched him and held him pretty easy, and he struggling and begging very pitiful for me to let him go and not kill him. I told him I warn't going to hurt him, and had made some nice soup for him; but he wouldn't touch it at first, and shoved the spoon away and said it made him sick to see it. But I persuaded him, and told him I would let him go if he would eat a little, first. So then he made me promise three or four times, and then he took a couple of spoonfuls; and straight off he got just wild and ravenous, and wanted it all. I fed him a cup full, and then carried the rest off and hid it; and so there I had to set, by the hour, and him begging for more; and about every half an hour I give him a little, and his eyes would blaze at the sight of it, and he would grab the cup out of my hands and take it all down at a gulp, and then try to crowd his mouth into it to lick the bottom, and get just raging and frantic because he couldn't.

Between times he would quiet down and doze; and then start up wild, and say "Lost, my God, lost!" and then see me, and recollect, and go to begging for something to eat again. I tried to get something out of him about himself, but his head was all wrong, and you couldn't make head nor tail of what he said. Sometimes he seemed to say he had been lost ten years, and sometimes it was ten weeks, and once I judged he said a year; and that is all I could get out of him, and no particulars. He had a little gold locket on a gold chain around his neck, and he would take that out and open it and gaze and gaze at it and forget what he was doing, and doze off again. It had a most starchy young woman in it, dressed up regardless, and two little children in her arms, painted on ivory, like some the widow Douglas had of her old anzesters in Scotland.

This kind of worry and sweat went on the whole day long, and was the longest day I ever see. And then the sun was going down, and no Tom and no Brace. This fellow was sound asleep, for about the first time. I took a look at him, and judged it would last; so I thought I would run out and water the mules and put on their side-lines and get right back again before he stirred. But the pack mule had pulled his lariat loose, and was a little ways off dragging it after him and grazing, and I walked along after him, but every time I got pretty close he throwed up his head and trotted a few steps, and first I knowed he had tolled me a long ways, and I wished I had the other mule to catch him with, but I dasn't go back after him, because the dark would catch me and I would lose this one, sure; so I had to keep tagging along after him afoot, coming as near to cussing the antelope meat as I dast, and getting powerful nervous all the time, and wondering if some more of us was going to get lost. And I would a got lost if I hadn't had a pretty big fire; for you could just barely see it, away back yonder like a red spark when I catched the mule at last, and it was plumb dark too, and getting black before I got home. It was that black when I got to camp that you couldn't see at all, and I judged the mules would get water enough pretty soon without any of my help; so I picketed them closer by than they was before, and put on their side-lines, and groped into the tent, and bent over this fellow to hear if he was there, yet, and all of a sudden it busted on me that I had been gone two or three hours, I didn't know how long, and of course he was out and gone, long ago, and how in the nation would I ever find him in the dark.

and this awful storm coming up, and just at that minute I hear the wind begin to shiver along amongst the leaves, and the thunder to mumble and grumble away off, and the cold chills went through me to think of what I had done and how in the world I was ever going to find him again in the dark and the rain, dad fetch him for making all this trouble, poor pitiful rat, so far from home and lost, and I so sorry for him, too.

So I held my breath and listened over him, and by Jackson he was there yet, and I hear him breathe—about once a minute. Once a week would a done me, though, it sounded so good to hear him and I was so thankful he hadn't sloped. I fastened the flap of the tent and then stretched out snug on my blankets, wishing Tom and Brace was there; and thinks I, I'll let myself enjoy this about five minutes before I sail out and freshen up the camp fire.

The next thing that I knowed anything about, was no telling how many hours afterwards. I sort of worked along up out of a solid sleep, then, and when I come to myself the whole earth was rocking with the smashingest blast of thunder I ever heard in my life and the rain was pouring down like the bottom had fell out of the sky. Says I, now I've done it! the camp fire's out, and no way for Tom or Brace to find the camp. I lit out, and it was so; everything drenched, not a sign of an ember left. Of course nobody could ever start a new fire out there in the rain and wind; but I could build one inside and fetch it out after it got to going good. So I rushed in and went to bulging around in the dark, and lost myself and fell over this fellow, and scrambled up off of him, and begged his pardon and asked if I hurt him; but he never said a word and didn't make a sound. And just then comes one of them blind-white glares of lightning that turns midnight to daytime, and there he laid, grinning up at me, stone dead. And he had hunks of bread and meat around, and I see in a second how it all was. He had got at our grub whilst I was after the mule, and over-eat himself and died, and I had been sleeping along perfectly comfortable with his relics I don't know how long, and him the gashliest sight I ever struck. But I never waited there to think all that; I was out in the public wilderness before the flash got done quivering, and I never went back no more. I let him have it all to his own self; I didn't want no company.

I went off a good ways, and staid the rest of the night out, and got most drownded; and about an hour or more after sun-up Tom and Brace come, and I was glad. I told them how things had went, and we took the gold locket and buried the man and had breakfast, and Brace didn't scold me once. Tom was about used up, and we had to stay there a day or two for him to get straightened up again. I asked him all about it, and he says:

"I got down to cinch up, and I nearly trod on a rattlesnake which I didn't see, but heard him go *bzzz!* right at my heel. I jumped most a rod, I was so scared and taken so sudden, and I run about three steps, and then looked back over my shoulder and my mule was gone—nothing but just white fog there. I forgot the snake in a second, and went for the mule. For ten steps I didn't hurry, expecting to see him all the time; but I picked up my heels, then, and run. When I had run a piece I got a little nervous, and was just going to yell, though I was ashamed to, when I thought I heard voices ahead of me, bearing to the right, and that give me confidence, knowing it must be you boys; so I went heeling it after you on a short-cut; but if I did hear voices I misjudged the direction and went the other way, because you know you can't really tell where a sound comes from, in a fog. I reckon you was trotting in one direction and me in the other, because it warn't long before I got uneasy and begun to holler, and you didn't hear me nor answer. Well, that scared me so that I begun to tremble all over, and I did wish the fog would lift, but it didn't, it shut me in, all around, like a thick white smoke. I wanted to wait, and let you miss me and come back, but I couldn't stay still a second; it would a killed me; I *had* to run, and I did. And so I kept on running, by the hour, and listening, and shouting; but never a sound did ever I hear; and whenever I stopped just a moment and held my breath to listen, it was the awfulest stillness that ever was, and I couldn't stand it and had to run on again.

"When I got so beat out and tired I couldn't run any more, I walked; and when the fog went off at last and I looked over my shoulder and there was a tall smoke going up in the sky miles across the plain behind me, I says to myself if that was ahead of me it might be Huck and Brace camping and waiting for me; but it's in the wrong direction, and maybe it's Injuns and not whites; so I wouldn't take any chances on it, but kept right on; and by and by I thought I could see something away off on the prairie, and it was Brace, but I didn't know it, and so I hid. I saw him, or something, twice more before night, and I hid both times; and I walked, between times, further and further away from that smoke and stuck to ground that wouldn't leave much of a track; and in the night I walked and crawled, together, because I couldn't bear to keep still, and was so hungry, and so scratched up with cactuses, and getting kind of out of my head besides; but the storm drove me up onto a swell to get out of the water, and there I staid, and took it. Brace he searched for me till dark, and then struck for home, calculating to strike for the camp fire and lead his horse and pick his way; but the storm was too heavy for that, and he had to stop and give up that notion; and besides you let the fire go out, anyway. I went crawling off as soon as dawn come, and making a good trail, the ground was so wet; and Brace found it and then he found me; and the next time I get down to cinch up a mule in the fog I'll notify the rest of you; and the next time I'm lost and see a smoke I'll go for it, I don't care if it comes out of the pit."

Chapter 8

WE WAS away along up the North Fork of the Platte, now. When we started again, the Injuns was two or three days ahead of us, and their trail was pretty much washed out, but Brace didn't mind it, he judged he knowed where they was striking for. He had been reading the signs in their old camps, all these days, and he said these Sioux was Ogillallahs. We struck a hilly country, now, and traveled the day through and camped a few miles up a nice valley late in the afternoon on top of a low flattish hill in a grove of small trees. It was an uncommon pretty place, and we picked it out on

account of Tom, because he hadn't stood the trip well, and we
calculated to rest him there another day or two. The valley was a
nearly level swale a mile or a mile and a half wide, and had a little
river-bed in it with steep banks, and trees along it—not much of a
river, because you could throw a brick across it, but very deep when
it was full of water, which it wasn't, now. But Brace said we would
find puddles along in its bed, so him and me took the animals and a
bucket, and left Tom in camp and struck down our hill and rode
across the valley to water them. When we got to the river we found
new-made tracks along the bank, and Brace said there was about
twenty horses in that party, and there was white men in it, because
some of the horses had shoes on, and likely they was from out Fort
Laramie way.

There was a puddle or two, but Brace couldn't get down the
banks easy; so he told me to wait with the mules, and if he didn't
find a better place he would come back and rig some way to get up
and down the bank here. Then he rode off down stream and pretty
soon the trees hid him. By and by an antelope darts by me and I
looked up the river and around a corner of the timber comes two
men, riding fast. When they got to me they reined up and begun to
ask me questions. They was half drunk, and a mighty rough looking couple, and their clothes didn't help them much, being old
greasy buckskin, just about black with dirt. I was afraid of them.
They asked me who I was, and where I come from, and how many
was with me, and where we was camped; and I told them my name
was Archibald Thompson, and says:

"Our camp's down at the foot of the valley, and we're traveling
for pap's health, he's very sick, we can't travel no more till he gets
better, and there ain't nobody to take care of him but me and aunt
Mary and Sis, and so we're in a heap of troub—"

"It's all a lie!" one of them breaks in. "You've stole them animals."

"You bet he has," says the other. "Why, I know this one myself;
he belongs to old Vaskiss the trader, up at the Fort, and I'm dead
certain I've seen one of the others somewheres."

"Seen him? I reckon you have. Belongs to Roubidou the blacksmith, and he'll be powerful glad we've found him again. I knowed him in a minute. Come, boy, I'm right down sorry for your sick pap, and poor aunt Mary and Sis, but all the same you'll go along back to our camp, and you want to be mighty civil and go mighty careful, or first you know you'll get hung."

First I didn't know what to do; but I had to work my mind quick, and I struck a sort of an idea, the best I could think of, right off, that way. I says to myself, it's two to one these is horse-thieves, because Brace says there's a plenty of them in these regions; and so I reckon they'd like to get one or two more while they're at it. Then I up and says:

"Gents, as sure as I'm here I never stole the animals; and if I'll prove it to you you'll let me go, won't you?"

"How're you going to prove it?"

"I'll do it easy if you'll come along with me, for we bought two mules that's almost just like these from the Injuns day before yesterday, and maybe they stole 'em, I don't know, but we didn't, that's sure."

They looked at each other, and says:

"Where are they—down at your camp?"

"No; they're only down here three or four hundred yards. Sister Mary she—"

"Has she got them?"

"Yes."

"Anybody with her?"

"No."

"Trot along, then, and don't you try to come any tricks, boy, or you'll get hurt."

I didn't wait for a second invite, but started right along, keeping a sharp lookout for Brace, and getting my yell ready, soon as I should see him. I edged ahead, and edged ahead, all I could, and they notified me a couple of times not to shove along so fast, because there warn't no hurry; and pretty soon they noticed Brace's trail, and sung out to me to halt a minute, and bent down over their saddles, and checked up their speed, and was mightily interested, as I could see when I looked back. I didn't halt, but jogged ahead, and kept widening the distance. They sung out again, and threatened me, and then I brushed by Brace's horse, in the trees, and knowed Brace was down the bank or close by, so I raised a yell and put up my speed to just the highest notch the mules could reach. I looked back, and here they come—and next comes a bullet whizzing by!! I whacked away for life and death, and looked back and they was gaining; looked back again, and see Brace booming after the hind one like a house afire, and swinging the long coils of his lariat over his head; then he sent it sailing through the air, and as it scooped that fellow in, Brace reined back his horse and yanked him out of his saddle, and then come tearing ahead again, dragging him. He yelled to me to get out of range, and so I turned out sudden and looked back, and my man had wheeled and was raising his gun on Brace, but Brace's pistol was too quick for him, and down he went, out of his saddle.

Well, we had two dead men on our hands, and I felt pretty crawly, and didn't like to look at them; but Brace allowed it warn't a very unpleasant sight, considering they tried to kill me. He said we must hurry into camp, now, and get ready for trouble; so we shoved for camp, and took the two new horses and the men's guns and things with us, not waiting to water our animals.

It was nearly dark. We kept a watch-out towards up the river, but didn't see anything stirring. When we got home we still watched from the edge of the grove, but didn't see anything, and no sign of that gang's camp fire; then Brace said we was probably safe from them for the rest of the night, so we would rest the animals three or four hours, and then start out and get as well ahead as we could, and keep ahead as long as this blamed Friday-antelope luck would let us, if Tom could stand the travel.

It come on starlight, a real beautiful starlight, and all the world as still and lovely as Sunday. By and by Brace said it would be a good idea to find out where the thieves was camped, so we could give it a wide berth when we started; and he said I could come along if I wanted to; and he took his gun along, this time, and I took one of the thieves' guns. We took the two fresh horses and rode down across the valley and struck the river, and then went

pretty cautious up it. We went as much as two mile, and not a sign
of a camp fire anywheres. So we kept on, wondering where it could
be, because we could see a long ways up the valley. And then all of
a sudden we heard people laugh, and not very far off, maybe forty
or fifty yards. It come from the river. We went back a hundred
yards, and tied the horses amongst the trees, and then back again
afoot till we was close to the place, where we heard it before, and
slipped in amongst the trees and listened, and heard the voices again,
pretty close by. Then we crept along on our knees, slow and
careful, to the edge of the bank, through the bush, and there was
the camp, a little ways up, and right in the dry bed of the river; two
big buffalo-skins lodges, a band of horses tied, and eight men
carousing and gambling around a fire—all white men, and the
roughest kind, and prime drunk. Brace said they had camped there
so their camp couldn't be seen easy, but they might as well camped
in the open as go and get drunk and make such a noise. He said
they was horse thieves, certain.

We was interested, and stayed looking a considerable time. But
the liquor begun to beat them, and first one and then another went
gaping and stretching to the tents and turned in. And then another
one started, and the others tried to make him stay up, because it was
his watch, but he said he was drunk and sleepy and didn't want to
watch, and said "Let Jack and Bill stand my watch, as long they like
to be up late—they'll be in directly, like as not."

But the others threatened to lick him if he didn't stand his
watch; so he grumbled, but give in, and got his gun and set down;
and when the others was all gone to roost, he just stretched himself
out and went to snoring as comfortable as anybody.

We left, then, and sneaked down to where our horses was, and
rode away, leaving the rapscallions to sleep it out and wait for Jack
and Bill to come, but we reckoned they'd have to wait a most
notorious long time first.

We rode down the river to where Brace was when I yelled to him
when the thieves was after me; and he said he had dug some steps
in the bank there with his bowie, and we could finish the job in a
little while, and when we broke camp and started we would bring

our mules there and water them. So we tied our horses and went down into the river bed to the puddle that was there, and laid down on our breasts to take a drink; but Brace says:

"Hello, what's that?"

It was as still as death before, but you could hear a faint, steady, rising sound, now, up the river. We held our breath and listened. You could see a good stretch up it, and tolerable clear, too, the starlight was so strong. The sound kept growing and growing, very fast. Then all of a sudden Brace says:

"Jump for the bank! I know what that is."

It's always my plan to jump first, and ask afterwards. So I done it. Brace says:

"There's a water-spout broke loose up country somewheres, and you'll see sights mighty soon, now."

"Do they break when there ain't no clouds in the sky?" I says, judging I had him.

"Ne'er you mind," he says, "there was clouds where this one broke. I've seen this kind of thing before, and I know that sound. Fasten your horse just as tight as you can, or he'll break loose presently."

The sound got bigger and bigger, and away up yonder it was just one big dull thundering roar. We looked up the river a piece, and see something coming down its bed like dim white snakes writhing along. When it went hissing and sizzling by us it was shallow foamy water. About twenty yards behind it comes a solid wall of water four foot high, and nearly straight up and down, and before you could wink it went rumbling and howling by like a whirlwind, and carrying logs along, and them thieves, too, and their horses and tents, and tossing them up in sight, and then under again, and grinding them to hash, and the noise was just awful, you couldn't a heard it thunder; and our horses was plunging and pitching, and trying their best to break loose. Well, before we could turn around the water was over the banks and ankle deep.

"Out of this, Huck, and shin for camp, or we're goners!"

We was mounted and off in a second, with the water chasing after us. We rode for life, we went like the wind, but we didn't have to use whip or spur, the horses didn't need no encouragement. Half way across the valley we met the water flooding down from above; and from there on, the horses was up to their knees, sometimes, yes, and even up to their bellies towards the last. All hands was glad when we struck our hill and sailed up it out of danger.

Chapter 9

OUR LITTLE low hill was an island, now, and we couldn't a got away from it if we had wanted to. We all three set around and watched the water rise. It rose wonderful fast; just walked up the long, gradual slope, as you may say, it come up so fast. It didn't stop rising for two or three hours; and then that whole valley was just a big level river a mile to a mile and a half wide, and deep enough to swim the biggest ship that was ever built, and no end of dim black drift logs spinning around and sailing by in the currents on its surface.

Brace said it hadn't took the water-spout an hour to dump all that ocean of water and finish up its job, but like enough it would be a week before the valley was free of it again; so Tom would have considerable more time than we bargained to give him to get well in.

Me and Tom was down-hearted and miserable on account of Jim and Peggy and Flaxy, because we reckoned it was all up with them and the Injuns, now; and so at last Tom throwed out a feeler to see what Brace thought. He never said anything about the others, but only about the Injuns; said the water-spout must a got the Injuns, hadn't it? But Brace says:

"No, nary an Injun.—Water-spouts don't catch any but white folks. There warn't ever a white man that could tell when a water-spout's coming; and how the nation an Injun can tell is something I never could make out, but they can. When it's perfectly clear weather, and other people ain't expecting anything, they'll say, all of a sudden, 'heap water coming,' and pack up in a hurry and shove for high ground. They say they smell it. I don't know whether that's so or not; but one thing I do know, a water-spout often catches a white man, but it don't ever catch an Injun."

Next morning there we was, on an island, same as before; just a level, shining ocean everywheres, and perfectly still and quiet, like it was asleep. And awful lonesome.

Next day the same, only lonesomer than ever.

And next day just the same, and mighty hard work to put in the time. Mostly we slept. And after a long sleep, wake up, and eat dinner, and look out over the tiresome water, and go to sleep again; and wake up again, by and by, and see the sun go down and turn it into blood, and fire, and melted butter, and one thing or another, awful beautiful, and soft, and lovely, but solemn and lonesome till you couldn't rest.

We had eight days of that, and the longer we waited for that ocean to play out and run off, the bigger the notion I got of a water-spout that could puke out such a mortal lot of water as that in an hour.

We left, then, and made a good day's travel, and by sundown begun to come onto fresh buffalo carcases. There was so many of them that Brace reckoned there was a big party of Injuns near, or else whites from the fort.

In the morning we hadn't gone five miles till we struck a big camp where Injuns had been, and hadn't gone more than a day or two. Brace said there was as many as a hundred of them, altogether, men, women and children, and made up from more than one band of Sioux, but Brulé's, mostly, as he judged by the signs. Brace said things looked like these Injuns was camped here a considerable time.

Of course we warn't thinking about our Injuns, or expecting to run across any signs of them or the prisoners, but Tom he found an arrow, broke in two, which was wound with blue silk thread down by the feather, and he said he knowed it was Hog Face's, because he got the silk for him from Peggy and watched him wind it. So Brace begun to look around for other signs, and he believed he found some. Well, I was ciphering around in a general way myself, and outside of the camp I run across a ragged piece of Peggy's dress as big as a big handkerchief, and it had blood on it. It most froze me to see that, because I judged she was killed; and if she warn't, it stood to reason she was hurt. I hid the rag under a buffalo chip, because if Brace was to see it he might suspicion she wasn't dead after all the pains we had took to make him believe she was; and just then he sings out "Run here, boys," and Tom he come running from one way and I the other, and when we got to him, there in the middle of the camp, he points down and says:

"There—that's the shoe-print of a white woman. See—you can see, where she turned it down to one side, how thin the sole is. She's white, and she's a prisoner with this gang of Injuns. I don't understand it. I'm afraid there's general trouble broke out between the whites and Injuns; and if that's so, I've got to go mighty cautious from this out." He looks at the track again, and says, "Poor thing, it's hard luck for her," and went mumbling off, and never noticed that me and Tom was most dead with uneasiness, for we could see plain enough it was Peggy's print, and was afraid he would see it himself, or think he did, any minute. His back warn't more than turned before me and Tom had tramped on the print once or twice—just enough to take the clearness out of it, because we didn't know but he might come back for another look.

Pretty soon we see him over yonder looking at something, and we went there, and it was four stakes drove in the ground; and he looks us very straight and steady in the eyes, first me and then Tom, and then me again, till it got pretty sultry; then he says, cold and level, but just as if he'd been asking us a question:

"Well, I believe you. Come along."

Me and Tom followed along, a piece behind; and Tom says:

"Huck, he's so afraid she's alive, that it's just all he can do to believe that yarn of ours about burying her. And pretty soon, now, like enough, he'll find out she ain't dead, after all."

"That's just what's worrying me, Tom. It puts us in a scrape, and I don't see no way out of it; because what can we say when he tackles us about lying to him?"

"I know what to say, well enough."

"You do? Well I wish you'd tell me, for I'm blamed if I see any way out—I wouldn't know a single word to say."

"I'll say this, to him. I'll say, suppose it was likely you was going to get knocked in the head with a club some time or other, but it warn't quite certain; would you want to be knocked in the head straight off, so as to make it certain, or wouldn't you ruther wait and see if you mightn't live your life out and not happen to get clubbed at all? Of course, he would say. Then I would put it at him straight, and say, wasn't you happier, when we made you think she was dead, than you was before? Didn't it keep you happy all this time? Of course. Well, wasn't it worth a little small lie like that to keep you happy instead of awfully miserable many days and nights? Of course. And wasn't it likely she would be dead before you ever run across her again?—which would make our lie plenty good enough. True again. And at last I would up and say, just you put yourself in our place, Brace Johnson: now, honor bright, would you have told the truth, that time, and broke the heart of the man that was Peggy Mills's idol? If you could, you are not a man, you are a devil; if you could and did, you'd be lower and hard-hearteder than the devils, you'd be an Injun. That's what I'll say to him, Huck, if the time ever comes."

Now that was the cleanest and slickest way out that ever was; and who would ever a thought of it but Tom Sawyer? I never seen the like of that boy for just solid gobs of brains and level headedness. It made me comfortable, right away, because I knowed very well Brace Johnson couldn't ever get around *that,* nor under it nor over it nor through it; he would have to answer up and confess he would a told that lie his own self, and would have went on backing it up and standing by it, too, as long as he had a rag of a lie left in him to do it with.

I noticed, but I never said anything, that Tom was putting the Injuns below the devils, now. You see, he had about got it through his noodle, by this time, that book Injuns and real Injuns is different.

Brace was unslinging the pack; so we went to him to see what he was doing it for, and he says:

"Well, I don't understand that white woman's being with this band of Injuns. Of course may be she was took prisoner years ago, away yonder on the edge of the States, and has been sold from band to band ever since, all the way across the Plains. I say of course that may be the explanation of it, but as long as I don't know that that's the way of it, I ain't going to take any chances. I'll just do the other thing: I'll consider that this woman is a new prisoner, and that her being here means that there's trouble broke out betwixt the Injuns and the whites, and so I'll act according. That is, I'll keep shy of Injuns till I've fixed myself up a little, so's to fit the new circumstances."

He had got a needle and some thread out of the pack, and a little paper bag full of dried bugs, and butterflies, and lizards, and frogs, and such like creatures, and he sat down and went to sewing them fast to the lapels of his buckskin coat, and all over his slouch hat, till he was that fantastic he looked like he had just broke out of a museum when he got it all done. Then he says:

"Now if I act strange and foolish, the Injuns will think I'm crazy; so I'll be safe and all right. They are afraid to hurt a crazy man, because they think he's under His special persecution" (he meant the Bad God, you know) "for his sins; and they kind of avoid him, and don't much like to be around him, because they think he's bad medicine, as they call it—'medicine' meaning luck, about as near as you can put it into English. I got this idea from a chap they called a naturalist.

"A war party of Injuns dropped onto him, and if he'd a knowed his danger, he'd a been scared to death; but he didn't know a war party from a peace party, and so he didn't act afraid, and that bothered the Injuns, they didn't know what to make of it; and when they see how anxious and particular he was about his bugs, and how fond of them and stuck after them he seemed to be, they judged he was out of his mind, and so they let him go his own gait, and never touched him. I've gone fixed for the crazy line ever since."

Then he packed the mule again, and says:

"Now we'll get along again, and follow the trail of these Injuns."

Doughface

MANY of the experiences of Sam Clemens, the boy, recurred in the mature author's memory again and again. For instance, in many notebooks and in published writings he recalled the death by fire of a tramp in the Hannibal jail shortly after the boy had smuggled matches to the prisoner. He also frequently remembered his coming upon the corpse of a murdered man one night when he sneaked into the office of his father, a justice of the peace. And he wrote many notes about his boyhood companion, Tom Nash, who became deaf and dumb as a result of his breaking through the ice on the Mississippi River.

Often, too, he recalled an experience he recorded in chapter fifty-three of *Life on the Mississippi*. While conversing with an old man during his visit to Hannibal in 1882:

> I asked about Miss _____.
> "Died in the insane asylum three or four years ago—never was out of it from the time she went in; and was always suffering too; never got a shred of her mind back."
> If he spoke the truth, here was a heavy tragedy, indeed. Thirty-six years in a madhouse, that some young fools might have some fun! I was a small boy, at the time; and I saw those giddy young ladies come tiptoeing into the room where Miss _____ sat reading at midnight by a lamp. The girl at the head of the file wore a shroud and a doughface; she crept behind the victim, touched her on the shoulder, and she looked up and screamed, and then fell into convulsions. She did not recover from the fright, but went mad.

141

Notebook 32a, which covers the period 20 June to 24 July 1897, refers
to the happening at three points in a series of notes concerning "Tom
Sawyer's Conspiracy." [1] In one entry he names the prankster, Roberta
Jones, also identified in this connection in "Villagers." In a notebook for
1902, Twain made another entry, apparently with the idea that he
might use the incident in a story about Tom and Huck and their gang
set fifty years after their youthful adventures: "Dough-face—old lady
now, still in asylum—a bride then. What went with *him?* Shall we visit
her? And shall she be expecting him in her faded bridal robes and
flowers?" Later in the same notebook he wrote, "doughface, but scare
no one mad." [2]

This version by Huck may have been written either in 1897 or in
1902. [3] The author entitled it "Huck Finn": I have given it a more
accurately descriptive title. Huck's narrative style adds little to the
effect, for the tale is singularly colorless.

---

[1] TS pp. 36, 45, 58.
[2] Notebook 35, TS pp. 12, 21.
[3] For the date, see Appendix B.

Doughface

WELL, I had a noble big bullfrog that I had traded a hymn-book for, and was all profit, becuz it never cost me anything, deacon Kyle give it to me for saving his daughter's life time she fell in the river off of the ferry boat going down to the picnic in Cave Holler, and warn't any use to me on account of my being able to get along without hymns, and I traded the bullfrog for a cat, and sold the cat for a false-face, a horrible thing that was awful to look at and cost fifteen cents when it was new, and so I was prospering right along and was very well satisfied.

But I lent it to Tom Sawyer and he lent it to Miss Rowena Fuller, which was a beautiful young lady and a favorite and full of spirits and never quiet but always breaking out in a new place with her inventions and making the whole town laugh, for she just lived for fun and was born for it. She was lovely in her disposition and the happiest person you ever see, and people said it took the sorrow out of life to see that girl breeze around and carry on, and hear her laugh, and certainly she done a lot of it, she was that lively and gay and pranksome.

She never meant any harm with her jokes, poor thing, but she never laughed any more after that time. She wouldn't ever done

143

what she done if she had thought what was going to come of it. But she didn't think, she got right to work on her project, and she was so full of it she *couldn't* think; and she was so full of laugh that she couldn't hold still, but kept breaking out in a fresh place all the time, just with antissipations. She was going to scare old Miss Wormly, which was a superstitious old maid and lived all alone and was that timid she was afraid of everything, specially of ghosts, and was always dreading them, she couldn't help it. Miss Rowena put on the false-face and got herself up in a shroud and started for Miss Wormly's about eleven at night, with a lot of young people trailing after her to see the fun; and she tiptoed in, and Miss Wormly was sitting by her lamp sort of half dozing, and she crept up behind her and bent around and looked her in the face, still and solemn and awful. Miss Wormly turned white like a dead person, and stared and gasped for a second, then she begun to scream and shriek, and jumped up and started to run, but fainted and fell on the floor. She was gone mad, poor old harmless lady, and never got over it. Spent all her days in the sylum, and was always moaning and crying, and many a time jumping out of her bed in the night, thinking the ghost was after her again. Poor Miss Rowena's life was spoilt, too, she never got up any more jokes and couldn't ever laugh at anything any more.

Tom Sawyer's Gang Plans
a Naval Battle

As EARLY as 1881 Mark Twain wrote to his friend James R. Osgood, asking him to secure and send to him several of Harper's dime novels concerning sailors—*Tom Cringle's Log, Green Hand, Sailor's Sweetheart,* and *The Cruise of the Midge.*[1] As Albert Stone has suggested,[2] he may have wanted these for his daughters. Since the books were more likely to appeal to masculine readers than to little girls, though, it seems more probable that they were for his own reading as potential sources. A notebook entry indicates that as late as 1900, he contemplated making use of sea terms in a story told by Huck Finn:

> Huck tells of those heros the 2 Irish youths who painted ships on Goodwin's walls and ran away. They told sea-adventures which made all the boys sick with envy and resolve to run away and go to sea—then later a man comes hunting for them for a small crime—laughs at their sailortalk (Get it from my "Glossary of Sea Terms").[3]

The following fragment may have been written soon after the entry quoted above.[4] The manuscript is numbered 129 to 138, which suggests

---

[1] *MTLP,* pp. 136–137.
[2] *IE,* p. 161.
[3] Notebook 33, TS p. 6.
[4] See Appendix B for dating information.

that it was once part of a longer work (the title here is mine). DeVoto's characterization of the fragment as "trivial and even perfunctory" is probably justified, though it may be that he goes a bit too far when he calls it "actually painful," [5] since the boys' arguments about the battle and the complications that arise are mildly amusing. Notes on the top of the final page of the manuscript, however, indicate that if the story had been continued it might well have become painful. The notes were "England expects" and "Kiss me, Hardy," and it was just as well for Mark Twain to stop before he had Tom utter these famous phrases.

---

[5] *MTW*, pp. 48–49.

Tom Sawyer's Gang Plans
a Naval Battle

W<small>E CATCHED</small> a little section of a raft floating down amongst the drift-wood, and Tom said now we had two line-of-battle ships we could fight a naval battle. So it was discussed, and some wanted to do one battle and some another, but finally we put it to vote and the battle of the Nile was elected. It was mainly on accounts of Tom Sawyer's influence, because he wanted to be Nelson. It took a whole evening after supper to plan it out and appoint everybody to his place. John Riggs was elected to be the French admiral, but he didn't like the position because he didn't think the French fit the best they could, that time, so he sejested that Tom could fight the battle of the Nile and he would fight the gorjious battle in Charles Second's time when the Dutch fleet everlastingly wiped out about a thousand British frigates, and he would be admiral Van Tromp and highst a broom for his flag.

Dick Fisher said you couldn't mix two battles together that was two hundred years apart, and was going into history, the way he always done, but they shut him up for insubordination, a-chipping in when nobody hadn't asked him, and him nothing but an ornery

low-down post-captain of a fifty-gun frigate, represented by three
mlasses barls lashed together, with an old pine door for a deck; so he
laughed at them for their marytime ignorance and told them to go
it, he didn't give a dern. That was more insubordination, and had to
be made an example of; he was on the point of being promoted to
be Captain Hardy on the flag-ship before he busted in with his
irrulevant history, but now for an example they reduced him to be a
Dutch commander named Van Wagner all through the battle until
time for Tom to be killed and him to swim over and catch him in
his arms and be Hardy and kiss him whilst he died. They was very
much put out and aggravated, and said if he didn't quiet down
now, blamed if they wouldn't degrade him to a quartermaster and
stop his grog. So he quieted down, as far as talk was concerned,
though he kept a throwing handsprings and baaing like a sheep and
crowing like a rooster, so as to interrupt the Council of War all he
could.

He was just that way, Dick Fisher was: always gay, and light-
hearted, and carrying on, nothing on his mind, good-natured, making fun of everybody and everything, there wasn't anything serious
in life to him, he would interrupt a dog-fight if he took the notion.

They counted up the forces, and there was twenty-two boys.
Some owned rafts, some owned barn-doors, some owned planks,
and some knowed of a little old played-out shanty away up Bear
creek that wasn't being lived in and could be pulled down and
would make seven elegant rafts—that is, the four sides, the two
roof-slants and the floor. It being a naval battle, there warn't no
boats allowed, except two canoes for the flag-ships, to carry orders;
and where signals at the mast-head was used for orders, the canoes
to paddle down the fleets and explain what the signals said; but the
canoes being on official business, was sacred, and couldn't be captured. Then there was two chaplain-canoes, to paddle amongst the
fleets and do burial service and dump the dead, and these was
sacred too. Them seven rafts was ranked for seventy-fours: four-
plank rafts was ranked for 50-gun ships; three-plankers was thirty-
sixes, barn-doors the same; two-plankers was single-deck 20-gun

brigs, and one-plankers was gun-boats. The fleets footed up like this:

BRITISH.		DUTCH.	
Flag-ship	1	Flag-ship	1
Line of Battle 74s	4	Line of Battle 74s	3
50-gun frigates	1	50-gun frigates	1
36-gun ship	1	36-gun ship	1
20-gun brig	2	20-gun brig	2
Gun-boats	3	Gun-boats	2
	12		10

So it didn't come out fair, being too much metal on the British side. Van Tromp was satisfied, just as it stood; said three 74s against four, and two gun-boats against three was plenty good enough for him; but Nelson wouldn't have it so; said he was willing to give odds, and was used to it, history showing such to be his experience from Cape Saint Vincent down, but he couldn't accept of none, his ruputation would not permit it. So there it was. Both admirals was stubborn and wouldn't take odds. Van Tromp said when it come to ruputations, turn to your history-book and look at his'n—he had one 'most two hundred years before Nelson was born. It was a fact, and it stung Tom Sawyer to his vitles; it was a sockdolajer, he couldn't get around it no way. There wasn't anybody could think of any way to fix it, so the battle was up a stump. Everybody was awful disappointed. Then Van Wagner pipes up and says—

"If it ain't mutiny to sejest it, I'll remark that there's a 50-gun frigate that ain't been counted in on the Dutch side, being the Rotterdam, which is mine."

Everybody reconnized that fact, and says—

"It's so; we didn't count-in them mlasses barls."

And Van Wagner went on.

"That leaves the Dutch short of the British only 24 guns. Now you let the British hand over a 20-gun brig and three gun-boats, and put one Dutch gun-boat out of commission, and there you are! —same metal on both sides."

It saved the battle, and everybody shouted and clapped their hands. All but little Jimmy Todd. He begun to cry, because his gun-boat was put out of commission; so they made him Dutch chaplain and appointed him to a canoe, and he was happy again. It looked like everything was all right, now, but it wasn't. Van Wagner pointed out that there was 21 vessels and 4 canoes in commission, being 25, and only 22 men. Not enough to go around.

They could all see it, and it made them sorrowful and vexed, it looked like we warn't ever going to get the battle arranged, we could fight six battles whilst we arranged one. Well, what had we better do? Van Tromp speaks up again, and says—

"You got to get a heap more men, that's what you've got to do. Flag-ship, with nothing on it but an admiral! There ain't no dignity about it. He couldn't handle her, anyway; it'll take ten to handle that steamboat stage, and I'd like to see you pole the Dutch flag-raft around with less. And look at the 74s. Seven of them; if you reckon you can handle them with any short of 21 boys, I'd like to see you try. And there's the 3 canoes. The fleets ain't fitten to go into action till you pull in 27 more men."

Everybody set quiet a thinking it over and sighing, and shaking their heads now and then. At last somebody says—

"Volunteers?"

But that wouldn't do; the regulations didn't allow no volunteers. So that settled that, and we thunk again, a spell. Then somebody says—

"Recruits?"

"Recruits, your granny," Tom Sawyer says, "they wouldn't join unless they could be officers."

That was so. So that settled that. By and by John Riggs says—

"We'll press them."

It raised a cheer, and everybody said it was splendid, and naval right down to the ground. So everything was all right, now, till Van Wagner says,

"If it ain't sedition to sejest it, you mutton-heads, how is 22 going to press 27?"

There was the misrablest silence the longest time and every

person down in the mouth, then John Riggs says, firm and decided,

"Dang the battle of the Nile, it ain't eligible. It ain't eligible the way it's planned. We got to start over again and reduce it so as to fetch it within our means."

Everybody cheered up again at that, and Tom asked him to map it out, and he done it.

"We'll have the fleets reduced to only just the two flag-ships and two canoes," he says. "One canoe to carry orders and one for a chaplain, and that leaves two ten-men crews for the flag-ships.

Tom Sawyer's Conspiracy

I

In 1884, along with a list of memories of Hannibal which Mark Twain thought that he might use "in this [unidentified] story," he made a notebook entry, "Pater-rollers and slavery"—a reference to the patrollers who guarded pre-Civil War Missouri towns against abolitionists and escaping slaves.[1] The group would figure prominently in "Tom Sawyer's Conspiracy." One can only guess what stimulated memory at this time. Possibly the author had been reading Return I. Holcombe's *History of Marion County, Missouri*. This account of Hannibal and other towns of the county was published in 1884; Orion Clemens had contributed to it; and a copy was in the humorist's library at the time of his death. It recalled that in 1842 the folk of Hannibal and nearby towns were "greatly troubled by the abolitionists" and "vigilance committees [i.e., patrollers] were appointed in every township, whose duty it was to keep vigilant watch and ward over the community."[2]

In June 1894, the author wrote an article, "A Scrap of Curious History," comparing recent events in France with events which allegedly took place in 1845 in humble Marion City, Missouri. Twain's account may well have been based upon Holcombe's book, although it

---

[1] Notebook 17, TS p. 20. Elsewhere in his notebooks the author frequently jotted down words from a Negro song about the patrollers.

[2] Pages 262–263.

took many liberties with the facts set forth there.[3] The story told by Twain went thus: Robert Hardy, a newly arrived New Englander, proclaimed himself an abolitionist and therefore was threatened by a mob. A minister, however, saved the Yankee by arguing that he was insane, and thereafter townspeople listened to Hardy's antislavery speeches with amusement. A change came when Hardy helped a slave escape to Illinois, killing a constable in the process. Hardy was tried and hanged. Thereupon a number of young men, one a pious printer, formed a secret abolitionist society with official costumes, passwords, grips, signs, and rituals. On posters containing pictures of skulls and crossbones, they issued warnings. Several of these details would recur in "Tom Sawyer's Conspiracy"—the fearsome abolitionists; the captured runaway slave; the secret society with its costumes, ceremonies, and warning posters; the pious printer; murder; and communal excitement and confusion.

A notebook entry of 1896 shows Mark Twain hitting upon the idea of relating these to a plot which Huck would describe: "Have Huck tell how one white brother shaved his head, put on a wool wig and was blackened and sold as a negro. Escaped that night, washed himself, and helped hunt *for himself* under pay." [4] A year later the author thought of using Huck himself as "the white brother": "Tom sells Huck for a slave." Some pages later in the notebook containing this entry, among items headed "For New Huck Finn," he writes "Huck," crosses it out, replaces it with "Tom" and concludes the sentence: "is disguised as a negro and sold in Ark for $10, then he and Huck help hunt for him after the disguise is removed." [5] This was the outline which would be adopted. Tom would disguise himself as a Negro, allow himself to be turned over to slave trader Bat Bradish (whose prototype is William Beebe in "Villagers") and then would escape, so that the folk of St. Petersburg would believe that the abolitionists were initiating a conspir-

---

[3] Twain's article is in *What Is Man? and Other Essays* (Definitive Edition, New York, 1923), XXVI, 182–192. The account in Holcombe's history—of events which actually took place in 1836 when Clemens was a year old—is on pp. 203–208. For a partial list of Twain's inaccuracies see Minnie M. Brashear, *Mark Twain, Son of Missouri* (Chapel Hill, 1934), p. 73.

[4] Notebook 31, TS p. 22.

[5] Notebook 32a, TS pp. 34, 58. In *MTW*, p. 49, Bernard DeVoto quotes a note wherein Huck still is the one who is to be disguised: "Marion City. Steal skiff. Turning Huck black and sell him." DeVoto dates this note "only a very few years before Mark's death"; but I see no evidence for his dating.

acy. A spate of additional working notes indicates that while unfolding this story Twain hoped—as he had in *Huckleberry Finn*—to freight his pages with details about life in an old-time Missouri village, e.g., "Paint Xmas Day and New Years . . . The serenaders . . . Skating on Mississippi—a desperate adventure on the ice . . . Corn-shucking and dance . . . The red-ear and the kiss." [6] A number of notes contain details in "Villagers 1840–3," which in fact the author wrote at this time, along with other Hannibal or St. Petersburg fragments.

He started to write this fragment in Weggis, Switzerland, in 1897 [7] and probably in the first spurt reached the end of chapter four and, to his annoyance, the winding-up of the only strand of plot that he had worked out. At this point a change in the kind of paper used suggests his habitual period of waiting for his depleted inspiration tank to refill. Then he returned to the manuscript again and worked on it in 1898, 1899, or 1900—perhaps in all three years. Working notes that have survived show the humorist pondering possible ways to keep his story going. Since the developments outlined are not used, they must have been unsatisfactory; but the new manuscript pages show that he finally decided upon a line of action. In chapter five Tom finds a reason for not following his plan to impersonate a slave—as a result of an interesting if improbable coincidence, another pair of conspirators have played a variation of Tom's trick; that is, another disguised white person has passed himself off to Bradish as an escaped slave and has become Bradish's captive. Soon Bradish is killed, the pseudoslave and his companion run away, and in chapter six Twain can embark upon the second part of his narrative.

The segment was to be a murder and detective story, concluding with a spectacular trial, a favorite pattern for Twain. D. M. McKeithan has pointed out significant elements in what might be called the detective theme—the Muff Potter plot—in *Tom Sawyer*: "an innocent man falsely accused of a crime . . . the introduction of evidence which seems to prove his guilt, and the late discovery of sensational new evidence or a surprise witness that saves the innocent man and identifies the unsuspected criminal in the closing hours of the trial." [8] Franklin Rogers has plausibly argued that between 1876 and 1883, while Mark

---

[6] Notebook 32a, TS pp. 57–58. The final phrase refers to the ancient custom at corn-huskings of awarding a kiss to any youth who comes upon a red ear of corn.

[7] For a consideration of the dating, see Appendix B.

[8] *Court Trials in Mark Twain and Other Essays* (The Hague, 1958), p. 25.

Twain was writing *Huckleberry Finn,* he planned to trot out this plot again, with Jim as the falsely accused man.[9] *Ah Sin,* a play which Twain wrote in collaboration with Bret Harte in 1877, also included a supposed murder, an unjustified accusation, and a clarification of the mystery. *Simon Wheeler, Detective* (which he wrote as a play in 1876/77 and in part as a novel between 1878 and 1898) utilized the same pattern. So did two published works of 1894 and 1896, respectively, *Pudd'nhead Wilson* and "Tom Sawyer, Detective."

In the present fragment Jim plays the role assigned to him in the discarded plan for *Huckleberry Finn*—that of the guiltless man charged with murder. Two witnesses, Fisher and Haines, offer damning evidence when he is tried; then (though the story breaks off before this part concludes) the surviving manuscript shows clearly that Tom was able to provide undisclosed evidence that would free Jim and convict the guilty parties.

Typically, the story would reveal that Mark Twain, who was of two or more minds about many matters, had an ambivalent attitude toward detectives and detective stories. He admired brilliant deductions and showed his admiration on several occasions by having Tom, Huck, and Pudd'nhead Wilson follow complex lines of reasoning to their conclusions. On the other hand, he was irked by pretentious and arrogant detectives in life and in books. As early as 1865 in a newspaper article he jeered at San Francisco's Detective Rose for making pompous and ridiculous deductions. Between 1876 and 1902 he fired shots at swaggering but bumbling detectives in a group of narratives—in a paragraph in *Tom Sawyer,* at much greater length in *Simon Wheeler* (in both its forms), in "The Stolen White Elephant," and in "A Double-Barrelled Detective Story."

In the second half of "Conspiracy," then, as in the first half, Twain followed customary pathways.

II

"Tom Sawyer's Conspiracy" made use of more than Mark Twain's typical plots. Like any story he set in St. Petersburg, it reached into its creator's boyhood for details of setting, for characters, and for happen-

---

[9] *Mark Twain's Burlesque Patterns* (Dallas, 1960), pp. 130–132.

ings. Geographically, it duplicates pre-Civil War Hannibal. Crawfish Branch, Catfish Hollow, Cardiff Hill, "Cold Spring where the mill is," Injun Joe's Cave, the deserted slaughterhouse, Hookerville, Jackson's Island (under different names), and the Illinois shore east of Hannibal all had their counterparts in actuality. The river figures prominently in the story as it had in the Hannibal days of Sam Clemens. It is a place for somnolent swimming or contemplation; it brings and carries away strangers who disturb the town's quietude. As in *Huckleberry Finn* and *Pudd'nhead Wilson*, the river is thought of as a highway which bears slaves downstream to harsh plantation masters or to Cairo where the Ohio may provide a route to freedom.

Characters based upon remembered Hannibalites, already used in earlier books, recur—Tom, Huck, Sid, Jim, Aunt Polly, the Widow Douglas, Miss Watson, and Judge Thatcher. Working notes in notebooks and on separate pages (see Appendix C) show that Mark Twain intended to use as prototypes other erstwhile Hannibal characters who appeared in "Villagers." [10]

Burrell's Gang derived from Murrell's Gang or Murrell's "Mystic Brotherhood," about whom the author had heard traditional yarns as a boy and about whom he had read as a man. [11] This gang, as he says in chapter twenty-nine of *Life on the Mississippi*, was "a colossal combination of robbers, horse-thieves, negro-stealers, and counterfeiters" who in the period of this story "projected negro insurrections." Legend had it that Murrell had used some of the rituals prominent in Mark Twain's story when initiating escaped Negroes, forcing them to take an oath and giving them a mystic sign and grip. In *Tom Sawyer* Twain had Tom and Huck find a treasure that the Murrell gang had buried. He probably remembered the abolitionists from his boyhood, for they had distributed leaflets, pamphlets, and handbills widely, setting an example for Tom. They had made the people of Hannibal and other Missouri villages very nervous.

Tom's deliberate acquisition of measles by climbing into bed with Joe

---

[10] Notes which accompany the manuscript in MTP are printed in this volume (Appendix C); others are in Notebook 32a. "Dat one-laigged nigger dat b'longs to old Misto Bradish" is mentioned by Jim in chapter eight of *Huckleberry Finn*.

[11] In *Life on the Mississippi*, Mark Twain quotes at length from "a now forgotten book which was published about half a century ago." The quotation duplicates several passages word-for-word from Augustus Q. Walton, *A History of the Detection, Conviction, Life and Designs of John A. Murel, The Great Western Land Pirate* . . . (Cincinnati, n.d.), pp. 34, 45, 57.

Harper is based upon an 1844 experience of Sam Clemens's. The good, old-fashioned doctor seems to have been modeled upon the Clemens family physician, Dr. Meredith, mentioned in the working notes for the story, as well as in "Villagers." Mark Twain had described strenuous treatments such as the doctor administers in half-a-dozen narratives, including *Tom Sawyer* and *Pudd'nhead Wilson*.

Tom's experiences as a printer and the strange technical expressions that Huck hears the printer use derive from young Sam Clemens's years as a printer's devil and tramp printer. (Mark Twain similarly derived humor from a reversed woodcut in "Fortifications of Paris" in 1870 and from typographical errors in *A Connecticut Yankee* and *Simon Wheeler, Detective*.) The esoteric official titles held by foreman Baxter in various secret societies are echoes of offices in pre-Civil War Hannibal societies and in the Masonic group of which Clemens himself was a member in the 1860's. The delight in sensational events, the morbidity, the excitability, and the moblike tendencies of the villagers are copied not only from the humorist's memories of his boyhood home town but also from his observations of mankind after leaving Hannibal. He had come to believe that men were, in Huck Finn's words, "a mighty ornery lot." This opinion was reinforced by the villagers' belief in the necessity of slavery, since, as Huck says, "they had to get their living." Moreover, the villagers could laugh at comedy deriving from slavery, a fact reflected in the boys' minstrel shows and their burnt-cork disguises. The author had written about minstrel shows and youthful imitations of them frequently in factual reminiscences and in fictional passages.

III

As he wrote this abortive narrative, Twain in his customary way drew upon literature as well as life for materials. And even this fragment testifies to some breadth in his reading.

Twain's lifelong liking for history shows itself time after time. Do Tom and Huck need a chain and a padlock and some keys? They can utilize those that they "used to play the Prisoner of the Basteel with." Telling Huck and Jim about a revolution, Tom is able to define such a movement as one "where there ain't only nine-tenths of the people satisfied with the gov'ment, and the others is down on it and rises up

full of patriotic devotion and knocks the props out from under it and
sets up a more different one." He is able to cite the American and the
French revolutions as examples. He recalls the careers of Cromwell and
Washington. The excited folk of St. Petersburg behave much in the
manner of mobs in accounts of the French Revolution by Carlyle and
others. When arguing for and organizing his "conspiracy," Tom refers
to the relatively obscure Georges Cadoudal as well as to the better
known Guy Fawkes and Titus Oates. He has also read about Bartholomew's Day—enough to have learned that "it was the Presbyterians
cleaning out the missionaries." To help run his conspiracy, Tom sets up
a Council of Three and a Council of Ten: his creator had read about
them while visiting Venice in 1867, and he had written about them in
chapter twenty-two of *The Innocents Abroad*.[12] In his account of the
French Revolution, Carlyle had written about passwords, secret grips,
and oaths like those figuring in this narrative.

Any story like this, which simultaneously accepts and rejects the
belief that detectives are admirable, not surprisingly reveals its author's
familiarity with and ambivalent attitude toward detective fiction.[13]
There is no satire in Huck's account in chapter five of Tom's deducing
at Bradish's cabin that Bradish's captive is white. Only admiration is
evident as Huck tells in chapter six of the way Tom determines that Bat
has died recently and then peers at tracks and deduces important facts
from them. "Jim's been here," he is able to say because he has recognized Jim's tracks. Tom's additional study of footprints shows that
"there [have] been four men there besides Bat and Jim." Following the
trail of the murderers, Tom makes other discoveries—that one has hurt
his left leg and limps, that he and his companion have stolen Captain
Haines's canoe, and that nevertheless they still are nearby.

All these details may have been suggested by detective stories which
the author knew or could have known. The following of footprints, of
course, was a commonplace in detective fiction. But Clemens's friend
Joe Twichell recently had introduced him to Sherlock Holmes; and
Memoirs of Sherlock Holmes (1894) contains a story, "The Silver

---

[12] He had also read about the groups in his friend Thomas Bailey Aldrich's
Story of a Bad Boy (1870), chapter nine, and he could have read about them in
Cooper's *The Bravo* (1831).

[13] "What a curious thing a 'detective' story is," wrote Twain in 1896. "And was
there ever one that the author needn't be ashamed of, except 'The Murders in the
Rue Morgue'?" (Notebook 30, TS p. 32).

Blaze," which not only tells about the following of footprints but also recounts a murder similar to the one in "Conspiracy" and describes the use of a duplicate key and the discovery among the murdered man's effects of a tallow candle and a watch. Doyle's "The Boscombe Valley Mystery" shows Holmes deducing from footprints that "the murderer is a tall man who limps with his right leg." [14] Tom's taking of a tallow mold of a footprint to use in his great trial scene has no direct parallel that I have found, but Holmes in *The Sign of the Four* (1890) mentions his famous monograph "upon the tracing of footsteps, with some remarks upon the uses of plaster of Paris as a preserver of impresses," and Mark Twain possibly had Tom use tallow because plaster of Paris was scarce in St. Petersburg.

Twain's reading of detective fiction must also have familiarized him with the aspects of detection which he satirized. Tom's remark that a detective "looks everywheres—he don't make any exceptions" is followed by this justification:

> First, he looks where he ain't likely to find anything—becuz that is where he'd druther find it, of course, on account of the showiness of it; and if he is disappointed he turns to and hunts in the likely places.

The remark about "likely places" recalls Dupin's argument in Poe's "The Purloined Letter." [15] During the 1870's, two decades before Doyle's stories about Holmes had become best sellers, Mark Twain had discovered Allan Pinkerton's gaudy detective stories and had made fun of some of their details in *Simon Wheeler, Detective*. The eye which Tom uses as an insignia in his reversed woodcuts is based upon the insignia of the Pinkerton agency, which bore a similar eye with the motto "We Never Sleep" beneath it. "The Sons of Freedom," the group of conspirators invented by Tom, quite possibly derived their fancy name and some of their tendencies from chapter eighteen of Pinkerton's novel, *The Spy of the Rebellion* (1883). What endlessly amused the humorist was the elaborate and often illogical theorizing of detectives

---

[14] Another possible source is a tale in *The Arabian Nights* cited by Tom Sawyer in "Tom Sawyer Abroad," chapter seven, wherein the wise man deduces from camel tracks: "I knowed a camel had been along, because I seen his track. I knowed he was lame in his off hind leg because he had favored that foot and trod light on it, and his track showed it."

[15] Not only did he refer to Poe's "The Murders in the Rue Morgue," but Mark Twain took details about the hunt for treasure in *Tom Sawyer* from "The Gold Bug."

such as Pinkerton recounted in each of his books. "What's common sense got to do with detecting, you leatherhead?" Tom, a worshiper of romantic conventions, asks Huck. "It ain't got *anything* to do with it. What is wanted is genius and penetration and marvelousness. A detective that had common sense couldn't . . . even make his living." Jake Flacker is one of Mark Twain's typical comic detectives, arrogant, mysterious, and no end ratiocinative as he reconstructs a murder in an account which Huck rightly describes as "clean, straight foolishness." When the villagers say that "it is the most astonishing thing the way a detective could read every little sign he come across same as if it was a book," they sound like Pinkerton, who says in "Byron as a Detective" (1876) [16] that diagrams of the heel marks that he has traced relate "the whole story as plainly as if it had been revealed in letter-press."

IV

"Tom Sawyer's Conspiracy" comes closer to completion than any other fragment in this collection. A few more pages would have ended the piece; even without them a reader can easily see how the story would have turned out. It had some merits, and its author must at least have liked parts of it. Although they may not rank among Huck's very best stylistic achievements, some passages are not to be scorned. The opening description of St. Petersburg in the spring and the later description of the storm—a favorite scene of Twain's—are evocative and moving. There is better than average satire in the boys' and Jim's discussions of civil wars, revolutions, insurrections, and conspiracies; in the account of the "good" doctor's ministrations; in the detailing of Mr. Baxter's activities in church and at lodge meetings "for the highsting up of the human race"; in the picture of Sam Rumford's valiant company on the march; in Tom's dissertation on the ways of detectives; and in the description of the frightened townsfolk "ranting up and down and carrying on and prophecying." Now and then a brief phrase recalls the comic style of the old Huck, as when he says that Jim "knowed me and Tom wouldn't let him be a slave long if industriousness and enterprise and c'ruption was worth anything," or when he speaks of feeling "as

---

[16] *Model Town and the Detectives. Byron as a Detective* (New York), p. 182.

happy and splendid as Sodom and Gomorrah or any other of them patriarchs."

A recurrent motif gives much of the narrative continuity and explores an important concern of the author. In the second paragraph, Tom says that Huck's and Jim's passive way of letting things happen instead of planning ahead "put double as much on Providence as there was any use in." Jim disagrees, *"You* can't relieve Prov'dence none, en he doan need yo' help, nohow." Then Tom and Jim have an argument which Tom wins by what Huck considers to be tricky logic. Thereafter references to Providence and discussions of it recur frequently, and not only Tom but others enter into them. The King, for instance, raises his hypocritical voice, as he had in *Huckleberry Finn,* in fulsome praise of Providence. In St. Petersburg after Bat's murder and Jim's arrest, "everybody was talking about the watchful inscrutableness of Providence, and thankful for it and astonished at it."

The author is voicing a disenchantment with the pious preachments of antebellum Hannibal which had been growing for many years. For a long time he had been sporadically attacking orthodox beliefs about Providence. In chapter three of *Huckleberry Finn,* written in 1876, he has Huck contrast the kind of Providence about which the Widow Douglas talks with the kind of Providence described by her sister, Miss Watson, noticing that one is benevolent while the other is ferocious. In chapter fifty-four of *Life on the Mississippi* (1883) he jests about his boyhood belief that Providence was deeply concerned with what happened to the boys of Hannibal. In his *Autobiography* at the time this fragment was written, he was satirizing the same belief; and a notebook entry of the period is explicit about his skepticism: "God cares not a rap for us—nor for any living creature." [17] The target of the fragment is the same, for it derides the belief that an august Providence concerns itself with such puny matters as the shenanigans planned by Tom to while away a summer.[18] The pessimistic author also attacks the belief that there is (as the King puts it) "a righteous overrulin' Providence" which works in unfathomable ways for the best and which, therefore, should

[17] Passages on Providence not cited or located in the text include MTN, p. 190 (an 1885 entry); pp. 360–363 (27 May 1898); Wilson's epigraph preceding chapter four of *Pudd'nhead Wilson* (1894); MTA, I, 133 (1898), MTE, p. 260 (1906).

[18] A working note reads, "But now you know it got to be *serious*—Providence changed the program."

be blindly trusted. The parent whose favorite daughter Susy had recently died, the author who was beginning to write "The Mysterious Stranger," was in no mood to accept such consolations.

Although "Tom Sawyer's Conspiracy" had a plot structure which could have been worked out to a fairly logical conclusion, although it had some stylistic bits which must have pleased its writer, and although it developed themes of interest to him, Mark Twain did not write the few pages that would have completed his story, and he made no effort to arrange for its publication. One is compelled to ask the reasons.

It is not difficult to suggest several. There are two plots, neither works out particularly well, and they are only loosely tied together. The conspiracy story starts slowly and once started does not yield enough satire, enough comedy, or enough interesting action to justify itself. One who is chiefly interested in a story of detection must plow through the conspiracy before encountering any mystery. Once the second plot has begun, the reader is called upon to accept a whole series of coincidences, any of which takes some painful swallowing—the working out of Tom's hoax to coincide precisely in nature and in timing with that of the King and the Duke, the simultaneous arrival at Bat's cabin of Fisher, Haines, and Jim, the encounter between the boys and the two confidence men on the steamboat, and, finally, the melodramatic arrival of the guilty pair in the courtroom at precisely the most exciting moment. No wonder Twain, in some of his working notes, considered making changes which would enable him to completely reconstruct his detective-story plot.[19]

The plot troubles alone need not have been fatal. Mark Twain had solved equally difficult plotting problems; he had eventually satisfied himself with *Pudd'nhead Wilson,* for instance, by amputating an extra plot. More important, probably, was the fact that at its best this story was doing little more than echo—not very effectively—his earlier writings. The account of Twain's work during this period, as H. S. Canby says, "sounds like the declining years of a skillful writer of best sellers, revamping his old successes after vitality is gone." [20] Finally, this narrative could not be shaped to enunciate the author's ideas about Providence and related matters nearly as well as the Eseldorf version of "The Mysterious Stranger," which Twain apparently started to write when he abandoned this manuscript.

---

[19] See Appendix C.
[20] *Turn West, Turn East* (Boston, 1951), p. 187.

Tom Sawyer's Conspiracy

Chapter 1

WELL, we was back home and I was at the Widow Douglas's up on Cardiff Hill again getting sivilised some more along of her and old Miss Watson all the winter and spring, and the Widow was hiring Jim for wages so he could buy his wife and children's freedom some time or other, and the summer days was coming, now, and the new leaves and the wind-flowers was out, and marbles and hoops and kites was coming in, and it was already barefoot time and ever so bammy and soft and pleasant, and the damp a-stewing out of the ground and the birds a-carrying on in the woods, and everybody taking down the parlor stoves and stowing them up garret, and speckled straw hats and fish-hooks beginning to show up for sale, and the early girls out in white frocks and blue ribbons, and schoolboys getting restless and fidgetty, and anybody could see that the derned winter was over. Winter is plenty lovely enough when it *is* winter and the river is froze over and there's hail and sleet and bitter cold and booming storms and all that, but spring is no good—just rainy and slushy and sloppy and dismal and ornery and uncomfortable, and ought to be stopped. Tom Sawyer he says the same.

Me and Jim and Tom was feeling good and thankful, and took

the dug-out and paddled over to the head of Jackson's island early Saturday morning where we could be by ourselves and plan out something to do. I mean it was Tom's idea to plan out something to do—me and Jim never planned out things to do, which wears out a person's brains and ain't any use anyway, and is much easier and more comfortable to set still and let them happen their own way. But Tom Sawyer said it was a lazy way and put double as much on Providence as there was any use in. Jim allowed it was sinful to talk like that, and says—

"Mars Tom, you ought not to talk so. *You* can't relieve Prov'dence none, en he doan need yo' help, nohow. En what's mo', Mars Tom, if you's gwyne to try to plan out sump'n dat Prov'dence ain' gwyne to 'prove of, den ole Jim got to pull out, too."

Tom seen that he was making a mistake, and resking getting Jim down on his projects before there was any to get down on. So he changed around a little, and says—

"Jim, Providence appoints everything beforehand, don't he?"

"Yessah—'deed he do—fum de beginnin' er de worl'."

"Very well. If I plan out a thing—*thinking* it's me that's planning it out, I mean—and it don't *go*, what does that mean? Don't it mean that it wasn't Providence's plan and he ain't willing?"

"Yessah, you can 'pen' 'pon it—dat's jes' what it mean, every time."

"And if it *does* go, it means that it *was* Providence's plan, and I just happened to hit it right, don't it?"

"Yessah, it's jes' what it mean, dead sho'."

"Well, then, it's right for me to go ahead and keep on planning out things till I find out which is the one he wants done, ain't it?"

"W'y, sutt'nly, Mars Tom, dat's all right, o' course, en ain' no sin en no harm—"

"That is, I can *suggest* plans?"

"Yassah, sutt'nly, you can *sejest* as many as you want to, Prov'dence ain' gwyne to mine dat, if he can look 'em over fust, but doan you *do* none of 'em, Mars Tom, excep' only jes' de right one—becase de sin is shovin' ahead en *doin'* a plan dat Prov'dence ain't satisfied wid."

Everything was satisfactry again. You see he just fooled Jim along and made him come out at the same hole he went in at, but Jim didn't know it. So Tom says—

"It's all right, now, and we'll set down here on the sand and plan out something that'll just make the summer buzz, and worth being alive. I've been examining the authorities and sort of posting up, and there's two or three things that look good, and would just suit, I reckon—either of them."

"Well," I says, "what's the first one?"

"The first one, and the biggest, is a civil war—if we can get it up."

"Shucks," I says, "dern the civil war. Tom Sawyer, I might a knowed you'd get up something that's full of danger and fuss and worry and expense and all that—it wouldn't suit you, if it warn't."

"And glory," he says, excited, "you're forgetting the glory—forgetting the main thing."

"Oh, cert'nly," I says, "it's got to have that in, you needn't tell a person that. The first time I ketch old Jimmy Grimes fetching home a jug that hain't got any rot-gut in it, I'll say the *next* mericle that's going to happen is Tom Sawyer fetching home a *plan* that hain't got any glory in."

I said it very sarcastic. I just *meant* it to make him squirm, and it done it. He stiffened up, and was very distant, and said I was a jackass.

Jim was a studying and studying, and pretty soon he says—

"Mars Tom, what do dat word mean—*civil?*"

"Well, it means—it means—well, anything that's good, and kind, and polite, and all that—Christian, as you may say."

"Mars Tom, doan dey fight in de wars, en kill each other?"

"Of course."

"Now den, does you call dat civil, en kind en polite, en does you call it Christian?"

"Well—you see—well, you know—don't you understand, it's only just a *name.*"

"Hi-yah! I was a layin' for you, Mars Tom, en I got you dis time, sho'. Jist a name! *Dat's* so. *Civil* war! Dey ain' no sich war. De

idear!—people dat's good en kind en polite en b'long to de church
a-marchin' out en slashin' en choppin' en cussin' en shootin' one
another—lan', I knowed dey warn't no sich thing. You done 'vent it
yo' own self, Mars Tom. En you want to take en drap *dat* plan,
same as if she was hot. Don't you git up no civil war, Mars
Tom—Prov'dence ain' gwyne to 'low it."

"How do *you* know, till it's been tried?"

"How does I know? I knows becase Prov'dence ain' gwyne to let
dat kind o' people fight—he ain' never hearn o' no sich war."

"He has heard of it, too; it's an old thing; there's been a million
of them."

Jim couldn't speak, he was so astonished. And so hurt, too. He
judged it was a sin for Tom to say such a thing. But Tom told him
it was so, and everybody knowed it that had read the histories. So
Jim had to believe it, but he didn't want to, and said he didn't
believe Providence would allow it any more; and then he got
doubtful and troubled and ontrustful, and asked Tom to lay low
and not sejest it. And he was so anxious that he couldn't be
comforted till Tom promised him he wouldn't.

So Tom done it; but he was disappointed. And for a while he
couldn't keep from talking about it and hankering after it. It shows
what a good heart he had; he had been just dead set on getting up a
civil war, and had even planned out the preparations for it on the
biggest scale, and yet he throwed it all aside and give it up to
accommodate a nigger. Not many boys would a done such a thing
as that. But that was just his style; when he liked a person there
wasn't anything he wouldn't do for them. I've seen Tom Sawyer do
a many a noble thing, but the noblest of all, I think, was the time
he countermanded the civil war. That was his word—and not a
half a mouthful for him, either, but I don't fat up with such, they
give me the dry gripes. He had the preparations all made, and was
going to have a billion men in the field, first and last, besides
munitions of war. I don't know what that is—brass bands, I reckon;
sounds like it, anyway, and I knowed Tom Sawyer well enough to
know that if he got up a war and was in a hurry and overlooked
some of the things, it wouldn't be the brass bands, not by a blame

sight. But he give up the civil war, and it is one of the brightest things to his credit. And he could a had it easy enough if he had sejested it, anybody can see it now. And it don't seem right and fair that Harriet Beacher Stow and all them other second-handers gets all the credit of starting that war and you never hear Tom Sawyer mentioned in the histories ransack them how you will, and yet he was the first one that thought of it. Yes, and years and years before ever they had the idea. And it was all his own, too, and come out of his own head, and was a bigger one than theirs, and would a cost forty times as much, and if it hadn't been for Jim he would a been in ahead and got the glory. I know, becuz I was there, and I could go this day and point out the very place on Jackson's island, there on the sand-bar up at the head where it begins to shoal off. And where is Tom Sawyer's monument, I would like to know? There ain't any. And there ain't ever going to be any. It's just the way, in this world. One person *does* the thing, and the other one gets the monument.

So then I says, "What's the next plan, Tom?"

And he said his next idea was to get up a revolution. Jim licked his chops over that, and says—

"Hit's a pow'ful big word, Mars Tom, en soun' mighty good. What's a revolution?"

"Well, it's where there ain't only nine-tenths of the people satis-fied with the gov'ment, and the others is down on it and rises up full of patriotic devotion and knocks the props from under it and sets up a more different one. There's nearly about as much glory in a revolution as there is in a civil war, and ain't half the trouble and expense if you are on the right side, because you don't have to have so many men. It's the economicalest thing there is. Anybody can get up a revolution."

"Why looky here, Tom," I says, "how can one-tenth of the people pull down a gov'ment if the others don't want them to? There ain't any sense in that. It can't be done."

"It can't, can't it? Much you know about history, Huck Finn. Look at the French revolution; and look at ourn. I reckon that'll show you. Just a handful started it, both times. You see, *they* don't

know they're going to revolute when they start *in,* and they don't
know they *are* revoluting till it's all over. Our boys started in to get
taxation by representation—it's all they wanted—and when they
got through and come to look around, they see they had knocked
out the king. And besides, had more taxation and liberty and things
than they knowed what to do with. Washington found out towards
the last that there had been a revolution, but *he* didn't know when
it happened, and yet he was there all the time. The same with
Cromwell, the same with the French. That's the peculiarity of a
revolution—there ain't anybody intending to do anything when
they start in. That's one of the peculiarities; and the other one is,
that the king gets left, every time."

"Every time?"

"Of course; it's all there is *to* a revolution—you knock out the
gov'ment and start a fresh kind."

"Tom Sawyer," I says, "where are you going to get a king to
knock out? There ain't any."

"Huck Finn, you don't have to have any to knock out, this time
—you put one *in.*"

He said it would take all summer, and break up school and
everything, and so I was willing for us to start the revolution; but
Jim says—

"Mars Tom, I's gwyne to object. I hadn't nothing agin kings
ontel I had dat one on my han's all las' summer. Dat one's enough
for me. He *was* de beatenes' ole cuss—now warn't he, Huck?
Warn't he de wust lot you ever see?—awluz drunk en carryin' on,
him en de duke, en tryin' to rob Miss Mary en de Hair-lip—*no* sah,
I got enough; I ain' gwyne to have nothing more to do wid kings."

Tom said that that warn't no regular king, and couldn't be took
as a sample; and tried his level best to argufy Jim into some kind of
reasonableness, but it warn't any use; he was set, and when he was
set once, he was set for good. He said we would have all the trouble
and worry and expense, and when we got the revolution done our
old king would show up and hog the whole thing. Well, it begun to
sound likely, the way Jim put it, and it got me to feeling oneasy,
and I reckoned we was taking too much of a resk; so I pulled out

and sided with Jim, and that let the stuffing out of the revolution. I was sorry to have Tom so disappointed again, and him so happy and hopeful; but ever since, when I look back on it I know I done for the best. Kings ain't in our line; we ain't used to them, and wouldn't know how to keep them satisfied and quiet; and they don't seem to do anything much for the wages, anyway, and don't pay no rent. They have a good heart, and feel tender for the poor and for the best charities, and they leg for them, too, and pass the hat pretty frequent, I can say that for them; but now and then they don't put anything in it themselves. They let *on* to economise, but that is about all. If one of them has got something on hand the other side of the river, he will go over in about nine ships; and the ferry-boat a laying there all the time. But the worst is the trouble it is to keep them still; it can't be done. They are always in a sweat about the succession, and the minute you get that fixed to suit them they bust out in another place. And always, rain or shine, they are hogging somebody else's land. Congress is a cuss, but we better get along with it. We always know what it will do, and that is a satisfaction. We can change it when we want to. And get a worse one, most of the time; but it is a change, anyway, and you can't do that with a king.

So Tom he give up the revolution, and said the next best thing would be to start an insurrection. Well, me and Jim was willing to that, but when we come to look it over we couldn't seem to think up anything to insurrect about. Tom explained what it was, but there didn't seem to be any way to work it. He had to give in, himself, that there wasn't anything definite about an insurrection. It wasn't either one thing nor t'other, but only just the middle stage of a tadpole. With its tail on, it was only just a riot; tail gone, it was an insurrection; tail gone and legs out, it was a revolution. We worried over it a little, but we see we couldn't do anything with it, so we let it go; and was sorry about it, too, and low spirited, for it was a beautiful name.

"Now then," I says, "What's the next?"

Tom said the next was the last we had in stock, but was the best one of all, in some ways, because the hide and heart of it was mystery. The hide and heart of the others was glory, he said, and glory was grand and valuable; but for solid satisfaction, mystery laid over it. It warn't worth while his telling us he was fond of mysteries, we knowed it before. There warn't anything he wouldn't do to be connected with a mystery. He was always that way. So I says—

"All right, what is your idea?"

"It's a noble good one, Huck. It's for us to get up a conspiracy."

"Is it easy, Mars Tom? Does you reckon we can do it?"

"Yes, anybody can."

"How does you go at it, Mars Tom? What do de word mean?"

"It means laying for somebody—private. You get together at night, in a secret place, and plan out some trouble against somebody; and you have masks on, and passwords, and all that. Georges Cadoudal got up a conspiracy. I don't remember what it was about, now, but anyway he done it, and we can do it, too."

"Is it cheap, Mars Tom?"

"Cheap? Well, I should reckon! Why, it don't cost a cent. That is, unless you do it on a big scale, like Bartholomew's Day."

"What is dat, Mars Tom? What did dey do?"

"I don't know. But it was on a big scale, anyway. It was in France. I think it was the Presbyterians cleaning out the missionaries."

Jim was disappointed, and says, kind of irritated—

"So, den, blame de conspiracy, down *she* goes. We got plenty Presbyterians, but we ain't got no missionaries."

"Missionaries, your granny—we don't need them."

"We don't, don't we? Mars Tom, how you gwyne to run yo' conspiracy if you ain' got but one end to it?"

"Why, hang it, can't we have somebody in the *place* of missionaries?"

"But would dat be right, Mars Tom?"

"Right? Right hasn't got anything to do with it. The wronger a conspiracy is, the better it is. All we've got to do is to have somebody in the place of the missionaries, and then—"

"But Mars Tom, will dey *take* de place, onless you explains to them how it is, en how you couldn't help yoself becase you couldn't git no mish—"

"Oh, shut up! You make me tired. I never see such a nigger to argue, and argue, and argue, when you don't know anything what you are talking about. If you'll just hold still a minute I'll get up a conspiracy that'll make Bartholomew sick—and not a missionary in it, either."

Jim knowed it wouldn't do for him to chip in any more for a spell, but he went on a mumbling to himself, the way a nigger does, and saying *he* wouldn't give shucks for a conspiracy that was made up out of just any kinds of odds and ends that come handy and hadn't anything lawful about it. But Tom didn't let on to hear; and it's the best way, to let a nigger or a child go on and grumble itself out, then it's satisfied.

Tom bent his head down, and propped his chin in his hands, and begun to forget us and the world; and pretty soon when he got up and begun to walk the sand and bob his head and wag it, I knowed the conspiracy was beginning to bile; so I stretched out in the sun and went to sleep, for I warn't going to be needed in that part of the business. I got an hour's nap, and then Tom was ready, and had it all planned out.

Chapter 2

I SEE in a minute that he had struck a splendid idea. It was to get the people in a sweat about the ablitionists. It was the very time for it. We knowed that for more than two weeks past there was whispers going around about strangers being seen in the woods over on the Illinois side, and then disappearing, and then seen again; and everybody reckoned it was ablitionists laying for a chance to run off some of our niggers to freedom. They hadn't run off any yet, and most likely they warn't even thinking about it and warn't ablitionists anyway; but in them days a stranger couldn't show himself and not start an uneasiness unless he told all about his business straight off and proved it hadn't any harm in it. So the town was considerable worried, and all you had to do was to slip up behind a man and say Ablitionist if you wanted to see him jump, and see the cold sweat come.

And they had tightened up the rules, and a nigger couldn't be out after dark at night, pass or no pass. And all the young men was parceled out into paterollers, and they watched the streets all night, ready to stop any stranger that come along.

Tom said it was a noble good time for a conspiracy—it was just as if it was made for it on a contract. He said all we had to do was to start it, and it would run itself. He believed if we went at it right and conscientious, and done our duty the best we could, we could have the town in a terrible state in three days. And I believed he was right, because he had a good judgment about conspiracies and those kind of things, mysteries being in his line and born to it, as you may say.

For a beginning, he said we must have a lot of randyvoozes—secret places to meet at and conspire; and he reckoned we better kind of surround the town with them, partly for style and partly so as there would always be one of them handy, no matter what part of town we might be in. So, for one he appointed our old hanted house, in the lonesome place three miles above town where Crawfish creek comes in out of Catfish hollow. And for another, mine and Jim's little cave up in the rocks in the deep woods on Jackson's island. And for another, the big cave on the main land three miles below town—Injun Joe's cave, where we found the money that the robbers had hid. And for another, the old deserted slaughterhouse on Slaughterhouse Point at the foot of town, where the creek comes in. The polecats couldn't stand that place, it smelt like the very nation; and so me and Jim tried to get him to change, but he wouldn't. He said it was a good strattyjick point, and besides was a good place to retreat to and hide, because dogs couldn't follow us there, on account of our scent not being able to beat the competition, and even if the dogs could follow us the enemy couldn't follow the dogs because they would suffocate. We seen that it was a good idea and sound, so then we give in.

Me and Jim thought there ought to be more conspirators if there was going to be much work, but Tom scoffed, and said—

"Looky here—what busted up Guy Fawkes? And what busted up Titus Oates?"

He looked at me very hard. But I warn't going to give myself away. Then he looked at Jim very hard—but Jim warn't going to, either. So then there wasn't anything more said about it.

Tom appointed our cave on Jackson's island for the high chief headquarters, and said common business could be done in the other randyvoozes, but the Council of State wouldn't ever meet anywhere but there—and said it was sacred. And he said there would have to be two Councils of State to run a conspiracy as important as this one—a Council of Ten and a Council of Three; black gowns for the Ten and red for the Three, and masks for all. And he said all of us would be the Council of Ten, and he would be the Council of Three. Because the Council of Three was supreme and could abrogate anything the other Council done. That was his word—one of his pile-drivers. I sejested it would save wages to leave out the Council of Ten, and there warn't hardly enough stuff for it anyway; but he only said—

"If I didn't know any more about conspiracies than you do, Huck Finn, I wouldn't expose myself."

So then he said we would go to the Council Chamber now, and hold the first meeting without any gowns or masks, and pass a resolution of oblivion next meeting and justify it; then it would go on the minutes all regular, and nobody could be put under attainder on account of it. It was his way, and he was born so, I reckon. Everything had to be regular, or he couldn't stand it. Why, I could steal six watermelons while he was chawing over authorities and arranging so it would be regular.

We found our old cave just as me and Jim had left it the time we got scared out and started down the river on the raft. Tom called up the Council of Ten, and made it a speech about the seriousness of the occasion, and hoped every member would reconnize it and put his hand sternly to the wheel and do his duty without fear or favor. Then he made it take an oath to run the conspiracy the best it

knowed how in the interests of Christianity and sivilization and to
get up a sweat in the town; and God defend the right, amen.

So then he elected himself President of the Council and Secretary, and opened the business. He says—

"There's a lot of details—no end of them—but they don't all
come first, they belong in their places; they'll fall in all right, as we
go along. But there's a first detail, and that is the one for us to take
hold of now. What does the Council reckon it is?"

I was stumped, and said so. Jim he said the same.

"Well, then, I'll tell you. What is it the people are a-worrying
about? What is it they are afraid of? You can answer that, I
reckon."

"Why, they're afraid there's going to be some niggers run off."

"That is right. Now, then, what is our duty as a conspiracy?"

Jim didn't know, and I didn't.

"Huck Finn, if you would think a minute you would know.
There's a lack—we've got to supply it. Ain't that plain enough?
We've got to run off a nigger."

"My lan', Mars Tom! W'y, dey'll hang us."

"Well, what do you *want*? What is a conspiracy *for*? Do you
reckon it's to propagate immortality? We've *got* to run risks, or it
ain't any conspiracy at all, and no honor in it. The honor of a
conspiracy is to do the thing you are after, but do it right and smart
and *not* get hung. Well, we will fix that. Now then, come back to
business. The first thing is, to pick out the nigger, and the next is,
to arrange about running him off."

"Why, Tom, we can't ever do it. There ain't a nigger in the town
that'll listen to it a minute. It would scare him out of his life, and he
would run straight to his master and tell on us."

He looked as if he was ashamed of me; and says—

"Now, Huck Finn, do you reckon I didn't know that?"

I couldn't understand what he was getting at. I says—

"Well, then, Tom Sawyer, if there ain't a nigger in the town that
will let us run him off, how can we manage?"

"Very easy. We'll *put* one there."

"Oh, cert'nly—that's very easy. Where are we going to get him?"

"He's here; I'm the one."

Me and Jim laughed; but Tom said he had thought it all out, and it would work. So then he told us the plan, and it was a very good one, sure enough. He would black up for a runaway nigger and hide in the hanted house, and I would betray him and sell him to old Bradish, up in Catfish hollow, which was a nigger trader in a little small way, and the orneriest hound in town, and then we would run him off and the music would begin, Tom said. And I reckoned it would.

But of course, just as everything was fixed all ship-shape and satisfactry, Jim's morals begun to work again. It was always happening to him. He said he belonged to the church, and couldn't do things that warn't according to religion. He reckoned the conspiracy was all right, he wasn't worried about that, but oughtn't we to take out a licence?

It was natural for him to think that, you know, becuz he knowed that if you wanted to start a saloon, or peddle things, or trade in niggers, or drive a dray, or give a show, or own a dog, or do most any blame thing you could think of, you had to take out a licence, and so he reckoned it would be the same with a conspiracy, and would be sinful to run it without one, becuz it would be cheating the gover'ment. He was troubled about it, and said he had been praying for light. And then he says, in that kind of pitiful way a nigger has that is feeling ignorant and distressed—

"De prar hain't ben answered straight en squah, but as fur as I can make out fum de symptoms, hit's agin de conspiracy onless we git de licence."

Well, I could see Jim's side, and knowed I oughtn't to fret at a poor nigger that didn't mean no harm, but was only going according to his lights the best he could, and yet I couldn't help being aggeravated to see our new scheme going to pot like the civil war and the revolution and no way to stop it as far as I could see—for Jim was set; you could see it; and of course when he was set, that was the end; arguments couldn't budge him. I warn't going to try; breath ain't given to us for to be wasted. I reckoned Tom would try, becuz the conspiracy was the last thing we had in stock and he would want to save it if he could; and I judged he would flare up and lose his temper right at the start, becuz it had had so much strain on it already—and then the fat would be in the fire of course, and the last chance of a conspiracy along with it.

But Tom never done anything of the kind. No, he come out of it beautiful. I hardly ever seen him rise to such grandure of wisdom as he done that time. I've seen him in delicate places often and often, when there warn't no time to swap horses, and seen him pull through all right when anybody would a said he couldn't, but I reckon they warn't any delicater than this one. He was catched sudden—but no matter, he was all there. When I seen him open his mouth I says to myself wherever one of them words hits it's agoing to raise a blister. But it warn't so. He says, perfectly cam and gentle—

"Jim, I'll never forget you for thinking of that, and reminding us. I clean forgot the licence, and if it hadn't been for you we might never thought of it till it was too late and we'd gone into a conspiracy that warn't rightly and lawfully sanctified." Then he speaks out in his official voice, very imposing, and says, "Summons the Council of Three." So then he mounted his throne in state, which was a nail-kag, and give orders to grant a licence to us to conspire in the State of Missouri and adjacent realms and apinages for a year, about anything we wanted to; and commanded the Grand Secretary to set it down in the minutes and put the great seal to it.

Jim was satisfied, then, and full of thankfulness, and couldn't find words enough to say it; though I thought then and think yet that the licence warn't worth a dern. But I didn't say anything.

There was only one more worry on Jim's mind, and it didn't take long to fix that. He was afeared it wouldn't be honest for me to sell Tom when Tom didn't belong to me; he was afeared it looked like swindling. So Tom didn't argue about it. He said wherever there was a doubt, even if it was ever so little a one, but yet had a look of being unmoral, he wanted it removed out of the plan, for he would not be connected with a conspiracy that was not pure. It looked to me like this conspiracy was a-degenerating into a Sunday school. But I never said anything.

So then Tom changed it and said he would get out handbills and offer a reward for himself, and I could find him, and not sell him but betray him over to Bat Bradish for part of the reward. Bat warn't his name; people called him that becuz he couldn't more than half see. Jim was satisfied with that, though I couldn't see where was the difference between selling a *boy* that don't belong to you and selling shares in a *reward* that was a fraud and warn't ever going to be paid. I said so to Tom, private, but he said I didn't know as much as a catfish; and said did I reckon we warn't going to pay the money *back* to Bat Bradish? Of course we would, he said.

I never said anything; but I reckoned to myself that if I got the money and Tom forgot and didn't interfere, me and Bat Bradish would settle that somehow amongst ourselves.

Chapter 3

W̲E̲ P̲A̲D̲D̲L̲E̲D̲ over to town, and Jim went home and me and Tom went to the carpenter shop and got a lot of smooth pine blocks that Tom wanted, and then to a shop and got an awl and a gouge and a little chisel, and took them to Tom's aunt Polly's and hid them up garret, and I stayed for supper and for all night; and in the middle of the night we slipped out and trapsed all over town to see the paterollers; and it was dim and quiet and still, except a dog or two and a cat that warn't satisfied, and nobody going about, but everybody asleep and the lights out except where there was sickness, then there would be a pale glow on the blinds; and a pateroller stood on every corner, and said "Who goes there?" and we said "Friends," and they said "Halt, and give the countersign," and we said we didn't have any, and they come and looked, and said, "Oh, it's you; well, you better get along home, no time for young trash like you to be out of bed."

And then we watched for a chance and slipped up stairs into the printing office, and put down the blinds and lit a candle, and there was old Mr. Day, the traveling jour. printer, asleep on the floor under a stand, with his old gray head on his carpet-sack for a pillow; but he didn't stir, and we shaded the light and tip-toed around and got some sheets of printing paper, blue and green and red and white, and some red printing ink and some black, and snipped off a little chunk from the end of a new roller to dab it with, and left a quarter on the table for pay, and was thirsty, and found a bottle of something and drunk it up for lemonade, but it turned out it was consumption medicine, becuz there was a label on it, but it was very good and answered. It was Mr. Day's; and we left another quarter for it, and blowed out the light, and got the things home all right and was very well satisfied, and hooked a hairbrush from Tom's aunt Polly to do the printing with and went to sleep.

Tom warn't willing to do business on Sunday, but Monday morning we went up garret and got out all our old nigger-show things, and Tom tried on his wig and the tow-linen shirt and ragged britches and one suspender, and straw hat with the roof caved in and part of the brim gone, and they was better than ever, becuz the shirt hadn't been washed since the cows come home and the rats had been sampling the other things.

Then Tom wrote out the handbill, "$100 Reward, Elegant Deef and Dumb Nigger Lad run away from the subscriber," and so on, and described himself to a dot the way he would look when he was blacked and dressed up for business, and said the nigger could be returned to "Simon Harkness, Lone Pine, Arkansaw;" and there warn't no such place, and Tom knowed it very well.

Then we hunted out the old chain and padlock and two keys that we used to play the Prisoner of the Basteel with, and some lampblack and some grease, and put them with the other things— "properties," Tom called them, which was a large name for truck which was not rightly property at all, for you could buy the whole outfit for forty cents and get cheated.

We had to have a basket, and there wasn't any that was big enough except aunt Polly's willow one, which she was so proud of and particular about, and it wasn't any use asking her to lend us that, becuz she wouldn't; so we went down stairs and got it while she was pricing a catfish that a nigger had to sell, and fetched it up and put the outfit in it, and then had to wait nearly an hour before we could get away, becuz Sid and Mary was gone somewheres and there wasn't anybody but us to help her hunt for the basket. But at last she had suspicions of the nigger that sold her the catfish, and went out to hunt for him, so then we got away. Tom allowed the hand of Providence was plain in it, and I reckoned it was, too, for it did look like it, as far as we was concerned, but I couldn't see where the nigger's share come in, but Tom said wait and I would see that the nigger would be took care of in some mysterious inscrutable way and not overlooked; and it turned out just so, for when aunt Polly give the nigger a raking over and then he proved he hadn't took the basket she was sorry and asked him to forgive her, and bought another catfish. And we found it in the cubberd that night and traded it off for a box of sardines to take over to the island, and the cat got into trouble about it; and when I said, now then the nigger is rectified but the cat is overlooked, Tom said again wait and I would see that the cat would be took care of in some mysterious inscrutable way; and it was so, for while aunt Polly was gone to get her switch to whip her with she got the other fish and et it up. So Tom was right, all the way through, and it shows that every one *is* watched over, and all you have to do is to be trustful and everything will come out right, and everybody helped.

We hid the outfit up stairs in the hanted house that morning, and come back to town with the basket, and it was very useful to carry provisions to Jim's big boat in, and cooking utensils. I stayed in the boat to take care of the things, and Tom done the shopping —not buying two basketfuls in one shop, but going to another shop every time, or people would have asked questions. Last of all, Tom fetched the pine blocks and printing ink and stuff from up garret, and then we pulled over to the island and stowed the whole boatload in the cave, and knowed we was well fixed for the conspiracy now.

We got back home before night and hid the basket in the woodshed, and got up in the night and hung it on the front door knob, and aunt Polly found it there in the morning and asked Tom how it come there, and he said he reckoned it was angels, and she said she reckoned so too, and suspicioned she knowed a couple of them and would settle with them after breakfast. She would a done it, too, if we had stayed.

But Tom was in a hurry about the handbills, and we took the first chance and got away and paddled down the river seven miles in the dugout to Hookerville, where there was a little printing office that had a job once in four years, and got a hundred and fifty Reward bills printed, and paddled back in the dead water under the banks, and got home before sundown and hid the bills up garret and had a licking, not much of a one, and then supper and family worship, and off to bed dog tired; but satisfied, becuz we had done every duty.

We went straight to sleep, for it ain't any trouble to go to sleep when you are tired and have done everything there was time to do, and done it the best you could, and so nothing on your conscience and nothing to trouble about. And we didn't take any pains about waking up, becuz the weather was good, and if it stayed so we couldn't do anything more till there was a change; and if a change come it would wake us. And it did.

It come on to storm about one in the morning, and the thunder and lightning woke us up. The rain come down in floods and floods; and ripped and raced along the shingles enough to deefen you, and would come slashing and thrashing against the windows, and make you feel so snug and cosy in the bed, and the wind was a howling around the eaves in a hoarse voice, and then it would die down a little and pretty soon come in a booming gust, and sing, and then wheeze, and then scream, and then shriek, and rock the house and make it shiver, and you would hear the shutters slamming all down the street, and then there'd be a glare like the world afire, and the thunder would crash down, right at your head and seem to tear everything to rags, and it was just good to be alive and tucked up comfortable to enjoy it; but Tom shouts "Turn out, Huck, we can't ever have it righter than this," and although he shouted it I could hardly hear him through the rattle and bang and roar and racket.

I wished I could lay a little bit longer, but I knowed I couldn't, for Tom wouldn't let me; so I turned out and we put on our clothes by the lightning and took one of the handbills and some tacks and got out of the back window onto the L, and crope along the comb of the roof and down onto the shed, and then onto the high board fence, and then to the ground in the garden the usual way, then down the back lane and out into the street.

It was a-drenching away just the same, and blowing and storming and thundering, a wild night and just the weather for ockult business like ourn, Tom said. I said yes; and said we ought to brought all the bills, becuz we wouldn't have another such a night soon. But he said—

"What do we want of any more? Where do they stick up bills, Huck?"

"Why, on the board that leans up against the postoffice door, where they stick up strayeds and stolens, and temperance meetings, and taxes, and niggers for sale, and stores to rent, and all them things, and a good place, too, and don't cost nothing, but an advertisement does, and don't anybody read it, either."

"Of course. They don't put up two bills, do they?"

"No. Only one. You can't read two at a time, except people that is cross-eyed, and there ain't enough of them for to make it worth the trouble."

"Well, then, that's why I fetched only one."

"What did you get 150 for, then? Are we going to stick up a new one every night for six months?"

"No, we ain't ever going to stick up any but the one. One's a plenty."

"Why, Tom, what *did* you spend all that money for, then? Why didn't you get only one printed?"

"On account of its being the regular number. If I had got only one, the printer would a gone soliloquising around to himself, saying 'This is curious; he could get 150 for the same money, and he takes only one; there's something crooked about this, and I better get him arrested.'"

Well, that was Tom Sawyer all over; always thought of everything. A long head; the longest I ever see on a boy.

Then come a glare that didn't leave a thimbleful of darkness

betwixt us and heaven, and you could see everything, plumb to the
river, the same as day. By gracious, not a pateroller anywheres; the
streets was empty. And every gutter was a creek, and nearly washed
us off of our feet the water run so deep and strong. We stuck up the
bill, and then stood there under the awning a while listening to the
storm and watching bunches of packing-straw and old orange boxes
and things sailing down the gutter when it lightened, and wanted
to stay and see it out, but dasent; becuz we was afraid of Sid. The
thunder might wake him up; and he was scared of thunder and
might go to the nearest room for comfort, which was ourn, and find
out we was gone, and watch and see how long we was out, so he
could tell on us in the morning, and give all the facts, and get us
into trouble. He was one of them kind that don't commit no sin
themselves, but ain't satisfied with that, but won't let anybody else
have a good time if they can help it. So we had to get along home.
Tom said he was too good for this world, and ought to be translated.
I never said anything, but let him enjoy his word, for I think it is
mean to take the tuck out of a person just to show how much you
know. But many does it, just the same. I knowed all about that
word, becuz the Widow told me; I knowed you can translate a
book, but you can't translate a boy, becuz translating means turning
a thing out of one language into another, and you can't do that with
a boy. And besides it has to be a foreign one, and Sid warn't a
foreign boy. I am not blaming Tom for using a word he didn't
know the meaning of; becuz he warn't dishonest about it, he used a
many a one that was over his size, but he didn't do it to deceive, he
only done it becuz it tasted good in his mouth.

   So we got home hoping Sid hadn't stirred; and kind of calculating on it, too, seeing how we was being looked out for in inscrutable
ways and how many signs there was that Providence was satisfied
with the conspiracy as far as we had got. But there come a little
hitch, now. We was on the roof of the L, and clawing along the
comb in the dark, and I was in the lead and was half way to our
window, and had set down frog-fashion, very gentle and soft, to feel
for a nail that was along there, becuz I had set down on it hard,
sometimes, when I warn't wanting to, and it was that kind of a nail

which the more you don't set down on it at all the more comfortable you can set down somewheres else next day, when there come a sudden sharp glare of lightning that showed up everything keen and clear, and there was Sid at his window watching.

We clumb into our window and set down and whispered it over. We had to do something, and we didn't know what. Tom said, as a general thing he wouldn't care for this, but it wasn't a good time, now, to be attracting attention. He said if Sid could have a holiday out on his uncle Fletcher's farm, thirty miles in the country, for about four weeks, it would clear the decks and be the very thing, and the conspiracy would glide along and be in smooth water and safe, by that time. He didn't reckon Sid was suspicioning anything yet, but would start in to watch us, and pretty soon he would. I says—

"When are you going to ask your aunt Polly to let him have the holiday, Tom—in the morning?"

"Why, I ain't going to ask her at all. That's not the way. She would ask me what was interesting *me* in Sid's comfort all of a sudden, and she would suspicion something. No, we must cunjer up some way to make her invent the idea herself and send him away."

"Well," I says, "I'll let you have the job—it ain't in my line."

"I'll study it over," he says, "I reckon it can be fixed."

I was going to pull off my clothes, but he says, "Don't do that, we'll sleep with them on."

"What for?"

"It's nothing but shirt and nankeen pants, and they'll dry in three hours."

"What do we want them dry for, Tom?"

But he was listening at Sid's door, to hear if he was snoring. Then he slipped in there and got Sid's clothes and fetched them and hung them out of the window till they was soaked, then he carried them back and come to bed. So then I understood. We snuggled up together, and pulled up the blankets, and wasn't overly comfortable, but of course we had to stand it. After a long thinking spell, Tom says—

"Huck, I believe I've got it. I know where I can get the measles. We've all got to have them some time or other anyway, and I better have them now, when they can do some good."

"How?"

"Aunt Polly wouldn't let Sid and Mary stay in the house if we had measles here; she would send them to uncle Fletcher's—it's the only place."

I didn't like the idea, it made me half sick; and I says—

"Tom, don't you do it; it's a fool idea. Why, you might die."

"Die, you pelican? I never heard such foolishness. Measles never kills anybody except grown people and babies. You never heard of a case."

I was worried, and tried to talk him out of it, and done my best, but it didn't do any good. He was full of it, and bound to try it, and wanted me to help him; so I give it up and said I would. So he planned it out how we was to manage it, and then we went to sleep.

We got up dry, but Sid's things was wet; and when he said he was going to tell on us, Tom told him he could go and tell, as fast as he wanted to, and see if him and his wet clothes could beat our dry ones testifying. Sid said he hadn't been out, but knowed we had, becuz he seen us. Tom says—

"You ought to be ashamed of yourself. You are always walking in your sleep and dreaming all kinds of strange things that didn't happen, and now you are at it again. Can't you see, perfectly plain, it's nothing but a dream? If you didn't walk, how comes your clothes wet? and if we did, how comes ourn dry?—you answer me that."

Sid was all puzzled and mixed up, and couldn't make it out. He felt of our clothes, and thought and thought; but he had to give it up. He said he judged he could see, now, it was only a dream, but it was the amazingest vividest one he ever had. So the conspiracy was saved, and out of a close place, too, and Tom said anybody could see it was approved of. And he was awed about it, and said it was enough to awe anybody and make them better, to see the inscrutable ways that that conspiracy was watched over and took care of, and I felt the same. Tom resolved to be humbler and gratefuller from this out, and do everything as right as he could, and said so; and after breakfast we went down to Captain Harper's to get the measles, and had a troublesome time, but we got it. We didn't go at it the best way at first, that was the reason. Tom went up the back stairs and got into the room all right, where Joe was laying sick, but before he could get into bed with him his mother come in to give him the medicine, and was scared to see him there, and says—

"Goodness gracious, what *are* you doing here! Clear out, you little idiot, don't you know we've got the measles?"

Tom wanted to explain that he come to ask how Joe was, but she shoo'd and shoo'd him to the door and out, and wouldn't listen, and says—

"Oh, do go away and save yourself. You've frightened the life out of me, and your aunt Polly will never forgive me, and yet it's nobody's fault but yourn, for not going to the front door, where anybody would that had any sense of discretion," and then she slammed the door and shut Tom out.

But that give him an idea. So in about an hour he sent me to the front door to knock and fetch her there; and she would have to go, becuz the children was with the neighbors on account of the measles, and the captain out at his business; and so, whilst I kept her there asking her all about Joe for the Widow Douglas, Tom got in the back way again and got into bed with Joe, and covered up, and when she come back and found him there, she had to drop down in a chair or she would a fainted; and she shut him up in another room until she sent word to aunt Polly.

So aunt Polly was frightened stiff, and shook so she could hardly pack Sid and Mary's things. But she had them out of the house in a half an hour and into the tavern to stay there over night and take the stage for her brother Fletcher's at four in the morning, and then went and fetched Tom home, and wouldn't let me come in the house; and she hugged him and hugged him, and cried, and said she would lick him within an inch of his life when he got well.

So then I went up on the hill to the Widow's, and told Jim, but he said it was a right down smart plan, and he hadn't ever seen a plan work quicker and better; and Jim warn't worried, he said measles didn't amount to anything, everybody has them and everybody's got to; so I stopped worrying, too.

After a day or two Tom had to go to bed and have the doctor. Me and Jim couldn't work the conspiracy without Tom, so we had to let it lay still and wait, and I reckoned it was going to be dull times for me for a spell. But no, Tom warn't hardly to bed before Joe Harper's medicine fetched his measles out onto the surface, and then the doctor found it warn't measles at all, but scarlet fever. When aunt Polly heard it she turned that white she couldn't get her breath, and was that weak she couldn't see her hand before her face, and if they hadn't grabbed her she would have fell. And it just made a panic in the town, too, and there wasn't a woman that had children but was scared out of her life.

But it crossed off the dull times for me, and done that much good; for I had had scarlet fever, and come in an ace of going deef and dumb and blind and baldheaded and idiotic, so they said; and so aunt Polly was very glad to let me come and help her.

We had a good doctor, one of them old fashioned industrious kind that don't go fooling around waiting for a sickness to show up and call game and start fair, but gets in ahead, and bleeds you at one end and blisters you at the other, and gives you a dipperful of castor oil and another one of hot salt water with mustard in it, and so gets all your machinery agoing at once, and then sets down with nothing on his mind and plans out the way to handle the case.

Along as Tom got sicker and sicker they shut off his feed, and closed up the doors and windows and made the room snug and hot and healthy, and as soon as the fever was warmed up good and satisfactry, they shut off his water and let him have a spoonful of panada every two hours to squench his thirst with. Of course that is dreadful when you are burning up, and nice cool water there for other people to drink and you can't touch it but need it more than anybody else; so Tom arranged to wink when he couldn't stand it any longer, and I watched my chance and give him a good solid drink when aunt Polly's back was turned; and after that it was more comfortable, for I kept an eye out sharp and filled him up every time he wunk. The doctor said water would kill him, but I knowed that when you are blazing with scarlet fever you don't mind that.

Tom was sick two weeks, and got very bad, and then one night he begun to sink, and sunk pretty fast. All night long he got worse and worse, and was out of his head, and babbled and babbled, and give the conspiracy plumb away, but aunt Polly was that beside herself with misery and grief that she couldn't take notice, but only just hung over him, and cried, and kissed him and kissed him, and bathed his face with a wet rag, and said oh, she could not *bear* to lose him, he was the darling of her heart and she couldn't ever live without him, the world wouldn't ever be the same again and life would be so empty and lonesome and not worth while; and she called him by all the pet names she could think of, and begged him to notice her and say he knowed her, but he couldn't, and once when his hand went groping about and found her face and stroked it and he took it for me, and said "good old Huck," she was broken-hearted, and cried so hard and mourned so pitiful I had to look away, I couldn't bear it. And in the morning when the doctor come and looked at him and says, kind of tender and low, "He doeth all things for the best, we must not repine," she—but I can't tell it, it would a made anybody cry to see her. Then the doctor motioned, and the preacher was there and had been praying, and we all went and stood around the bed, waiting and still, and aunt Polly crying, and nobody saying anything. Tom was laying with his eyes shut, and very quiet. Then he opened them, but didn't seem to notice, much, or see anything; but they kind of wandered about, and fell on me; and steadied there. And one of them begun to sag down, went shut, and t'other one begun to work and twist, and twist and work, and kind of squirm; and at last he got it, though pretty lame and out of true—it was a wink. I jumped for the fresh cold water, tin pail and all, and says "Hold up his head!" and put it to his lips, and he drunk and drunk and drunk—the very first I had had a chance to give him in a whole day and night. The doctor said, "Poor boy, give him all he wants, he is past hurting, now."

It warn't so. It saved him. He begun to pull back to life again

from that very minute, and in five days he was setting up in bed,
and in five more was walking about the floor; and aunt Polly was
that full of joy and gratefulness that she told me, private, she
wished he *would* do something he had no business to, so she could
forgive him; and said she never would a knowed how dear he was
to her if she hadn't come so near losing him; and said she was glad
it happened and she'd got her lesson, she wouldn't ever be rough on
him again, she didn't care what he done. And she said it was the
way we feel when we've laid a person in the grave that is dear to us
and we wish we could have them back again, we wouldn't ever say
anything to grieve them any more.

Chapter 4

ALL THE first week that Tom was sick he wasn't very sick,
and then for a while he was, and after that he wasn't, again, but was
getting well; so he lost only the between-time. Both of the other
times he worked on the conspiracy—first to get it all shaped out so
me and Jim could finish it if he died, and leave it behind him for
his monument; and the other time to boss it himself. So the minute
I come down to help take care of him he said he wanted some type,
and to learn how to set them up; and told me to go to Mr. Baxter
about it. He was the foreman of the printing office, and had Mr.
Day and a boy under him and was one of the most principal men in
the town, and looked up to by everybody. There warn't nothing
agoing for the highsting up of the human race but he was under it
and a-shoving up the best he could—being a pillow of the church
and taking up the collection, Sundays, and doing it wide open and
square, with a plate, and setting it on the table when he got done
where everybody could see, and never putting his hand anear it,
never pawing around in it the way old Paxton always done, letting
on to see how much they had pulled in; and he was Inside Sentinel
of the Masons, and Outside Sentinel of the Odd Fellows, and a
kind a head bung-starter or something of the Foes of the Flowing

Bowl, and something or other to the Daughters of Rebecca, and something like it to the King's Daughters, and Royal Grand Warden to the Knights of Morality, and Sublime Grand Marshal of the Good Templars, and there warn't no fancy apron agoing but he had a sample, and no turnout but he was in the procession, with his banner, or his sword, or toting a bible on a tray, and looking awful serious and responsible, and yet not getting a cent. A good man, he was, they don't make no better.

And when I come he was setting at his table with his pen, and leaning low down over a narrow long strip of print with wide margins, and he was crossing out most everything that was in it and freckling-up the margins with his pen and cussing. And I told him Tom was sick and maybe going to die, and—

There he shut me off sudden, and says, prompt and warm—

"*Him* die? We can't have it. There's only one Tom Sawyer, and the mould's busted. Can I do anything? Speak up."

I says—

"Tom says, can he have—"

"*Yes;* he can have anything he wants. Speak out," he says, all alive and hearty and full of intrust.

"He'd like to have about a handful of old type that you hain't got any use for, and—"

Then he broke in again and sung out to Mr. Day, and says—

"Tell the devil to go to hell and fetch a hatful; and quick about it."

It give me the cold shivers to hear him. In about a minute Mr. Day says—

"The devil says hell's empty, sir."

"All right, fetch a hatful of pie."

That made my mouth water, and I was glad I come. Then the boy fetched a couple of oyster cans full of old type; it had to be old, there warn't any new in the place; and Mr. Baxter told him to fetch a stick and a rule.[1] And last, he told him to fetch an old half-case,

---

1. *Hell,* printer's term for broken and otherwise disabled type. 2. *Printer's Devil,* apprentice. 3. *Pi,* printer's term for a mass of mixed-up type. 4. The (composing) stick and rule are used in setting the type.—EDITOR. [Mark Twain's own footnote.]

which he done; it was the size of a wash-board, and was all sepa-
rated up into little square boxes. Then they pasted A's and B's and
C's and so on on the boxes, to show which boxes they belonged in
—two sets, capital letters and little ones; and Mr. Baxter told the
boy to go with me and help carry the things and learn Tom how to
set the type. And he done it.

He learnt Tom, and Tom set up all the type in the oyster cans
and then put all the letters where they belonged in the case, setting
up in bed and using up about two days at it. Bright? Tom Sawyer?
I should reckon so. Inside of five days he had learnt himself the
whole trade, and could set up type as well as anybody; and I can
prove what I am saying. Becuz, that day he set up this, and I took it
over and Mr. Baxter printed it, and when he took up the print he
was astonished, and said so; and give me a copy for myself, and one
for Tom, and I've got mine yet.

COMPOSITION

The nδble art of print£ing called by some typoGrap*hy the art*
Preservative of Arths was fistr discivered up a lane in a *tower* by
cuittng letters on birch pags not knowing they woud print and nat
expecting it Zut they did by aÄcident hence theGerman name for
type to thais day buchstaban althoughtl ma∂e of metal ever since let
all the nations bless the name fo Guttingburg andFowst whica done
done‡ iⲦ амеɳ¿

TOM SAWYER
Prinⱼerx

When Mr. Baxter printed it and took it up and looked at it the
tears come in his eyes, and he says—

"Derned if any comp. in christiandum can lay over it but old
Day, and *he* can't when he's sober."

It made Tom mighty proud when I told him, and well it might.
But the strain of composing of it out of his head thataway, and
setting it up without anybody's help, and the general excitement of
it and anxiousness it cost him to get it ackurate, was too many for
him and knocked him silly and laid him out, and the sickness went

for him savage; and so that was the last thing he ever done till the day the doctor says—

"Huck, he's convalescent."

I warn't prepared, and fell flat in my tracks where I was. But when they throwed water on me and I come to and they told me what the doctor was trying to mean when the word fell out of him, I see it warn't so bad as I reckoned.

Now some boys quits repenting as soon as they are getting well, and goes to getting worldly again, and judging they hadn't ought to have got flustered so soon, it wasn't necessary, but it warn't so with Tom, he said he had a close shave and ought to be grateful to Providence, and was; and man's help warn't worth much, and man's wisdom warn't anything at all—look at ourn, he says.

"Look at ourn, Huck. We went for measles. It shows how little we knowed and how blind we was. What good was measles, when you come to look at it? None. As soon as it's over you wash up the things and air out the house and send for the children home again, and a person has been sick all for nothing. But you take the scarlet fever and what do you find? You scour out the place, and burn up every rag when it's over and you're well again, and from that very day no Sid and no Mary can come anear it for six solid useful weeks. Now who thought of scarlet fever for us, Huck, and arranged it, when we was ignorant and didn't know any better than to go for measles? Was it us? You know it warn't. Now let that learn you. This conspiracy is being took care of by a wiser wisdom than ourn, Huck. Whenever you find yourself getting untrustful and worried, don't you be afraid, but recollect about the scarlet fever, and remember that where that help come from there's more to be had. All you want is faith; then everything will come out right, and better than you can do it yourself."

Well, it did look so; there wasn't any way to get around it. It was the scarlet fever that saved the game and kept Sid up country, and it wasn't us that thought of it.

It was real summer by now, and Tom was well and hearty, and the weather and everything suitable and ready for us to go ahead.

So we took our little printing office over to the island to have it handy any time we might want it; and I fished all the afternoon, and smoked and swum and napped, whilst Tom took his chisels and things and one of his blocks, and carved this on it.

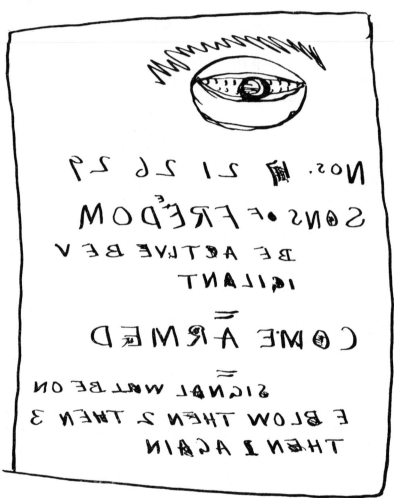

Then he dabbed it over with black ink, and dampened some white printer's paper and laid it on, and a piece of blanket on that and a heavy smooth block on top of that and give it a good hammering with his mallet, and then took off the paper and it was printed very beautiful, but by gracious it was all wrong-end first and you had to stand on your head to read it. Well, it beat me, and it beat Tom. There warn't any way to understand how it come like that. We took and looked at the block, but the block was all right, it was only the printing that was crazy. We printed it again, but it come wrong again, just the same. So then we studied it out and judged we had got at the trouble this time; we put the paper underneath and turned the block upside down on it and printed it. But it never done any good; it was as crazy as it was before.

Tom said that when he set up type in the stick it read from left to right and upside down, but he hadn't reckoned Mr. Baxter would leave it so, but would fix it right before he printed it, and of course he done it, becuz it was right when it come back printed, but *we* couldn't learn that juglery out of our own heads, we would have to wait and get him to tell us the secret; and we reckoned he would, if we swore we wouldn't tell anybody; and Tom was willing to do that, and so was I.

Tom was ever so disappointed, after all his hard work, and I was very sorry for him, to see him setting there all tired and idle and low spirited; but all of a sudden he got excited and glad, and said it was the luckiest thing that ever happened, and the very thing for a conspiracy, becuz it was so strange and grisly and mysterious, and looked so devilish; and said it would scare the people twice as much as it would if it was in its right mind, and all ship-shape and regular, the common old way; and says—

"Huck, it's a new thing, and we've discovered it, and will go down to prosperity along with Guttingburg and Fowst, and be celebrated everywheres, and can take out a patent on it and not let anybody use it except for conspiracies, and not even then unless they have a pure character and are the best people in the business."

So it come out right, after all. And it's mostly so, when things is looking the darkest, Tom said, you only have to wait, and be trustful, and keep your shirt on.

And I asked him who was the Sons of Freedom, and he said the people would think it was the ablitionists, and it would scare the cold sweat out of them. And I asked him what that nut was for, at the top, and he said it wasn't a nut, it was an eye and an eyebrow, and stood for vigilance and was emblumatic. That was him—all over; if a thing hadn't a chance in it somewheres for the emblumatics it warn't in his line, and he would shake it and hunt up something else.

He said we must have a horn of a solemn deep sound, for the Sons of Freedom to make the signal with; so we chopped down a hickory sapling and skinned it and got a wide strip of bark that was plenty long enough, and went home to supper, and carried it to Jim that night, and he twisted it into a tapering long horn, and we took it into the Widow Douglas's woods on the front slope of the hill towards the town and Jim clumb the highest tree and hid it there. Then home and to bed; and slid out, away in the night, and down to the river street, and slipped into Slater's alley when the paterollers was asleep, and so up back behind the blocks and come out through that crack that was betwixt the julery shop and the post-office, and tacked our bill onto the board, and back the way we come, and home again.

At breakfast in the morning a person could see that aunt Polly was kind of excited about something, becuz she was nervous and absent-minded, and kept getting up and going to the window and looking out, and muttering to herself; and once she sweetened her coffee with salt and it made her choke and strangle; and she would take up her toast and start to butter it and forget what she was doing and lay it down; and when Tom put the little Webster spelling book in the place of it when she was staring haggard towards the window she buttered that and took a bite, and lost her temper and throwed the book across the house, and says—

"There, hang the thing, I'm that upset I don't know what I'm a doing. And reason enough. Oh, dear, you little know what danger you're in, poor things, and what danger we're all in."

"Why, what is it, aunt Polly," Tom says, like he was surprised.

"Don't you see the people flocking down street and flocking back, and talking so excited, and most of them gone half crazy? Why there's an awful bill sticking up, down at the postoffice, and the ablitionists are going to burn the town and run off the niggers."

"Goodness, aunt Polly, it ain't as bad as that, I reckon."

"What do you know about it, you numscull! Hain't Oliver Benton been here, and Plunket the editor, and Jake Flacker, and told me all about it, and do you reckon you are going to lay abed asleep and then come down here a-reckoning and a-reckoning and a-reckoning, and suppose that *that* is going to count for anything when a person has been listening to grown people that don't go reckoning around, but digs up the cold facts and examines them and *knows?*"

She wouldn't let him say a word, but said if we was done breakfast, clear out and get hold of everything that was going on, and come and tell her, so she could prepare for the worst. We was glad of the chance; and when we got out in the street we see that everything was working prime, and couldn't be no better; and Tom said if he had died he would always regretted it.

Down at the postoffice you couldn't get anear it. Everybody was there, and scrowging in to get a look at the bill, going in red and coming out pale and telling all about it to them that was on the outside edge pawing and shouldering to get in.

Jake Flacker the detective was the biggest man in town, now, and everybody was cringing to him and trying to get something out of him, but he was mum, and only wagged his head as much as to say, "Never you mind, just leave this thing to me, don't you worry;" and people whispered around and said, "I bet you he knows them rascals, and every move they make in the game, and can put his hand on them whenever he wants to—look at that eye of his'n; you can't hide nothing from an eye like that." And Colonel Elder said the bill was a most remarkable one and proved that these warn't no common ornery canail, but blackhearted biggots of the highest intelligents. It pleased Tom to hear him say that, for he was the most looked up to of any man in town, and come from old Virginia and belonged to the quality. Colonel Elder said the bill was done in a new and ockult and impossible way, and showed what we was coming to in these abandund days; and that seemed to make every-body shudder.

And that warn't all the shuddering they done. They shivered every time the signals was mentioned. They said they would wake up some night with their throats cut and them awful sounds dinging in their ears. And then somebody noticed that the *kind* of sound it was going to be warn't named distinct in the bill. Mostly they reckoned it was a horn, but said there warn't no proof of it; it might be blows on a anvil, Pete Kruger the German blacksmith said; and Abe Wallace the sexton said yes, and it might be blows on a bell, too. And then they *all* up and cussed the uncertainty of it, and said they could stand it better, and maybe get some sleep, too, if they knowed what it was.

Colonel Elder spoke up again, and said yes, that was bad, but the uncertainty about the date was worse.

"That's so," they said; "we don't know when they're coming—the bill don't say. Maybe it's weeks, maybe it's days,—"

"And maybe it's to-night," says the Colonel, and that made them shiver again. "We must take time by the firelock, friends; we must get ready; not next week, not to-morrow, but to-day." They give a little shout, and said the Colonel was right. He went on and made them a speech and braced them up, then Claghorn the justice of the peace made one, and by this time everything was booming and the most of the town was there and they turned it into a public meeting; and whilst the iron was hot, Plunket the editor got up and spoke, and praised up Colonel Elder, which was in the last war and at the battle of New Orleans, and knowed all about soldiering, and was the man they needed now. And he moved to elect him Provo Marshal and set up martial law in the town, and they done it. And then the Colonel he thanked them for the honor they done him, and ordered Captain Haskins and Captain Sam Rumford to call out their companies and go into camp in the public square, and put details all about town to guard it, and issue ball cartridge, and have them in uniform, and all that. So then the meeting broke up, and we started along.

Tom said everything was working splendid, but it didn't seem so to me. I says—

"How are we going to get around, nights? Won't the soldiers watch us and meddle with us? We are tied, Tom, we can't do a thing."

"No," he says, "it's going to be better for us than ever, now."

"How?"

"They'll want spies, and they can't get them. They know it. And Jake Flacker's no good. He don't know enough to follow the fence and find the corner. I've got a ruputation, on account of beating the Dunlaps and getting the di'monds, and I'll manage for us—you'll see."

He done it, too. The Colonel was glad to have him, and wanted him to get some more, if he could, and he would put them under him. So Tom said all he wanted was me and Jim. He said he wanted Jim to spy amongst the niggers. The Colonel said it was a good idea, and everybody knowed Jim and could trust him; so he give Tom passes, for us and him, and that fixed us all right.

Then we went home and told about everything except spying and the passes; and soon we heard drums and a fife away off, and it come nearer, and pretty soon Sam Rumford's company went a marching by—tramp, tramp, tramp, all the feet a-rumbling down just as regular, and Sam a-howling the orders, "Shoul--der--ARMS! by the left file, for--word!" and so on, and the fifes a-screaming and the drums a-banging and a-crashing so you couldn't hear yourself think, by George it was splendid and stirred a person up, and there was more children along than soldiers; and the uniforms was beautiful, and so was the flag, and every time Sam Rumford whirled his sword in the air and yelled, it catched the sun and made the prettiest flash you ever see. But aunt Polly she stood there white and quivery, and looked perfectly gashly. And she says—

"Goodness only knows what is coming to us. I am *so* thankful Sid and Mary——oh, Tom, if you was only with them."

It was Tom's turn to shiver—and mine, too; and we done it. The next thing, she would be arranging for him to go out somewheres in the country where some family had had scarlet fever and would take him. Tom knowed it, and knowed there wasn't any time to waste; so we went out back to fetch some wood for the kitchen, and paddled over to the island to think up what we better do to get around this trouble; and Tom set down, off by himself, and thought it out, and took a pine block and carved this on it and printed a lot of them with red ink.

We fetched them home, and away in the night we went spying around and showing the passes when the soldiers stopped us, and stuck one on Judge Thatcher's door and fifteen others, and on aunt Polly's; becuz Tom said if we didn't stick them on anybody's door but aunt Polly's the people might suspicion something. We had lots of them left, but Tom said he reckoned we would need them.

In the morning—it was Wednesday—it made another big stir, and them that had them on their doors was thankful and glad, and them that hadn't was scared and mad, and said pretty rough things about the others, and said if they warn't ablitionists they was pets of them, anyway, and they reckoned it was about the same thing. And everybody was astonished to see how the S. of F. gang had managed to come right into the town and stick up the things under the soldiers's noses; and of course they was troubled and worried about it, and got suspicious of one another, not knowing who was a friend and who wasn't; and some begun to say they believed the town was full of traitors; and then they shut up, all of a sudden, and got afraid to say *anything;* and got a notion that they had already said too much, and maybe to the wrong people.

I never see a person do such a noble job of cussing as the Colonel; and Tom he said the same. And he had up the captains to headquarters and said it was scandlous, and said he couldn't have things going on like this, and they'd got to keep better watch, and they promised they would.

Tom told me to set down the name of everybody I heard talking against people that had our protection-paper on their doors, and he done the same.

Aunt Polly was comforted to have the paper on her door, and not scared any more, like she was; but Mrs. Lawson the lawyer's wife come in, in the morning, and made her feel bad about it. She let on she didn't know aunt Polly had one, and said thank goodness *she* hadn't any, and didn't want it, but at the same time whoever wished to be protected by ablition secret gangs and warn't ashamed of it was welcome for all *her.* And when aunt Polly colored up a little and couldn't say anything, she got up and says "but maybe I'm indiscreet, please forgive me," and went out very grand, and aunt Polly's comfort was most all gone.

That night we stuck the papers on all the doors we took the names of, and stuck one on Mrs. Lawson's, too. It shut up a lot of people's mouths, and made Mrs. Lawson quiet; and comfortabler, too, than she was before, I reckon. And we found Jake Flacker standing watch asleep down by the lumber yard, and stuck one on his back. Me and Tom went about town in the morning, and lo and behold some of the papers was missing from some of the doors— five—and there was five papers on doors that we hadn't put them on.

And he said wait till next morning and we would see something more that was fresh. And it was so. Everybody that had a paper had wrote his name on it to keep people from stealing it, for it was all over town how they was being smouched. Aunt Polly had her name on her paper, wrote large and plain, and the same with Mrs. Lawson.

When Saturday come all the town that hadn't the papers was tuckered out and looked seedy, becuz they had set up the most of three nights listening for the signals, and then laid down to sleep in their clothes when they couldn't keep awake any more. Then, just as the excitement was wavering a little and getting ready to go down, on account of no signals yet, the paper come out and started it all up again; for it was full of it, and just wild about it; and it had extracts from papers in Illinois and St Louis about it, and showed how it was traveling and making the town celebrated; and so everybody was proud as well as worried, and read the paper all through, and Tom said they hadn't ever done that before. So he was proud, too, and said it was a good conspiracy, and we would go ahead, now, and give it another boom.

Chapter 5

So everything was all right, now, and we went around in the night and stuck up the reward-bill for the runaway nigger-boy; and Jim was along, on spy-business. Then we laid the plans for next afternoon—like this. Towards evening me and Tom would go up to the hanted house on Crawfish Branch, and whilst Tom was in there dressing to play nigger, I would go on up to Bat Bradish's and tell him I knowed where the nigger was that was advertised, and would show him the place if he would give me some of the money when he got the reward. Then I would fetch him and turn Tom over to him, chain and all, and Tom was to have the extra key along, and unlock the chain in the night and escape and go back to the hanted house and change clothes again and wash up, in the Branch, and carry his nigger clothes home; and Jim would blow the horn-signals in the high tree at midnight and set the town wild; and in the morning of course Bat would come to town and tell about his nigger that was escaped, and that would make everybody sure that the ablishonists *was* on hand to a certainty; and that would fire things up worse than ever and make the conspiracy the best success we ever had; and Tom could be a detective and help hunt for himself, and have a grand time.

So next afternoon towards dusk we come in sight of the hanted house, and was about to step out of the woods into the open, but Tom pulled me back, and said somebody was coming down the Branch. And it was so. It was Bat Bradish. So Tom told me to go and meet up with him and tell him, and then get him out of the way until Tom could go and dress in the hanted house. I left Tom waiting in the bushes and went out and when I got to where Bat was I told him about the nigger. But stead of jumping at the chance he looked kind of bothered; and scratched his head and cussed a little, and said he had just *got* one runaway nigger a half an hour ago, and couldn't manage two in these skittish times; did I reckon I could keep watch of mine a few days and then come?

I didn't know anything else to do, and of course it could take some of the tuck out of the conspiracy and Tom wouldn't like that, so I done the best I could the way things stood and told him I reckoned I could manage it. That cheered him up and he said I wouldn't lose anything by it, he would look out for that; and said the nigger he had got was a splendid one and had a five hundred dollar reward on him, and he had bought the chance off of the man that found him for two hundred cash and would clear about three hundred, and a profitable good job, too. He was going down to town now to see the sheriff and make his arrangements. As soon as he was out of sight down the Cold Spring road I whistled to Tom and he come and I told him the bad news.

It just broke his heart. I knowed it would. He had been imagining all kinds of adventures and good times he was going to have when he was washed up and hunting for himself, and he couldn't seem to get over it. It looked to me, in a private way, like Providence was drawing out of the conspiracy; and so, by and by I made a mistake and said so. It made him pretty fierce, and he turned on me and said I ought to be ashamed of myself—a person without any trust, and not deserving any blessings; and then he went on and give me down the banks; and said how could *I* know but this was one of the most mysterious and inscrutablest moves connected with the whole conspiracy? He had got a good start, now, so I knowed everything was going to be comfortable again; for if I let him alone and didn't interrupt, he would hammer right along with his arguments till he proved to himself that this *was* a planned-out move and belonged in the game. And sure enough, he done it. Then he was gay and cheerful right away, and said he was glad it happened and said he was foolish and wicked for losing pluck merely because *he* couldn't see the design straight off. I let him alone and he rattled along, and finally he got the notion that maybe he had guessed out what the new design was—it was for him to go yonder and trade places with that nigger. And so he was going straight to dress and get ready; but I says—

"Tom Sawyer, that's a five-hundred-dollar nigger; you ain't a five-hundred-dollar nigger, I don't care *how* you dress up."

He couldn't get around that, you know; there warn't any way. But he didn't like to let on that I had laid him out; so he talked random a minute, trying to work out, then he said we couldn't tell anything about it till we had *seen* the nigger. And said, come along.

I didn't think there was any sense in it, but I was willing to let him down as easy as I could, so we struck out up the hollow. It was dark, now, but we knowed the way well enough. It was a log house, and no light in it; but there was a light in the lean-to, and we could see through the chinks. Sure enough it was a man, and a hearty good strong one—a thousand-dollar nigger, and worth it anywhere. He was stretched out on the ground, chained, and snoring hard.

So then Tom wanted us to go in and look at him good. But I wouldn't do it. I warn't going to fool with a strange nigger in the night in a lonesome place like that, I will get you to excuse me, I says. Tom said, all right, I needn't if I didn't want to, nobody was forcing me. Then he pulled the latch-string easy and got down on his hands and knees and crope in, and I kept my eye to the chink to see what would happen. When Tom got to the other end where the nigger was, he took up the candle and shaded it with his hand and examined the nigger, which had his mouth wide open to let the snore out. I see Tom looked surprised at something; and I reckoned it was something the nigger said in his sleep, becuz I heard him growl out something. Then Tom took up the nigger's old battered shoes and turned them this way and that, examining them like a detective, and something fell out of one of them, and he picked it up, and looked around the place a little, here and there, same as a detective would, then set the candle back and crope out, and says come along.

So we went to the hanted house and struck up over Cardiff Hill, and Tom says—

"I reckon this'll learn you to have trust next time, Huck Finn."

"What will?"

"Well, there was a plan and a program, wasn't there?"

"There *was*, yes—and it got busted."

"Did, did it? According to the plan and the program a runaway nigger was going to escape from there to-night—ain't that so?"

"Yes."

"Well, it's going to happen."

"Shucks—what are you talking?"

"It was going to be a white nigger wasn't it?"

"Yes."

"All right, *that's* going to happen."

"Tom, you don't mean it."

"Yes I do."

"Honest Injun, Tom, is that man white?"

"Honest Injun, Huck, he is."

"Why, it's the most astonishing thing I ever see."

"Huck, it's the very same game we laid out to play ourselves. Providence hasn't changed anything in the program except just the *person*—that's all. *Now* I reckon you'll have trust hereafter."

"Why Tom, it's the strangest thing that ever—"

"Happened? I *told* you it was the most mysterious and inscrutablest design in the whole conspiracy. I reckon you believe me now. *We* don't know what the change is made for Huck, but we know one thing—it was for the best."

He said it very solemn, and it made me feel thataway. Well, it was all very wonderful and strange. It made us kind of quiet a while, then I says—

"Tom, how'd you know he is white?"

"Oh, a lot of things. They couldn't fooled old Bat if he had good eyesight. Huck, for one thing, the inside of that nigger's hands are black."

"Well, what's the matter of that?"

"Why, you idiot, the inside of a nigger's hands *ain't* black."

"That's so, Tom, I didn't think of it."

"And he talked some words in his sleep; he talked white, not nigger; hasn't learnt to talk nigger in his sleep, yet."

"Tom, what makes you think he's going to get out to-night."

"Evidence of it in his shoe."

"Something fell out of it; was that it?"

"Two things fell out; I put one back. It was a key. But I tried it in his padlock first, and it fitted."

"By gracious!"

"He's playing our scheme to a dot, don't you see?"

"Why, Tom, it just beats anything that ever was. Say—what was the other thing that fell out?"

"I didn't put that back—I've got it yet."

"Lemme see it, Tom; what is it?"

But he put me off, and said it was too dark to see it; so I knowed he was working one of his mysteries and I'd got to wait till it suited him to come out with it. I asked him how he come to look in the nigger's shoe. He sniffed, and says—

"Huck Finn, hain't you got any reasoning powers at all? Where *would* a detective look? He looks everywheres—he don't make any exceptions. First, he looks where he ain't likely to find anything— becuz that is where he'd druther find it, of course, on account of the showiness of it; and if he is disappointed he turns to and hunts in the likely places. But he's *got* to examine everything—it's his business; and he must remember all about it at the trial, too. I didn't want to find the things in the shoe, of course—"

"Why, Tom?"

"Didn't I just *tell* you why? Becuz it was the likely place. A white nigger that's playing a swindle knows his new marster might take a notion to search him; so *he* don't hide his suspiciousest things in his pockets, does he?"

"Well, now, I wouldn't a thought of that, but I reckon it's so, Tom. You think of everything and you notice everything."

"A detective's got to. I noticed everything in that lean-to, and can tell all about it, from the musket on the hooks with no flint in the lock to Bat's old silver-plated watch hanging under the shelf with the minute-hand broke off the same length as the hour-hand and you can't come within two weeks of telling what time of day it is, to save you; and I noticed—"

All of a sudden I thought of something—

"Tom!"

"Well?"

"We are just foolish."

"How?"

"To be fooling along here like this. The thing for us to do is to rush to the sheriff's and tell him, so he can slip up here and catch this humbug and jail him for swindling Bat."

He stopped where he was, and says, very sarcastic—

"You think so, do you?"

It made me feel sheepish, but I said "Yes," anyway, though I didn't say it very confident.

"Huck Finn," he says, kind of sorrowful, "You can't ever seem to see the noblest opportunities. Here is this conspiracy weaving along just perfect, and you want to turn him in in this ignorant way and spoil it all."

"How is that going to spoil it, Tom Sawyer?"

"Well, just look at it a minute," he says, "and I reckon you'll see. How would a detective act? I'll ask you that. Would he go in that simple girly way and catch this humbug and make him tell where the other one is, and then catch the other one and make him hand out the two hundred dollars, and have the whole thing over and done with before morning and not a rag of glory in it anywhere? I never see such a mud turtle as you, Huck Finn."

"Well, then," I says, "What *would* he do? It looks like the common sense way, to me, Tom Sawyer."

"Common sense!" he says, as scornful as he could. "What's common sense got to do with detecting, you leatherhead? It ain't got *anything* to do with it. What is wanted is genius and penetration and marvelousness. A detective that had common sense couldn't ever make a ruputation—couldn't even make his living."

"Well, then," I says, "What *is* the right way?"

"There's only one. Let these frauds go ahead and play their game and get away, then follow them up by *clews*—that's the way. It may take weeks and weeks, but is full of glory. Clews is the thing."

"All right," I says, ruther aggravated, "have it your own way, but I think it's an assful way."

"What is there assful about it, Huck Finn?"

"It's assful because you mayn't ever catch them at all, and when you do they've spent all of Bat's two hundred and he can't get it back. Where's the sense in that?"

"Don't I tell you there ain't any sense *in* detecting,—I never see such a clam. It's nobler—and higher—and grander; and who cares for the money, anyway?—the glory's the thing."

"All right," I says, "go it—I ain't interfering. What's your plan?"

"Now you're getting into your right mind. Come along, and I'll tell you as we climb. These two frauds think they are safe—they don't know there's any detectives around, in a little back settlement like ourn. They'd never think of such a thing. It makes them our meat. Why? Becuz the nigger will wash up, and both of them will get up some new disguises so as Bat and anybody else won't know them, and like as not they'll stay here a while and try to play some more swindles. Now then, the plan is this. Whenever you and Jim sees a stranger, you let me know. If he's the nigger, I'll reconnize him; and I'll let him alone till I catch him with another stranger— then we'll take them into camp."

"You might get the wrong ones."

"You leave it to me—I'll show you."

"Is that the whole plan, Tom?"

"You'll find it's a plenty. You lay for strangers and tell me—that's all I want."

So then we went ahead and clumb the tree and found Jim there and told him the whole thing, and he said it was splendid, and believed it was the best conspiracy that ever was, and was coming along judicious and satisfactory. And about half past one in the morning he blowed the signals and it was a perfectly horrible noise, enough to make a person turn in his grave; and then we pulled out for town to sample the effects.

Chapter 6

I⁢T COULDN'T a been better, it couldn't a been finer. Tom said so his own self, and Jim said the same. The whole town was out in the streets, taking on like it was the Last Day. There was lights in all the houses, and people ranting up and down and carrying on and prophecying, and that scared they didn't know what they was about. And the drums was rumbling and the fifes tooting and the soldiers tramp-tramping, and Colonel Elder and Sam Rumford shouting the orders, and the dogs howling—it was all beautiful and glorious.

When it got to be about an hour before dawn Tom said he must get back to Bat's place, now, so as to get footprints and other clews while they was fresh, so he could begin to track out the escaped nigger. He knowed his aunt Polly would be uneasy about him, but

it wouldn't do for him to go there, he might get locked up for
safety, and that could make no end of trouble with the conspiracy,
so he told Jim to go and explain to her how he was out on detective
work, and ask her permission and comfort her up; then he could
rush and overtake us. Me and Tom struck out up the river road,
then, and got to Bat's just in the gray of the dawn.

And by gracious! Right before the lean-to was Bat Bradish
stretched out on the ground, and seemed to be dead, and was all
bloody; and his old musket was laying there with blood and hair on
the barrel; and the lean-to was open and the nigger gone, and
things upset and smashed around in a great way, and plenty of
footprints and clews and things, all a person could want. Tom told
me to rush for the undertaker—not the new one, give the job to the
old one, Jake Trumbull, which was a friend of ourn—and said he
would come along and catch up with me as soon as he had got the
clews tallied up.

He was always quick, Tom was. I warn't out of sight at the turn
of the river road when I looked back and see him waving his hat for
me. So I run back, and he says—

"We needn't go for help, Huck, it's been 'tended to."

"What makes you reckon so, Tom?"

"I don't reckon anything about it, I know it. Jim's been here."

And sure enough he had. Tom had found his tracks. Of course
he had come the short way over the hill and beat us, becuz we come
the long way, up the river road. I was dog-tired, and glad we didn't
have to go for anybody. I went behind the house, out of sight of the
dead man, and set down and rested whilst Tom examined around
amongst the clews. It warn't but a few minutes till he come and
said he was through, and said there'd been four men there besides
Bat and Jim, and he had their prints, but nobody's prints was inside
the lean-to except Bat's and the white nigger's and another man's
—the nigger's pal, he reckoned. He said Jim and two of the men
was gone for help by the short way over the hill, and the nigger and
his pal had made for the creek, and we would take out after
them—come along.

It was an easy trail, through mangy poor little grass-patches with bare dust between; and where the tracks struck the dust they bored in heavy and showed that the men was running as hard as they could go. Tom says—

"They don't know the country very well, you see; or they're too excited; or they've got pointed a little wrong on account of it's being dark. Anyway, if they don't slew to the left pretty soon they'll get into trouble."

"Looks like it," I says; "they're aiming for the jumping-off place."

The jumping-off place was twelve foot high, and had low bushes on it, and even in the daytime an ignorant person wouldn't know it was there till he was over it. We chased the tracks plumb to the edge. Then we pulled off to the left and clumb down and got the trail again at the jumping-off place and followed it fifty yards to the Branch. The Branch was uncommon high but had begun to fall; so there was a flat wide belt of half-dry mud at the edge, shriveling and stinking, and Tom says—

"Good luck, Huck, the pal hurt his left leg when he fell over the jumping-off place, it only makes a dragging-print here, and the nigger had to help him along. It's a clew, don't you know!"

He would trade pie for a clew, any time. Next, he says—

"They've got old Cap. Haines's canoe; hooked it, I reckon."

Said he knowed it by the print the bow made in the mud. It might be—I didn't know. I had stole the canoe lots of times, but never noticed. I says—

"Now we can go home. They're safe in Illinois by this time and we ain't going to hear of them no more."

But he said no, it might be and it mightn't be; he wouldn't jump to no conclusions about it—best way was to go ahead and find out; and says—

"The only way to ascertain a thing is to *ascertain;* guessing ain't any good. And besides—look at it all around. Suppose this pal's leg is broke? Is he going to strike for Illinois and the everlasting woods? No; he'll want a doctor. They haven't been in town—they'd have been in jail in two minutes, becuz they're strangers; it ain't any healthy place for strangers in these conspiracy times. They've come from up river or over river; they know Bat; they've traded with him before, some time or other. *If* the leg's broke they've got to have a doctor—"

"Well then, they've gone to town, Tom."

"In Cap. Haines's canoe?—from close to the murder?—a canoe that they stole, you can bet on it—it's the kind of folks they are. *I* don't think they've gone to town."

"Well, I don't, nuther, come to think. What will they do, Tom?"

We was tramping along down the Branch, all this time. Tom thought a while, then says—

"Huck, if they had plenty of time, they could manage, but I reckon they haven't. Nearest town up-stream, twenty-five miles— an all-day trip with one paddle; nearest town down-stream, twenty-one miles—five hours; but it wouldn't do any good; the news of the murder will be there to-day, and even if they sunk Haines's canoe and stole another, people would still want to know where they got that leg." After studying a little, he says "I hope they've done that. I hope they've had the time. We'd have them before night, dead sure!"

"Good!" says I.

We went tramping along, Tom a-watching for clews. Pretty soon he shook his head and pulled a long breath, and says—

"No, it won't work, Huck; they're around here somewheres— they hadn't the time."

"How do you know?"

"Well, the nigger overslept or something, the pal didn't turn up till hours after he oughter, and so the thing didn't come off till towards dawn."

"What makes you think that, Tom?"

"Becuz Bat was warm yet, when we got there; I felt of him, under his waistcoat."

It give me the cold shivers; I wouldn't a done it.

"Go on," I says.

"The nigger has got to wash up and change to white folks' clothes before he can go and smuggle a doctor to his pal, and like enough the pal's got a disguise, too. The nigger's got another suit, anyway—that's sure. He would want to make his change pretty soon after he escaped, before he met up with anybody. So I reckon the clothes must be hid around here somewheres, not very far. Well, by the time the washing and dressing and paddling three miles was done it would be daylight and they would be chased and caught as they passed the town, I don't care which side of the river they went down. If they've tried it they've made a mistake."

Well, when we had gone along down about a half a mile and was abreast the stretch of bushes back of the hanted house, right there we struck the trail again. Tom says—

"Ain't it curious? They got in ahead of us on our scheme all around: play counterfeit-nigger like we was going to do, and jump our dressing-room, too. They've been around here before, Huck."

The canoe warn't anywhere in sight; they had hid her or turned her loose, we didn't know which, and didn't care anyway, it warn't any matter. We crope through the bushes and there was the trail plowing straight for the house through the high weeds where the garden used to was. The windows was still boarded up the way me and Tom done it the summer before, the time we let on to be a gang of counterfeiters and used to go there and cut out tin money in the night and contribbit it to the mishonary business Sundays, and she was looking awful lonesome and mournful, the way she always done. Tom said we'd got to get down on our hands and knees and crawl through the weeds, and go very, very slow, and not make the least noise or they might hear us. I says—

"Who? Me? I reckon I see myself a doing it. If you want to go and get into trouble with them hellions," I says, "it's your instincts and it's all right, and I'll wait for you; but nary a peg do I budge."

So he took his course with his little compass and started, and I watched, out of the shadder of the bushes. He done it first rate. You would see the tops of the weeds wiggle a little, and after a quiet spell they would wiggle again, a little further along—the slowest business; but always I could keep track of him, and always he was getting ahead. So he got there by and by, and I waited the dullest longest time, and got afraid they had grabbed him and choked him to death; but at last I see by the weeds that he was coming again, and I was awful glad. As soon as he got to me he says—

"Come along, it's all right—they're there. I crep' through the hole where the hogs get under the house, and it was dark as pitch in there and in the house, and I stuck my head up through the busted place in the floor—"

"What a fool!"

"Fool yourself!—they couldn't see me; and couldn't if it had been light—our old counterfeiter-chest was in the way. And I didn't see them, either, but I've heard them talk. I was 'most as close to them as I am to you, now. If I had had a walking stick I could a punched them with it. But I wouldn't."

"Well, then, you've got *some* sense left, but not enough to hurt, Tom Sawyer. What did they say?"

"Talked about the scrimmage."

"Like enough—but what did they *say?*"

"Lots."

Then he said he was too tired to walk down to town, and no hurry anyway—we must jump in the river and float down on our backs—which was satisfactry to me; but I knowed I had got all I was going to get about that talk for just now. Them old roosters had laid another mystery, and he warn't ready to have it hatched out yet.

Just where the Branch goes into the river we struck a mortal piece of good luck. Some person had come ashore and left his skiff pulled up, with the oars in the rollocks, and warn't anywhere in sight; so we borrowed it, Tom saying something grateful about Providence, and we got in and pulled out a good piece and laid down in her and lit the pipes and let her float. It was very comfortable after all the hard work we'd been through. By and by Tom says—

"It warn't in the plan, but of course it's there for the best."

"What ain't in the plan?"

"The murder. It's a kind of a pity, becuz there warn't any real harm in Bat Bradish, but as long as it had to be somebody I reckon it's as well it's him, and it *does* give this conspiracy a noble lift, now *don't* it, Huck? We'd be mean not to be grateful. And more trustful than ever, too. Why, Huck, a body wouldn't think it, but a person can see, now, that a conspiracy that is conducted right is just as good as a revolution. Just as good and ain't half the trouble."

"Looks so to me, Tom."

"Huck, it's just like a revolution in some ways—a person that hadn't had any experience couldn't tell it from a revolution. You see, it starts in for one thing, and comes out another; starts in in a little small way to worry a village, and murders a nigger-trader. Yes, sir, it's got all the marks of a revolution; and the way it's prospering along now, I believe it could be nursed up and turned *into* a revolution. All it wants now is capital, and something to revolute about."

Well, he was started, and so I let him alone. It was the best way. He would think it out, and gild it up, and put the ruffles on it, and I could lay still and rest, and that suited me.

Just as we struck into town and went ashore by the Cold Spring where the flour mill is, here comes Higgins's Bill, the one-legged nigger, hopping along on his crutch, very much excited and all out of breath and says—

"Marse Tom, ole Jim want you en Huck to come to de jail quick as you kin—dey's got him, en jammed him in, seh."

"What for?"

"Killin' ole Bat Bradish."

I says—

"Great jeeminy!"

But Tom's face lit up pious and happy—it made me shiver to see it; and he give Bill a dime, and says, quite ca'm—

"All right; run along; we are a coming." Bill cleared out and we hurried up, and Tom says, kind of grateful, "Ain't it beautiful, the way it's developing out?—*we* couldn't ever thought of that, and it's the splendidest design yet. *Now* you'll be trustful, I reckon, and quit fretting and losing confidence."

"Tom Sawyer," I says, "What in the nation is there splendid about it?" I was mad, and grieved, and most crying. "There's our old Jim, the best friend we ever had, and the best hearted, and the

whitest man inside that ever walked, and now he's going to get
hung for a murder he never done, I just *know* he never done it, and
whose fault is it but this blame conspiracy, I wish it was in—"

"Shut up!" he says, "You can't tell a blessing from a bat in the
eye, I never see such an idiot—always flying at everything Providence does, you ought to be ashamed of yourself. Who's running
this conspiracy?—you? Blame it, you are hendering it every way
you can think of. Old Jim get hung? Who's going to let him get
hung, you tadpole?"

"Well, but—"

"Hush up! there ain't any well about it. It's going to come out all
right, and the grandest thing that ever was, and just oceans of glory
for us all—and here you are finding fault with your blessings, you
catfish. Old Jim get hung! He's going to be a hero, that's what he's
going to be. Yes, and a brass band and a torchlight procession on
top of it, or *I* ain't no detective."

It made me feel good and satisfied again, I couldn't help it. It was
always just so. He had so much confidence it was catching, and a
person always had to knock under and come to his notions.

We had our passes, and was officials, so we shouldered through
the crowd at the jail door and the sheriff let us in, though he
wouldn't let anybody else. Tom told me private not to know anything, and he wasn't going to know anything himself—he would do
the talking for us both, to the sheriff. He done it. The sheriff didn't
get anything out of him. Old Jim was scared most to death, and was
sure he was going to be hung; but Tom was ca'm, and told him he
needn't worry, it warn't going to happen; and so it warn't ten
minutes till Jim was ca'm, too, and all cheered up and comfortable.
Tom told Jim the officers wouldn't ask him any questions, and if
visitors got in and asked him questions he must say he couldn't
answer anybody but his lawyer. Then Jim went ahead and told us
his tale.

He didn't find aunt Polly at home, of course she was out getting
her share of the scare; so he was after us pretty soon, and hurried
up, reckoning he could catch up with us, but we went the long way
by the river road and he went the short one over Cardiff Hill; so it

wasn't light, yet, when he got to Bat's place, and he stumbled over Bat and fell on him; and just as he was getting up a couple of men come running, and grabbed him, and it was Buck Fisher and old Cap. Haines, and they said they had heard the murdersome row and was glad they catched him in the act. He was going to explain, but they shut him up and wouldn't let him say a word—said a nigger's word warn't any account anyway. They felt of Bat's heart and said he was dead, then they took Jim back over the hill and down to the jail, and spread the news, and then the town was that beside itself it didn't know *what* to do. Tom studied a while, and says, kind of thoughtful—

"It could be better. Still, it ain't bad, the way it is."

"Good lan', Mars Tom, how you's a talkin'! Here I is, wid de man's blood all over me, en you—"

"That's all right, as far as it goes—a good point, a very good point; but it don't go far enough."

"How does you mean, Marse Tom?"

"By itself it ain't any evidence of a motive. What we want's a motive."

"What's a motive, Marse Tom?"

"A *reason* for killing the man."

"My goodness, Marse Tom, I never *killed* him."

"I know. That's the weak place. It's easy to show that you *probably* killed him, and of course that is pretty good, but it can't hang a man—a white one, anyway. It would be ever so much stronger if you had a *motive* to kill him, you see."

"Marse Tom, is I in my right mine, or is it you? Blame my cats if I kin understan'."

"Why, plague take it, it's plain enough. Look at it. I'm going to save you—that's all right, and perfectly easy. But where's the glory of saving a person merely just from jail. To save him from the gallows is the thing. It's got to be murder in the first degree—you get the idea? You've got to have a *motive* for killing the man—*then* we're all right! Jim, if you can think up a rattling good motive, I can get you put up for murder in the first degree just as easy as turning your hand over."

He was all excitement and hope, but Jim—why, Jim could hardly get out his words he was that astonished and scared.

"Why, Marse Tom—why, bless yo' heart, honey, *I* ain't in no sweat to hunt up dish-yer—"

"Hold still, I tell you, and think of a motive! I could have thought up a dozen while you are fooling away all this time. Look here, did Bat Bradish like you?—did you like Bat?"

That seemed to jostle Jim. Tom saw it, and followed it right up. Jim dodged this and that and t'other way, but it didn't do any good, Tom chased him up and found out it was Bradish that was at the bottom of it the time old Miss Watson come so near selling Jim down the river and Jim heard about it and run away and me and him floated down to Arkansaw on the raft. It was Bradish that persuaded her to sell Jim and give him the job of doing it for her. So at last Tom says—

"That's enough. That's a motive. We are all right, now, it's murder in the first degree, and we'll have a grand time out of it and when we get through you'll be a hero, Jim. I wouldn't take a thousand dollars for your chances."

But Jim didn't like it a bit, and said he would sell out for ten cents, and glad to. Tom was very well satisfied, now, and said we would tell the district attorney—which is the lawyer for the prostitution—all about the motive, and then things would go right along. Then he arranged with the sheriff for Jim to have pipes and good vittles and everything he wanted, and said good-bye to Jim, promising we would come every day and amuse him some more. Then we left.

Chapter 7

THE TOWN was booming. Everybody was raging about the murder, and didn't doubt but Jim was in with the Sons of Freedom and been paid by the gang to murder the nigger-trader, and there'd be more—every man that owned niggers was in danger of his life; it was only just the beginning, the place was going to swim in blood, you'll see. That is what they said. It was foolish talk, that talk about Jim, becuz he had always been a good nigger, and everybody knowed it; but you see he was a free nigger this last year and more, and that made everybody down on him, of course, and made them forget all about his good character. It's just the way with people. And the way they was taking on about Bat Bradish you would a thought they had lost a angel; they couldn't seem to get over grieving about him and telling one another no end of sweet little beautiful things he had done, one time or another, which they had forgot till now; and it warn't no trouble, nuther, becuz they hadn't ever happened. Yesterday there wouldn't anybody say a good word for the nigger-trader nor care a dern about him, becuz everybody despised nigger-traders, of course; but to-day, why, they couldn't seem to get over the loss of him, nohow. Well, it's people's way; they're mostly puddnheads—looks so to me.

Of course they was going to lynch Jim, everybody said it; and they just packed all the streets around the jail, and talked excited, and couldn't hardly wait to commence. But Cap'n Ben Haskins, sheriff, was inside, and the mob that started in there without an invite would have a sickly time, and knowed it; and Colonel Elder was outside, and that warn't healthy for a mob, and they knowed it. So me and Tom went along; we warn't worried about Jim. Tom let the *motive* leak out where it would get to the attorney for the prostitution; then we got in the back way at his aunt Polly's and got something to eat and didn't have any trouble becuz she was out enjoying the excitements and hunting for Tom; and from there we went up in the woods on the hill to get some sleep where we wouldn't be in the way, and Tom made his plans.

He said we would 'tend the inquest to-day, and be on hand at the Grand Jury to-morrow, but our evidence wouldn't go for anything against Cap. Haines's and Buck Fisher's, and Jim would be brought in for first degree all right. His trial would come off in about a month. It would take that long for the pal's leg to get so he could walk on it. Then we must have it fixed so that when the trial was just going against Jim we could snatch the two frauds into court and clear Jim and make a noble sensation, and Jim would be a hero and we would all be heroes.

I didn't like it; I was scared of it; it was too risky; something might happen; any little hitch, and Jim's a goner! A nigger don't stand any show. I said we ought to tell the sheriff and let him go and get the men *now*—and jail them, and then we'd have them when we wanted them.

But Tom wouldn't listen to it for a minute. There warn't anything stunning about it. He wanted to get the men into the court without them suspicioning anything—and then make the grand pow-wow, the way he done in Arkansaw. That Arkansaw business had just pisoned him, I could see it plain; he wouldn't ever be satisfied to do things in a plain common way again.

Well, we couldn't keep awake any longer, so we reckoned we would sleep an hour, and then step down to the inquest. And of course when we woke it was too late. When we got down there it was over, and everybody gone—corpse and all. But it warn't much matter, we could go to the Grand Jury to-morrow.

Why, we had slept away past the middle of the afternoon and it was coming on sundown. Time to go home for supper; but Tom said no, he wanted to make sure of his men; so we would wait till night and he would step to the hanted house and listen again. I was very willing for him to do it, it would make me feel easier; so we struck down the Branch and slid past, and down to the river and up it a quarter of a mile under the bluff and went in swimming and stayed in till an hour after dark, then come back and Tom crope through the weeds to the house, and I waited.

I waited and waited, and it was awful lonesome and still and creepy there in the dark, and the hanted house so close. It was not actually very long, but it seemed so, you know. At last Tom come a tearing through the weeds and says—

"Oh, poor Jim, poor Jim, he'll be hung— they're gone!"

I just fell flat, where I was. Everything was swimming, it seemed to me I was going to faint. Then I let go and cried, I couldn't help it and didn't want to. And Tom was crying, too, and said—

"What did I ever do it for?—Huck what *did* I do it for! I had them safe, and I could a saved Jim spite of anything anybody could do, if I only hadn't been a fool. Oh, Huck you wanted me to tell the sheriff, and I was an idiot and wouldn't listen, and now they've got away and we'll never see them again, and nothing can save Jim, and it's all my fault, I wish I was dead."

He took it so hard, and said so many hard things about himself that I hadn't the heart to say any myself, though I was going to, and had them on my tongue's end, but you know how it is, that way. I begun to try to comfort him, but he couldn't bear it, and said call him names, call him the roughest ones I knowed, it was the only thing could do him any good; and then he broke out and abused himself for taking for *granted* the man's leg was broke, and maybe it was only sprained—of *course* it was only sprained, it was perfectly plain, now. Then he had a sudden idea, and said—

"Come!"

So we went tearing down the road for town; said maybe the men would make for the next town below, and we would catch the steamboat and beat them. As we passed the Cold Spring the boat went by; when we got to the wharf she was pulling in the stage, but we jumped for it and made it. People yelled at us to know where we was bound for, but we never took any notice, and went up on the harricane roof and away aft, and set down in the sparks to watch for the canoe, and forgot all about the Grand Jury, but Tom said it wasn't any matter, nothing could save Jim but to find the *men*.

Tom couldn't talk straight and connected, he was gone clean off of head by the disastersomeness of what was come to Jim on accounts of him letting the men get away; and pretty soon he seen, himself, that his mind was upside down, becuz he says—

"Huck, I'm so miserable it has knocked all the judgment out of me. Don't you know there ain't any sense in us being on this boat?"

"Why, Tom?"

"Becuz it's in the plan I made on the broken-leg theory, and the leg *ain't* broke. The man don't have to hunt a doctor, and he can go wherever he wants to. And they *have* gone to Illinois and the everlasting woods—it's the rightest place and the safest for them. Huck, they went the minute it was dark, and if we had went in swimming at the mouth of the Branch 'stead of a quarter of a mile above, we'd a *seen* them. I wish we was back to town, I'd give a million dollars. We would get on their trail and tree them in their camp quick and easy, because the pal's leg is hurt and he can't go a yard without help. Huck, we've got to get back there the minute we can—what a fool I've been to forget that broken-leg theory and come on this boat."

Well, I could see it now, myself; I didn't think of it before. But I didn't say anything mean; his mind warn't to blame for getting out of true, when you come to think. Anybody's would. I was starting in to encourage him up, but he busted out bitter and aggravated, and says—

"The luck has turned against us, there ain't any getting around it —look at this!"

It was rain. I was sorry enough for him to cry.

"It's going to wipe out the trail." He begun to get perfectly desprate, and said if any harm come to Jim he would square up the best he could—he would blow his brains out, he wouldn't miss them.

I couldn't bear to see him in so much trouble, so I tried to soothe him up, and told him *we* couldn't know where the men went to, becuz we didn't know the men, and so how could we know how they would act? Mightn't they belong to Burrell's Gang?

"Yes—prob'ly *do*. What of it?"

"Wouldn't they be safe if they was with the Gang?"

"Perfectly. Go on."

"Fox island is their den, ain't it?"

"Yes."

"How far from here?"

"Hundred and seventy mile."

"They can make it in four nights in a canoe and lay up and hide daytimes, and so how do *we* know they ain't making for home?"

"Lemme hug you, Huck! There's one level head left, anyway. If we can head them off before they get there, and have a sheriff with us—Huck, if they are ahead of us we'll catch up on them inside of an hour and make this boat chase them down. I bet you we're all right, Huck. Rush! Go down on the foc'sle and watch; I'll go in the pilot house and watch. If you see them, give three whoops as loud as you can, and I'll have the pilot all ready and anxious for business. Rush!"

So we both rushed. He was all right again and hopeful, and I was glad I thought of that idea, though I didn't take no stock in it, much. I knowed Tom's notion that the men had broke for Illinois was worth six of it. He would know it, too, when his mind got settled, then we would go home, and if that pal's leg was much hurt there would be new trails in a day or two, and not so very deep in the woods, either.

It was as dark as pitch on the foc'sle, and I fell over a man, and he storms out—

"What in hell are you doin'!" and grabbed me by the leg.

I sunk right down where I was, pulpy and sick, and begun to whimper, for it was the King's voice! Another voice says—

"Seems to be only a boy, you old hog—*he* didn't do it a-purpose. You've got no bowels—and never had any."

By George, it was the Duke!

And there I was!

The King spoke up again—

"A boy, are ye? Why didn't you *say* so? I took you for a cow. What do you want here—hey? Who are ye? What's your name?"

Of course I didn't want to answer, but I knowed I had to. But I tried to make my voice different—

"Bill Parsons, please sir."

"Ger-reat Scott!" says the Duke, setting up, and poking his face in mine, "what's brought *you* here, Huck Finn?"

He talked ruther thick, and I judged he was drunk; but that was all right, becuz if the Duke was more good-natureder one time than another it was when he was drunk. I had to tell them about myself, I knowed there warn't any way to get around it; so I done it as judicious as I could, caught sudden thataway, and unloaded con-

siderable many lies onto them. When I got done they grunted, and
the Duke says—

"Now tell some truth for a change."

I started painting again, but the Duke stopped me, and says—

"Wait, Huckleberry, you better let me help, I reckon."

My time was come, and I knowed it. He was sharp, and he
would begin to chase me up with questions and follow me right to
my hole. Of course I knowed his game, and was scared. The time I
let Jim get away, down there in Arkansaw, it took a pile of money
out of him and the King's pocket, and they had me, now. They
wouldn't let up till they found out where Jim was—that was
certain. The Duke begun; then the King begun to shove in questions, but the Duke shut him up and told him he was only botching
the business, and didn't know enough to come in when it rained. It
made the King pretty grouty.

It warn't long till they had it out of me—Jim was in jail, in our
town.

"What for?"

Now the minute the Duke asked that, I see my way perfectly
clear. If Jim was to get clear they could come with their sham
papers and run him South and sell him, but if I showed them he
was going to get hung, and hung for sure, they wouldn't bother
about him no more, and we would be shut of them. I was glad I had
that idea, and I made up my mind to put the murder on Jim and do
it strong.

"What for?" the Duke says.

"Murder," I says, perfectly ca'm.

"Great guns!"

"Yes," I says, "he done it, and he done right—but he *done* it,
ain't any doubt about that."

"It's an awful pity, becuz he warn't a bad nigger at bottom; but
how do you know he done it?"

"Becuz old Cap. Haines and Buck Fisher come on him in the
very act. He had hit a nigger-trader over the head with his own
musket, and stumbled and fell on him, and was getting up when
the men come running. It was dark, but they heard the row and

warn't far off. I wisht they had been somewheres else. If Jim hadn't fell he might a got away."

"Too bad. Is the man really dead?"

"I reckon so. They buried him this afternoon."

"It's awful. Does Jim give in that he done it?"

"No. Only just says it ain't any use for a nigger to talk when there's two white men against him."

"Well, that's so—hey, Majesty?"

"Head's level for a nigger—yes."

"Why, maybe he *didn't* kill the man. Any suspicious characters around?"

"Nary."

"Hasn't anybody seen any?"

"No. And besides, if there'd been any, where's their *motive*? They wouldn't kill a man just for fun, would they?"

"Well, no. And maybe Jim hadn't any motive, either."

"Why, your grace, the motive's the very worst thing against him. Everybody knows what he done to Jim once, and two men heard Jim tell him he was going to lay him out for it one of these days. It was only talk, and I know it, but that ain't any difference, it's white man's talk and Jim's only a nigger."

"It does look bad for Jim."

"Poor old Jim, he knows it. Everybody says he'll be hung, and of course he hain't got any friends, becuz he's free."

Nobody said anything, now, and I judged I had put it home good and strong, and they would quit bothering about Jim, and me and Tom would be let alone to go ahead and find the men and get Jim out of his scrape. So I was feeling good and satisfied. After a little bit the Duke says—

"I've been a thinking. I'll have a word with you, Majesty."

Him and the King stepped to the side and mumbled together, and come back, and the Duke says—

"You like Jim, and you're sorry for him. Now which would you druther—let him get sold down South, or get hung?"

Chapter 8

IT WAS sudden. It knocked me silly. I couldn't seem to understand what his idea was. Before I could come to myself, he says—

"It's for you to say. Now and then and off and on me and the
King have struck Jim's trail and lost it again; for we've got a
requisition for Jim from the Governor of Kentucky onto the Governor of Missouri and his acceptans of the same—all bogus, you
know, but the seals and the paper, which is genuwyne—and on
them papers we can go and grab Jim wherever we find him and
there ain't anybody can prevent us. First and last we've followed
that trail but first and last we've followed it to Elexandry, sixty mile
above here. Lost it again, and give it up for good and all, and took
this boat there towards the middle of the afternoon to-day—"

"Not knowin' that a righteous overrulin' Providence—"

"Shut up, you old rum-barrel, and don't interrupt. It's with you,
Huck, to save him or hang him. Which is it?"

"Oh, goodness knows, your grace, I'm anxious enough—tell me
how."

"It's easy. Spose Jim murdered a man down yonder in Tennessee
or Mississippi or Arkansaw fourteen months ago when you and Jim
was helping me and the King run the raft, and me and the King
was going to sell Jim for *our* nigger, becuz he *was* ourn, by rights of
discovery, we having found him floating down the river without
any owner—"

"Yes, and he's ourn *yit*," says the King, in that snarly way of
his'n.

"Stick your feet in your mouth and stop some of your gas from
escapin', Majesty. Spose Jim done that, Huck—murdered a planter
or somebody down there. Take it in? Get the idea?"

"Not by a blame' sight I don't. Jim never done it. Jim warn't
scasely ever out of my sight a day on a stretch; and if he—"

"There—don't be a fool. Of course he never done it; *that* ain't the idea. The idea is—*spose* he done it. See? Spose he *had* a done it. *Now* you see?"

"No, I don't."

"Shucks! Why, blame it, you couldn't try him up here till *after* you had tried him down there, could you? Got to take his murders in the order of preseedence, hain't you? 'Course. Any idiot knows that much. Very good. Now then, here's the scheme that'll give us back our nigger and save your black chum's life. To-morrow in Sent Louis we'll go to a friend of ourn that's in a private business up a back alley and got up our papers for us, and he'll change them so as to fit the case the way it stands now; change them from nigger 'escaped from service' to murder—murder done by Jim down South, you know. Then we'll come straight up here to-morrow or next day and show the papers and take Jim down South and sell him—not in Kentucky, of course, but 'way down towards the mouth of the river, where Missouri couldn't ever get on his track when she found she'd been played. See it *now*, don't you?"

By gracious I felt that good, I reckon the angels don't feel no better when they looks down Sabberday morning and sees the Catholic kids getting roped into the Presbyterium Sunday school. Well, the world, it's curious, thataway. One minute your heart is away down and miserable, and don't seem to be no way out of your troubles, and next minute some little thing or another happens you warn't looking for and just lifts her to your teeth with a bounce, and all your worries is gone and you feel as happy and splendid as Sodom and Gomorrah or any other of them patriarchs. I says to myself, it's nuts for Tom Sawyer, this is. And it's nuts for Jim, too. Jim's life's safe by this game, if they play it good, and if he ain't in England and free again three months after they sell him it'll be becuz we've forgot how to run niggers out of slavery and better quit the business.

So I told them to count me in, the 'rangement was satisfactry to me. They was very much pleased, and shuck me by the hand; the first time they ever come down onto my level like that, I reckon. And I said I wanted to help if they'd tell me how; and the Duke says—

"You can be a prime help, Huck, and you won't lose nothing by it, nuther. All you got to do is, keep mum—don't talk."

"All right, I won't."

"Tell Jim, if you want to; tell him to look awful scared and guilty when he sees us and finds we are sheriff's officers and hears what we've come for—it'll have a good effect; but he mustn't show that he has seen us before. And *you* mustn't. You want to be particular about that."

"I won't let on to know you, your grace—I'll be particular."

"That's the idea. Say—what are you doing on this boat?"

It took me ruther sudden, and I didn't know what to say, so I said I was traveling for my health. But they was feeling good, now, and unparticular; so they laughed and asked me where was the resort, and I said the town down yonder where the lights is showing; so they let me go, then, and told me good-bye and said there was going to be trouble in the chicken coops of that resort before morning, but they reckoned I would pull through all right.

I cleared for the pilot house, feeling first rate; then I remembered I had forgot to watch for the canoe, but I didn't care; I knowed there hadn't been any or the pilot and Tom would a seen it and chased it down. The mud-clerk was up there collecting our passages, and me and Tom come down on the texas roof, and I whispers and says—

"What do you think—the King and the Duke's down on the foc'sle!"

"Go 'long—you don't mean it!"

"Wish I may never die. You want to have a sight of them?"

"Well, I should reckon! Come along."

So we flew down. They was celebrated in our town on accounts of me and Jim's adventures with them, and there wasn't a person but would give his shirt for a look at them—including Tom. The time Tom saw them down in Arkansaw it was night, and they was tarred and feathered and the public was riding them on a rail in a torchlight procession and they was looking like the pillar of cloud that led Moses out of the bulrushers; but of course he would like to see them without the feathers on, becuz with the feathers on you couldn't tell them from busted bolsters.

But we didn't make it. The boat was sidling in to the wharfboat, and of course the mates had cleared the foc'sle and there warn't anybody there but a crowd of deckhands, now, bustling with the freight. They was red and vivid in the shine of the fire-doors and the torch-basket, but it was pitch dark everywheres else and you couldn't see anything. So we hopped ashore and took out to the upper end of the town and found a long lumber raft there and went out and set down on the outside edge of it with our legs in the water and listened to the quietness and the little waves slapping soft against it, and begun to talk, and watch out for the canoe, and it was ever so summery and bammy and comfortable, and the mosquitoes a singing and the frogs agoing it, the way they do, such nights.

So then I told Tom the scheme and said we must keep mum, and not tell anybody but Jim. It cheered him up and nearly made him gay; and he said Jim was safe now; if we didn't find the men the Duke's plan would save him, sure, and we would have good times running him out of slavery again, and then we would take him over to England and hand him over to the Queen ourselves to help in the kitchen and wait on table and be a body-guard and celebrated; and we would have the trip, and see the Tower and Shackspur's grave and find out what kind of a country we all come from before we struck for taxation and misrepresentation and raised Cain becuz we couldn't get it.

But he said he'd got his lesson, and warn't going to throw any more chances away for glory's sake; no, let glory go, he was for business, from this out. He was going to save Jim the *quickest* way, never mind about the showiest.

It sounded good, and I loved to hear it. He hadn't ever been in his right mind before; I could see it plain. Sound? He was as sound as a nut, now. Why, he even said he wished the King and the Duke would come and take Jim out of jail and out of town in the *night*, so there wouldn't be nary a sign of gaudiness and showiness about it, he was done with pow-wow, and didn't want no more. By gracious that made me uncomfortable again, it looked like he'd gone off his balance the *other* way, now. But I didn't say nothing.

He said the new scheme was a hundred times the most likeliest, but he warn't going to set down and take it easy on that account, becuz who knows but the Duke and the King will get into jail down there, which is always to be expected, and mightn't get out till it was too late for Jim's business—

"*Don't,* Tom!" says I, breaking in, "don't let's talk about it, don't let's even *think* about it."

"We've got to, Huck; it's in the chances, and we got to give all the doubts a full show from this out—there ain't going to be any more taking things for granted. We'll hunt for the *men* a couple of days while we're waiting—we won't throw any chance away." After a spell he drawed a sorrowful deep breath and says, "it was a prime good chance before the rain—I wish we hadn't come down here."

We watched faithful, all night till most daylight, and warn't going to go to sleep at all, but we did; and when we woke up it was noon and we was disgusted; and peeled and had a swim, and went down to town and et about 64 battercakes and things and felt crowded and better; and inquired around and didn't hear of the canoe, and a steamboat come along late and we got home at dark and Jim was slated for first degree and Bat was in the ground, and everybody was talking about the watchful inscrutableness of Providence, and thankful for it and astonished at it, but didn't das't to say so right out.

And after 64 more we went to jail and comforted Jim up and told him about the new plan, and it joggled him considerable, and he couldn't tell straight off whether to be glad or not, and says—

"By jimminies, I don't mo'n git outer one scrape tell I gits in a wuss one." But when he see how down-hearted it made Tom to hear him say that, he was sorry, and put his old black hand on Tom's head and says, "but I don't mine, I don't mine, honey, don't you worry; I knows you's gwyne to do de bes' you kin, en it don't make no diffunce what it is, ole Jim ain't gwyne to complain."

Of course it was awful to him, the idea of the King and the Duke getting a grip on him again, and he could scasely bear to talk about it; still, he knowed me and Tom wouldn't let him be a slave long if industriousness and enterprise and c'ruption was worth anything; so he quieted down, and reckoned if the Queen was satisfied with him after she tried him and found he was honest and willing, she would raise his wages next year; and Tom said she was young and inexperienced and would, he knowed it. So it was all satisfactry, and Tom went along home, and told me to come too, and I done it.

His aunt Polly give him a hiding, but it didn't hurt—nor me, neither; we didn't care for it. She was in a towering way, but when we explained we had been over on t'other side of the river fishing, about a couple of days and nights, and didn't know the horn-signal had blowed and scared the town to death and there'd been a murder and a funeral and Jim done it, she forgot she was mad at us, and wouldn't a sold out her chance for a basket of money, she being just busting to tell the news.

So she started in, and never got a dern thing right, but enjoyed herself, and it took her two solid hours; and when she got done painting up the show it was worth four times the facts, and I reckon Tom was sorry he didn't get her to run the conspiracy herself. But she was right down sorry for Jim, and said Bat must a tried to kill Jim or he never would a blowed his brains out with the musket.

"*Did* blow them out, did he, aunt Polly?"

"Such as he had—yes."

Then company come in to spend the evening, and amongst them was Flacker the detective, and he had been working up his clews and knowed all about the murder, same as if he'd seen it; and they all set with their mouths open a listening and holding their breath and wondering at his talents and marvelousness whilst he went on.

Why, it was just rot and rubbage—clean, straight foolishness, but them people couldn't see it. According to him, the Sons of Freedom was a sham—it was Burrell's Gang, and he had the clews that would prove it. Burrell's Gang—it made them fairly shudder and hitch their chairs clos'ter together when he said it. He said there was six members of it right here in town, friends of you all, you meet up and chat with them every day—it made them shudder again. Said he wouldn't mention no names, he warn't ready yet, but he could lay his hands on them whenever he wanted to. Said they had a plan to burn the town and rob it and run off the niggers, he had the proofs; and so they went on a shuddering, enough to shake the house and sour the milk. Said Jim was in leagues with them, he had the facts and could prove it any day; and said he had shaddered the Sons to their den—wouldn't say where it was, just now; and he come onto provisions there cal'lated to feed sixteen men six weeks —(ourn, by jings!) And found their printing 'rangements, too, and lugged them off and hid them, and could show them whenever he got ready. Said he knowed the secret of the figures that was printed on the bills with red ink, and it was too awful to tell where there was senstive scary women. That made everybody scrunch together and look sick. And he said the man that got up them bills warn't any common ornery person, he was a gigantic intelleck, and was prob'ly the worst man alive; and he knowed by some little marks on the bills that another person wouldn't notice and wouldn't under-stand them if he did, that it was Burrell his own self that done it; and said there warn't another man in America could get up them bills but Burrell. And that very Burrell was in this town this minute, in disguise and running a shop, and it was him that blowed the signal-horn. Old Miss Watson fainted and fell onto the cat when she heard that, and she yowled, becuz it was her tail that got hurt, and they had a lot of trouble to fetch her to. And last of all, he said Jim had two 'complices to the murder and he seen their footprints—dwarfs, they was, one cross-eyed and t'other left-handed; didn't say how he knowed it, but he was shaddering them, and although they had escaped out of town for now, he warn't worrying, he allowed he would take them into camp when they was least expecting of it.

Why that was me and Tom—I never see such an idiot. But the company was charmed to death with that stuff, and said it was the most astonishing thing the way a detective could read every little sign he come across same as if it was a book, and you couldn't hide nothing from him. And they said this town would a lived and died and never knowed what started the row and who done it if it hadn't been for Flacker, and they was all under obligations to him; but he said it warn't nothing, it was his perfeshon, and anybody could do it that had practice and the gifts.

"*And* the gifts! you may well say *that*," says Tom's aunt Polly; and then they all said it.

She was soft on detectives, becuz Tom had an ambitiousness thataway, and she was proud about what he done that time down at his uncle Silas's.

Chapter 9

WE WAS over the river before daylight next morning, and as soon as the dawn come we begun to search for them foot-tracks. Tom had the measures of the two men's tracks—length and width; and he had the heels exact, just as they was printed in the ground in the lean-to, becuz he had run tallow into them from the candle and made thin moulds, and then traced them around on a leaf which he tore out of Bat's grocery-store book and done it with Bat's pen. The prints was like anybody else's to me, except the pal's left heel, which had a little of the north-east corner gone, and it oughter been the other one, to do us any good, I reckoned, becuz it was the left one he dragged after he hurt it falling down the jumping-off place, and the corner wouldn't show, now, if he was still a-dragging it; but Tom said I was a sap-head, and said if it dragged couldn't we see the drag-mark. Well, that was so; so then I didn't say no more.

We started work about a mile above the ferry on the Illinois shore. There was a low place where you could land a lame man there, and it was the only one above the ferry—the rest was all bluff bank ten foot high, like a wall, at this stage of the river. There was considerable many tracks, some fresh and some old, but if the ones we wanted was there they was too old to show up, now. We went out in the woods a piece and struck down-stream and went as far as the ferry, and found tracks in places, but they warn't the right ones. There wasn't a place for miles below the ferry where they could land; so we struck out on the ferry road and hunted the ground on both sides of it away out double as far as a lame man could get to in the time they had, since they started, but we hadn't any luck.

We stuck to it all day, and went back next day and ransacked again—rummaged the whole country betwixt the landings, plum till dark. It warn't any good. Next day we went down and rummaged Jackson's island—no tracks there but Flacker's; and he had lugged off our print-works, and some of our feed, too. So then we crossed to our shore and went to the cave, but that warn't any use, becuz the soldiers was there that Colonel Elder sent on accounts of the pow-wow the conspiracy made, and if any strangers had tried to get in there it would a been hark from the tomb for them.

We had to give it up, then, and paddled along home. Tom was down in the mouth again, becuz Jim would have to go down South with the King and the Duke, now, and could have a terrible rough time before we could run him out of slavery and break for England. But pretty soon he jumps up, all excited and glad, and says—

"We're fools, Huck, just fools!"

"Tain't no news," I says, "but what's the matter now?"

"Why, we're in luck—that's what's the matter."

"Skin it to me," I says, "I'm a listening."

"Well, you see, we didn't find the men, and ain't ever going to; so Jim hangs, for dead sure, now, if he stays here—ain't it so? And so it's splendid that he's going to be sold South, and I'm glad you run across the Duke and the King. It's the best thing that ever happened, becuz—"

"Shucks," I says, "is it any more splendider now than it was two minutes ago? You was 'most sick about it, then. How is it such good luck?"

"Becuz he ain't agoing to *be* sold South."

It sounded so good I come near jumping up and cracking my heels; but I held in, becuz I don't like disapp'intments, and says—

"How you going to prevent it?"

"Easy. We're just fools for not thinking of it sooner. We'll go down the river with them on the same boat, and when we get to Cairo we're in a free State, and we'll say, now then, the most you can get for Jim down South is a thousand dollars—you can get that right *here* for him!"

So then I *did* jump up and crack my heels, and says—

"It's splendid, Tom. I'm in for half of the money."

"No you ain't."

"Yes I am."

"No you ain't. If it hadn't been for the conspiracy Jim wouldn't been at that place, and wouldn't be in no trouble now. It's my fault, and I foot the bill."

"It ain't fair," I says. "How did I come to hog half of the robber's money and get so rotten flush? Was it my smartness? No, it was yourn. By rights you ought to took it all, and you wouldn't."

And I stuck to him till he give in.

"Now then," I says, "we ain't such fools as you think, for not thinking about this sooner. We couldn't buy Jim *here*, becuz he's free and there ain't anybody to buy him of. We couldn't buy him of anybody *but* the King and the Duke, and can't buy him of *them* till he's on free ground where we can run him up the Ohio and into Canada and over to England—so we've thought of it plenty soon enough, and ain't fools, nuther."

"All right, then, we ain't fools, but ain't it lucky that we went down the river when there warn't the least sense in it, and yet it was the very thing that met us up with the King and the Duke, and we can see, now, Jim would be hung, sure, if it hadn't happened. Huck—something else in it, ain't there?"

He said it pretty solemn. So I knowed he had treed the hand of Providence again, and said so.

"I reckon you'll learn to trust, before long," he says.

I started to say "I wisht *I* could get the credit for everything another person does," but pulled it in and crowded it down and didn't say nothing. It's the best way. After he had studied a while he says—

"We got to neglect the conspiracy, Huck, our hands is too full to run it right."

I was graveled, and was agoing to say "Long's we ain't running it anyway—'least don't get none of the credit of it—it ain't worth the trouble it is to us," but pulled it in and crowded it down like I done before. Best way, I reckon.

After supper we went to the jail and took Jim a pie and one thing and another and told him how we was going to buy him at Cairo and run him to England, and by Jackson he busted out and cried; and the pie went down the wrong way and we had to beat him and bang him or he would a choked to death and might as well a been hung.

Jim was all right, now, and joyful, and his mournfulness all went away, and took his banjo, and 'stead of singing "Ain't got long to stay here," the way he done since he got into jail, he sung "Jinny git de hoecake done," and the gayest songs he knowed; and laughed and laughed about the King and the Duke and the Burning Shame till he 'most died; it was good to see him; and then danced a nigger breakdown, and said he hadn't been so young in his heart since he was a boy.

And he was willing for his wife and children to come and see him now, if their marsters would let them—and the sheriff; he couldn't bear the idea of it before. So we said we would try for it, and hoped we'd have them there in the morning so he could see them and say good-bye before the King and the Duke come up on the boat.

That night we packed our things, and in the morning I went to Judge Thatcher and drawed eight hundred dollars, and he *was* surprised, but he didn't get no information out of me; and Tom drawed the same, and then we went to 'range about Jim's wife and children, and their marsters was very good and kind, but couldn't spare them now, but would let them come before long—maybe next week—was there any hurry? Of course we had to say no, that would answer very well.

Then we went to the jail and Jim was dreadful sorry, but knowed it couldn't be helped and he had to get along the way things was; but he didn't take on, becuz niggers is used to that.

We chattered along pretty comfortable till we heard the boat coming, but after that we was too excited to talk, but only fidgeted up and down; and every time the bolts and chains on the jail door rattled I catched my breath and says to myself, that's them a-coming! But it wasn't.

They didn't come at all. We was disappointed, and so was Jim, but it warn't any matter, they was prob'ly in the calaboose for getting drunk and raising a row, and would turn up to-morrow. So then we hid the money and went a-fishing.

Next day Jim's trial was set for three weeks ahead.

No Duke and no King, yet.

So we allowed we would wait one more day, and then if they didn't come we would go down to Sent Louis and go to the calaboose and find out how long they was in for.

Well, they didn't come; so we went down. And by George they warn't in the calaboose, and *hadn't* been!

It was perfectly awful. Tom was that sick he had to set down on something—he couldn't stand.

What to do we didn't know; becuz the calaboose was the only address them bilks ever had.

Then we went and tried the jail. No use—they hadn't been there, either.

It was getting to look right down scary; I knowed it, and Tom knowed it. But we'd got to keep moving, we couldn't rest. It was a powerful big town—some said it had sixty thousand people in it, prob'ly a lie; but we searched it high and low for four days just the same, particularly the worst parts, like what they call Hell's Half-Acre. But we couldn't run across them; they was gone—clean gone, just the same as if they had been blowed out, like a candle.

We got downer and downer in the mouth, we couldn't make it

out nohow. Something had gone and happened to them, of course, but there warn't no guessing what, only we knowed it was serious. And could be mighty serious for Jim, too, if it went on so. I reckoned they was dead, but I didn't say so, it wouldn't help Tom feel any better.

We had to give it up, and we went back home. And not talking much; there warn't anything to talk about, but plenty to think. And mainly what to say to Jim, and how to let on to be hopeful.

Well, we went to the jail every day, and pretended we warn't uneasy, and let on to be pretty gay, and done it the best we could, but it was pretty poor and wouldn't fooled anybody but old Jim, which believed in us. We kept it up more than two weeks, and it was the hardest work we ever had and the sorrowfulest. And always we said it was going to come out all right, but towards the last we couldn't say it hearty and strong, and that made Jim suspicion something, and he turned in and went to bracing *us* up and trying to make us cheerful, and it 'most broke us down, and was the hardest of all for us to bear, becuz it showed he had as good as found out we hadn't any real hope, and so he was forgetting to be troubled about himself he was so sorry for us.

But there was one part of the day that we warn't ever in the jail. It was when the boat come. We was always there, and seen everybody that come ashore. And every now and then, along at first, as the boat sidled in I would think I saw them bilks in the jam on the foc'sle and nudge Tom and say "There they are!" but it was a mistake; and so towards the last we only went becuz we couldn't help it, and looked at the passengers without any intrust, and turned around and went away without saying anything when they had all come ashore. It seemed kind of strange: last month I would a broke my neck getting away from the King and the Duke, but now I would druther see them than the angels.

Tom was pale, and hadn't any appetite for his vittles, and didn't sleep good, and hadn't any spirits and wouldn't talk, and his aunt Polly was worried out of her life about him, and believed the Sons of Freedom and their bills and their horn had scared Tom into a sickness; and every day she loaded him up with any kind of medicine she could get aholt of; and she watched him through the keyhole, and 'stead of giving it to the cat he took it himself, and that just scared her crazy; and she said if she could get her hands on the Son of Freedom that scattered them bills around she believed to gracious she would break his leg if it was the last act.

Me and Tom had to be witnesses, and Jim's lawyer was a young man and new to the village, and hadn't any business, becuz of course the others didn't want the job for a free nigger, though we offered to pay them high. They hated to go back on Tom, but they was plenty right enough, they had to get their living and the prejudices was pretty strong, which was natural. Tom reconnized that; he wouldn't be lawyer for a free nigger himself, unless it was Jim.

Chapter 10

THE MORNING of the trial Tom's aunt Polly stopped him and warn't going to let him go; she said it warn't any place for boys, and besides, they wouldn't be allowed—everybody was going and there wouldn't be room; but Tom says—

"There'll be room for me and Huck. We're going to be witnesses."

She was that astonished you could a knocked her down with a brickbat; and shoved her spectacles up on her forehead and says—

"*You* two! What do *you* know about it, I'd like to know!"

But we didn't stop to talk, but cleared out and left her finishing fixing up; becuz she was coming, of course—everybody was.

The court-house was jammed. Plenty of ladies, too—seven or eight benches of them; and aunt Polly and the Widow Douglas and Miss Watson and Mrs. Lawson, they all set together, and the Thatchers and a lot more back of them—all of the quality. And Jim was there, and the sheriff.

Then the judge come in and set down very solemn, and opened court; and Mr. Lawson made a speech and said he was going to prove Jim done it by two witnesses, and he had a *motive*, and would prove that, too. I knowed it didn't make Tom feel good to hear him say that.

Jim's young lawyer made a speech and said he was going to prove an *allyby*—prove it by two witnesses; and that it warn't done by Jim but by a stranger unknown. It made everybody smile; and I was sorry for that young man, becuz he was nervous and scared, and knowed he hadn't any case, and so couldn't talk out bold and strong like Mr. Lawson done. And he knowed everybody was making fun of him, too, and didn't think much of him for being a free nigger's lawyer and a nobody to boot.

Flacker he went on the stand and give his idea of how it all happened; and mapped it out and worked his clews, and everybody held their breath and was full of wonderment to hear him make it so plain and clear, and nothing in the world to do it with but just his intellects.

Then Cap. Haines and Buck Fisher told how they catched Jim as good as in the very act; and how poor old Bat was laying there dead, and Jim just getting up, having caved his head in with the musket and slipped and fell on him.

And then the musket was showed, with rust and hair on the barrel, and the people shuddered; and when they held up the bloody clothes they shuddered some more.

Then I told all I knowed and got back out of the way; and hadn't done no good, becuz there wasn't anybody there believed any of it, and the most of them *looked* it.

Then they called Tom Sawyer, and people around me mumbled and said, "'Course—couldn't happen 'thout *him* being in it; couldn't do an eclipse successful if Tom Sawyer was took sick and couldn't superintend." And his aunt Polly and the women perked up and got ready to wonder what kind of 'sistance he was going to contribbit and who was going to get the benefit of it.

"Thomas Sawyer, where was you on the Saturday night before the Sunday that this deed was done?"

"Running a conspiracy."

"Doing what?" says the judge, looking down at him over his pulpit.

"Running a conspiracy, your honor."

"This sounds like a dangerous candor. Tell your story; and be careful and not reveal things that can hurt you."

So Tom went on and told the whole thing, how we got up the conspiracy and run it for all it was worth; and Colonel Elder and Captain Sam set there looking ashamed and pretty mad, for 'most everybody was laughing; and when he showed that it was us that was the Sons of Freedom and got up the scare-bills and stuck them on the doors, and not Burrell, which Flacker said it was, they laughed again, and it was Flacker's turn to look sick, and he done it.

So he went on telling it, straight out and square, and no lies, all the way down to where Jim come down out of the tree after he blowed the signal-horn and we all went into the town and sampled the excitement—and you could see the people was believing it all, becuz it sounded honest and didn't have a made-up look; and so the *alliby* was getting to look right down favorable, and people was nodding their heads at one another as much as to say so, and looking more friendlier at Jim, too, and Mr. Lawson warn't looking so comfortable as he was before; but at last come the question—

"You say the prisoner was to go and report to your aunt, and then follow you. What time was that?"

And by Jackson Tom couldn't tell him. We hadn't noticed. Tom had to guess; it was all he could do, and guessing warn't worth much. It was mighty bad—and it showed in people's faces. Mr. Lawson was looking comfortable again.

"Why were you three going to Bradish's house?"

Then Tom told them *that* part of the conspiracy; how he was going to play runaway nigger and I was going to play him onto Bradish, but Bradish had already got one—and so on; and how Tom examined the nigger in the night and see that he warn't a nigger at all, and had a key in his shoe, and he judged he was going to escape, and he wanted to be there and get the clews and hunt him down after he got away. And the people and the judge listened right along, and it was just as good as a tale out of a book.

And he told how me and him got there at daylight and see Bat laying dead, and he told me to go for the undertaker, and then found Jim's track and called me back and said it was all right, Jim had been there and of course *he* was gone to tell about the murder.

A lot of them smiled at that, and Mr. Lawson laughed right out.

But Tom went right along, and told how we followed the tracks to the hanted house and he crope in under there and listened and heard the murderers talk, but didn't see them.

"Didn't see them?"

"No, sir;" and he told why.

"Imaginary ones, maybe," says Mr. Lawson, and laughed; and a lot of the others laughed, too, and a fellow close to me says to a friend, "he better stopped when he was well off—he's got to embroiderin', now." "Yes," says the other one, "he's spiling it."

"Go on," says the judge; "tell what you heard."

"It was like this. One was a thrashing around a little now and then and growling, and the other one was groaning; and by and by the one that thrashed around says in a low voice, 'Shut up, you old cry-baby, and let a person get some sleep.' Then the groaner says, 'If your leg was hurt as bad as mine, you'd be a cry-baby too, I reckon, and it's all your fault, anyway; when Bradish come and catched us escaping, if you had a helped me 'stead of trying to prevent me, I would a busted his head right there in the lean-to, 'stead of outside, and he wouldn't a had a chance to yell and fetch them men a-running, and we wouldn't a had to take a short cut and hurt my leg and have to lay up here and p'raps get catched before the day's over—and yet here you are a-growling about cry-babies, and it shows you hain't got no real heart, and no Christian sentiments and bringing up.' Then the other one says, 'The whole blame's your own, for coming three or four hours late—drunk, as usual.' 'I warn't drunk, neither; I got lost—ain't no crime in that, I don't reckon.' 'All right,' says the other one, 'have it your own way, but shut up and keep still now; you want to be thinking up your last dying speech, becuz you're going to need it on the gallows for this piece of work, which was just unnecessary blame foolishness, and I'll be hung too, and serve me right, for being in such dam company.' The other one wanted to growl some more about his leg, but this one said if he didn't shut up he would pull it out and belt him over the head with it. So then they quieted down and I come away."

When Tom got done it was dead still, just the way it always is when people has been listening to a yarn they don't take no stock in and are sorry for the person that has told it. It was kind of miserable, that stillness. At last the judge he cleared his throat and says, very grave—

"If this is true, how is it you didn't come straight and tell the sheriff? How do you explain that?"

Tom was working at a button with his fingers and looking down at the floor. It was too many for him, that question, and I knowed it. How was he going to tell them he didn't do it becuz he was going to work the thing out on detective principles and git glory out of it? And how was he going to tell them he wanted to make the glory bigger by making it seem Jim killed the man, and even crowded him into a *motive,* and then went and told about the motive where Mr. Lawson could get on it—and so just by reason of him and his foolishness the murderers got away and now Jim was going to be hung for what they done. No, sir, he couldn't say a word. And so when the judge waited a while, everybody's eyes on Tom a fooling with his button, and then asked him again why he didn't go and tell the sheriff, he swallowed two or three times, and the tears come in his eyes, and he says, very low—

"I don't know, sir."

It was still again, for a minute, then the lawyers made their speeches, and Mr. Lawson was terrible sarcastic on Tom and his fairy tale, as he called it, and so then the jury fetched Jim in guilty in the first degree in two minutes, and old Jim stood up and the judge begun to make his speech telling him why he'd got to die; and Tom he set there with his head down, crying.

And just then, by George, the Duke and the King come a-working along through the crowd, and worked along up front, and the King says—

"Pardon a moment, your honor," and Tom glanced up; and the Duke says—

"We've got a little matter of business which—"

Tom jumps up and shouts—

"I reconnize the voices—it's the murderers!"

Well, you never see such a stir. Everybody rose up and begun to stretch their necks to get a view, and the sheriff he stormed at them and made them set down; and the King and the Duke looked perfectly astonished, and turned pretty white, I tell you; and the judge says—

"Why do you make such a charge as this?"

"Becuz I know it, your honor," Tom says.

"How do you know it—you said, yourself, you didn't see the men?"

"It ain't any difference, I've got the proofs."

"Where?"

He fetched out the leaf from Bat's book and showed the drawing, and says—

"If this one hasn't changed his shoes, this is the print of the left one."

And it *was*, sure enough, and the King looked very sick.

"Very good indeed," says the judge. "Proceed."

Tom fetched a set of false teeth out of his pocket, and says—

"If they don't fit the other one's mouth he ain't the white nigger that was in the lean-to."

Tom Sawyer: A Play
in Four Acts

I

In the spring of 1874 Clemens heard that out in San Francisco actor John T. Raymond was staging and starring in an unauthorized dramatization of the humorist's portion of *The Gilded Age*. He threatened to enjoin performances, paid playwright Gilbert B. Densmore for his script, rewrote the drama in a few weeks, and in July copyrighted the new version of the play, which was performed as *Colonel Sellers*. This version, with Raymond in the title role, became a great success and during the many years of its performance brought the author $20,000.[1] In August 1874, before it was staged, theatrical producer John Augustin Daly asked the humorist to write "something for my company & my theatre." "I think," Daly continued, "I could put you on the road to a good thing."[2]

Encouraged by Daly's coaxing, the success of *Colonel Sellers*, and letters from others interested in producing plays associated with his name, Mark Twain asked his friend William Dean Howells on 13 July 1875 to dramatize the still unpublished *The Adventures of Tom Sawyer*, saying, "I believe a good deal of a drama can be made of it."

[1] *MTHL*, II, 861–863.
[2] *MTHL*, I, 34, n. 2.

Howells refused on 19 July, partly because "I don't see how anybody can do that but yourself." Even before receiving Howells's refusal, Twain must have applied for a copyright.[3] For on 21 July he secured one by submitting this synopsis:

TOM SAWYER.

A Drama.

By Mark Twain—(Samuel L. Clemens)

Containing:

Tom Sawyer, Jeff Thatcher, Huck Finn, Joe Harper, Ben Rogers, Alfred Temple, "Jim," etc., *Boys;* Becky Thatcher, Mary, etc., *Girls;* Aunt Polly, the Widow Douglas, Judge and Mrs. Thatcher, Mrs. Harper, Mr. Dobbins, (schoolmaster,) Muff Potter, Injun Joe, etc., *Elderly People.*

Whitewashing the Fence, and selling privileges to do the same. Bible presentation to Tom Sawyer, on purchased tickets. Fight with Alfred Temple. Tom's art-lesson and love-scene with Becky; tick-trade with Huck; tick-squabble in school with Joe Harper. Battle of Public Square Heights. The broken Sugar-bowl. Tom gets ready to die under Becky's window, and gets drenched. The midnight murder in the graveyard by Injun Joe, witnessed by Huck and Tom. Their bloody oath in the tan-house. Frightened by the stray dog. Potter accused by Injun Joe at the inquest, and confesses. "Examination Day" at school. Teacher's bald head gilded, and his wig removed by a suspended cat. Teacher's anatomical book torn by Becky; Tom accuses himself at the last moment, and takes the whipping. The pirating expedition to Jackson's Island by Huck Finn the Red-Handed, the Black Avenger of the Spanish Main, and the Terror of the Seas. Tom returns and eaves-drops. Hears conversation between Aunt Polly, Sid, Mary, and Mrs. Harper, appointing date of funeral of the three runaway boys. Goes back to Island, and in midst of their own funeral the three lads march down the aisle. Tom afterward explains to Aunt Polly why he "did not leave the bark."

Trial of Muff Potter. At latest moment Tom Sawyer called to witness stand, and when his damaging tale is half finished, Injun Joe breaks away and escapes.

Tom, and Huck Finn the Pariah of the village of St. Petersburgh, hunt for hidden treasure under dead trees, and in haunted houses. Secreted in haunted house they see Injun Joe and a stranger come there to bury a trifle of money; in digging the hole, an ancient box of gold coin is found, which they conclude to carry off and hide in "No. 2 under the cross," to

---

[3] *MTHL*, I, 95–96. I infer that the author applied for his copyright before he heard from Howells on the basis of the dates of the letter and of the copyright entry. The text which follows was obtained from the copyright office.

the serious disappointment of the lads. The boys search room No. 2 in the Temperance Tavern, and find only clandestine whiskey and Injun Joe drunk and asleep.

Huck dogs Injun Joe and the stranger at midnight to Widow Douglas's, then informs the Welchman Jones of the intended burglary and mayhem, and the widow is saved.

The pic-nic. Tom and Becky lost during three days in MacDougal's cave. Tom sees Injun Joe in there, who flies. Search for the children. Tom accidentally finds a way out, together with Becky. Reception in town. Injun Joe starves to death in the cave.

Tom takes Huck to cave; they dig under figure of the cross, and get the treasure. Widow Douglas takes Huck into her family, and distresses the life out of the vagabond with her cleanly, systematic, and pious ways. He, Tom, and Joe Harper turn robbers, and so make use of the cave.

FIFTY YEARS LATER.—Ovation to General Sawyer, Rear-Admiral Harper, Bishop Finn, and Inspector Sid Sawyer, the celebrated detective.

HARTFORD.

1875.

Some phrasings in this synopsis strongly suggest that it was written before the play was. The "etcs." in the list of characters, for instance, indicate an uncertainty which one who has written a play would not be likely to have. After saying that the boys attend their own funeral, Twain says, "Tom afterward explains to Aunt Polly why he 'did not leave the bark.'" The indefinite "afterward" suggests that the scene during which this explanation is offered has not been developed. Again: "Huck dogs Injun Joe and the stranger at midnight to Widow Douglas's, then informs the Welchman Jones of the intended burglary and mayhem, and the widow is saved." Here too the paucity of details seems to indicate a scene still in the planning stage. It is noteworthy, too, that the synopsis summarizes events in the order of their occurrence in the novel, with very few omissions. These facts and the correspondence and the dating of the copyright all raise doubts that any of the play had been written before this synopsis was.

Shortly afterward Twain evidently wrote at least some of the drama outlined here. In a letter of 14 August 1876 he states that although he forgot to include in his novel "a ridiculous spelling-scene, historical and arithmetical classes, etc (country school fashion,) . . . I have it in the play." [4] A fragment of a note in the Estelle Doheny Collection, St.

---

[4] The letter is to the son of Moncure Conway, the author's British agent (TS, MTP).

John's Seminary, Camarillo, California, outlines the scene in similar words (see Appendix C).

Other notes in the Doheny collection outline Acts IV and V as the humorist planned to write them, and they conform to the outline used to procure the copyright. In the first of two scenes of Act IV, the villagers were to discuss and lament the supposed death of the boys and to plan their funeral, as they do at the start of chapter seventeen of the novel. In the second scene, Tom was to return to his home at night, as he had in chapter fifteen of the book, and hear his Aunt Polly and her friends talking about his death. Act V was to dramatize the latter part of chapter seventeen, which showed the boys returning to their own funeral:

> Curtain discovers funeral well along. Three coffins. Make it a love-feast. Brethren asked to speak. 3 do. Preacher concludes. General burst of weeping. The boys crawl from under pews—preacher staring—everybody faces around—the ragged piratically dressed chaps come forward. General rejoicing. Everybody forgives. The 3 take back their compliments. Ain't anybody goin' to be glad Red's back? Yes, I will! Amy steals to Tom's side—Gracie to Joe's and as concourse breaks up they name the day. *Curtain.*

A memorandum in parentheses adds that the boys are to "discard their caps for plumed paper ones—wear tin swords, turn their coats, get flashy sashes, false horse-pistols etc.," and appear "in this preposterous gear."

Whether Twain got this far in the dramatization one cannot be sure, but after outlining Act V, even he must have realized that he was in bad trouble. I say "even he" because Mark Twain was quite capable of planning and writing unactable plays. On 25 February 1874 he wrote to his friend Mrs. Fairbanks: "I have written a 5-act play, with only one (visible) character in it—only one human being ever appears on the stage during the 5 acts—but the interest is not in *him* but in two other people who never appear at all. It may never be played . . . [but] it is at least novel & curious." [5] This "curious" invention has not survived, but a fragment of another (equally grotesque) has—a burlesque *Hamlet* with a long-winded comic character boldly inserted into Shakespeare's play. If this monstrosity had been completed and produced on the scale of Act I and the one scene of Act II, its performance would have been

---

[5] *MTF*, p. 183.

interminable. And again, in 1890, Twain would write a dramatization of *The Prince and the Pauper* that producer Daniel Frohman calculated "would have taken two nights to perform." [6]

Capable though he was of such fecklessness, Twain must have noticed that his outlined five acts had carried him through less than half of his synopsis. Thus, as a play foreshadowing O'Neill's *Mourning Becomes Electra* (but much duller), the completed drama would have taken hours, perhaps days, to perform. Twain may have noticed another difficulty: if all the scenes outlined were staged in order, more than thirty-five scene changes would have been necessary—an utterly impractical number.

At any rate, late in 1875 or early in 1876, the humorist sounded out Henry J. Byron, British actor, theater manager, and playwright, about collaborating on a dramatization of *Tom Sawyer*. (Byron's play *Our Boys* had just started a record run, and Clemens knew him as a humorist.) The letter of inquiry, however, was misplaced, and before Byron found it and answered it some months later, Clemens had Moncure Conway, his agent in England, approach another dramatist, Tom Taylor. Taylor, editor of *Punch* and a prolific writer of plays of many sorts, declined for reasons that one can infer from the letter Twain wrote on 14 August 1876:

> I agree with Mr. Taylor, that the story *as it stands* is doubtless not dramatizable; but by turning and twisting some of the incidents, discarding others and adding new ones, that sort of difficulty is overcome by these ingenious dramatists. But I haven't the head to do it.

Taylor's refusal made possible another approach to Byron, the humorist's "first choice any way." As late as 28 November, Conway told Clemens, "I have addressed to Miss Lee the great impersonator of 'Jo' in Bleak House [an inquiry about her playing a role in] Tom Sawyer but have no reply yet." [7] But I have come upon no evidence that Byron made an attempt at collaboration.

---

[6] The burlesque *Hamlet* in its incomplete state has been published in *Mark Twain's Satires & Burlesques,* ed. Franklin R. Rogers (Berkeley, 1967), pp. 55–86; for Frohman's comment, see Rodman Gilder, "Mark Twain Detested the Theatre," *Theatre Arts,* XXVIII (February 1944), 115.

[7] Letters cited include: SLC to Moncure Conway 24 July 1876, Columbia; SLC to Conway 10 August 1876, TS in MTP; one from Conway to SLC 28 November 1876 in SLC Scrapbook 1872–78, MTP; SLC to Conway's son, Eustace Conway, 14 August 1876, TS in MTP.

II

Between 1876 and 1878, Twain helped write the comedy *Ah Sin* in collaboration with Bret Harte, and he himself wrote the comedy "Cap'n Simon Wheeler, the Amateur Detective." Each play was composed rapidly, and each, he thought, was wonderful. But after the former had been produced briefly, he called it "a most abject & incurable failure!" And after the latter had been put aside for a while and then reread, he characterized it as "dreadfully witless & flat." [8] Nevertheless it took the humorist only a few years to forget his failures, and in 1883 and 1884 he again busied himself frantically with dramatic writing. He persuaded Howells to come to Hartford and collaborate with him on a new play, *Colonel Sellers as a Scientist*, later called *The American Claimant*. When this was finished, he admired it inordinately and, even before prospective producers had been allowed to read it, he began negotiations for its production at what would have been highly advantageous terms for its authors. Whereas other Twain plays had been too long to produce, this evidently was too short—or so Raymond indicated when he finally was allowed to see it.[9] In the end, abandoning hope for this narrative in dramatic form, Twain rewrote and published it as fiction. While still trying to get the Sellers play produced, he proposed that he and Howells write a historical tragedy, and quickly turned out a version of what was to be the climactic scene. Then he conceived of another collaboration which he and Howells might attempt—a play set in the Sandwich Islands, and he heaped up notes to be used in writing it. Work on these abortive plays did not keep him from completing dramatic versions of both *The Prince and the Pauper* and *Tom Sawyer* during this period.[10]

The history of the latter play followed the customary pattern: to the author's delight, he found himself writing at a prodigious speed. He read the finished product and admired his handiwork. Cockily he

---

[8] *MTHL*, I, 206, 246.

[9] *MTBus*, pp. 227–241, 276. Said Raymond: "If the play is altered and *made* longer I should be pleased to read it again."

[10] *MTB*, pp. 763–764. For details about the dating of the latter, see Appendix B of this volume.

negotiated to have it produced, while visions of millions danced through his head. But he failed to find a producer. And in time he was driven to recognize that his drama had little or no merit.

In four weeks, he boasted to Howells on 13 February 1884, "I have written one 4-act play [*Tom Sawyer*], & 2½ acts of another [*The Prince and the Pauper*]." [11] Even though some of this version of the comedy evidently was lifted bodily from the earlier play, and although some merely had to be revised, the speed with which Twain wrote was remarkable. Some notes kept with the manuscript indicate how he achieved such speed: he jotted down the content and page numbers of promising passages in the Toronto edition. "Dead cat—good.—64–9 (all good graveyard stuff)" says one note; "152 [Aunt Polly on Tom's essential goodness, chapter fourteen] Must come in." Additional notes suggest where bits can be worked into scenes other than those where they occur in the novel: "Tom's love scene—before school-blackboard. 71–78 (It can come in, all right, at school. . . .)"; "Add on 78 (Do you love rats?) after 71—before school takes in." "232—also 241 [the boys' discussion of treasure hunting] This in the graveyard or on island before murder . . ." indicating that at this stage the author was unsure whether the dig for the treasure would take place in the cemetery where the doctor is killed or on Jackson's Island—although the treasure would be moved. Eventually Twain eliminated the Jackson's Island episode, and references to it disappeared.

He was eager to end each act, in the fashion of the day, with a memorable action. "Tom's flogging ends one act," he wrote. He reminded himself to have Potter "carried off to jail" as another act ends. Again, "One act to close with Tom's testimony in court and flight or manacling of Injun Joe and Muff's gratitude." Next he set down an exchange to occur in this scene:

Tom—Huck I can't stand it (struggling).
Huck—O, Tom *don't* ruin us!

At the end of the page containing this note Twain hit upon a way to eliminate a scene shift: "(Hold court in school-house with black-boards around.)" The play follows this suggestion after Teacher Dobbins

---

[11] *MTHL*, II, 471. The latter play was finished by 13 March 1884; Howells believed that it was "altogether too thin and slight" and "not more than half long enough" (*MTHL*, II, 485).

explains that the classroom will become a courtroom because the regular courtroom is too small.

After making such jottings and having decided which settings to use, the author (so far as one can guess on the basis of surviving notes) wrote a synopsis of each act (several synopses of Act IV, since he had trouble concluding several lines of action in it). He used only four settings: Act I, street before Tom's home; Act II, moonlit graveyard; Act III, country schoolroom; Act IV, the cave. He then proceeded to write the acts in full, frequently revising. The typescript for the play was prepared on three separate typewriters, possibly by different typists. Although the reason is obscure, I suspect the author had his manuscript typed in a hurry so that he could quickly get the play staged and start earning vast sums of money.[12] A large share of Act II was rewritten after it had been typed; the typed pages have been crossed out and the new portion in Mark Twain's hand has been inserted.

Completed on 29 January 1884, the play was copyrighted at once—on 1 February. The copyright was secured on the basis of the submission to the copyright office of a scene-by-scene synopsis. This summary is completely in accord with the dramatization, and therefore it presumably was written after the play was completed (see Appendix C).

Mark Twain was so pleased with this piece of work that even before he had finished it he was pondering on the cast which might properly perform it and trying to dictate terms. "I want Louis Aldrich to play Tom Sawyer's part, & Parsloe to play Huck Finn," he informed his business agent, Webster. "I think it would be a strong team—& have all the boys & girls played by grown people." He told Webster that the actor who played Tom must do so "till it is down to where it pays him only an average of $300 or $400 *a month* clear & above expenses, for a *whole season.*" Alternately with instructions to peddle the still unproduced Sellers play, he sent Webster comments on the new drama and instructions about arranging its production. "Tom Sawyer is *finished,*"

---

[12] In Act I–III, pp. 1–3 are in italic upper and lower case type (type *A*), 4–10 are in roman full capitals (type *B*), 11–27 in *A*, 28–31 in *B*, 32–35 in *A*, 36–43 in *B*, 44–51 in *A*, 52–top half of 67 in *B*, bottom half of 67–74 in *A*. Several of the shifts occur in the middle of a page of holograph manuscript, and about the same number at the top of a holograph manuscript page. The typescript of Act IV is in standard pica type. Although no holograph version has been found for Act IV, pp. 8, 11, 20, 22, and 26 are only partly filled, suggesting that the typist began work before the manuscript was completed, and typed the pages in batches as the author finished them.

he happily reported on 8 February, "& it is a *good* play—a good *acting* play." At the same time (probably because Aldrich and Parsloe had not jumped at the chance to sign for roles), he wanted to have James Lewis approached.[13] The reasons are indicated in a note in the Mark Twain Papers (Paine 159):

> The principal girls in this play can as well be full grown, (and fat or lean) and merely *dressed* as children. The burlesque will do no harm.
> *Jim* can be burlesqued also—a negro boy 6 feet high or 6 feet through.
> It is only Huck and Tom that must not be burlesqued.
> If Mr. Lewis and Miss Rehan had the parts of Tom and Huck, the rest would be undifficult.

The idea of having a woman play Tom or Huck or having actresses play both was not new. The author had spoken of having both roles played by women in a letter to Howells dated 13 July 1875, and he had mentioned the possibility to Conway on 24 July 1876. In notes written during 1884, he spoke of having Marie Burroughs in one role and Ada Rehan in the other, or of teaming up Lewis with Miss Rehan.[14]

Eventually the play was submitted to Daly, along with stern instructions about the casting, the premiere date, and the royalty arrangement.[15] On 27 February 1884 Daly rejected the chance to stage the play and incidentally commented upon the idea of giving the leading roles to adults:

> I fear that *Tom Sawyer* would not make a success at my theatre. After a very close reading I must disagree with you on the point that grown up people may successfully represent the boys & girls of your piece. Tom might be played by a clever comedian as a boy—but the other parts would seem ridiculous in grown peoples hands.

On the letter, Clemens wrote a note to his business agent, "Send & get the play, Charley."[16]

One hears no more about the author's attempting to dramatize his novel, but exactly a year later Clemens informed Howells that he had sold dramatic rights to *Tom Sawyer* "on a royalty & it is to be exploited presently in New York." Not having seen the manuscript, he added, he

---

[13] *MTBus*, pp. 232–235.
[14] *MTHL*, I, 95; *MTBus*, p. 257.
[15] *MTBus*, pp. 256–257. I assume that the "notes" on these pages were not written in May 1884, as seems to be indicated, because Daly's refusal, cited in the next footnote, was written some months before May.
[16] *MTBus*, pp. 236–237.

knew nothing about the dramatization. A play dramatizing the picnic
scene from *Tom Sawyer* was given on 11 June 1885 at the Star Theatre
in New York; and either this play or another titled *Tom Sawyer* ran for
a week in June 1890, another week in June 1891 at the Third Avenue
Theatre, New York, and a third week in January 1892 at the Harlem
Theatre.[17]

Meanwhile—perhaps after seeing one of these productions—Clemens had decided that his novel just could not be dramatized. Before he
left his summer residence near Elmira, New York, in 1887, a letter from
Susquehanna, Pennsylvania, dated 3 September 1887, and signed by
W. R. Ward reached him. Under the letterhead of the Kittie Rhoades
Theatrical Company it informed him that "we have taken the liberty to
try and dramatize your 'Tom Sawyer.'" Might the company advertise
this as the humorist's work? On the envelope, the recipient wrote, "For
Unmailed Letters," with the idea that the request and his unsent reply
would be included in an article that he was planning. Part of the
unmailed reply went:

> You are No. 1365. When 1364 sweeter and better people, including the
> author, have "tried" to dramatize Tom Sawyer and did not arrive, what
> sort of show do you suppose you stand? That is a book, dear sir, which
> cannot be dramatized. One might as well try to dramatize any other
> ⟨sermon.⟩ hymn. Tom Sawyer is simply a hymn, put into prose form to
> give it a worldly air.[18]

The play, the author continued, like all the dramatizations preceding it,
would "go out the back door the first night. . . . I have seen Tom
Sawyer's remains in all the different kinds of dramatic shrouds there
are."

III

A dramatization of a novel by Mark Twain which did not have to be
draped in a shroud was the actor Frank Mayo's version of *Pudd'nhead
Wilson*. Brander Matthews tells how Mayo succeeded in writing a play
which had a long run:

---

[17] *MTHL*, II, 520–521.
[18] ALS in MTP. The unmailed answer and what was, according to Clemens,
the mailed answer are in *MTL*, II, 476–479.

He simplified Mark's story and he amplified it; he condensed it and he heightened it; he preserved the ingenious incidents and the veracious characters; he made his profit out of the telling dialog; and he was skilful in disentangling the essentially dramatic elements of Mark's rather rambling story.[19]

Although in adapting *Tom Sawyer* for the stage Mark Twain simplified and condensed his story, and although he more or less managed to preserve most of "the veracious characters," he did not do these things satisfactorily,[20] and he failed to make other changes such as Mayo made.

Twain simplified his story by excluding many scenes—the Sunday school and church episodes, the wholesale conversions and backslidings of the boys of the village, for instance. Understandably, he did not dramatize two scenes which would have required the services of trained cats—the one in which Tom fed his aunt's pet the pain-killer and the one in which another cat removed the wig from Dobbins. He did not have Tom show off before Becky's home; he did not have Tom and Huck sign the secret pact in blood; and he did not include the thrilling scene wherein the two boys were trapped by Injun Joe and the stranger in the haunted house. He left out the whole of the Jackson's Island episode—the boyish pirates' idyllic adventures, Tom's secret visit to Aunt Polly, and the startling appearance of the boys at their own funeral. And since these and other omitted bits are memorable, it might be argued that he failed to preserve "the ingenious incidents."

Moreover, he had trouble of a sort that pestered him in writing most of his novels and all of his plays—the relating of incidents to an overall plot. When he wrote his only successful dramatization, one recalls, Twain used a plot supplied by someone else. When, in 1877, the producer John Brougham read "Cap'n Simon Wheeler, The Amateur Detective," he found it "altogether too diffuse in its present condition for dramatic representation. . . ."[21] Collaborating with Harte and

---

[19] "Mark Twain and the Theater," in *Playwrights on Playmaking and Other Studies of the Stage* (New York, 1923), p. 180.

[20] The boys lost their potential for growth. Muff Potter became more virtuous and hence a less believable and a simpler character than he was in the novel: he tries to get out of robbing the grave, and he fights the doctor not because he wants money but because the doctor insults him. Dobbins, too, is simplified and is robbed of the acidity that he shows in the novel.

[21] *MTB*, pp. 596. Matthews, *Playwrights*, p. 183, notices that as a playwright Twain "could not organize a structure with the necessary and harmonious connection and relation of its parts."

Howells on plays, the humorist depended upon them to supply plots, and even then the plays turned out badly.

The novel *Tom Sawyer* had a unity thrust upon it because, as an attack on Sunday-school, Good-and-Bad-Boy fiction, it showed how a real boy grew up; and although there were digressions, several persistent narrative strands showed a boy maturing. Each began with a childish action and concluded with a more mature one: the relationship of Tom and Becky, for instance, began with puppy love and a boyish courtship and ended with the boy's accepting punishment in place of the girl and with his comforting and protecting her in the cave. The Jackson's Island episode began with boyish thoughtlessness and ended with a display of mature concern for others. The Muff Potter strand began with a childish shrinking from duty and ended with Tom's testifying in court, despite danger. Tom talked irresponsibly with Huck at the start; at the end he assumed a grown-up role. Because childlike actions cluster in early chapters and more mature ones in later chapters, there is an overall development.[22]

In the play, only the line of action involving Muff Potter suggests Tom's maturing, and it does so sketchily because Twain did not carry over into the play the boy's struggle with his conscience about helping Muff, which was developed at length in the novel. The action therefore loses much significance. The Jackson's Island happenings disappear. The love story loses its relevance, for while the novel develops the changing relationship between Tom and Becky, the play inexplicably divides Tom's affections between Becky and another girl. Tom's relationship with Becky therefore shows no development whatever.[23] And as the drama ends, instead of talking in an adult fashion, Tom is mocking Aunt Polly by standing on his head. Not only does the overall structure of the novel disintegrate in the play; the character of Tom which that structure revealed loses much of its lifelike complexity.

---

[22] "So endeth this chronicle," says the Conclusion. "It being strictly a history of a *boy*, it must stop here; the story could not go much further without becoming the history of a *man*." See Walter Blair, "On the Structure of *Tom Sawyer*," *Modern Philology*, XXXVII (August 1939), 75–88; Hamlin Hill, "The Composition and the Structure of *Tom Sawyer*," *American Literature*, XXXII (January 1961), 379–392.

[23] Where in the novel Tom shows that he is maturing by gallantly taking Becky's punishment, in the play he says, "I cannot tell a *lie*—it was Alfred *Temple!*" and he stands by while Alfred is whipped. In the book, Tom shows bravery by rescuing Becky in the cave; in the play Huck joins Tom in saving both Becky and Amy.

In addition to the narrative which shows Tom's maturing, the quality in the novel that led Twain to speak of it as a hymn helped it achieve a degree of unity. This quality was the book's atmosphere—a unique blend of the idyllic and the terrifying. As DeVoto says,

> It is a hymn: to boyhood, to the fantasies of boyhood, to the richness and security of the child's world, to a phase of American society now vanished altogether, to the loveliness of woods and prairies that were the Great Valley, to the river . . . It is wrought out of beauty and nostalgia. Yet Mark is nowhere truer to us, to himself, or to childhood than in the dread which holds this idyl inclosed. The book so superbly brings the reader within its enchantment that some reflection is required before he can realize of what ghastly stuff it is made—murder and starvation, grave-robbery and revenge, terror and panic, some of the darkest emotions of men, some of the most terrible fears of children, and the ghosts and demons and death portents of the slaves.[24]

One who searches for reasons why this "enchantment" is not carried over into the play finds several. A remarkably large number of descriptive passages do much to create both idyl and terror in the book: peaceful St. Petersburg bathed in sunshine, its breezes filled with the perfume of flowers; the town at night, warm in moonlight; the drowsy church and schoolroom; "nature in a trance" in the woods on Cardiff Hill and on Jackson's Island; the dark and weatherbeaten graveyard with winds moaning through its trees; the old tanyard at night, silent except for the lugubrious howls of a dog straying nearby; the frightening thunderstorms; the deadly silent haunted house; the labyrinthian cave. Mark Twain found no satisfactory substitute for these passages in the play. In the book, too, on many occasions the author unfolds Tom's thoughts and feelings—the workings of the boy's conscience, his moments of delight, tenderness, loneliness, melancholy, and fear. Nothing in the play persuades one that Tom feels any of these deeply. Beyond the fact that the author was forced by his medium to show only exteriors, another reason is that he so determinedly concentrated upon the broadest comedy. In the play burlesque looms large—in the first-act whitewashing of the calf by the boys, in the scene in Act III where Aunt Polly mistakenly believes that Huck is praying when he is playing mumblety-peg, in the final moments of Act IV wherein Tom engages in acrobatics, and in a dozen only slightly less obvious scenes. And the broad comedy plays hob with the audience's empathy, robbing even the

---

[24] *The Portable Mark Twain* (New York, 1946), pp. 32–33.

most pathetic scenes of pathos, even the most melodramatic scenes of suspense.

A final difficulty, related to this one, resulted from Twain's failure to make individual scenes diverting or engrossing. Robert A. Wiggins has noticed that the humorist had a habit of "concentrating upon the scene or episode as the chief structural element." "His fiction," Wiggins continues, "abounds in memorable scenes remembered out of their context." [25] In this dramatization, Twain similarly concentrates upon episodic units. But inexplicably he gallops through scenes that might have been developed through action and loafs through scenes which consist mainly of talk. The murder scene, for example, he might well have prolonged to develop excitingly, and the trial scene he might have filled with suspense, but both are too brief in the play to build to any sort of a climax.

Contrast what he does in Act I: He starts with an attenuated, desultory discussion by two little girls of their strange notions about love, pausing only to force dollops of exposition down the audience's throats. Next he brings in the Negro boy Jim to engage in a soliloquy enlivened by a minimum of action (he eats a cake). Next Jim talks with Muff Potter—more exposition. After the pair departs, Aunt Polly enters, speaks at length, talks briefly with Mary, and they leave. Now Tom enters and perpetrates a long soliloquy. Only after all this relatively static talk, briefly interrupted by some banging firecrackers, does Twain provide a few minutes of action in Tom's fight with Alfred Temple and the whitewashing of the fence. The concentration upon talk at the expense of action is typical.

Such proportioning, natural enough for a comic lecturer who so consistently created laughter by artfully presenting chatter which meandered in a seemingly artless way, marred this dramatic composition. Twain himself evidently saw that a conversation between Tom and Huck in Act II, drawn from three chapters of *Tom Sawyer* and one of *Huckleberry Finn,* stretched too long. He chopped out the part taken from the as yet unpublished *Huck.* But his reluctance to do so is shown by his marginal comment: "Might a trifle of this be preserved and thrust in back yonder . . . ?" A wonderful talker who appreciated his own artistry had a hard time shutting up even one of his invented characters.

---

[25] "Mark Twain and the Drama," *American Literature,* XXV (November 1953), 282.

There were other reasons why even in an era when inferior dramas often did very well, this dramatization never found a producer; but those which have been detailed here are enough to account for its failure. Mark Twain's letter of 1890 to Daniel Frohman which condemned Mrs. Abby S. Richardson's dramatization of *The Prince and the Pauper,* ironically enough, applies equally well to his own dramatization of *Tom Sawyer:*

> I should have perceived that Mrs. Richardson's contract to dramatize the book had not been fulfilled; that she had . . . got as far away from the book as she could; that she had merely transferred *names* from the book, and often left the *characters* that belonged to them behind; that whenever she meddled with a high character she lowered its tone; that whenever she took an incident from the book, she distorted and damaged it. . . .[26]

He scolded others; himself he could not scold.

---

[26] Dated 2 February 1890, in the Estelle Doheny Collection, St. John's Seminary, Camarillo, California.

Tom Sawyer

(TIME—40 YEARS AGO.)
SCENE—A MISSOURI VILLAGE ON
MISSISSIPPI RIVER.

Act I.

Pull up garters—no, re-tie them. Two girls of ten near a village house; smart summer dresses of fashion of 40 years ago —hair in two long plaited tails down back, ends tied with ribbon. They are nibbling long striped sticks of candy. Broad Leghorn hats, with long broad ribbons.

Gracie Miller—I'll tell you something Bessie Thompson told me if you'll never tell anybody I told you.

Amy Lawrence—O will you. Good. I won't ever tell.

G—'Pon your word and sacred honor?

A—'Pon my word and sacred honor.

G—'Deed and deed and double deed?

A—'Deed and deed and double deed—O do tell me, won't you, Gracie?

G—Well, I don't know. Wait till I tie my (*turns her back to audience and ties her garter*). I'm afraid you'll tell.—And besides—

258

A—O I'll never tell. What is it, now, Gracie?

G—I don't think I ought to tell you, Amy, because sometimes you know things and you won't ever tell me.

A—Gracie Miller! You ought to be ashamed of yourself. I never never *never* knew anything and didn't tell you. I always run and tell you the first thing. Who did I run and tell, the time that my brother Jim was sliding on cellar door and stuck a splinter in his heart?

G—Well, what of *that? That* wasn't anything.

A—It *wasn't,* wasn't it? Didn't you say I was a dear good *thing* for telling you before I told anybody else, and you said you'd never forget me as long as ever you *lived,* and any time you had anything to tell you'd go as straight as ever you could walk and tell me?— *there* now. And every single solitary time we have a new crop of kittens at home, who do I run and tell first? Why you—you!—so *there* now!

G—'Mf. I don't care anything about your old kittens. I reckon we've got cats enough; yes, and *thousands* of kittens—bran new ones—every week.

A—O yes, of course you do.

G—Well we *do,* Miss. Nine *hundred* anyway—and I *know* it.

A—Gracie Miller, what you've said is not half of it true, and you *know* it; and so it's a *sin;* and the dreadfulest *kind* of a sin. It's *arson,* that's what it is.

G—I don't care what it is. And I don't care what you *think* about it—so *there.* I don't like you *anyhow.*

A—(*Crying.*)—Gracie Miller, you're just as spiteful and ugly and disagreeable as you can *be,* and I don't like you one *bit,* and I *never* did—and I hope you won't ever ask to swing on our *gate* any more in this *world;* for I shouldn't ever wish such characters to swing on it.

G—Nobody wants to. I'd rather go without happiness all my *days* than swing on a gate with people that it's a dishonor to swing on a gate with.

A—Gracie Miller, I'll never speak to you again as long as I *live*—never.

G—(*Crying.*)—I don't *want* you to speak to me. I wouldn't answer you if you *did*.—There, you can take back your old doll—I wouldn't *have* it. (*Throwing it down spitefully.*) Give me *mine*.

A—(*Throwing down a similar rag doll.*) Take it and *welcome*.— I wouldn't soil my *hands* with it.

> (*They pick up the respective dolls and turn away crying. They pause apart and sob awhile, eyeing each other askance. Then Amy addressing vacancy.*)

A—I'm sure I don't care. I reckon I know something *too*. And what's more, I'll never *tell*.

> (*G—pricks up her ears, but does not respond. A—continues presently.*)

A—Somebody's come to *town*. I know who it is.

G—(*To vacancy.*)—I know of somebody that's come to town— this very *day*, too. And I reckon I know his *name*, too. (*A. is interested.*) And I know something that somebody said about Tom Sawyer.

A—(*To vacancy.*) Tom *Sawyer!*

G—Nobody knows it but *me*. I'd a *told* somebody if they'd a *behaved*.

> (*Both girls edge toward each other sheepishly—both afraid to make the first advance toward reconciliation. Wiping their eyes on their aprons they edge together back to back—presently A. furtively looks over G.'s shoulder and then timidly passes her doll around. G. looks at it a moment, takes it, passes her doll, which A. takes. Then*)

A—I didn't mean anything by what I said, Gracie.

G—(*facing around*) Didn't you, Amy? Well, I didn't mean anything by what *I* said. If you'll make up, *I* will.

A—I'm agreed! O you dear! (*They kiss.*) I'll give you a bite of my *candy* if you'll give me a bite of yours. (*They measure and take the biggest bites they can, and then examine to see who got the best of it.*)

G—(*munching*) I love you better than anybody in the *world*, Amy.

A—(*munching and talking thickly*) And I love *you* better than anybody in the world, Gracie. You don't despise our cats *now*, DO you, Gracie?

G—No I *love* them; and I can swing on your *gate*, now, *can't* I, Amy?

A—Yes, just as much as ever you *want* to. I want you to come to my house just whenever you *can*; and I'll come to *your* house, too.

G—O, how nice! Amy, I'll *tell* you that, now, if you want me to.

A—O, *do*, Gracie, *that's* a love.

G—(*whispering mysteriously but loudly*) Ben Rogers says you and Tom Sawyer's *engaged!*

A—O, what a *story!*

G—O, you needn't try to look so! I've *caught* you!—Why your face is as red as *fire!* Now own up, Amy—DO, I won't tell a breathing soul—and then I'll tell *you* something.

A—Will you, Gracie? *Will* you, now?

G—I will, *indeed.*

A—(*diffidently and mysteriously*)—Well, he's pestered me so long that at last I *did* tell him I—I—(*Heaving her apron over her head*) loved him just a tiny tiny *little* bit!—

G—O, that's so nice! It's *so* nice! And when is it going to *be?*

A—What?

G—Why, the *wedding?*

A—O, I—I—well I never *thought* of that.

G—Never *thought* of it! Why there must be a *wedding*, of course.

A—Yes I reckon that is so. When would *you* have it?

G—O, I'd have it right *away*. It's *ever* so much fun.

A—Why? Have *you* ever been married?

G—Only once.

A—Is it a *real* wedding?

G—O, no, just *pretend*, you know.

A—Who did you marry?

G—The. Lawson.

A—Why *I* never knew that. What broke it *off?*

G—Nothing broke it off; I'm a *widow* now.

A—Why how can *that* be? The. *Lawson* isn't dead.

G—I know; but we only *pretend.*

A—Oh,—I see.

G—Yes, I wanted to go into mourning, and so I thought I'd be a *widow.*

A—What did you want to do *that* for?

G—Well, I think mourning's nice, and besides I wanted to do like young Mrs. Beesom. (*Impressively*) Every day, she goes to her husband's grave and cries around and carries flowers there.

A—Yes, but you didn't have any *grave,* and then it's so far to the graveyard, too.

G—I know, but there's a *ridge* in our back yard, where they put *tur*nips under in the winter, and I make believe it's a *grave,* you know. I pretend to be in *mourning,* and go there and *cry,* and have *such* a good time. And I've got a long piece of *stovepipe* standing up on the ridge, and it looks *just* like a monument.

A—O, how nice! I wish *I* was a widow.

G—Well you can be one. All you do, you marry Tom Sawyer, and then pretty soon you let on that he has got the measles or the whooping cough and *died,* and then if you can get a piece of stovepipe I'll let you have part of my grave, and—

A—O, it would be too lovely for *anything;* but I couldn't *bear* to think of Tom being *dead.* I—I—I'll tell *you,* Grace, but nobody *else.* I don't love Tom just a tiny tiny *little* bit. Let me whisper to you—I love—him—more—than—*sour*-grass! (*Hides face in apron.*) Gracie, don't you ever *tell.*

G—O, it's splendid—it's just *too* charming. *I* won't ever tell. Deed and deed and *double* deed I won't. Mayn't I come to the wedding?

A—O, of *course!* But *widows* don't go, do they?

G—No, they don't go to circuses, nor weddings, nor funerals, nor hardly *any* kinds of frolics at *all*—because it isn't *proper,* you know —but then I'll go into *second* mourning for a while, and *then* I can.

A—How do you go into second mourning?

G—O, *that's* easy. Do you see this little bow of black ribbon pinned on the top of my hat? Well that means I'm in full *mourn-ing.*—But if I take that off and put on a *lavender*-colored bow, I'll be in *second* mourning,—and *then* you can carry on as much as ever you want to.

A—That's good. Gracie, who *is* it that's come to town?

G—Why it's a boy from St. *Louis.*

A—From St. *Louis!* My! he must be *grand!*

G—'Deed they *say* he is. His name's Alfred *Temple*—ain't it a sweet name? And they say he dresses in Sunday clothes all the *week.*

A—No! Why his folks must be EVER so rich.

G—Yes, they say they *are.* They say his father's worth more'n a thousand *dollars.*

A—O dear, that must be *heaps* of money! How much *is* a thousand dollars?

G—I don't know. But I reckon it's sixteen or seventeen *barrels* full—they *say* it is. They say that boy wears *gloves,* Sundays; and standing *co*llars; and they say he wears a *necktie* every single day of his life—just the same as a *man* would. Goodness, won't the boys *hate* him!

A—*Hate* him! Why they'll heave mud at him till he'll look like *Adam.*—I mean before he was whitewashed. I hope Tom *Sawyer* won't get into trouble with him, but I know he *will.* Well, of course they'll all try to *whip* him, just because he's a *new* boy. And then, you know, they won't *stand* a boy that's so plaguey *respectable*— and a *city* boy, at *that.* But I wish I could *see* him—I never *saw* a *city* boy, and I've so *wanted* to!

G—So have *I.*—Amy, are you going to the *war* this afternoon?

A—I *want* to go, but—

G—But *what?*

A—Well, you know *Tom's* captain of the Bengal *Tigers,* and it might make *talk.* Are *you* going?

G—Yes, I'd *like* to go, but I reckon I won't.

A—*I* know why!

G—*Why,* now?

A—You know very *well!* Who's captain of the Bloody *Avengers?* Ah!—

G—'Mf! Who cares for Joe *Harper?* I'm sure I don't.

A—O, Gracie *Miller*, what a *fib!*

G—Well, I *don't* care for that cripple. At least I don't care *much*.

A—O, how you *talk.* Why *everybody* knows. Now own *up*, Gracie. You're not going to keep anything from *me*, are you? You wouldn't do *that?*

G—Well, Amy, I *won't*—but you mustn't ever *tell*, WILL you? (*In confidential tone.*) As soon as I'm out of mourning, we're going to get *engaged.* Now *please* don't tell. Amy, guess what he gave me to *remember* him by forever and ever and *ever?*

A—O what *was* it? *Please* tell me.

G—A beautiful brass *door*-knob—and it's hardly battered a *bit. There* it is. (*Producing it.*)

A—O, what a *love* of a thing! (*Impressively:*) Gracie, I should think every time you looked at this, it would make you *better* and *nobler.*

G—It *does*, Amy. I put it under my head, every *night.*—I mean to keep it and love it as long as ever I *live.* And when I die I want flowers in my coffin, and I want my hands crossed on my breast— *so*, like Johnny *Patterson's* was, that *died*—and I want to hold this door-knob just so—(*in her clasped hands*).

A—O, that will be lovely. *So* lovely! Everybody will talk about it. I mean to ask Tom to give *me* a door-knob just *like* it, when he finds one; and he's *likely* to, because he's always away off in the woods and all sorts of strange places, digging for *treasures*—treasures buried by pirates and *robbers* and such people, you know. And if he finds a treasure, and there's a *door*-knob amongst it, and I *ask* him for it, I know he'll *give* it to me—and I WILL ask him—I'll ask him the first thing, when I *see* him. Gracie, when is the *war* going to come off?

G—About 3 o'clock this afternoon. Haven't you been invited?

A—O, yes, Tom *always* invites me, but I forgot the *time.* What is it *about*, this time?

G—Well—let's *see. Last* Saturday the battle was because the Bloody Avengers said the Bengal Tigers were *aristocrats.* Saturday *before* it was because the Bengal Tigers said the Bloody Avengers were *chicken*-thieves. I think it was so *late*, last Saturday, before the war was *over*, that they didn't fix *up* what to fight about *this* time—so I heard one of the boys say they were going to fight *first* and then settle what it was about *after*wards. Now you come to *my* house and stay till the *war*, and I'll show you all my things, and my grave and my monument, and let you see me *cry*.

A—O, *that* will be nice. Gracie, don't you ever, *ever* tell! (*Exhibits a cake, skips to the cottage door and deposits it on the step.*)

G—O, my! Is that for *Tom?*

A—Yes. Don't you ever *tell*.

G—*I* won't. Will he know who put it there?

A—Yes. I promised I'd do it—it's a *love* gift. And it's got a beautiful, beautiful little *love*-letter in*side* of it. Come along—come along! *Run!*

(*Exit both.*)

(*Enter from the cottage door, a darkey boy—Jim—playing a jewsharp.*)

Jim—Gitt'n' pooty *warm* in dah. Ole missis she don't *like* de way Mars Tom's been a doin'. She 'clar she mos' half a mind to make him *work* to-day. Dat won't suit Mars *Tom, I* tell you! Yah-yah-yah! Mars Tom he want to go to de *war*. I reckon Mars *Sid* gittin' Mars Tom into dis trouble. Mars Sid he de *good* boy. *He* like to go to de *Sunday* School; but ef you give Mars *Tom* he choice, wether he'll go to de *Sunday* school er to de *prar*-meeting, w'y mos'ly he gen'ally druther go to de *circus*. But Mars Tom he mighty good to *me*; gives me *lots* o' things; but Mars Sid *he* don't never do nothin' like dat. He too awful *good*, I reckon. Yah-yah-yah. (*Picks up Tom's cake, crams it all into his mouth and goes to munching it and looking around for more, and talking and munching with full mouth all the time.*) No in*deedy*, Mars Sid he de *nice* boy. *He* never git a lick—don't never ketch *him* in no mischief. Dat cake mighty *good*; somebody *drap* dat, I reckon. (*Making ghastly efforts to swallow it.*) But 'pears to *me* like dey'd sumf'n *in* dat cake. I reck'n it's a *noos*paper. *Feel* like a noospaper—*tas'* like a noospaper—an' I bet she *is* a noospaper, *too*. Wonder what dey want to put her in de *cake* fer—fer to fill *up*, I reck'n. It's *k'yerlessness* to take 'n' wase a *noospaper* dat-away. (*Gets it down with a final frightful struggle, and caresses his stomach, not altogether gratefully.*) By jing, she's down, at *las'*. But I ain't gwyne to subscribe no *mo'* for dat paper. (*Sits down and works patiently at a coarse comb and piece of paper trying to construct a musical instrument.*) Ole Missis she do *love* Mars Tom, for *all* he up to so much *devilment*, and jes' pester de *life* outen her.—She don't *like* to *lick* Mars Tom, but den my goodness she *got* to lick him *sometimes*. *All* boys is got to be licked—case if you don't lick 'em dey don't *'mount* to nuffin. Ole Injun Joe *he* say dey ain't wuff a dam—(*or substitute a spasm of the stomach in place of the dam*). I wisht I das't to swah like dat Injun Joe—I don't see why dey *hab* a debble, for to keep a body in a *sweat* all de time. I wisht *I's* de debble—'I' jings I'd warm Mars *Sid* sometimes, I don't reckon. Yah-yah-yah. O, no, I reckon not! Yah-yah-yah. Well, *I* don't see dat axe nowhah.—*I* can't split de kindlin' wood if I can't find de *axe*. I reckon maybe it's in de back *yard*—or down *suller*,—or in de *kitchen* som'ers. I'll go *see*. I can't never remember what I done wid de axe.—If ole missis ketch me loafin roun' heah, she take an' bust me wide *open*—DAT she will. Dah's ole Muff *Potter*—HE kin fix dis comb, *I* bet you. *He* know how to do mos' *anything*. (*Enter ragged good-natured loafer.*) Mars *Potter*, I wisht you'd fix dish yer *comb* fer me—somehow she won't *go*. (*Getting up.*)

Muff. Lemme *see* it, Jim. (*Tries it.*) Your *paper's* too *rumply*, Jim, *that's* what's the trouble. (*Gets a lot of boy's rubbish out of his pocket, selects a piece of paper, fits it, plays a tune.*)

Jim. (*Trying it successfully.*) I's much *obleeged* to you, Mars *Muff*, 'DEED I is. I *knowed* you could fix it. Waz you lookin for Mars *Tom*?

Muff. No, I was looking for Injun *Joe*. Have you seen him?

Jim. Yes, sir, I *has*, en what's *more* en dat, I's *felt* him, too. He come by heah 'bout a half an hour ago—en *'course* he fetch me a wipe side de *head*—he *always* do—I wish somebody'd take en *kill* dat ornery *half*-breed, dat's 'ut *I* wisht.

Muff. What does he do *that* for, Jim?

Jim. I dono. But I reckon maybe he's 'fraid I'll fogit dat I *laugh* at him wunst when he 'uz *drunk* en a ole sow run 'twix' his *laigs* en up*sot* him. Dat 'uz mo' en a year *ago;* but he allays fetch me one side de *head,* every time *sence*—when I don't see him a-comin' *fust.* What does you want to see dat rubbage fer, Mars Muff?—what does you want 'long o' *him?*

Muff. O nothing, (*going*) nothing particular. Which way'd he go?

Jim. Down todes Dr. *Robberson's.* (*Going; and tuning up on the comb.*) I's mighty much *obleeged* to you fer fixin dish yer ole *pianner* fer me, Mars Muff—she go fust-*rate,* now, *'deed* she do.

Muff. O, that's all right, Jimmy.

(*Exit both.*)

Aunt Polly and Mary.

Aunt Polly—(*flying out at the door, fire crackers tied to a long string behind her or the popping of them heard before she appears.*)—Tom *Sawyer!* (*Pause.*) You *Tom*—! well, I lay if I get hold of you I'll—T-o-m *Sawyer!* (*Pause—listening.*)

Mary. (*Looking about.*) Aunty, he isn't here *anywhere.*

A. P. Well, look around, look around, child. (*Mary moves off, shading her eyes with her hand, peering rearward.*) I never did see the beat of that boy. Y-o-u-u *Tom!*

Mary. How did it *happen,* aunty?

A. P. Happen? Why, whilst I was threatening to make him *work* to-day for playing hookey *yesterday,* and just turned around a minute to reach for my switch and give him a *trouncing,* he hitched that dreadful string of *crackers* to my dress behind, and set them *off;* and of course before I could come to my right senses, he was out and gone. Y-o-u-u *Tom!* Keep a sharp lookout, Mary. Don't you see anything of him *yet?*

Mary. No. But I'll go further. (*Moving off*) Which way did he go?

A. P. Bless your heart, how should *I* know? I thought the *world* was coming to an end; how could *I* think to look which way the scamp *went.* (*Smiles, and says aside, gently*)—Hang the boy, can't I ever *larn* anything? Hasn't he played tricks enough on me for me to be looking *out* for him by this time? But *old* fools are the *biggest* fools, they say. Can't learn an *old* dog new *tricks,* as the saying is. But deary me, he never plays them *alike* two days, and so how's a body to *know* what's coming? He appears to know just how long he can torment me before he gets my *temper* up; and he knows if he can manage to put me *off* for a minute, or get out of my *sight,* it's all *gone* again, and I can't hit him a *lick.* (*With a sigh.*) I'm not doing my *duty* by that boy, and that's the *truth,* goodness *knows.* Spare the rod and spoil the *child,* as the good book says. I'm laying up sin and suffering for us *both,* I *know.* He's full of the old *scratch,* but laws-a-me, he's my own dead *sister's* boy, poor thing, and I haven't got the *heart* to lash him, somehow. Every time I let him *off,* my conscience does *hurt* me so; and every time I *hit* him my old heart most *breaks.* Well-a-well, man that is born of woman is of few days and full of *trouble,* as Scripture says, and I reckon it's *so.* I'll just be *obliged* to make him work, to-day, to punish him and make him see the *enormity* of touching off fire-crackers right under a person's nose when her back is turned and she unpre*pared* for it and not *expecting* anything. It's mighty *hard* to make him work *Saturdays,* when all the boys are having *holiday;* but he *hates* work more than he hates anything *else,* and I've *got* to do *some* of my duty by him or I'll be the *ruination* of the child.

    Mary. (*Reappearing.*) I can't see a *sign* of him *anywhere,* aunty.

    A. P. Well, come *along* then, and never *mind.* (*Pause—reflecting.*) Mary, would you make him work to-day?

    Mary. There, aunty dear, you are weakening *already.* you won't make him work to-day, if *that's* what you want to know.

    A. P. (*Bridling.*) Go in the *house!* —and stop your *impudence.* I'm *not* weakening, at *all.* I've provided a great quantity of *whitewash,* and a new *brush;* and I've told him a dozen *times* that if he ever misbehaved *again* I'd make him whitewash this *fence;* and I tell you right *now*—and *here*—that as sure as the sun is in the *sky,* if he ever misbehaves another single *time,* I WILL make him whitewash it.

Mary. (*Aside—laughing clandestinely*) I *knew* she couldn't do it—she's too soft-hearted.

A. P. (*Observing her a moment, severely*)—Go in the *house*, I tell you!

(*Exit both into the house.*)

Tom Sawyer (*in gaudy General's uniform.*) (*Glides in, stealthily, on white pine stilts, dragging a dead rat on a string. Dismounts. Examines rat—swings it.*)

Tom. (*Solus.*) It's a *noble* good rat. (*Goes looking around for the cake, talking.*) Nobody but a *goose* would have *sold* it for a *fish-hook*—but Tom *Hooker* doesn't know anything. (*Stands in an awkward, uncomfortable attitude a moment.*) No——yes—— no——yes, they *are* b'George! There's a *hole* in my pocket, *sure*, and those fishing worms are getting *out*. (*Pulls out a handful of apparently squirming worms and counts them.*) There's five gone—I had nineteen. (*Kicks—apparently shakes out one or two; kicks again, no result.*) Well, I've got *three* back *anyway*; never mind the other two. (*Sits on floor.*) I wonder what I'll *do* with them, now. I can't trust that *pocket* any more. (*Reflects a while—then puts the lot in his cap without comment, and puts his cap on. Gets up and glances around again.*) Now what has ever become of that *cake*? I can't find it *anywhere*. (*Pause—reflects—manner changes.*) She said she'd leave a cake—with a *love*-letter in it—and *this* is the way she keeps her *word*. (*Pause.*) Well—it just means *this*: Tom Sawyer's not *good* enough for her; and she's gone and taken up with somebody *else*—that's what it means. Very well, Miss *Amy*, (*sitting down and propping his jaws in his hands*) if a person's heart is *nothing* to you, and you can break it and never *care*, and just *gloat* over his sufferings (*snuffling*) and be *happy*, and him so *miserable*, and rejoice in seeing him go *down*, and get to be *dissipated* and de*spised*, and fill a drunkard's *grave*, (*over-come by his feelings*)— well, let it *be* so, since it *must* be so—and since you are de*termined* to *have* it so, and may you always be *happy*, and never come to see and feel what you've *done*, and how you've blighted a person that *loved* you so—(*taking off his cap and fondling the worms tearfully*)

—and who was always thinking of *you*, and trying to make your life sweet and bright and *heavenly*, and got all these *worms* for you, and was going to give you this *very rat*—(*gets up and sadly throws the worms and the rat aside, snuffling.*) They're nothing to me, *now*. They have lost all that made them noble and beautiful. They were a *joy* to me, as long as I could think of *her* having them, and they reminding her of *me* whenever she looked at them—but that is all gone *by*, now. No—let them go—rats and worms are for the gay and happy—they cannot cheer, they cannot *heal*, a broken heart. (*Pause—then gloomily.*) Well, since it must be so—since it is forced upon me, be it so: I will lead a life of crime. (*Suspiciously —jealously*)—But who is this other she has cast me off for? Some proud *rich* person? Of *course*—I might have *known* it. They are all *alike*. Is it that *new* boy? Is it that St. *Louis* boy? I just *know* it is. Well if I don't make him climb a— I reckon that's him coming, *now*. (*Pause—weakening.*) He's *bigger'n* I *expected*. (*Pause.*) I wonder if it isn't nobler just to *scorn* him,—and not take the least *notice* of him—no more than if he was a *dog*. (*Pause.*) He's *considerable* bigger than I *reckoned* he'd be. (*Pause.*) Aunt *Polly* says if you *despise* a mean low scoundrel that's *injured* you, and don't take the least *notice* in the *world* of him, it cuts him to the *heart*—and hurts him a *hundred* times worse than it would to *whip* him till he couldn't stand *up*. It shows him that you are too proud to dirty your *hands* with such characters.

> (*Enter Temple, neatly dressed, and simpering along daintily and complacently. The boys eye each other contemptuously— sidle warily round each other, still eyeing.*)

Tom. I can *whip* you.

Alfred Temple. I'd like to see you *try* it.

T. Well, I can *do* it.

A. No you can't, *either*.

T. Yes, I *can*.

A. No you *can't*.

T. I *can*.

A. You *can't*.

T. Can.

A. Can't.

(*Uncomfortable pause.*)

T. What's your *name?*

A. 'Tisn't any of your *business.*

T. Well I'll *make* it my business.

A. Well, why *don't* you?

T. If you say much, I *will.*

A. Much—much—much. *There,* now.

T. O, you think you're mighty *smart,* DON'T you. I could whip you with one *hand* tied behind me.

A. Well, why don't you *do* it?—you *say* you can.

T. Well I *will,* if you fool with me.

A. O yes—I've seen whole *families* in the same *fix.*

T. Smarty! You think you're *some,* now, *don't* you. O *what* a hat!

A. You can *lump* that hat if you don't like it. I dare you to knock it *off;* and anybody that'll take a *dare—*

T. You're a *scrub!*

A. You're *another.*

T. You're *another*—and a *fighting* one, and dasn't take it *up.*

A. Aw—take a *walk!*

T. Say—if you give me much more of your lip I'll thrash you till you can't stand *up.*

A. O, of *course* you will.

T. Well, I *will.*

A. Well why don't you *do* it, then? What do you keep *saying* you will, for? Why don't you *do* it? It's because you're *afraid.*

T. I *ain't* afraid.

A. You *are.*

T. I *ain't.*

A. You *are.*

(*Another pause, and more eyeing and sidling around. Presently they are shoulder to shoulder, and pushing each other.*)

T. Get *away* from here!

A. Get away *yourself!*

T. I *won't.*

A. I won't *either.*

(So they stand, each shoving against the other, and panting, but neither getting an advantage. Then each relaxes his strain with watchful caution.)

T. You're a *sheep!* I'll tell my big *brother* on you, and he is seven feet *high* and can whip you with his little *finger.*

A. What do *I* care for your big brother? I've got a brother that's bigger than *he* is, and can throw him over that *fence,* too, just as easy as *nothing.*

T. *(Contemptuous snort)* 'Mf.

A. *(snort)* 'Mf yourself.

(Tom draws a line on the ground.)

T. I dare you to step *over* that, and I'll whip you till you can't *crawl.*

(A. promptly steps over, and the two stand stomach to stomach.)

A. Now you *said* you'd do it, now let's *see* you do it.

T. Don't you *crowd* me, now; you better look *out.*

A. Well, you *said* you'd do it, why don't you *do* it?

T. For two cents I *will* do it.

    (A. takes two coppers from his pocket and holds them out with derision.)

T. *(Contemplates them a moment, then turns away and starts slowly off, with his nose in the air.)* I scorn to have anything to *do* with such low characters. I wouldn't dirty my *hands* with you. I *want* to fight—and I can hardly keep *from* it—and I could whip you in two *seconds* if I *wanted* to, but I don't *want* to, because my aunt Polly she doesn't *like* fighting, and she says—

A. *(Mockingly and with great derision)* O, it's his aunt *Polly,*— the dear old—

T. *(facing about—in passionless tone, but very significantly)*— Hold *on*—you want to go mighty *careful,* now, when you talk about *her.*

A. *Why* do I?

T. *(Slowly, but in a tone which means business.)*—Because if you were to say just one, single, little, disrespectful *word*—

A. *(Interrupting)*—I'll say a *hundred.* She's an old—

(*Tom is into him in a second—rattling fight—A. down at last, Tom astride him pounding his face.*)

T. (*A blow*) O, she *is*, is she? (*Blow*) She *is*, is she? (*and so on*) (*The family burst out from the house, meantime. Jim dances around with delight, Mary and Sid horror-stricken, Aunt Polly indignant.*)

Mary. O, Tom!

Sid. What a dreadful *spectacle!*

Jim. Gib it *to* him, Mars Tom—gib it *to* him. (*Is slapped sprawling by aunt Polly.*)

(*Aunt Polly dives in, snatches Tom off by the slack of his jacket collar. Alfred hobbles off half crying, rubbing his bruises, mumbling threats, and exit.*)

Aunt Polly. (*Contemplating Tom.*) You incorrigible boy. Now what do you *think* of yourself?

T. (*Head down, fumbling with his buttons sheepishly—pause —then meekly.*) I—I didn't *go* to do it.

A. P. (*Outraged*) Good land, he didn't *go* to do it! It did *itself,* I suppose. Tom, I've as good a mind as ever I had in my life to—(*suddenly seizes him and runs her hand through his hair.*) Well if you haven't been in swimming *again.* Your hair's damp.

T. (*Aside*) O, hang it, I thought I'd got it *dry.* (*Aloud—glancing up furtively.*) Presspiration.

A. Oh—well, it's lucky for you it *is.*

Mary. (*With glad solicitude.*) Dear, I'm glad he's innocent for *once!*

Sid. Yes, you could *know* he hasn't been in swimming, because you sewed *up* his collar, and it's *still* sewed.

T. (*Aside—suspiciously*) Now you better look *out,* Mr. Siddy.

A. P. (*Examining.*) Yes, *that's* so. Well, it's lucky for *you,* Tom, that it is so. For dear me, it won't do for me to be overlooking *all* your—

Sid. (*Reflectively*) I was thinking—no, I was mistaken—I *remember,* now, you *did* sew it with *black* thread.

T. (*aside*) All right, Mr. Siddy, I'll *lick* you for that!

A. P. I never did anything of the *kind*. I sewed it with *white* thread. Let me *see* it. (*Examines again. Contemplates Tom, sorrowfully, shaking her head. Pause—gravely takes him by the ear, and leads him into the house, the others following.*) Come along—no more holiday for *you*, THIS day.

Tom. Please, aunt Polly, oh, *please* let me off this *once*, and I'll never *never* do a thing again that you don't want me to. *Please,* aunty, *please—please*—just this *once*.

(*Exit all.*)

Enter Tom with long handled brush and bucket of white-wash.

Tom. (*Solus.*) It's such a *lovely* day—and I got to *work*. All the boys in town having *holiday*, and I got to be at *this* kind of thing. (*Surveying the job.*) A hundred thousand yards of board *fence*, forty-seven thousand feet *high*—(*sighing*) dear, I wish I'd died when I was a *baby* and wouldn't *minded* it. (*Passes his brush lazily along the top board once or twice—and compares it with what has yet got to be done; is discouraged and stops.*) It *isn't* any use—I *never* could do it all.

(*Enter Jim jewsharping, with tin pail.*) Say, Jim, *I'll* fetch the water, if you'll whitewash some.

Jim. Dasn't, Mars Tom. Ole Missis, she'd take en tar de *head* off'n me.

T. Sho. Perfect *nonsense. She* wouldn't hurt a *fly*. Jim, I'll give you six *marbles* if you will.

Jim. Mars Tom, I wisht I *could*, but—en *besides* I got sumfin de matter in my *stomach*, kaze I reck'n I done et sumfin 'at don't 'gree wid me, an'— (*rubbing stomach*)—

T. I'll give you all the marbles I've *got*—and my *stilts*—and a piece of *chalk*—and my tin *horn*—and a *rat*—and 17 *fishing* worms —and—(*Jim is about to yield—sets his pail down, while Tom is taking out his marbles.*) (*Aunt Polly appears at the door and gives them a look—Jim flies, and Tom gets immediately to work—Aunt Polly re-enters, closes door, and pulls down the blinds—or leaves them down as they were.*)

T. (*Makes a dash or two and quits.*) O dear, the *boys* will be coming along, directly, and I can't look them in the *face* I'll be so ashamed. And they'll make *fun* of me. Oh, I just can't *bear* it. (*Gets about 20 worthless odds and ends from his bulging pockets and contemplates them.*) No, it isn't any *use*—I can't *hire* them to help me—I'm not *rich* enough. They'll only just stand around and make *fun* of me. There comes Ben *Rogers*, NOW, the very worst one of the *lot*, to make fun of a person. (*With a sudden glad inspiration*) O, I've got it—I know what I'll do. (*Goes to whitewashing, carefully and deliberately*)

> Enter Ben Rogers. (*Eating an apple and rolling a hoop. Stops and stares.*)

Rogers. Hel-lo. You're up a stump, *ain't* you!

> (*Tom absorbed in his work—apparently doesn't hear. Surveys his work with the eye of an artist—adds another touch. Keeps stepping back, surveying, with head on one side, and carefully retouching.*)

Rogers. Hi-*yi!* Got to *work*, hey?

T. (*Suddenly glancing over his shoulder.*) Why, it's *you*, Ben. I wasn't *noticing*. (*Resumes work.*)

R. I'm going in swimming. Don't you wish *you* could? But of course you'd rather *work*, WOULDN'T you? *Course* you would.

T. (*Indifferently—and still retouching.*) What do you *call* work?

R. (*astonished.*) Why, Caesar's ghost, ain't *that* work?

T. Well, maybe it *is*, maybe it *isn't*. All *I* know is, it suits Tom Sawyer.

R. O, *come*, now, you don't mean to let on you *like* it?

T. (*Still artistically retouching.*) *Like* it? Well, I don't see why I shouldn't like it. Does a boy get a chance to whitewash a fence every day?

> (*This puts the thing in a new light. Rogers grows deeply interested. Watches Tom a while, then says.*)

R. Say, Tom, let *me* whitewash a little.

> (*Tom considers—reflects—half passes the brush to Rogers— changes his mind, and resumes work.*)

T. No—no, I reckon it wouldn't *do*, Ben. You see, aunt Polly's very particular about this fence—right here on the *street*, you know —but if it was the *back* fence I wouldn't mind, and *she* wouldn't mind. Yes, she's very particular about this fence; it's got to be done just *so*; I reckon there isn't one boy in a *thousand*, maybe *two* thousand, that can do it the way it's got to be done.

R. No—is *that* so? O, *come*, now; lemme just *try*—only just a *little*. I'd let *you*, if you was *me*, Tom.

T. Ben, I would *like* to—I would *indeed*; but aunt Polly—well, *Jim* wanted to do it, but she wouldn't *let* him; *Sid* wanted to do it, but she wouldn't let *Sid*. Now don't you see how I'm *fixed*? If you were to tackle this fence, and anything was to *happen* to it—

R. O *shucks*, I'll be just as *careful*. Now lemme *try*—I'll give you the core of my *apple*.

T. (*Reflecting—then reluctantly.*) Well, *here*. No, Ben; now *don't*—I'm afraid—

R. (*Anxiously, eagerly*) I'll give you *all* of it. And my *hoop*.

T. Well, then, *all* right—a body can't *resist* you. But be *mighty* careful, Ben. (*Gives up the brush, takes the hoop, goes off and sits on barrel, swinging his legs and munching.*) (*Aside.*) Now that isn't any slouch of a *trade*. (*Reflectively*) Now *that's* curious. Long as it was *work*, he couldn't been *hired* to do it, and don't *want* to do it; but the minute it's something he can't *get* to do, he's just *freezing* to *buy* in. Now the *other* boys—(*with sudden inspiration*)—why I reckon they're all *alike*! *Jim*! Come *here*, Jim.

(*Enter Jim with pail of water.*)

Jim. Jings! Gim *me* de core, Mars Tom, gim *me* de core!

Tom. *Like* to, Jim, but there ain't going to *be* any. Got something better for you than *that*, ANYway—(*privately, in a low voice.*) Jim, there's a chance for you to make 15 *marbles*.

Jim. No!—is *dat* so?

T. Yes. Now keep *quiet*, don't say anything to *any*body, but you go and get the *other* whitewash bucket and the *old* brush, and slip them in amongst the gooseberry bushes over yonder inside the back *gate*, where I can *find* them.

Jim. I'll have 'em dah in less'n a half a *minute*.

T. And then, Jim, you fly around and hook all the *other* brushes and whitewash you can find amongst the neighbors' back sheds.

Jim. Shan't hatter go *fur*, Mars Tom. Jist to nigger Bill de *whitewasher's*. He ain't *home*, and I'll jist gobble every las' one he's got.

T. All right, now—*rush*.

(*Exit Jim.*)

Business. From now on for a while, Jim hurries across the stage (the middle or background of it) every minute or so, each time with a couple of buckets and a couple of brushes—makes no utterance except an occasional "whoosh" indicative of sultriness and heavy exertion.

(*Enter Huck Finn in rags, and wearing battered plug hat.*)

Huck. (Glancing at Rogers.) What's *he* up to?

T. O, nothing—he's just having some *fun*.

H. Funny kind of *fun!* Is *he* going with us?

T. No. *Nobody's* going but you and me.

H. Well, I've come to see what time we better *start*.

T. Why, about *midnight*.

H. All right. I've got a pick and a shovel.

T. So've *I*. That's all we *want*.

H. Sure you can get *out?*

T. O, yes, aunty and everybody'll be *asleep*, then, and I can get out at the *window*.

H. Well, where'll I *meet* you?

T. O, in the graveyard.

H. You just bet you I *won't!*

T. Why?

H. Because *I'm* not going into no *graveyard* by myself, at no sich time o'night.

T. Shucks, what you '*fraid* of? But it isn't any matter; I'll meet you up at the end of our *lane*. Will *that* do?

H. Yes, that'll answer.

T. All right. (*Looking off, r.*) Hello! (*Rolling of drums and music of fifes in distance on both sides.*)

H. It's the *armies,* going to the *war.*

T. So 'tis. Well, *my* brigade will have to fight it out without a *general* THIS time.

(*Enter with music and banners, in good military order, the two armies of boys—one boy smoking corn-cob pipe—(an officer) (from l. and r.) in cheap but showy uniforms (Tom's opposers in red, his own men in blue or yellow sashes, wooden guns,—officers with tin swords, riding prancing and cavorting broomsticks.—The red general, Joe Harper, in the lead of his army on crutches.) (A minor officer is on tall red stilts.) He approaches and stumps around Ben Rogers, greatly interested. Both armies break ranks without orders, and crowd around.*)

Tom. Don't go too *near* there, Joe Harper.

Joe. Why?

Tom. Because it's a mighty particular *job.* I'm only letting Ben do some of it for a *favor.*

Joe. For a *favor?*

Tom. Yes—and because he can do it *better* than any other boy in town.

Joe. O, git *out! He* do it better than any boy in town! I *like* that!

Tom. Well, he *can.*

Joe. (*Dismounting from crutches.*) Shucks, you just gim *me* a hold of that brush a minute.

Tom. No, Joe, I can't *let* you. It's a *very* particular job.

1 Boy. I'll bet I can beat Ben Rogers. Tom, just *let* me.

2 Boy. (*interrupting*) No, let *me,* Tom, I got here *first.*

3 Boy. You *didn't.* I was here 'fore *you.* Tom, mayn't I try, just ever so *little?*

(*They all crowd around struggling and saying*)—

All—Let *me,* Tom—please let me.

Tom. (*retreating l.*)—No, boys, I *can't*—now don't *ask* me—*you* know I would if I *could,* but it's such a particular job, and aunt Polly she—(*springing free of them*) Sol—jers—attention! *You* call yourself *soldiers*—and act *this* way, just like a low-down *mob!* It's enough to make a General ashamed of the human *race* to *see* it! General *Harper*, if it suits *you* to see the Bloody *Avengers* act so, all *right;* but it don't *suit* ME to see the Bengal *Tigers* behave so. If the Bengal Tigers ever do such a thing *again*, I *resign*—I won't *command* such troops. And if the Bloody *Avengers* ever do so any more, I'll never stoop to fight them *again*. I'm agoing *out* now, to get some more *whitewash*. If the armies want to go along and talk *business*, all *right;* but they've got to go *like* armies, they can't go like an *insurrection. Now* then! General Harper, set your troops in *order*, and I'll do the same with *mine*. Brigade—attention!

Joe Harper. Brigade, attention!

(*Alternately they give the several necessary orders and put the two armies through the manual of arms—then march and countermarch all about the stage, making of the whole thing as correct and handsome a military display as they can, and in no sense a burlesque—and finally march off, with drums and music, under their two leaders.*)

Huck. Ben, what makes Tom so dreadful particular about that old *fence?*

Rogers. (*Swabbing off the sweat.*) I don't know, but he wouldn't let me *touch* it at first; said *Jim* wanted to, and *Sid* wanted to, but he couldn't *let* them, it was so particular; and so I had to *buy* a chance. I gave him an apple and my hoop. (*Resuming his work.*)

Huck. Well, that beats anything I ever *struck!* I should think *any*body could *white*wash.

R. Well, I suppose anybody *can* do it *rough*—but Tom he thinks—

Huck. Gim *me* that brush a minute!

R. I *can't*, Huck. Tom don't *allow* it.

H. Why I only want to try just a *minute*, Ben, *that's* all.

R. Well, I can't *do* it, Huck, 'thout you ask *Tom*.

H. Will you, *then?*

R. I will if he *says* so. But I know you can't *persuade* him—I tried *that* enough. You'll have to *give* him something.

H. What'll he *charge*, Ben?

R. O, *I* don't know. You'll have to go and find out for your*self.*

H. All right, I'll *do* it.

(Exit, eagerly.)

(*Enter Young Dr. Robinson, Muff Potter, and Injun Joe (the half-breed), and talk apart.*)

Muff. It's five dollars, *anyway?*

Dr. R. Yes.

Muff. And *you* furnish wagon and everything?

Dr. R. Yes, I furnish *everything.*

Muff. What time of *night?*

Dr. R. Well, we want to be there an hour or two after midnight.

Muff. And if we get *caught?*

Dr. R. I'll stand by you in the *courts*—I'll see you through. Is it all *settled,* now?

Muff. Yes—I reckon we're satisfied; ain't we Joe?

Joe. Yes. ——*Wait.* You going *with* us?

Dr. R. I'm not going *with* you—THAT wouldn't be best—each of us must arrive by himself, and from a different direction—but I'll be there when you come, or very soon *after.*

Joe. (*Aside*) All right. Insults an Injun, years ago—and thinks it's *forgotten!* It might happen to be a bad *night* for *him.*

Dr. R. Now if everything's arranged, come along, and I'll tell you where to get a sack to *carry* it in, and where to borrow a wagon and horse when nobody's *looking.*

Muff and Joe. All right.

(Exit the Three.)

(*Enter the crowd of boys, each with a pail and brush, and fall eagerly to work, whitewashing the fence, the trees, the door-steps, the barrel and the house. Man crosses with a practicable black calf, and they whitewash it when he isn't looking, but is staring at the workers and saying "Well upon my word, I do believe old Polly Sawyer's gone crazy."*

Presently enter Tom, on Joe Harper's crutches, and wearing one of the boys' red jackets, Huck's plug hat, and smoking that cob pipe.)

Tom. Come, pay in *advance!* We don't *trust,* here. Pay up, pay up before you *begin.*

> (*They crowd forward and empty at Tom's feet their bulging pockets of all conceivable odds and ends—marbles, chalk, twine, balls, apples, bits of glass, door-knobs—anything and everything that will make a show—then hurry eagerly to work ——also those tall red stilts.*)

Tom. (*Discards the crutches, mounts the red stilts, and leans up against the house or a stage-box, contemplating the laboring armies and his plunder*)—It's a noble *day*—I've broke the *crowd!*

> (*Mary appears in the door and stands there.*)

Mary. (*aside, transfixed*)—Well, upon my *word!* There's aunt Polly in yonder crying her eyes out because she's been so hard-hearted as to make that poor boy *work! (Shouting within)* Aunt Polly! Aunt Polly—just come *here!*

> (*Aunt Polly appears in the door, with her face hid in her apron, crying. Removes it and takes a look. Puts up her hands piously and says*)

A. P. Well, for the land's *sake!*

(TABLEAU. CURTAIN.)

Act II.

SCENE 1.

A Graveyard by Moonlight.

> (*Tom and Huck enter with spades and picks. Huck also has a dead cat. They sit.*)

Huck. (*Evidently scary and uncomfortable.*) Blamed if I *like* this kind of a place, Tom.

Tom. Shucks, what will you care what kind of a *place* it is, if we find about a ton or a ton and a half of buried *treasure*—gold, and silver, and *diamonds,* and such things?

H. Well, I *wouldn't* care, *then.* But *will* we, Tom?

T. I don't know; but we can pitch in and *try,* soon as we are rested. Everybody *says* that Murrell's gang used to bury treasures around on this very hill-top, years ago. Look *here,* Huck, YOU never told me before about saving the widow Douglas from being murdered and robbed. How is *that?*

H. Well, I never told *any*body. I *had* to tell *some*body, so as to *save* her; and so I told the old *Welsh*man, *Jones,* what I'd overheard that villain say; and when the right night come, he was on hand with his gun, and saved the widow's *life,* and come mighty near getting the *robber,* too—*did* hit him with a bullet.

T. When was it?

H. Three weeks ago.

T. Well, upon my *word!* And don't the widow know *yet,* that it was *you* that kept her from being killed?

H. Deed she *don't! Nobody* knows but *Jones,* and he swore to me he'd never *tell.*

T. Why, what a goose you *are.* You'd be a *hero*—THAT's what you'd be—you'd be a *hero.* Everybody would talk about you and *call* you a hero. Huck you're just a *fool.* I wish it was *me—I* wouldn't fool away any such chance to be glorious and celebrated —*I'd* tell, precious *quick.*

H. Well, I'll bet you *wouldn't*—if you knowed who the man *was* that was going to do the *murdering.*

T. Why—who *was* it, Huck?

H. (*hesitatingly and cautiously*) Tom, will you swear on your sacred word and honor wish you may drop stone cold in your tracks if you ever ever *ever* tell?

T. I swear it *all,* Huck; I never never never *will* tell. Now tell me, Huck. Who *was* it?

H. (*rises, and tip-toes around, listening and watching—detects no sound—tip-toes to Tom, shades his mouth with his hand and says in Tom's ear*)—It was Injun *Joe!*

T. (*Immensely startled*) Good gracious Caesar's ghost land of Goshen heavens and *earth!* Well, you'd *better* keep still. Why if he ever found out it was you that prevented him, he'd *drown* you just as he would a *pup.*

H. 'Course he would. *I* don't want to be no hero on any such *terms.*

T. Neither would *I, I* tell you. They say he never forgives and he never *forgets,* and he'll always get even on a person that crosses him.

H. Well, let's not *talk* about it any more—I can't *bear* it.

T. They say he's been seen around town *again,* lately.

H. (Scared) No—when?

T. Two or three days ago.

H. O, Tom, don't *talk* about it any more!

T. All right, then, I *won't. (Swabbing his face.)* My, Huck, it's a long way to lug the spades and shovels such a hot night.

H. Deed it *is,* Tom—and I've had this old *tom-*cat, be*sides.*

T. Lemme *see* him, Huck. *My,* he's pretty stiff! Where'd you *get* him?

H. Bought him off'n a boy.

T. What did you *give?*

H. I give a Sunday-school ticket and a *bladder* that I got at the slaughter-house.

T. Where'd you get the *ticket?*

H. Bought it off'n Ben *Rogers* two weeks ago for a *hoop-*stick.

T. Say—what are dead cats *good* for, Huck?

H. Good for? Cure *warts* with.

T. No? Is *that* so? I know something that's *better.*

H. I bet you *don't.* What *is* it?

T. Why, *spunk* water.

H. Spunk water! I wouldn't give a *dern* for spunk water.

T. You *wouldn't,* wouldn't you? D'you every *try* it?

H. No, I hain't. But Bob *Tanner* did.

T. Who *told* you so?

H. Why, *he* told Jeff *Thatcher,* and Jeff told Johnny *Baker,* and Johnny told Jim *Hollis,* and Jim told Ben *Rogers,* and Ben told a *nigger,* and the nigger told *me. There,* now.

T. Well, what *of* it? They'll *all* lie. Anyway all but the *nigger,* I don't know *him.* But I never saw a nigger that *wouldn't* lie. But *say* —how do you cure 'em with dead *cats?*

H. Why, you take your cat and go and get in the graveyard, long about *midnight,* where somebody that was wicked has been buried; and when it's midnight a devil will come, or may be two or *three,* but you can't *see* 'em, you can only *hear* something like the wind, or may be hear 'em *talk;* and when they're taking that feller *away,* you heave your cat after 'em and say, "Devil follow *corpse,* cat follow *devil,* warts follow *cat,* *I'*m done with ye." That'll fetch *any* wart.

T. Sounds right. D'you ever try it, Huck?

H. No, but old Mother *Hopkins* told me.

T. Well, I reckon it's *so,* then, becuz they say she's a witch.

H. Say! Why, Tom, I *know* she is. She witched *pap.* Pap says so his own *self.* He come along one day, and he *see* she was a *witching* him, so he took up a rock, and if she hadn't dodged he'd a *got* her. Well, that very night he rolled off'n a shed wher' he was layin' drunk, and broke his *arm.*

T. Why that's *awful.* Say, Hucky, when you going to try the cat?

H. To-night. I reckon the devils'll come after old Hoss Williams to-night. We'll try it, when we're done *digging.*

(*Huck gets out a percussion-cap box and opens it.*)

Tom. Say, Huck, what's *that?*

H. Nothing but a *tick.*

T. Where'd you *get* him?

H. Out in the *woods,* last week.

T. What'll you *take* for him? (*Examining the tick.*)

H. I don't know. I don't want to *sell* him.

T. All right. It's a mighty *small* tick, *anyway.*

H. Oh, *anybody* can run a tick down that don't *belong* to them. *I'*m satisfied with it. It's a good enough tick for *me.*

T. Sho, there's *ticks* a plenty. I could have a *thousand* of 'em if I *wanted* to.

H. Well, why *don't* you? Becuz you know mighty well you *can't.* This is a pretty early *tick,* I reckon. It's the first one *I'*ve seen **this** year.

T. Say, Huck, I'll give you my *tooth* for him.

H. Less *see* it.

(*Tom got out a bit of paper and carefully unrolled it. Huckleberry viewed it wistfully. The temptation was very strong. At last he said.*)

H. Is it *genuwyne?*

T. Look for yourself.

(*Tom lifted his lip and showed the vacancy.*)

H. Well, all right, it's a trade.

(*Tom enclosed the tick in the percussion-cap box.*)

T. Well, if we're going to find any *treasure* to-night, per'aps we'd better begin to get to *work*, Huck.

H. All right, Tom. Where'll we dig?

T. Oh, 'most anywhere.

H. Why, is it hid all *around?*

T. No, in*deed* it isn't. It's hid in mighty particular *places*, Huck —sometimes on *Islands*, sometimes in rotten chests in a graveyard under the end of a limb of an old dead *tree*, just where the shadow falls at midnight; sometimes under the floor in ha'nted *houses.*

H. Who *hides* it?

T. Why, *robbers*, of course—who'd you *reckon? Sunday*-school sup'rintendents?

H. I don't know. If it was mine I wouldn't hide it; I'd *spend* it and have a good *time.*

T. So would I; but *robbers* don't do that way, they always *hide* it and *leave* it there.

H. Don't they come *after* it any more?

T. *No*, they *think* they will, but they generally forget the *marks*, or else they *die.* Anyway it lies there a long time and gets *rusty*; and by-and-by somebody finds an old yellow paper that tells how to find the *marks*—a paper that's got to be ciphered over about a *week*, because it's mostly *signs* and hy'rogli*phics.*

H. Hyro—*which*licks?

T. Hy'rogli*phics*—PICTURES and things, you know, that don't *mean* anything.

H. Have *you* got one of them papers, Tom?

T. No.

H. Well, then, how you going to find out the *marks?*

T. I don't *want* any marks. They *always* bury it under a ha'nted house, or on an island, or under a dead tree that's got one *limb* sticking out. Well, there's lots of dead-limb trees around *here*—dead *loads* of 'em.

H. Is it under *all* of them?

T. How you *talk. No.*

H. Then how you going to know which one to *go* for?

T. Go for *all* of 'em.

H. Why, Tom, it'll take all *summer.*

T. Well, what of *that?* Suppose you find a brass pot with a hundred *dollars* in it, all rusty and *gay,* or a rotten chest full of *di'monds.* How's *that?*

(*Huck's eyes glowed.*)

H. That's *bully,* plenty bully enough for *me.* Just you gimme the hundred *dollars,* and I don't want no *di'monds.*

T. All right. But I bet you *I'm* not going to throw off on di'monds. Some of 'em's worth twenty dollars *apiece.* There ain't *any,* hardly, but's worth six bits or a *dollar.*

H. No. Is *that* so?

T. Cert'nly—*any*body'll tell you so. Haven't you ever seen one, Huck?

H. Not as *I* remember.

T. Oh, *kings* have *slathers* of them.

H. Well, *I* don't know no *kings,* Tom.

T. I reckon you *don't.* But if you were to go to *Europe* you'd see a *raft* of 'em hopping around.

H. Do they *hop?*

T. Hop your *granny!* NO.

H. Well, what did you *say* they did, for?

T. Shucks, I only meant you'd *see* 'em—not *hopping,* of *course* —what do they want to *hop* for? But I mean you'd just *see* 'em—scattered *around,* you know, in a kind of a general *way.* Like that old hump-backed *Richard.*

H. Richard? What's his *other* name?

T. He didn't *have* any other name. Kings don't have any but a *given* name.

H. No?

T. But they *don't.*

H. Well, if *they* like it, Tom, all *right;* but *I* don't want to be a king and have only just a *given* name, like a *nigger.* But say— where you going to dig *first?*

T. Well, *I* don't know. S'pose we tackle this old dead limb tree *here.*

H. I'm agreed.

(*So they mark where the shadow falls and get to work. They work and converse alternately.*)

T. Say, Huck, if we find a treasure here, what you going to *do* with your share?

H. Well, I'll have a pie and a glass of soda every *day,* and I'll go to every circus that comes *along.* I'll just *waller* in 'em. I'll *bet* I'll have a gay time.

T. Well, ain't you going to *save* any of it?

H. Save it? What *for?*

T. Why, so as to have something to *live* on by-and-by.

H. Oh, *that* ain't any use. *Pap* would come back to thish yer town some day and get his claws on it if I didn't hurry *up,* and I tell you *he'd* clean it out pretty quick. What you going to do with *yourn,* Tom?

T. I'm going to buy a new drum, and a sure-'nough sword, and a red necktie, and a bull pup, and get *married.*

H. Married!

T. That's it.

H. Tom, you—why you ain't in your right *mind.*

T. Wait—*you'll* see.

H. Well, that's the foolishest thing you could *do,* Tom. Look at pap and my mother. *Fight!* why they used to fight all the *time. I* remember, mighty well.

T. That's nothing. The girl *I'm* going to pick out won't fight.

H. Tom, I reckon they're all *alike.* They'll *all* comb a body. Now you better *think* about this a while. I *tell* you you better. What's the *name* of the gal?

T. It ain't a *gal* at *all*—it's a *girl.*

H. It's all the *same,* I reckon; some says *gal,* some says *girl*— *both's* right, like enough. Anyway, what's her *name,* Tom?

T. I'll tell you some time—not now.

H. All right—*that'll* do. Only if you get *married* I'll be more lonesomer than *ever.*

T. No you *won't,* you'll come and live with *me.*

H. Consound it, do they *always* bury it as deep as this?

T. Sometimes—not *always.* Not *generally.*

H. Where you going to dig *next,* after we get *this* one?

T. I reckon maybe we'll tackle the old tree that's over on Cardiff Hill, back of the widow's.

H. I reckon that'll be a good one. Blame it, we must be in the wrong *place.* What do *you* think?

T. It *is* mighty curious, Huck. I don't *understand* it.

H. Same time, we *can't* be wrong. We spotted the shadder to a *dot.*

T. I know it, but then there's *another* thing.

H. What's *that?*

T. Why we only *guessed* at the time. Like enough it was too *late* or too *early.*

(*Huck dropped his shovel.*)

H. *That's* it. That's the very *trouble.* We got to give this one *up.* We can't ever tell the right *time,* and besides, this kind of thing's too *awful,* here this time of night, with witches and ghosts a fluttering around so. I feel as if something's *behind* me all the time; and I'm afeared to turn *around,* becuz maybe there's others in *front* a waiting for a chance. I been creeping all over ever since I *got* here.

T. Well, I've been pretty much so *too,* Huck. (*After a pause.*) They nearly always put in a *dead* man when they bury a treasure under a *tree,* to look *out* for it.

H. Lordy!

T. *Yes,* they do, I've *always* heard that.

H. Tom, I don't like to fool around much where there's dead people. A body's *bound* to get into trouble with 'em, *sure.*

T. I don't like to stir 'em up, *either,* Huck. (*Impressively.*) S'pose this one here was to stick out his skull and *say* something!

H. Don't, Tom! It's *awful!*

T. Well it just *is*, Huck, I don't feel comfortable a *bit.* . . . sh! what's *that?* (*They listen.*)

H. It's the devils, *sure*—coming to carry off Hoss Williams's body to the bad place. Look here, I ain't going to stay here another m—

T. Keep still! It wasn't anything but the wind amongst the trees. (*Digging.*)

H. O *come,* Tom, let's—

T. 'George! I've *struck* something! Huck, I do believe we've *got* it!——No——old coffin, maybe———no it ain't, it's a *box.* Here—you shove your spade down *there*—no, *there*—that's right——now *heave* on it———not so fast———now, *that'll* do.——— Oho, you see it *is* a box, your*self!*——It's rather a *little* one— ain't bigger than a cigar box, but———(*hoisting it out*)—*my* but she's *heavy* enough! (*Excitedly*) Huck, if it's money, we're rich! (*Preparing to crush in the top.*)

H. *Hurry,* Tom, and let's see!—hurry!

(*Tom smashes in the top, grabs a handful of coin, lets it run through his fingers.*)

T. Every cent of it's old gold *coins!* Huck, we're *rich!*—*that's* what we are, we're *rich!*

H. *Rich?*—just with *that* little?

T. That *little,* you igno*rammus!* Why you unutterable *fool,* there ain't less than four hundred million *dollars,* there.

H. (*Gravely*—*after a pause.*) And the box's worth *something*— it's a real good *box,* Tom.

T. *Hang* the box! Why, don't I tell you you're *rich?* Why, Huck, you've got all the money you *want,* now. You can't spend it in a hundred thousand years. Huck, looky *here*—you can spend two dollars a day every day as long as you *live,* and you can't spend all of *your* share—maybe two and a *half.*

H. Tom are you in earnest?

T. Huck, just as sure as I'm standing here, I'm in right down dead earnest. And it's *so,* too.

H. (*Fervently.*) Well, Tom, if it *is* so, you can just bet on *one* thing. This county's 40 mile wide; and day after to-morrow when they want to find out who's bought up all the *pie*, you take and send 'em to Huck *Finn*.

T. You're going for the *pie*, then?

H. (Fervently.) Early. *Early*. If I don't eat up'ards of a mile and a half of pie every day for seven *year*, I wish I may *bust*.

T. Well, you *will* bust—as you call it. *(Looking around, poking around.) I'm* going to drive an *omnibus*—that's what *I'm* going to do. I'll drive an omnibus or *die. (Finds a long sack.) Here's* the thing *we* want. Shan't have to *hide* the money, *now*—carry it *home*, turn *about*. Hello, it's got three *water*-melons in it. *(Huck arrives with the box of money.)* Somebody's been *stealing* them, and heard *us*, and dropped it and *ran*, I reckon. *(Puts the box in.)* Now we'll lug the whole thing down to the old *saw*mill, and eat the melons, and count the *money*, and—sh!

H. Jump, Tom, it's the devils *this* time, I heard 'em, *sure! (Both boys jump and hide. Enter Injun Joe. Huck, gasping.)* Goodness gracious, it's Injun Joe!

Injun Joe. (aside.) Not here *yet*—and I've been gone an *hour* on the lookout. *(Ruminates—strikes an idea.)* Ah, *I* know what I'll do! I'll take my sack—

Both boys. (aside—and sick.) His sack!

Joe. Yes, I'll take my sack *(shouldering it)* and slip down the old road, and cut across by the—

(Exit, talking to himself.)

T. Consound him, he's got our *money!*

H. (Scared.) O, keep still, keep *still*—he might turn around, any minute, and come *back* here—and besides—sh!

T. There's *more* coming!

(Enter Dr. Robinson and Muff Potter. Potter is slightly tight. He is whittling a heavy stick.)

Doctor. (angrily.) And besides, with your sneaking and *shirking*, you've caused a good hour's *delay*. Ten to one Injun Joe's been here, and given us up, and gone *home* again.

Muff. (ugly) I sneaked and shirked because I was sorry I'd ever *promised* to help you rob a *grave*, and I wanted to get *out* of it, and not come at *all*. And what's more, you've called me just *enough* hard names, this last ten minutes, and I want you to *stop* it.

Dr. What! Why, you scum of the earth—

Muff. (*Getting close*)—*Stop* it, I tell you!

Dr. You filthy, impudent loafer—

(*Muff attempts to take him by the collar.*)

Dr. (*Striking him with his open hand*)—What're you trying to do!

Muff. (*Drunkenly striking back*) Don't you *hit* me. I don't 'low no man to hit *me*.

Dr. (*shoves him violently*) Keep *off*.

(*Muff, aroused—recovers, surges drunkenly forward, drops his knife and club, he and the doctor collar each other and struggle.*)

(*Enter Injun Joe—skulks eagerly forward, snatches up the knife and jumps behind a tree.*)

H. It's Injun Joe again! *Come!* (*wants to drag Tom away.*)

T. Stay where you *are!* You want him to *see* you?

Injun Joe. (*aside—watching, nervously fingering the knife*) I've got him, sure! (*bright moon again.*)

(*Dr. snatches himself loose and springs for Tom's shovel; Muff grabs up his club, and the two rush upon each other, Injun Joe gliding around behind the doctor; as the doctor fells Muff, Joe stabs the said doctor. Both men fall and lie still.*)

(CURTAIN)

[Act III]

[SCENE 1]

Village Schoolhouse.

(*Large blackboard, etc. Alfred Temple discovered alone.*)

Alfred. (*solus*) Well, I've got here ahead of Mr. Tom Sawyer for *once*. If I can't fix him *one* way, I can *another*. (*Meddles around, and opens Tom's desk. Enter Amy Lawrence and comes roguishly smiling and tip-toeing toward him.*) Here—his spelling-book will do.—(*Opens it and pours ink on the page—closes it, lifts up lid of desk—is just softly laying the book within, when Amy says*)

Amy. (*over his shoulder*)—Boo!

Alfred. (*Scared*) O laws! (*Lid slams down with a bang.*) Why, Amy, how you *startled* me!

Amy. (*lifting the lid and getting the book in spite of his efforts to prevent—opens it, looks him over, solemnly, puts back the book*) I —would—be—*ashamed* of myself!

Alf. (*Trying to get hold of her hand*)—Amy—

Amy. (*repulsing him*) Don't *touch* me! (*Scanning him*) What a low creature you *are*!

Alf. If you'll only let me *explain*—

Amy. Don't *speak* to me! I'll never love you *again*. And if Tom Sawyer had treated me *right*, I would go just as straight as I could *walk*, and *tell* him! (*Moving away.*)

(*Alfred accompanies her, pleading, in dumb show.*)

Amy. O, I'll never tell him. You needn't be so *scared*. I wouldn't speak to Tom Sawyer for (*listens in dumb show*) what?

(*Alf.—more dumb show*)

Amy. (*Scornfully*) You did it for *fun*! It's great *fun*, to get a boy a whipping that you darsn't try to whip *yourself*! Go 'way from me —I de*spise* you!

(*Exit both L.*)

(Enter Becky Thatcher (R.) and sits at a desk,—cons her book. Presently, enter Tom, munching an apple.)

Tom. *(aside)* Why that's the new *girl* that's come to town. *My,* but she's pretty!

(Edges sheepishly toward her—she looks up, whirls her back on him, buries herself in her studies. Tom edges closer—finally sits gingerly down on her other side. She whirls her back on him again. Tom lays his apple cautiously by her elbow. She steals a glance around—shoves the apple away. Tom puts it back. She glances around again—sees the apple, but turns away her head without molesting it. Tom softly pushes it around in front of her.)

Tom. *Please* take a bite—I don't want it *all.*

(She glances around, but arrives at no conclusion. Tom begins to draw painfully on a slate, tongue in cheek, and following his motions with his head—hiding his drawing with his other hand. The girl's curiosity is aroused—timidly tries to see the picture—Tom still shades it with his hand. Presently she pleads—)

Becky. Let *me* see it—*won't* you?

T. If you'll take a *bite,* I will.

(She takes a very little one.)

T. Shucks, *that* ain't a bite. Take a *big* one.

B. I *can't.* That's as big a one as I *can* take.

T. Sho, let *me* show you.

B. Well, you do it *for* me.

(Tom crams the apple into his mouth, bites out a prodigious chunk, which he hands to her; bites out one for himself, and they both go to contentedly munching.)

B. *(mouth full)* Now let me see it. *(Tom reveals the picture.)* *(With happy astonishment)* Why as I *live,* if it isn't a real shure-nuff *house!* Dear me, I wish *I* could draw like that. Do you reckon you could make it *big*—on the *black-board?*

T. O, *easy!*

B. O, do, *do! (Tom draws it large on black-board.)* O, how lovely!—now make a *man. (Tom makes a man—see Chapter 6 of*

"Adventures of Tom Sawyer" for these drawings.) O, it's a perfectly *beautiful* man! Now make *me* coming along. (*Tom does it*)
O dear, it's too lovely for *anything*—why it's *just* as if I was looking
in a *looking*-glass!

T. I can draw *anybody*—just every bit as good as *that*, too—anybody I ever *saw*.

B. *Can* you, really? I do wish *I* could draw.

T. It's *easy*, *I'*ll learn you.

B. Oh, *will* you? *When?*

T. At *noon* every *day*. Do you go home to dinner?

B. I'll stay if *you* will.

T. *Good*—that's a go. What's your *name?* (*They sit down
again.*)

B. Becky *Thatcher*. What's *yours?* Oh, *I* know. It's Thomas
Sawyer.

T. That's the name they *lick* me by—here in *school*. I'm *Tom*
when I'm *good. You* call me Tom, *will* you?

B. Yes.

(*Now Tom began to scrawl something on the slate, hiding the
words from the girl. But she was not backward this time. She
begged to see. Tom said:*)

T. Oh, it ain't anything.

B. Yes it *is.*

T. No it *ain't;* you don't want to see.

B. Yes I *do,* INDEED I do. *Please* let me.

T. You'll *tell.*

B. No I won't—deed and deed and *double* deed I won't.

T. You won't tell *anybody* at *all?* Ever as long as you *live?*

B. No, I won't ever tell *any*body. *Now* let me.

T. Oh, *you* don't want to see!

B. Now that you treat me so, I *will* see, Tom—(*and she put her
small hand on his, and a little scuffle ensued. Tom pretending to
resist in earnest, but letting his hand slip by degrees till these
words were revealed: "I love you."*)

B. (*Reading*) I *love* you. Oh, you bad *thing! (And she hit his
hand a smart rap, but reddened and looked pleased nevertheless.
Tom was swimming in bliss. He said*)

T. Do you love *rats?*

B. *No,* I *hate* them.

T. Well, I do *too*—LIVE ones. But I mean *dead* ones, to swing
round your head with a *string.*

B. No, I don't care for rats much, *anyway.* What *I* like is
chewing gum.

T. Oh, I should *say* so! I wish I had some *now.*

B. *Do* you? *I've* got some. I'll let you chew it a while, but you
must give it *back* to me.

(*That was agreeable, so they chewed it turn about, and dan-
gled their legs against the bench in excess of contentment.*)

T. Were you ever at a *circus?*

B. *Yes,* and my Pa's going to take me *again* sometime, if I'm good.

T. *I've* been to the circus three or *four* times—*lots* of times.
Church ain't a *circumstance* to a *circus.* There's things going on at a
circus all the *time.* I'm going to be a *clown* in a circus when I grow
up.

B. Oh, *are* you! *That* will be nice. They're so *lovely*—all spotted *up.*

T. Yes, *that's* so. And they get *slathers* of money—most a dollar a *day,* Ben *Rogers* says. Say, Becky, were you ever *engaged?*

B. What's *that?*

T. Why engaged to be *married.*

B. No.

T. Would you *like* to?

B. I reckon so. I don't know. What is it *like?*

T. *Like?* Why it ain't like *anything.* You only just tell a boy you won't ever have anybody but *him,* ever ever *ever,* and then you *kiss,* and that's *all.* ANYbody can do it.

B. *Kiss?* What do you *kiss* for?

T. Why *that,* you know, is to—well, they *always* do *that.*

B. Everybody?

T. Why *yes,* everybody that's in *love* with each other. Do you remember what I wrote on the *slate?*

B. Ye—yes.

T. What *was* it?

B. I shan't *tell* you. (*Bashfully—throwing apron over her head and then off again.*)

T. Shall *I* tell *you?*

B. Ye—yes—but some other *time.*

T. No, *now.*

B. No, not now—to-*morrow.*

T. Oh, no, *now,* PLEASE, Becky. I'll *whisper* it; I'll whisper it *ever* so *easy.* (*Becky hesitating, Tom took silence for consent, and passed his arm about her waist and whispered the tale ever so softly, with his mouth close to her ear. And then he added*) Now *you* whisper it to *me*—just the *same.*

> (*She resisted for a while, and then said*)

B. You turn your *face* away, so you can't *see,* and *then* I will. But you mustn't ever *tell* anybody—WILL you, Tom? Now you *won't* —WILL you?

T. No, indeed, in*deed* I won't. *Now,* Becky.

> (*He turned his face away. She bent timidly around till her breath stirred his curls, and whispered.*)

B. I—*love*—you.

(*Then she sprang away and ran around and around the desks
and benches, with Tom after her, and took refuge in a corner
at last, with her little white apron to her face. Tom clasped her
about her neck and pleaded.*)

T. Now Becky, it's *all* over—all over but the *kiss.* Don't you be
afraid of *that*—it ain't *anything* at *all.* PLEASE, Becky.

(*And he tugged at the apron and the hands. By-and-by she
gave up and let her hands drop; her face, all glowing with the
struggle, came up and submitted. Amy puts her head in at
door, sees this, and goes off boo-hooing—but T. and B. don't
hear her. Tom kissed the red lips, and said*)

T. Now it's all *done,* Becky. And always after this, you know,
you ain't ever to love anybody but *me,* and you ain't ever to *marry*
anybody but *me,* never never and for *ever.* WILL you?

B. No, I'll never love anybody but *you,* Tom, and I'll never
marry anybody but you, and you ain't to ever marry anybody but
me, either.

T. *Certainly.* Of *course.* That's *part* of it. And *always,* coming to
school, or when we're going *home,* you're to *walk* with me, when
there ain't anybody *looking*—and *you* choose me *and I* choose *you*
at *parties,* because that's the way you *do* when you're engaged.

B. It's so *nice.* I never *heard* of it before.

T. Oh it's *ever* so nice and jolly. Why me and Amy *Lawrence*—
(*The big eyes told Tom his blunder, and he stopped confused.*)

B. Oh, *Tom!* Then *I* ain't the *first* you've ever been engaged to!
(*The child began to cry. Tom said:*)

T. Oh, *don't* cry, Becky. I don't *care* for her any more.

B. Yes you *do,* Tom—you *know* you do.
(*Tom tried to put his arm about her neck, but she pushed
him away and turned her face to the wall, and went on crying.
Tom tried again, with soothing words in his mouth, and was
repulsed again.*)

T. Becky, it's just as *true* as anything I ever *said*—it is all *off*
between Amy Lawrence and me—it is in*deed.* We haven't *spoken*
for *weeks.* It came of her not leaving me a *note* that she *promised*

she would—and of her running with that St. *Louis* boy that's come to town—and she goes with him all the *time*, YET—and this very *morning* I met her and wanted to explain and make it all *up* with her, and she *wouldn't*; and said she'd never *speak* to me again. (*Pause.*) Becky, I—I don't care for *anybody* but you.

(*No reply—but sobs.*)

 T. Becky, (*pleadingly*) Becky, won't you *say* something?

  (*More sobs. Tom got out another apple, bit a hunk out of it and passed it around her so that she could see it, and said*)

 T. Please Becky, won't you *take* it?

  (*She struck it to the floor and marched out crying. Exit. Tom sat down at a desk, put his head on his arms and apparently cries.*)

  (*Enter Amy Lawrence—passes by Tom with her scornful nose in the air, not deigning to look at him. She stands, arms akimbo before blackboard.*)

 Amy. (*Half crying, but admiring.*) O, they are *too* LOVELY for this *world*—(*sudden access of anger*) but I just *know* he made them for *her*—hateful *thing!* (*Frantically rubs out the pictures; then goes mooning around.*) Why if the *key* isn't in the teacher's *desk!* I'd just give the *world* to know what it is he puts in there every day, done up in a *rag.* **I** believe it's a CRUCIFIX—*heaps* of people think he's a *Catholic,* and some talk right *out* and *say* so. And many and *many's* the time he puts his head in this desk and appears to be *praying* to something—and I believe he *is.* (*Keeps an eye on Tom—gets out the rag, exposes a whisky bottle—puts it to her nose*) Pah! (*Bottle falls and breaks. She stands horrified and speechless. Tom rises and gazes. She begins to cry.*) Tom Sawyer, you're just as *mean* as you can *be,* to sneak up on a person and—and—

 Tom. I haven't sneaked up on anybody.

 Amy. (*Crying violently*) You ought to be *ashamed* of yourself, Tom Sawyer; you *know* you're going to *tell* on me; and oh, what *shall* I do, what SHALL I do! I'll be *whipped*—and I *never* was whipped in school. (*Stamping her foot*) Be so mean, if you want to! I know something that's going to happen!—you just *wait*—YOU'LL see! Hateful, hateful, *hateful!* (*Goes off crying to hang up her bonnet and shawl.*)

(*Cracked school-bell overhead begins to ring. Tom gazing after Amy musingly, meantime.*)

Tom. (*aside*) What a curious kind of a fool a *girl* is. Never been *whipped* in SCHOOL! Shucks, what's a *whipping?* That's just *like* a girl—they're so thin-skinned and chicken-*hearted.* Well, of course I ain't going to tell old Dobbins, but what *of* it? Old Dobbins will ask who it *was?* Nobody'll *answer.* Then he'll do just the way he *always* does—ask first one and then t'other, and when he comes to the right girl *he'll* know it, without any *telling.* Girls' faces *always* tell on them. *They* haven't got any backbone. She'll get *thrashed.* Well, it's a kind of a tight *place* for Amy, because there ain't any way *out* of it. (*Tom conned the thing a moment longer, and then added:*) All *right,* though; she'd like to see *me* in just such a fix—let her sweat it *out.* (*Pause*) Now suppose this was in a *book;* (*sudden happy inspiration*) and *you* didn't *mind* a whipping, and she *did.* What would *happen?* Why, you'd generously *save* her! All right—I know what *I'll* do!

(*Tom goes with a heroic swagger, hangs up his hat, and goes to his seat. Enter a scrambling swarm of hot and panting boys and girls in dresses of 40 years ago, and hang up their things and hustle to their places, and go to whispering, cuffing, punching each other, catching flies, giggling, etc.*

Enter Old Dobbins, the schoolmaster—approaches his desk —stands portentously over his broken bottle—a hush falls upon the school, pupils all stare, and wait. Dobbins mounts his throne, without a word. Raps with his rule. Silence.)

Dob. Children, the court room being very *small,* a larger place is required for this afternoon's important session. The use of this room having been requested, I shall be obliged to dismiss you much *earlier* than usual.

All. (*with noisy enthusiasm*) O, goody!

Dob. (*Raps*) Silence! The trial has gone *against* your poor humble old helper and *friend,* Muff Potter (*sorrow in the school*) and the court will meet in this room, presently, to pronounce upon him the dreadful sentence of *death*. (*Tom starts, and leans his head on his hand and toys idly with his pen.*) Ah, let this miserable business sink *deep* into your *memory*; take the lesson of it to your *hearts*, and never allow your bitter passions to *master* you—so that *you* may be spared poor *Muff's* fate. (*Presently.*) Get to your lessons.

> (*After Dobbins says "Get to your lessons," he goes into a brown study, and the boys and girls get to scuffling, pinching, sticking pins in each other—a boy sits down on a pin, says "ouch" cuffs his neighbor. Spit-balls are thrown, pea-guns are used, etc., fly-catching goes on. Buzz of study from some of the better children. Dob. abstracted—mutters occasionally, "Poor Muff"*)

Dobbins. First class in history come forward and recite.

> (*A boy and a girl step forward.*)

D. William, who discovered America?

W. Clumbus.

D. Correct. Where was he born?

W. Clumbus, Ohio.

D. Sarah, where was he born?

S. Genoa, Italy. (*Pronounce it Ge-no-ah.*)

D. Correct. Go up head. (*They change places.*) What was the date of the discovery?

S. Eighteen sixty-four.

D. William, what was the date of the discovery?

W. Fourteen ninety-two.

D. Correct. Go up head. (*They change again.*) What *country-man* was he?

W. Irishman.

D. Sarah, what countryman was he?

S. Italian, sir.

D. Right. Go up head. What was his religion?

S. Pressbyterian.

D. Nonsense. *William?*

W. Catholic, sir.

D. Correct. Go up head. (*They change*) What did he say when the new world burst upon him in the early dawn?

W. (*hesitating*) He—he said Gee—*whillikins!*

D. Idiot! Sarah, what did he *say?*

S. (*hesitating*) He—he said, Almost thou persuadest me to be a Chris—

D. (*interrupting with rising anger*) This is *brutal* ignorance! *William*—mind you go *carefully,* now—what did he *say?*

W. (*Confused and scared*) He—he said, Consider the lilies of the valley, how they—

D. (*Furious—interrupting—fetching a whack or two with his switch.*) Go to the *dunce*-block, sir! Sarah, *answer* me—what did Columbus *say,* when the new world burst upon his vision?

(*William goes and dons the tall paper dunce-cap and mounts the block.*)

S. (*Confused and scared*) He—he said, What shall it *profit* a man though he gain a whole *world* and—

D. Go to your *seat!*—you are a disgrace to the *school!* Benjamin Rogers, I will hear your *grammar* lesson. (*Rogers comes forward.*) How many persons constitute a *multitude?*—parse the sentence: How many persons constitute a *multitude.*

R. How is a *noun,* COMMON noun, third *person,* neuter *gender*—

D. Wait, sir! What did you say *how* was?

R. Noun, sir.

D. Noun, you stupid! It's a *preposition.* Go *on.*

R. How is a *preposition, common* preposition, third *person,* feminine *gender,* indicative *mood,* present *tense,* and refers to *many.* MANY is an auxiliary verb—

D. (*interrupting*) It isn't a *verb* at *all,* it's an *adjective.*

R. Many is an *adjective,* possessive *case,* comparative *degree,* second *person,* singular *number,* and agrees with its *object* in number and *person.*

D. What *is* its object?

R. Multitude. PERSONS is a reflexive *pronoun*—

D. Stop! Benjamin Rogers, have you *studied* this lesson at *all?*

R. Yes, sir.

D. I do not like to be *severe* with you; but I *must* say, that for the *best* grammar scholar in the *school,* you are making but a poor show *out* of it. What is *multitude?*

R. Multitude is an auxiliary interjection, and—

D. (Sadly) There!—Ah, mine is a *disheartening* trade. (*to Rogers*) *You* have *talent*, you have even *genius*, for *grammar*, yet you are wasting your gift through criminal *heedlessness*. Go to your *seat*, I have no heart to *punish* you. To *think* that you can stand up here, without apparent *shame*, and call *multitude* an auxiliary *interjection*, when I have told you over and over and *over* again, that it is a copulative *conjunction*. (*Rogers retires*) Come *forward*, Joseph Harper, and say your *multiplication* table. (*Harper comes, on crutches, and recites glibly; Dobbins sits abstracted and does not hear him. Presently mutters: "That poor poor fellow!—I can't get him out of my mind—or my heart!"*)

Harper. Twice one is *two*, twice two're *four*, three tums four're *twelve*, four tums four're nine*teen*, five tums six're twenty-*seven*, five tums seven're thirty-*four*, six tums eight're forty-*nine*, seven tums nine're fifty-*four*, eight tums ten're seventy-*two*, 'leven tums nine're fifty-*six*, 'leven tums 'leven're ninety-*eight*, twelve tums ten're a *hundred* and *ten*, twelve tums eleven're a hundred and 'leven, twelve tums twelve're a hundred and sixty-*four*. (*Pause— and swabs off the sweat.*)

D. (Rousing himself slightly) What are you *waiting* for? Why don't you say your multipli*cation* table?

H. I *did* say it, sir.

D. Oh—I didn't *hear*. Did you say it *all?*

H. Yes, sir.

D. Did you make any *mistakes?*

H. No, sir.

D. That is very *well*. I will mark you *perfect*. You may do your *sums* now.

(*D. relapses into abstraction, H. does a lot of absurd sums, in vast figures, on the blackboard, somewhat after this pattern:*

$$
\begin{array}{r}
167 \\
42 \\
213 \\
111 \\
\underline{18} \\
1384.
\end{array}
$$

Then rubs them out. D. mutters "Ah, poor Potter!")

D. (Rousing.) What are you rubbing them *out,* for?

Small boy. Please, mayn't I go *out?*

D. What do you want to go *out* for?

S. B. Noth'n.

D. Well, go *'long,* then.

Another boy. Please mayn't I *too,* sir?

D. One at a *time.* Go to your *seat.* (*To Harper.*) Why did you rub the sums *out?*

H. I didn't know you wanted to *see* 'em, sir.

D. You *didn't?* (*Wearily*) Well, it's no matter. I hope you did them *right.*

H. Yes, sir, I *did.*

D. Pay *attention,* now. If A has a barrel of *apples,* and sells an eighth of them to *B,* and a quarter of them to *C,* and *half* of them to *D,* and gives an eighth of them to the *poor,* what *remains?*

H. (*Pause*) The *barrel,* sir.

D. (*Reflective pause.*) Correct. I didn't *think* of that. You may go. (*H. retires to his seat.*) Class in declamation.

(Several come forward and recite "You'd scarce expect one of my age," "The Boy Stood on the Burning Deck," "The Assyrian came down like a wolf on the fold," with stilted elocution and cast-iron gestures, the teacher saying absently, from time to time, "Very good" "Very good indeed" "Admirably done," etc. (To himself) "Who could ever have dreamed of his killing any one!")

D. General class in orthography.

(The school forms in line. D. gives out Baker, Lady, Rabbit, Cooper, and these are spelt correctly.)

D. Cataplasm.

1st. pupil. C, a, t, cat, t, y, catty,—

D. Next.

2d. pupil. C, a, t, cat, e—

D. Next.

3d. C, a, w, t, cat—

D. Next.

4th. C, a, double t, cat—

D. Next.

5th. K, a,—

D. Next.

6th. C, a, g, h, t, cat—

D. *Next!* (*irritated*)

7th. C, a, u, g, h, t, cat—

D. Nᴇxᴛ!

Tom Sawyer. C, h, e, i, g, h,—

D. What are you trying to *do?*

Tom. (*Meekly*) That's the way it's spelt in *my* book, sir.

D. Nonsense! It's not spelt so in *any* book.

Tom. Yes, sir, it's spelt that way in *mine.* I *thought* it wasn't spelt right, but I asked my aunt *Polly* and she reckoned it was spelt in that large way because most likely it was a book that was made for people that are hard of *hearing,* and—

D. There, that's *enough* of absurd *excuses.* Edward Tompkins, bring me Thomas Sawyer's *book.* (*It is brought.*) *Now* we shall see.

Dob. (*Displaying ink.*) Thomas Sawyer, how did *that* come?

Amy. (*aside*) O, it's too *bad!* I've a notion to—but I *won't:* he'll tell on *me.*

Tom. (*aside*) Now *that's* what she meant when she said she knew of something going to *happen!* Sʜᴇ did that! Very *good*—by and by when I *save* ʜᴇʀ, it'll just spread sackcloth and ashes of *remorse* on her head!

Dob. Thomas Sawyer, do you *hear* me? How did this *come?*

Tom. (*meekly*) I don't know, sir.

Dob. You don't *know!* Didn't *you* do it?

Tom. (*Meekly*) No, sir.

Dob. Who *did* do it?

Tom. I don't kn—know, sir.

Dob. Why do you *hesitate?* Look me in the *eye.* You su*spect* somebody. Who *is* it?

Tom. N—nobody, sir.

Dob. This is *enough* of this. Take off your *jacket.*

Amy. (*half rises.*) (*aside*) O, dear, *dear!* (*Sits down again, distressed.*)

> (*Tom is whaled. Alf Temple, whom Tom cannot see, enjoys it in dumb show.*)

Dob. (*Solemnly*) Before dismissing the school, I have *another* account—and of greater *importance*—to settle. (*Picks up piece of the bottle—holds it up.*) Who among you dares to invade his teacher's desk, like a *thief,* and meddle with his *property?* Who broke this? (*Pause—silence.*)

Amy. (*aside, in fright*) O, now I shall be *whipped!* (*Pause— glancing toward Tom*) Why don't he *tell?*

Dob. (*Solemnly and slowly, impressively*) *Somebody* here knows who *did* this thing—and that somebody shall *speak*—for I will *know!* I charge that person who carries upon his conscience that guilty knowledge, to hold up his *hand.*

> (*A waiting breathless pause of some seconds, then Tom Sawyer's right hand goes slowly up.*)

Amy. (*staring through her tears—aside*) O, *dear,* it's just as *mean* of him—

Dob. Thomas Sawyer, who broke this *bottle?*

> (*Tom rises slowly, turns and looks slowly about the room— then his eye meets the master's.*)

Tom. (*solemnly*) I cannot tell a lie—it was Alfred *Temple!*

Amy. (*aside—gratefully*) O how *lovely* in him!

Alf. (*astounded*) It's a *lie,* sir—I—

Dob. Silence! Not a word *out* of you! You bear the very *marks* of a sneak! Off with your *jacket!*

> (*Gives him a fearful whaling, and he howls all the way through, while Tom stands gravely with his hand in his breast, in the attitude of a self-admiring hero. With the last cut—*)

Dob. School is dismissed.

> (*Amy flies to Tom, puts her hands on his shoulders and her mouth to his ear—*)

Amy. O, what a *noble* DARLING!—I *never* shall forget you for this!

Slide the scene.

[SCENE 2]

(*A front scene while schoolhouse is being turned into a tempo-
rary court-house. Enter Huck and sits down on the ground.
Drives a peg an inch long, deep into the ground, and goes to
playing "mumbly-peg." Goes through the various operations,
and at last when he is on his knees trying to pull the peg out
with his teeth, enter aunt Polly. She stands contemplating
Huck with pleased surprise. Uplifts her hands.*)

A. P. (*fervently*) I could *hug* him for it! That ever I should have
lived to see *this*! I'll *join* him. (*joins her hands in front of her
bosom, drops her head reverently, closes her eyes, and moves her
lips as if in prayer.*)

(*Huck continues to work and tug at the peg with his teeth a
reasonable time, then—*)

Huck. Rot the thing, I can't git it *out!*

A. P. (*opens her eyes with a start, and sets them severely upon
the unconscious boy. Huck gets down to his work again. A. P. goes
and bends over him, adjusts her spectacles and gazes down. Stands
so, some seconds, then lifts H. slowly by the ear.*) What're you
trying to *do?*

H. (*humbly*) Please mam, trying to pull the *peg* out.

A. P. (*gently*) You poor motherless ridiculous thing!—and I
thought you were *praying*. Pity but you *would*, Huck. You'd be the
better for it, child, you'd be the *better* for it. You look *hungry*—had
your *dinner?*

H. (*hesitatingly*) Y-yes'm.

A. P. When?

H. Y-yistiddy.

A. P. (*gives him a hunk of cake from reticule*) There; I was
taking it to the trial to give to that poor unfortunate Muff Potter;
because I don't want him to feel *friendless*, you know—he's got
enough trouble without *that*. But I'll get him *another* cake.

H. (*with solicitude.*) What do you reckon they'll *do* with him?

A. P. Haven't you *heard?* Huck they're going to *hang* him.

Huck. (*aside*) O, dear, that ain't no news to ME, the way me and Tom have ha'nted that *trial.*

A. P. O, it seems too BAD. Poor soul, it's only his very *first* murder. ——You seen my *Tom?*

H. No'm.

A. P. (*going*) He didn't come home to *dinner,* the *scamp.* (*resignedly*) But I didn't *expect* him—I *never* do.

(*exit.*)

(*Crowd of Sunday-dressed citizens drift past, going to the trial— they can speak of it, if necessary.*)

(*Enter Tom in a hurry.*)

Huck. Tom, I been waiting around *ever* so long for you. I've got bad *news.*

Tom. No?—what *is* it?

H. Injun Joe don't *live* in the ha'nted *house* up the Stillhouse HOLLOW.

T. Well, then, good-bye to that *money*—we shan't ever *find* it! We've tracked out every out-of-the-way place he *could* live in; and so now we've just got to give it *up.* Huck, it's *mighty* hard luck!

H. Well, it just *is,* Tom. But we can't help it—ther' ain't no *way.* (*pause*) *Tom?*

T. Yes?

H. (*hesitating—fumbling his buttons*)—I—I

T. (*depressed*) I know what you're going to say.—You can't keep away from the *trial.*—Well—*I'm* weakening, *too.* I reckon it wasn't any use to *say* to each other that we'd keep away. Huck, it's *horrible* to sit there and see that poor Muff's life given away by that *half-* breed, but I can't any more keep away than if it was a *candle* and I was a *moth.* Come *along*—it ain't any *use.* We *can't* keep away. (*going*)

H. Tom we must keep the *other* promise, though. We musn't *say* one WORD. Injun Joe would break loose and *kill* us, right *there!* We mustn't let out a single *syllable,* Tom.

T. I know it. We got to keep perfectly *mum.* Poor old Muff! (*Exit both.*)

[SCENE 3]

THE COURT-ROOM. Aunt Polly prominent. "O-yes, O-yes,
O-yes! the honorable court will now come to order," *etc. (Poll
the jury?) The usual formalities and solemnities of opening
court. Injun Joe in gaudy new finery (he being now rich) in a
prominent place—for he was chief witness. Tom and Huck
steal in together, in the background, distressed, scared.*

The Judge. Mr. Sheriff, bring in the prisoner.

(*The Sheriff and a deputy go out and return supporting Muff
on either side, he being weak, bowed, broken and humbled by
what he has gone through. They sit.*)

(*Citizens, aside*) (*remarks?*)

The Judge. Prisoner, (*Muff shrinks, and looks up, with the
appealing expression of a dumb animal in distress*) a most painful
duty devolves upon me. To have to speak the words which doom to
death a fellow-creature is necessarily a painful office—*always*—and
surely it is the *more* painful when the person against whom the
doom is pronounced is one whose previously gentle and harmless
life, and kindly *ways*, have won and *kept* the friendly interest of *all*
men; whose tireless loving offices, and sympathies, and eager
helpfulness in their small affairs have made him the idol of *all
children*—

T. (Held back by Huck) O, Huck, I can't *stand* it, I *must*—

H. O, *please* Tom,—*please*—he'd kill us right *here*.

1. Cit. Ah, poor fellow!

Judge.—and whose goings and comings have been so blameless
that *all* will say *this* for him, that he has never had but one single
enemy—HIMSELF. To have to pronounce the awful sentence of
death against such a man, then, is indeed a hard duty. I *would*, for
your sake, for *mine*, for poor beset and tempted human *nature*, that
there were a *doubt*. But—there is *no* doubt—no softening circumstance—no palliation. In a moment of passion heightened and exag-

gerated by *drink*, you committed that most hideous of all crimes, *murder*. This is proved by the testimony of the witness known as Injun *Joe*, who *saw* the act, and was unable to *prevent* it.

T. (*aside*) O, Huck!

Judge. You have not been able to *deny* it. This is con*fession* of the crime. At midnight, in a lonely place, you drove your cruel knife into the body of a defenseless fellow-being—at the very *moment*, as the testimony *shows*, that he was imploring you to *spare* him for the sake of these (*indicating with a gesture*) his unoffending *wife*, and these his innocent *little* ones, whom you have so often danced upon your *knee*.

(*Muff bursts into sobbings.*)

Citizens.—Ah.

T. (*struggling with Huck*)—Huck, how *can* I—

Judge. (*solemnly*) Prisoner, have you anything to say why sentence of death should not be pronounced against you?

(*Muff struggles to his feet, looks wildly about—gulps, swallows, puts his hand to his throat—gradually grows quieter— turns his eyes slowly till they rest sorrowfully upon the widow and children—pauses—mournfully shakes his head, sinks down, puts his face in his hands and rocks to and fro.*)

(*Tom covers his face with his hands and seems to cry— Huck whispering in his ear.*)

Judge. (*solemnly*) The prisoner will *rise.* (*Muff is assisted to his feet, and stands with bowed head. The black cap is put on him, Tom and Huck staring and choking—a pleased interest or a damned smile in Injun Joe's face.*) It is the sentence of the court that you be taken hence to the *jail*, and thence on Friday the 14th. of August, to the place of execution, at 12 o'clock, *noon*; and that there you be hanged by the neck till you are *dead*—and may God have mercy on your—

Huck. (*immensely excited—to the struggling Tom and giving him a shove*)—Go *on*, Tom!

Tom. (*stepping swiftly forward and raising his hands*) O, *wait* —I was *there*, and I saw the killing *done!* (*Sensation—aunt Polly half rises—seats herself again, and uses her fan a moment, then*

fixes her gaze on Tom. Tom goes rapidly on.) I was behind a
tree—with *another* person—and he will give his *name* if you want
it—and I saw the two men *quarreling,* and Muff Potter threw
down his knife and the *stick* he had; and then they *collared* each
other and *struggled,* and *another* man came creeping up out of the
bushes, (*Injun Joe interested*) and *watching*—creeping up towards
that *knife*—and *grabbed* it and turned up his *sleeve,* and went
creeping and tip-toeing around, waiting for a *chance*—and then the
doctor tore loose and jumped for a *spade,* and Muff jumped for his
stick, and rushed at the doctor, and the doctor knocked the senses
clear out of him with the *spade*—and in that very *second* that *other*
man jumped for the *doctor* and drove the *knife* into him! (*Great
sensation—people rise to their feet—Muff Potter too—Injun Joe
very uneasy*) It was bright *moonlight,* (*Injun Joe rises, scared*) and
I saw that man as plain as I see him *now*—and there he *stands!*
(*pointing.*)

> (*Injun Joe makes a break.*)

Judge and Sheriff. Seize him!

> (*Injun Joe tears his way through the crowd, crashes through
> window at back of stage, and escapes, a dozen men chasing
> after him.*)

> (*Muff gropes his way to Tom, falls on his knees, and takes
> hold of his hand with both of his, and mutely fondles it with
> his face and kisses it. Pause—then aunt Polly comes slowly
> and sternly forward, adjusting her spectacles—stands contem-
> plating Tom severely a moment, then says:—*)

A. P. Well. I'll be bound *you'd* be mixed up in it, what*ev*er it
was.

(Tableau. Curtain.)

Act IV.

SCENE: *In the cave. Many avenues open into it. In mid-stage, a
big rock. At back of stage,* (*concealed*) *a hole covered with a bridge
of brittle boards. Dim light.* (*In the closing scene, when crowd*

*comes winding in from the various avenues with torches, then a
strong light, and the cave is seen to be gorgeous.)*

    *Enter Huck and Tom, with an inch of candle, dragging them-
    selves along, exhausted with fatigue. Throw themselves down.*

Huck. (*Despairingly.*) Tom, we're *goners*, and ther' ain't no
help for it. We'll never find our way out of this awful tangle in the
world!

    Tom. (*Disgusted.*) Now what a fool notion *that* is!

    Huck. It *ain't* a fool notion, *either.* How long we been in this
cave?

    Tom. I don't know. How's a body going to tell, where it's pitch
dark all the time, and night and day just alike?—just the same
color.

    Huck. Well *I* know. We been in here a *week*—I know it by just
how awful long it *seems,* and because I'm so hungry and tired.

    Tom. A week your granny!—we'd be *dead,* you idiot!

    Huck. Well how long do *you* think?

    Tom. Lemme see. We've had two long sleeps. And the rest of the
time we've been tramping.—It *seems* a week, or a month, or a year,
or along there somewhere, because it's so dismal and lonesome and
still; but I'll bet it isn't over two days and nights.

    Huck. Shucks, you think I could get as hungry as *I* am in two
days and nights? (*Makes frantic grabs and darts at a bat, Tom
helping. They fail to catch him and sit down again.*) Tom, I'd give
thirty-five dollars for that bat, if I had the money, and that was the
price of a bat, and you couldn't get 'em no cheaper. If I wouldn't,
I'm a *nigger.* (*Pause—Droopingly.*) Tom, it's awful to be lost this
way.

    Tom. (*Impatiently.*) *Shucks,* how you *talk!* We *ain't* lost!

    Huck. Ain't *lost!* Well I'd like to know what you *call* it, then?

    Tom. (*Irritated.*) Look a here, Huck Finn, how in the mischief
can we be *lost,* when we know where we *are?* You answer me *that.*

    Huck. We *don't* know where we are.

    Tom. What's the *reason* we don't? We're in the *cave,* ain't we?
And we *know* we're in the cave, don't we? I never *saw* such an ass!

    Huck. Now Tom Sawyer, that's just all *bosh. I* don't see no

difference, wurth a *cuss,* between being lost where you *don't* know
where you are, and being lost where you *do* know where you are.
And in *my* opinion, there *ain't* none.

Tom. Well if you ain't the mullet-headedest ignorammus that
ever—why look a *here:* Suppose you were lost out *doors*—right
out in the open *world,* in a general *way*—*every*where; you may well
call THAT lost, because you couldn't have any *idea* where you
were;—but in a *cave* that isn't more than seven miles long and a
half a mile deep at the very out-*side,* and has got a thousand miles
of crevices and passages in it, and you can go wherever you please,
and always put your hand on yourself whenever you *want* to—the
idea of calling that *lost!* Huck Finn, I never *saw* such a flat-head as
you!

Huck. Well I reckon maybe you are right. I hadn't thought of it
that way. (*Pause.*) But I can tell you *one* thing, Tom, I don't feel
so rotten much better *off,* now that I *ain't* lost, than I did before,
when I thought I *was.* If we ever git *out*—

T. If we ever get out! Why of *course* we'll get out, look here,
(*Telling it off on his fingers*) how does this thing stand? Why, *this*
way. All the girls and boys come down the river three miles, and
they come into this cave, to have a picnic and a *lark.* They get to
playing hide and whoop amongst the *passages.* They keep it up a
long *time.* You and I give them the *slip* and go wandering off to
plan another trip to the haunted house to hunt for Injun Joe's
money—

H. (*Interrupting with enthusiasm*) My *souls,* Tom, I was that
glad, three weeks ago, when we heard about 'em finding that
drownded Injun down the river at Saverton, and everybody said it
was Injun Joe, *sure,* that for as much as fifteen minutes I didn't
care if we *never* found the money, I was so dog-gone grateful!

T. And well you *might* be; because when *your* name got into the
papers along with *mine,* that let *you* in for some of his affections,
you see, and he wouldn't *forget* you, you know.

H. (*Scared.*) O, *don't,* Tom. Don't *talk* about it!

T. Why what are you afraid of *now?*

H. I know—but don't *talk* about it, Tom, in this dark place.

T. Well! then, I *won't*—where *was* I? Very good: we wandered off and got l— (*Shudder from Huck*) and the rest of the children got *lost.* We hunted and hunted, but had to give them up to—to— their *fate,* poor things. Well that wasn't *our* fault—we did the best we could for them.

H. Well, I only wish somebody had a took as much trouble for *us,* Tom—*rot* 'em!

T. Well they *will,* you muggins.

H. (*Eagerly*) How, Tom?

T. Those children *missed* us, didn't they?

H. Yes—yes—go—on!

T. Couldn't find hide nor hair of us?

H. Yes, yes, go on!

T. When they got home they told Aunt Polly—

H. Go *on* Tom!

T. And she raised the *town*—just as sure as you are born she did —and consequently there ain't a doubt in the world but this old cave's been brim *full* of people and *torches* ever *since!*

H. (*Throwing a hand-spring*) We're *saved* Tom, sure as *guns!* (*Throws another handspring or so, and subsides, happy.*)
　　　(*Tom's attention attracted to something—glides to the spot— dumb show of delight, returns.*)

T. Perfectly plain *case.*

H. (*Apprehensively*) But Tom, why don't they *find* us?

T. Hang it, how can they find *us* when we're not *lost?* It's a perfectly plain case that *they're* lost them*selves.*

H. (*In despair*) Then what *can* we do, Tom?

T. *Do?* Why turn out and *find* them. They'll be grateful all their *days.*—And they *ought* to be.

H. Well, come right *along* Tom. (*In new distress*) But how can *we* hunt for anybody? Candle's all used up but just this little *piece.*

T. You go and look *yonder.* (*Pointing*)
　　　(*Huck can't find it. Tom comes and shows him a couple of candles.*)

H. Good! Ain't that *luck.*
　　　(*They light them and throw away the small piece.*)

T. We're all right *now*—come along.

(*They wander off and find that hole, boarded over.*)

T. (*Motioning Huck back*) Hold on! Here's something boarded over. An old salt*petre* pit I reckon. (*Huck comes and looks*) Huck I tell you we've got into a mighty far-away part of this *cave!*

H. How do you *know?*

T. Because these boards are so *rotten.* Nobody has crossed them for twenty *years* I guess—may be a *thousand.* He would break *through.*

H. That's no sign. A person could *jump* over.

T. O, he *could*, could he? Suppose *you* do it?

H. (*Shrinking*) I—I don't *want* to.

T. Huck, you're *afraid* to.

H. Well, what *of* it? I'd dare *any*body to do it.

T. Do you dare *me?*

H. Yes, I *do.*

T. All right. I dare you to *follow*—and anybody that'll take a dare—

H. Will steal a *sheep*, I know. Go ahead.

(*Tom steps back, and after a few false starts, makes a running leap and barely lands on the other side, his hat falling off on Huck's side.*)

H. (*Goes through the same program, his hat falls off—he just barely clears the hole.*) Tom, I ain't going to try *that* any more—not if I *know* myself.

T. Well I don't want to, either. But how are we going to get our hats?

(*They study over this problem.*)

T. (*Brightening.*) Why Huck, if this is nothing, but a salt*petre* pit, it may not be 4 feet *deep.* Let's drop a *rock* through between the *boards*, and listen for it to strike *bottom.*

H. All right.

T. (*Bending over and dropping the rock.*) Now—listen! (*They listen intently 3 or 4 seconds.*) There!—Whe—ew! Huck, this hole's 4,000 feet *deep!*

H. (*Impressively.*) And we've been idiots enough to jump *over* it! Do you want your *hat?*

T. Hat?—*no.* What does a body want with his *hat* in the *house?* Come along—we ain't going to get *sun*-struck.

(*Exit.*)

(*Enter (front, L.) Amy Lawrence and Becky Thatcher, with an inch of candle. Exhausted, leg-weary. They sit down.*)

Becky. (*Begins to cry.*) O, Amy, I can't bear it any *longer!* It seems years and *years* that we've been lost; and I'm *so* tired and frightened and hungry!

Amy. There—lay your head in my lap, Becky—and *don't* give up, dear, *don't* cry. *We'll* be found.

Becky. (*Brightening a little.*) Do you believe it, Amy? *Do* you, really and *truly* believe it?

Amy. I do, really and *truly,* deed and deed and *double* deed. I *know* it!

Becky. O, say it *again,* Amy—keep *on* saying it, it does sound *so* good!

(*Sitting and embracing.*)

Amy. Becky, it's just as *sure!* Why, Tom Sawyer—

Becky. (*With a sigh.*) He's *your* Tom—ain't he, Amy?

Amy. Yes, he *is,* and—

Becky. (*Regretfully.*) I wish he was *my* Tom.

Amy. (*Generously.*) Why you can have *half* of him, Becky, if you want to.

Becky. (*Joyously.*) *May* I, Amy?

Amy. *Yes,* you may—I don't want *all* of him.

Becky. (*Worshipingly.*) Amy Lawrence, you are just too good and *noble!* For this world. (*Rapturously embracing and kissing her.*) There—you *lovely* love, what did you start to *say* about him?

A. Why *this.* Do you think Tom Sawyer is a kind of person to go out of this cave and leave *us* in here *lost?* I thank you, *no!* I just know as well as well can *be,* that he stayed *behind* when the rest went home, and he's in this cave *yet, hunting* for us.—That's the kind of a boy Tom *Sawyer* is, I'd have you to know. (*Aside.*) Why *that's* done her *good*—she's *nodding.* Well, let her go to *sleep.* (*Nodding herself.*) I'll take care of her. When I can't (*Drowsily.*) —can't—can't keep awake any longer, I'll wake her up, (*Gapes.*) and *she* can keep watch a while, and I'll—I'll—I'll take—a—little —nap. (*Gapes, mutters incoherently, very drowsily.*) then—if—if —I should die before I—wake,—I—I—

> (*Both girls asleep. One of them moves her foot, in sleep, and puts the candle out.*)
> (*Injun Joe enters L. candle in hand to slow music. He peers and pokes around, in a bad fright.*)

Joe. (*Solus.*) I can't *stand* this! I've got to leave! It can't be *all* imagination—for days and *days* I've heard the sound of distant *voices,* and *seemed* to catch the glimmer of distant *lights.* I'm all worn out with *dodging* and *running;* I'd give the *world* for an hour's sleep! Sh! (*Pauses to listen.*) And it's all on account of—ah, if I *could* get my hands on those cursed *boys!* (*Listens again.*) No, it's *imagination.* I'm all wrought *up* for want of *sleep.*—(*Wearily, despondently.*) O, I don't *dare* to leave the cave—it's *death* to do it. (*Pause, holds up candle, looks up at the walls, pleased surprise.*) Why, *here!*—these walls are clear and *clean,* instead of all clouded up with *names* and *dates* done with *candle*-smoke. It means that this part of the cave is never *visited*—and *I* never was in it before. No,—*wait; here* are some (*Reading.*) "J. B. W., 18*11;* H. M., 1803; William Bacon, 1806; R. L. G., 18*15.*" That's all. The latest is 18*15*—25 years *ago.* Ah, *this* is safe—they'll never come *here.* I'll fetch the money, and *hide* it.

> (*Exit L.*)

> (*Enter Tom and Huck bareheaded R. Tom discovering the girls.*)

Tom. Looky *here,* Huck! (*Bending over the girls.*) *Amy!*
> (*The girls start up, rubbing their eyes, then staring.*)

Amy. (*Springing at him and throwing her arms around his neck and crying for joy.*)—O, *Tom* I'm so glad! (*She lets go, and embraces Becky.) There* what did I *tell* you? I KNEW he'd come! *You* hug him! *half* of him's *yours!*

Becky. (Diffident and whimpering and twisting her apron.) I—I *would* if it was *dark.*

Tom. (Blows out his candle, hugs her.)

Becky. Is it all made *up,* Tom? You haven't got anything *against* me?

Tom. No! What are you *talking* about child? Do you think I would hold anything against a *girl? Come*—sit *down* and *rest* a minute—I'm *dog*-tired. *(They all sit.)* Just *explain,* now. What in the world are you girls doing *here*—and all by *yourselves?*

Amy. (Surprised.) Why, don't *you know?*

Tom. Don't I know *what?* What should *I* know?

Amy. (Alarmed.) Tom, haven't you been hunting for *us?*

Tom. Why, *no!* What do you *mean?* Are you *lost?*

Becky. (Breaking down.) O! oh, oh, ever, ever, ever since the *picnic!*

Tom. My goodness!

Becky. Yes. How long have *you* been in here?

Tom. Same length of *time.* Huck and I haven't been *out* yet.

Both girls. (In despair.)—O, dear, *dear!*

Amy. And didn't you know *we* were *lost?*

Tom. No! I never heard of it 'till this minute.

Amy. O, Tom, *Tom,* it's *dreadful!* Then we're *all* lost! And we'll never, never *never* get out, I just *know* it! O dear dear, *dear!*

Tom. Nonsense, Amy—how you talk; *we're* not lost. It's our *parents,* and aunts and uncles and things.

Becky. Why Tom, are *they* in here?

Tom. Of *course* they are—*somewhere.* Don't you suppose they'd come to hunt for *us? Certainly* they would—and they've got lost *themselves.*

Both Girls.—O, *goody!*

Tom. No, it isn't *goody,* either. Because we've got to hunt *them.* It isn't going to do for us to leave them in here to *starve,* is it?

Amy. (With loving effusion.) O, *Tom,* how *good* you are! You *always* think of everybody else before you do of *yourself.*

Tom. (With simple sincerity.) I'm *made* so. There isn't any *merit* in it.

Becky. O, I'm *so* hungry!

Tom. (Gets out a crust and divides it between them.) I've saved and saved this along for a close *place.* I'm glad I *did* it, now.

(*The girls eat ravenously.*)

Amy. But Tom, you're hungry *yourself.* (*Pressing the crust on him.*) *Take* some of it, Tom. (*He won't.*)

Becky. Tom *do* take some of mine—*do.* (*Pressing it on him.*)

Tom. No, I don't *want* it. I don't *honest,* I'm not *hungry.* Had a *bat.*

(*A moment of munching silence, the girls tugging ravenously at the bread, Tom and Huck observing them with hungry interest.*)

(*Enter Injun Joe stealthily, his water-melon sack over his shoulder. Discovers the children, starts violently, with a gasp of fright, then gets out his knife and goes creeping and stealing towards them. The girls discover him and scream. He drops his bag with a crash. Tom and Huck jump for the rock in mid-stage, and Joe jumps for them, the girls either paralyzed or continue to scream. The boys move round and round the rock, as around a table, keeping it always between themselves and Joe. Quick work, quick dodging required. Finally, all stand at bay and watching each other. Tom whispers a word in Huck's ear, Huck nods intelligently. Tom makes a feint toward the front, shouting.*)

Tom. Now Huck!

(*Joe skips in that direction to intercept, Huck flies rearward, Tom flies after him, Joe flies after both. Race for life. Huck makes a mighty spring, clears the hole, Tom does likewise and exit, but Injun Joe crashes through the rotten boards with a death-howl, and disappears.*)

(*Tom and Huck stealthily re-appear, and bend over the hole. The girls come running.*)

Tom. It's *awful* Huck!

Huck. (*Shuddering and turning away.*) Makes a body *sick* to *think* of it!

Amy. O, dear, *dear*, let's get away from this dreadful place. (*Both girls sob with fright.*) O, Tom, we're all going to be killed, or *die*, or something, in this horrible cave, I just *know* it, Tom!

Tom. (*Leading them away.*) Now don't you girls worry a *bit*. It's all *right*, and it's all going to come *out* right. The minute I find these poor old people, I'll take you right out of the *cave*. But we *mustn't* leave *them* in here *lost*—it won't *do*—it ain't *right*. Why you'd never hear the *last* of it in those mushy *Sunday*-school books—

(*Exit all, R.C.*)

(*Enter R.C. and from several other avenues, with torches, the whole town, and file in and out and round and about, and so reach at last the front of the stage. They assemble—weary and also despondent.*)

Judge Thatcher. Friends, once more I will urge what I began to urge early in this long-drawn, heart breaking search. It is not the work for *women,* and now that our hopes have wasted away, until it can not be really said that we *have* any hope left— (*Sobs, or groans or something from people.*) and we are expecting the *worst* and *must* expect the worst— (*More emotion from the people—mothers and aunts and sisters of Becky and Amy.*) and may come at any moment upon mournful *evidences* of the futility of all our efforts— (*More groans and sharp ones.*) it *can* not be well for the women to stay, and they MUST not. I beg them, I *implore* them to go *home.*

Aunt Polly. (*Straightening up out of her despondent attitude*) Go HOME, Judge Thatcher? And leave *my* TOM behind? Have —you—lost—your—*mind?* If it's a hundred *years*, I'll never stir a *step* out of this place till I get my *boy!* (*Puts her face in her apron, and sobs by* convulsion, *not* sound—*soon controls herself and uncovers her face again.*) If he is to be found crushed and disfigured at the bottom of some *abyss*, let it *be* so; it is God's will—but I shall be there! and none but these old hands, that have nurtured him and caressed him, and been laid a thousand times in blessing upon his head—when he was *asleep*—(*Do not* emphasize *this unconscious irony*) shall compose his limbs, and close the eyes that were the sunshine of my *life*. I shall be *there*; oh, God *knows* I shall be *there*, to *touch* him, *fondle* him, hold his head in my lap, love him, *lament* him; oh, my darling—my darling, the unceasing *joy* and *torment* of my happy old age! (*Breaks wholly down and sobs.*)

(*Meantime, Mary and Ben Rogers, bearing candles, have wandered, rearward. They discover the hats and the hole. Mary screams. All the crowd rush thither. The men take off their hats and stand reverently—the women all crying. Presently—*)

Judge Thatcher. I *feared* it—I feared it would turn *out* so. Poor lads they have found a *grave* down there, and the little girls *with* them—wandering about in this horrible place in the dark; for doubtless their candles gave out *long* ago.

(*Aunt Polly takes up Tom's hat, kisses it, presses it to her bosom.*)

Widow Douglas. Poor Huck Finn, nobody takes up *his* hat—nobody *wants* it. It seems *pitiful*; and yet he *earned* his friendlessness, poor outcast. I don't believe there was a *bit* of *harm* in him, but then there was no *good*, either. I wish in my heart that that poor thing had done *one* good action—*something, anything*, to make *somebody* want to say to that forsaken relic, "Come you *shan't* lie here—*I* will take you up." (*Pause.*) I will do it *myself*. (*Takes up the battered old plug gingerly*) It seems like forsaking a human *being* to leave it there. Poor Huck, he was *always* good-hearted—*no*body can deny *that*.

Judge Thatcher. Come, friends, we have a mournful task before us—let us not tarry *here*. (*Supports Aunt Polly and leads the way. All follow down and gather in front.*)

Aunt Polly. (*Getting a switch from out the folds of her dress and contemplating it.*) O, my poor dead boy! To *think* that while *he* was wandering to his *grave* in this black place, and perhaps thinking *lovingly* of *me*, I was thinking of *him* such thoughts as *this!*—(*Crying.*) It is too cruel, it is *too* cruel! (*Throwing it down.*) O, to the last day of my ruined life, I will never lay my hand in punishment upon a living creature *again.*—(*Pause.*) O, he is gone, he is *gone,* he is GONE!—I cannot cannot *bear* it! (*Kneels down sobbing, with her face in her hands—they all kneel with backs to the front, and hide their faces.*) Lord be merciful to me a *sinner!* (*Goes on, apparently praying to herself.*)

(*The children appear at the rear centre.*)

Tom. Sh-h! *There* they are!—lost, sick, and *discouraged*—pleading, for *help.* What did I tell you?—what did I *tell* you? It's the most extraordinary triumph I've ever achieved in my *life*—and yet I believed from the *start* I could do it. I've found this whole *gang!* (*Pause—impressively.*) Huck, we'll be *heroes* for this. It'll be in the papers—maybe in *books.* Sh-h! Now do as I *tell* you—we'll work off a sur*prise* on them.

(*Tom whispers something in the ear of each—then the others disappear, and Tom blows out his candle and creeps down and stretches himself on the floor behind Aunt Polly, and begins to snore—snores two or three times and stops. Aunt Polly starts —looks up with a happy surprise in her face—listens—hears nothing more—shakes her head.*)

Aunt Polly. (*Resignedly.*) It was only imagination. But for a *moment* I really thought it was *him*—oh, *dear*—dear! (*Pause— musingly.*)—And what *music* it was! (*Tom begins to snore again.*) That—why—that's not imagi——(*Turns slowly, rises, her eye falls on Tom. Snatches him in her arms.*) O, my darling, my darling! (*Holds him at arm's length and devours him with her eyes.*)—O, he *is* alive, O, my *own* precious Tom! (*Hugs him again.*)—(*Holds him at arm's length again.*)—O, you darling, you pr—*ecious!*—(*Snatches up the switch and applies it vigorously.*) —I'll tan you, I'll tan you, you good for nothing scamp!—(*Laying it on.*)—here I've been trapsing around this hole 2 or 3 days and nights, hunting for *you,* you *trash!* and (*Hugging him.*) O, my *darling* I am so grateful, so *grateful,* so unspeakably—(*Giving him a parting half-dozen whacks, throws down the switch, clasps and uplifts her hands and face.*)—O, receive the *spirit* of a gratitude which an *eternity* of *speech* could not express in words!

Mrs. Lawrence. O, *you* are rich, but *my* child is *still* lost and I shall never again—

(Tom snatches Amy from concealment and she jumps into her arms.)

Mrs. T. Then I *only* am bereaved—Oh, my lost, lost *darling,* is there *no* hope, is there no—

(Tom snatches Becky from her concealment and she jumps into her mother's arms.)

(Huck wanders diffidently out from his concealment.)

T. *(Going to him)* Here! You want to all welcome *Huck, too* you know.

Several. *(Crowding about him)* Huck *is* welcome.

T. It's been kept a secret a good while, but there are reasons why it isn't any use to keep it a secret any *more*—Huck risked his life to save the widow Douglas's and was the cause that it *was* saved—the time Injun Joe planned to *kill* her.

(The widow goes for Huck.)

A.P. We've had enough of this place, and now we'll *leave* it I reckon.

T. *(To his aunt)* *(Coming forward)* Wait a moment, before you go. This is not *regular*. There is no *climax*. It would not happen so in a *book*.

A.P. *Hang* your *books*. Nothing suits *you* unless it happens as it would in a *book*. I want to get out of this *place*. I don't care anything *about* the books.

T. Aunt Polly it would not be *regular*. Now just a *word* that's all. It is a happy *day*—a *great* day—full of splendid *episodes*. My *own* humble efforts—

A.P. *(Interrupting)* What have *you* done. I want to know.

T. Huck was *lost*. I *found* him and restored him to—to *society*. Two young *maidens* were lost, I *found* them, and restored them to their *parents*. You people were all lost. I *found* you and restored you to—to your country and your *flag*.

A.P. O, *go* on!

T. This *money*—some four hundred millions of *dollars,* I reckon

—was lost. I found it—*Huck* and I found it—and will restore it to —to *circulation*. (*Empties the money on the floor.*)

Everybody. What! (*They swoop towards it.*)

T. There—contain your curiosity—we'll tell you all *about* it at *home.* Mr. Alf *Temple,* yonder, has been a grand *hero* for two or three weeks, because he found a drowned *Injun* down by *Saverton,* and was likely to get the town's two hundred dollars *reward* offered for Injun *Joe* dead or alive. *Was* likely—but *ain't* likely any *longer.* It wasn't Injun *Joe!*

Alf. T. It *was* Injun Joe!

T. It *wasn't.*

A.P. Hush *up!* How do *you* know?

T. Because Injun Joe was standing *here* an hour ago!

A.P. (*Frightened.*) Goodness!

(*General disposition to stampede.*)

T. Hold on—stay where you *are*—you're not in any *danger.*

A.P. Because *you're* here I suppose.

T. Yes, that's *partly* the reason. Injun Joe came blustering in here an hour ago, with his knife and tried to *scare* me. He *succeeded.* For I was unpre*pared.* Huck and I fled for our *lives.* He *followed.* We *cleared* that hole yonder, but—

Several. (*Anxiously*) But *what?*

T. He *didn't.* He's reposing at the bottom of it *now.*

Several. (*Sensation*) Dead?

T. Likely—the hole's four thousand feet *deep.* We *sounded* it.

First. This is *prodigious!*

Second. What a lucky *riddance!*

A.P. Poor, poor *fellow!*

Tom. He's down there—on account of Huck and *me.* And if Mr. Alf *Temple* don't object, we'll produce him and take the *reward.*

A.P. It's dreadful! But Tom, you *are* a kind of a some sort of a hero by *accident,* after *all.*

Tom. Then if I by these humble achievements have earned your favor, grant me your blessing upon my *nuptials.*

A.P. (*Backing off and inspecting him.*) Your *what?*

Tom. Nuptials.

A.P. Nuptials!

Tom. Nuptials.

A.P. What *do* you mean, child?

Tom. I am going to get *married.*

A.P. Is the world coming to an end.

Tom. (*Leading forward Amy and Becky.*) Please give us your blessing.

A.P. Goodness *sake,* are you going to marry *both* of them?

Tom. That's the—that's the *idea.*

A.P. Well, this *is* like a book—too *much* like a book altogether. (*Lifts him gradually by the ear.*) Tom, do you really *want* to get married?

Tom. Ow!—y—*yes'm.*

A.P. (*Still lifting.*) *Reflect* upon it—it is a serious step. *Do* you want to marry?

Tom. I—I don't *know'm.*

A.P. (*Still lifting.*) But *do* you?

Tom. Ow!—*no'm!*

A.P. (*Still lifting.*) Make perfectly *sure,* Tom.

Tom. No, *no*—I don't *want* to get married. I *am* sure.

A.P. (*Letting go.*) Very *well* then. Get right down on your knees and say you're *sorry* for ever *thinking* of such ridiculous *outrageous nonsense*—and don't you get up till I *tell* you. (*She faces the audience—he kneels behind her. As soon as her back is turned, he stands on his head.*) Well, he *is* a good, obedient *boy*—there's no *denying* that. A body can't *stay* put out with him. When he knows he's in the wrong, he's so *humble.* (*Curtain beginning to descend.*) He's not so obedient when he's *away* from you, because he's so *forgetful,* poor Tom; but as long as you're *by,* it keeps him re-minded of what you told him to *do,* and then he'd sooner *die* than— (*Turns and catches him standing on his head—he flirts down on his knees again—she stands contemplating him severely.*)

(CURTAIN.)

EXPLANATORY
NOTES

Explanatory Notes

Jane Lampton Clemens

43.5–7 I knew her well . . . days' journey apart.] From his birth in 1835 until 1852, Clemens lived with his family. Between the latter year and 1861, he saw his mother frequently. In 1861, he and his brother left for Nevada, and thereafter he saw her only during brief visits.

47.7–24 I knew that . . . the executioner] See also *MTA*, I, 83–84, 87.

48.12 The Earl] See *MTHL*, I, 301–302 and II, 869–871.

49.8–9 Manifestly, training and association can accomplish strange miracles.] This is a favorite theme of the author, developed in *Huckleberry Finn, Connecticut Yankee, Pudd'nhead Wilson, What Is Man?*, and *The Mysterious Stranger* (1916).

49.31 The "nigger trader" was loathed by everybody.] William B. Beebe, considered in "Villagers."

50.17–20 A woman . . . sold to a Mr. B.] Jennie, who had accompanied the Clemenses on the trip from Tennessee to Missouri in 1835.

51.6 hard and tedious journey] As the letter in MTP shows, John Marshall Clemens made this trip during the winter of 1841/42. The debtor was William Lester. Three years later Clemens still was trying to collect.

51.11   conscience to hold him to it.] Clemens silently omitted some details at this point, but succeeded in shortening without distorting his father's account of the transaction.

52.4–8   She was a dancer . . . seventy years before.] This passage suggests that Clemens may have used Orion's sketch in writing his essay. Orion wrote: "To the last Mrs. Clemens maintained dancing to be innocent and healthful. Even in the last year of her life she liked to show a company the beautiful step and graceful movement she had learned in her youth." Mrs. Clemens lived with Orion during her last years.

52.5–6   as capable a [dancer] as the Presbyterian church could show among its communicants.] Jane joined the Presbyterian Church of Hannibal in 1843. Orion, in a brief sketch of his mother (see Appendix C) described her as a "good Baptist."

A Human Bloodhound

69.4   my father] No one has presented any evidence that the tendency toward philosophical speculation which characterizes the narrator's father was characteristic of John M. Clemens, the father of Samuel L. Clemens.

69.7   Harbison's] In chapter ten of The Adventures of Tom Sawyer, Huck and Tom, hiding in an old tannery, hear a dog howling and guess that it is Bull Harbison.

69.11   the Corpse] This is one of the names given to Godkin, "perhaps the name that had the widest currency," in "Indiantown." See WWD, p. 165.

Huck Finn and Tom Sawyer among the Indians

92.13–14   aunt Sally . . . Missouri] As DeVoto notices in his comments on the story: "A slight indication that Mark has confused Aunt Sally with Aunt Polly." Because he seldom reread his books, the author sometimes had trouble remembering the names of his characters.

101.1   It was . . . camp] "The loss of animals being one of the most serious of troubles, the camp should be so situated as to give the greatest possible security to the waggons and picket line against the sneaking attempts of thieves during the darkness. The ground should be sufficiently level to permit the tents being properly pitched; the sward should be thick, that rain may not render the camp muddy; the grass short, to secure against accident by fire. A few trees add greatly to the beauty and comfort of a camp . . . The camp should be in close vicinity to water . . ." (Richard Irving Dodge, *The Plains of the Great West and Their Inhabitants, Being a Description of the Plains, Game, Indians, &c. of the Great North American Desert* [New York, 1877], p. 69. Hereafter this book will be cited as *The Plains*).

102.6   There was . . . Injuns] Cf. Mark Twain, "The Noble Red Man," *The Galaxy*, X (September 1870), 428: "In June, seven Indians went to a small station on the Plains where three white men lived, and asked for food; it was given them, and also tobacco. They stayed two hours, eating and smoking and talking, waiting with Indian patience for their customary odds of seven to one to offer, and as soon as it came they seized the opportunity; that is, when two of the men went out, they killed the other the instant he turned his back . . . then they caught his comrades separately . . ."

102.30   one named Hog Face] "Any personal defect, deformity of character, or casual incident furnishing ground for a good story, is eagerly seized upon as a fit name. 'Powder Face,' the war chief of the Arrapahoes . . . is known . . . by the title which was given him from having his face badly burned by an explosion of powder when he was a young man" (Richard Irving Dodge, *Our Wild Indians: Thirty-Three Years' Personal Experience Among the Red Men of the Great West* [Hartford, 1883], p. 228. Hereafter this book will be cited as *Our Wild Indians*). It should be mentioned that long before he read Dodge, in "Niagara" (1869) Twain had given Indians names such as Laughing Tadpole, Gobbler-of-the-Lightnings, Benificent Polecat, and Roaring Thundergust.

103.34   minute . . . for it;] "By nature he [the Indian] is a perfect child, and when he wants anything he wants it with all his heart and mind and soul, immediately and without reference to anything else. . . . the Indian will give anything he possesses for the merest bauble to which he takes a fancy" (*Our Wild Indians*, p. 263).

104.17   And they . . . us.] Notebook 3 (1865), TS p. 8 has an item written by Clemens when he was visiting Angels' Camp in California: "Pi Ute war dance on hills back of Angels'."

104.20–21   the one . . . Man-afraid-of-his-Mother-in-law,] " 'Man-afraid-of-his-horses,' received, it is said, his name from having, on the occasion of an attack on his camp by hostile Indians, saved his horses but left his family in the hands of the enemy" (*Our Wild Indians*, p. 228). In his adaptation of this name, Twain made use of an old, sure-fire joke.

106.30–35   the Injun . . . Flaxy,] ". . . the Germaine girls . . . were captured on the banks of Smoky Hill River in Western Kansas, on September 10, 1874. The family consisted of father, wife, and seven children; six of whom were girls, whose ages ranged between five and twenty-one years. The following is the account given by Catherine . . . 'The next morning I went down the river's bank to drive up the cattle, and when returning heard shouts and yells. Running towards the waggon I saw my poor father shot through the back and my mother tomahawked by a big Indian. They were both scalped while yet living. . . . Rebecca seized an axe and attempted to defend herself. She was soon overpowered, and knocked down insensible. While lying on the ground covered with blood, several Indians outraged her person. Then they tore her clothes off and covered her up with bedclothes from the waggon. These were set on fire, and my darling sister was burned to death. Stephen was killed next, his scalp being taken. Sister Johanna and myself were placed side by side, and they came up to inspect us and see which one they should kill. The choice fell on poor Johanna, and she was shot through the head. Tying us—Sophia, Lucy, Nancy, and myself—they hurried us across the prairie, going south. My clothes were torn from me. I was stripped naked, and painted by the old squaws, and made the wife of the chief who could catch me when fastened upon the back of a horse which was set loose on the prairie. . . . I was made the victim of their desires—nearly all in the tribe . . ." (William Blackmore, "Introduction" to *The Plains*, pp. 1–li).

107.22–24 And he told . . . book.] In "The Noble Red Man," *The Galaxy*, X (September 1870), 428, Twain writes of Indian cruelty between June 1868 and October 1869, citing "Dr. Keim's excellent book" as his authority: *"Husbands were mutilated, tortured, and scalped, and their wives compelled to look on. . . .* their favorite mutilations cannot be put into print."

109.7–8 he said . . . anything more,] "This and later passages," says DeVoto in his notes on this fragment, "are the most formidable evidence yet for the notion that Tom was Mark's presentation of the Don Quixote theme."

114.25 an Injun is patient;] "The Indian is patient and cunning; he relies on these qualities for the surprise of his enemy" (*Our Wild Indians*, p. 437). "The Indian's great delight is the attack of a wagon train. . . . For days he will watch the slow-moving line, until he knows exactly the number and character of armed men that defend it" (*Our Wild Indians*, pp. 451–452).

115.4–5 an Injun . . . hurry.] "In a close contest, or if the Indians have cause to be exceptionally angry, the wounded man is promptly dispatched. If there be plenty of time and no danger apprehended, the unfortunate prisoner will have full experience of the ingenuity in torture of these fiends" (*Our Wild Indians*, p. 529).

115.15–16   I know . . . nigger,] "An Indian will never take the scalp of a colored soldier, nor does he give any reason for it; all to be got out of him by way of explanation is, 'Buffalo soldier no good, heap bad medicine'" (*Our Wild Indians*, p. 517).

115.35–
116.2   this is nothing . . . retaliate on.] ". . . the Indians believe that the manes or shades of the departed slain in battle require to be appeased by the death of the slayer, if possible; or, failing his, by that of some one of the slayer's nation or tribe.

"In the spring of 1873 a band of Cheyennes on a marauding expedition to New Mexico were surprised by troops, and some six or eight killed. When the survivors reached home with the news, the most fearful excitement prevailed throughout the Indian camp, and a party was at once made up to go to the settlements to obtain white victims in retaliation. Fortunately for the unprepared settlers, but most unfortunately for themselves, a small party of surveyors were at work on the route of the Indian march. They were set upon by the Indians, who, when they had killed a number sufficient to appease the shades of their slain friends, returned satisfied to their encampment without molesting the settlers" (*Our Wild Indians*, p. 182).

117.1   Poor . . . her.] "I have before said that the Indians are fond of children. In their raids on each other and on the whites those children which are large enough to help themselves a little, and not so large as to be likely to have strong affection or memory, are carried off to the tribe and adopted into it. These foster children are treated by the Indians as their own . . ." (*The Plains*, p. 394).

118.22   he said no . . . first,] What these other fish were is never made clear.

119.25   Brace Johnson . . . man.] As the headnote preceding this fragment indicates, Huck's description of Brace is much like Custer's description of Wild Bill Hickok which Clemens may have seen as early as 1872.

120.21   moreover . . . religion.] "The power of earnestness is well exemplified in the influence that the Indian religion obtains over the white trappers and 'squaw-men' who live with them. Nine-tenths are sooner or later converted to the Indian idea, and many of them have firm faith in their power of making 'medicine'" (*Our Wild Indians*, p. 108).

120.23   Injuns . . . two Gods,] "In common with the best of the plains Indians, the Cheyenne believes in two gods, equals in wisdom and power.

"One is the '*good god,*' aiding the Indian, to the best of his ability, in all his undertakings, whether good or bad, and (without reference to abstract right or morality, of which the Indian has no conception) always and under all circumstances his friend and assistant. From him comes all the pleasurable things of life: warmth, food, joy, success alike in the chase, love, and war.

"The other is the '*bad god,*' always his enemy, and injuring him at all times and places, when not restrained by the power of the good god. From the bad god comes all pain, suffering, and disaster. He brings the cold, he drives away the game, and through his power the Indian is tortured with wounds or writhes in death.

"Constant conflict, of which the Indian is the subject, is going on between the two gods, with constantly varying results. Having no inward sense of right and wrong, and no idea of any moral accountability, either present or future, the Indian attributes to the direct action of one great power all the good, and to the other great power all the bad, that may happen to him. For his devoted and unremitting services on behalf of the Indian the good god demands nothing in return—no adulation, no prayers, not even thanks. He is the Indian's friend, as the bad god is his enemy, for some inscrutable reason of his own, which the Indian does not undertake to divine.

"While the Indian believes in another life after death,

the power of the two gods does not extend to it, but is restricted entirely to benefits or injuries in this world . . ." (*The Plains*, pp. 272–273).

Cf. the purported teachings of a governess, Miss Foote, to the Clemens children in 1881 or 1882 (Edith Colgate Salisbury, *Susy and Mark Twain* [New York, 1965], p. 143).

122.11   a regular fog.] Custer had told of the coming of a similar fog, and of a detachment of cavalry which got lost in it, traveled for an hour in a semicircle, and attacked its own camp because it mistook it for an Indian village (*The Galaxy*, XIV [May 1872], 613–614). *The Plains* (pp. 48–49), however, contains more details corresponding to those in Mark Twain's story. After telling about several men who were crazed because they lost their sense of direction on the plains, Dodge writes:

"Once in Texas, when quite a young man, I went hunting with the acting post surgeon, an enthusiastic sportsman, but a very nervous excitable man. . . . a heavy fog settled down upon us, completly shutting out the sun and all landmarks. . . . The doctor . . . soon developed a symptom of the plains insanity—'to keep moving.' . . . My plan was to find a comfortable position, go into camp, and remain quiet until the sun appeared. He would not hear of it; and I had to go with him to save him from himself. . . .

"We were wandering objectless in a circle. After a great deal of persuasion I got the doctor to go into camp. We had nothing to eat, and had found no water. He could not sleep, and by morning was almost insane. The fog still enveloped us, but he would not remain in camp; and I thought action best for him, who was, in addition to his other troubles, now tormenting himself with the certainty of dying of hunger and thirst. . . . [Eventually the fog lifted.] We had wandered . . . for more than twenty-five miles from the post."

126.5–6   a little . . . chain] Mrs. Richard Holliday of Hannibal during Clemens's boyhood wore an ivory miniature picturing her father. She was the prototype of the Widow Douglas. (*SCH*, pp. 157–158).

129.28　　Sioux was Ogillallahs.] The names and locations of Indian tribes which are mentioned by Brace are contained in a table at the conclusion of *The Plains*, pp. 441–448.

134.13–14　　"There's . . . now."] Dodge, in *The Plains* (pp. 81–85) writes at length about waterspouts. "The quantity of water poured from the clouds, and the effect produced," he says, are apparently incredible, but "the facts are perfectly known to every plainsman." Like Brace, he knows that when such a storm breaks horses should be tethered at once and that such storms may come even when the sky is clear. Dodge described "the most remarkable" of six or eight such storms which he had been in: "My company was encamped for the summer on a bluff bank about twenty-five feet high, at the foot of which was the dry sandy bed of a stream. . . . About eleven o'clock on a clear, bright, beautiful starlight night . . . I heard a distant roaring, rushing sound, now more now less distinct, but gradually swelling in power. . . . I rushed out and placed myself on the edge of the bank overlooking the sand. In a few moments a long creamy wave, beaten into foam, crept swiftly with a hissing sound across the sand. This appeared to be only a few inches in depth. Following with equal speed, and at a distance of about sixty feet behind the advance of this sheet, was a straight, unbroken mass of water of at least four feet in height. The front of this mass was not rounded into a wave, but rose sheer and straight, a perfect wall of water. From this front wall the mass rose gradually to the rear, and was covered with logs and *débris* of all kinds, rolling and plunging in the tremendous current. In ten minutes from the passage of the advance wave, the water at my feet was at least fifteen feet deep, and the stream nearly half a mile wide.

"It was three days before this stream was fordable, and fully a month before it returned to its normal con-

dition. . . . The rain which furnished all this water was
a waterspout of probably an hour's duration."

137.10   shoe-print . . . woman.] "Next morning the command,
at an early hour, started out to take up this Indian trail
which they followed for two days as rapidly as possible;
it becoming evident from the many campfires which we
passed, that we were gaining on the Indians. Wherever
they had encamped we found the print of a woman's
shoe, and we concluded that they had with them some
white captive" (*The Life of the Hon. William F. Cody,
Known as Buffalo Bill the Famous Hunter, Scout and
Guide, An Autobiography* [Hartford, 1879], p. 255).

137.24   four . . . ground;] "The rule is this. When a woman is
captured by a party she belongs equally to each and all,
so long as that party is out. . . . The husband or other
male protectors killed or dispersed, she is borne off in
triumph to where the Indians make their first camp. . . .
If she resists at all her clothing is torn off from her
person, four pegs are driven into the ground, and her
arms and legs, stretched to the utmost, are tied fast to
them by thongs. Here, with the howling band dancing
and singing around her, she is subjected to violation after
violation, outrage after outrage, to every abuse and in-
dignity, until not unfrequently death releases her from
suffering" (*The Plains,* pp. 395–396).

139.18–19   "Now . . . all right.] Dodge, in *Our Wild Indians* (pp.
220–223), claims that Indians never confine or maltreat
madmen because they believe such men to be "directly
under the malevolent influence of the Bad God." He tells
the story of "a prominent scientist . . . in pursuit of
knowledge on the Upper Missouri":

> In a country full of hostile Sioux, without a blanket or
> mouthful to eat, he started alone, armed only with his
> butterfly net and loaded only with his pack for carrying
> specimens. One day, when busily occupied, he suddenly
> found himself surrounded by Indians. He showed no fear,
> and was carried to the village. His pack was found loaded
> with insects, bugs, and loathsome reptiles. The Indians

decided that a white man who would come alone into that country unarmed, without food or bedding, for the accumulation of such things, must be crazy; so, the pack having been destroyed as 'bad medicine,' the doctor was carefully led out of camp and turned loose.

DeVoto suggests that Robert Montgomery Bird's *Nick of the Woods* (1837) may have been influential here. Mark Twain shows familiarity with it in chapter 55 of *Life on the Mississippi*. In Bird's novel Nathan Slaughter paints himself with lizards, snakes, skulls, and other pictures and inspires fear in the Indians by pretending that he is having an epileptic fit.

Tom Sawyer's Conspiracy

163.1–3   Widow . . . Watson] Widow Douglas had appeared in both *Tom Sawyer* and *Huckleberry Finn;* her sister Miss Watson figured in the latter book. On Miss Watson's death, her slave Jim had been given his freedom in her will. Nevertheless, Miss Watson is anachronistically revived and appears throughout this piece.

163.5–6   summer days . . . now] This passage greatly resembles the opening paragraph of the recently published "Tom Sawyer, Detective" (1897).

165.18   Jimmy Grimes] Grimes is modeled after Jimmy Finn and General Gaines, two of Hannibal's town drunkards. Both names were set down in working notes; one identifies Gaines as the new town drunkard, and another recalls that Gaines was an ex-keelboatman.

165.28   Christian, as . . . say.] The argument here is much like Huck and Tom's discussion of the Crusades in chapter one of *Tom Sawyer Abroad*.

167.4   Stow] Harriet Beecher Stowe's *Uncle Tom's Cabin* had been published serially in 1851 and 1852. The passage seems to place Huck's recounting of the antebellum happenings of the story in the postwar period.

168.27   Miss Mary] In chapters 24 through 29 of *Huckleberry Finn*, the King and the Duke attempted to dupe the Wilks girls, "Mary [Jane] en de Hair-lip." Jim had stayed aboard the raft during these chapters, so he could not have known about the events first-hand.

170.3–4   he was . . . before.] See "It was always nuts for Tom Sawyer—a mystery was." (Chapter two of "Tom Sawyer, Detective.")

178.20–21 Elegant Deef and Dumb Nigger Lad] Variations of this disguise were often employed by Clemens: cf. Injun Joe's disguise in *Tom Sawyer*, the Duke's in *Huckleberry Finn*, and that of Jake Dunlap in "Tom Sawyer, Detective."

184.24–25 Can't you . . . dream?] Similarly in chapter 15 of *Huckleberry Finn*, Huck persuades Jim that an actual experience was a dream.

188.29   Inside Sentinel] The Royal Arch Masons and the Knights Templar were not chartered in Hannibal until the 1860's. The Odd Fellows Mystic Lodge, No. 17, was chartered in the town on 29 July 1846, and officers mentioned in this passage were active in the organization.

193.2   wrong-end first] Clemens had used the joke about the reversed cut in the Buffalo *Express*, 17 September and 15 October 1870, and in the *Galaxy* for November 1870.

197.10–11 beating the Dunlaps] refers to Tom's exploits in "Tom Sawyer, Detective."

207.16   blowed the signals] About once a month Hannibal's rowdies rode around the streets and roused the sleeping villagers until an ordinance passed in 1845 made it a misdemeanor to disturb the peace "by blowing horns, trumpets or other instruments."

211.11   struck the trail] Working note B2 (Appendix C) outlines another line of action following this.

213.18   Higgins's Bill] A note on Tom's mention of Bull Harbison in chapter ten of *Tom Sawyer* comments on usage:

"If Mr. Harbison had owned a slave named Bull, Tom would have spoken of him as 'Harbison's Bull,' but a son or a dog of that name was 'Bull Harbison.'" Notebook 32a, TS p. 59, has: "Introduce Higgins that one-legged nigger," and a working note refers to "One-legged Higgins (Bradish's nigger)." In chapter eight of *Huckleberry Finn*, Jim tells a story about "dat one-laigged nigger dat b'longs to old Misto Bradish."

218.11　the way . . . Arkansaw] refers to Tom's successful activity in "Tom Sawyer, Detective."

221.21　By George . . . Duke!] Notebook 32a, TS p. 60, has: "Bram Stoker says reintroduce the red-haired girl and the King and Duke." Bram Stoker, whom the humorist had known for several years, was the author of *Dracula*. Working notes which mention the King, the Duke, and Mary Jane Wilks indicate that the humorist reread the chapters of *Huckleberry Finn* in which they appear.

222.8–10　The time . . . pocket] This reference to chapter 31 of *Huckleberry Finn* contains two incorrect details: Huck had not allowed Jim to get away, and instead of losing money on Jim, the Duke and the King had gained forty dollars by turning him over to Silas Phelps.

223.18　Everybody knows . . . once] Presumably, the King and the Duke could not know this, since Huck had never told them the truth about the ownership of Jim.

226.32　time . . . Arkansaw] Huck's memory of the details as set forth in chapter 33 of *Huckleberry Finn* is quite accurate.

227.21　hand him . . . ourselves] The reference to the queen places this after 1837, when Victoria succeeded to the throne. A little later Tom's statement that the queen "was young and inexperienced" places the story not long after 1837, in contrast to the H. B. Stowe reference.

231.10–11　what he . . . Silas's] refers to Tom's feats in "Tom Sawyer, Detective."

233.6   Cairo . . . free State] Cairo was in Illinois, a free state; so were other towns all the way between St. Petersburg and Cairo on the Illinois side of the river. A later speech of Huck's (p. 233.20–25) more clearly justifies the boys' waiting until Jim gets to Cairo.

234.20   The Burning Shame] the disgraceful performance of the King and the Duke in Bricksville as described in chapter 23 of *Huckleberry Finn*. The caper was given this name in the manuscript, but for the book Clemens changed it to the Royal Nonesuch. Jim was on the raft and could not have witnessed it.

APPENDIXES

APPENDIX A

Villagers of 1840–3:
A Biographical Directory

NAMES AND identifying phrases for persons who appear in "Villagers of 1840–3" are ordered alphabetically below. When traces of the person have been found outside Mark Twain's manuscript, biographical facts are presented. The chief sources of information include: Return Ira Holcombe, *History of Marion County, Missouri* (St. Louis, 1884); C. P. Greene, *A Mirror of Hannibal* (Hannibal, 1905); Albert Bigelow Paine, *Mark Twain: A Biography* (New York, 1912, 1935); Minnie M. Brashear, *Mark Twain: Son of Missouri* (Chapel Hill, 1934); Samuel C. Webster, *Mark Twain: Business Man* (Boston, 1946); and—preeminently—notations by Dixon Wecter on a typescript copy of the manuscript and Wecter, *Sam Clemens of Hannibal* (Boston, 1952). In addition, I have made use of the published writings of Mark Twain and the unpublished writings in the Mark Twain Papers in the University of California at Berkeley.

Villagers Who Are Named

ARMSTRONG, JESSE. He was purportedly a distant cousin of Clemens, but, as Wecter discovered, the events in this "biography" had no relation to his life. Instead, they are based upon a sensational murder which took place in Hannibal in 1888 long after Clemens had left. The husband was Amos J. Stillwell, a prosperous businessman; the lover, Dr. Joseph Carter Hearne, twenty-three years Stillwell's junior and a prosperous surgeon. As in this account, the husband was murdered in the night with an axe secured on the premises, the widow's share of the inheritance was substantial ($40,000), and the pair married a year later. Followed to the train by a jeering mob, they moved to California. Dr. Hearne was tried and acquitted in 1895. It is possible that Clemens heard the details from his sister, since Stillwell had been associated with her husband's St. Louis firm in the 1850's. The incident may have been recalled to his memory some years after he wrote "Villagers," during his visit to Hannibal in the spring of 1902. The following summer at York Harbor, he related to William Dean Howells and possibly outlined part of a story about an unspecified notorious happening in the town of his youth (*MTB*, p. 1177). In 1908 Minnie T. Dawson told the story in *The Stillwell Murder, or a Society Crime*, published in Hannibal.

BECKY. Probably Becky Penn, since a later paragraph refers to a sister who has been identified as Arzelia Penn. "The long dog" was a minstrel routine.

BEEBE, [WILLIAM B.] He was a forwarding and commission merchant who shipped frequently between Hannibal and New Orleans. He carried on a traffic in slaves and probably was the hated "nigger trader" mentioned by Mark Twain in his *Autobiography*, I, 124. "Tom Sawyer's Conspiracy" contains a character who resembles him and is a slave trader, Bat Bradish. Beebe figures again as a slave trader in the "Schoolhouse Hill" version of "The Mysterious Stranger," and his son Henry, under the name Henry Bascom, is portrayed as a schoolyard bully. A note for that piece reads: *"Henry Bascom (Beebe) the bully new rich man and slave trader."* John Marshall Clemens and the elder Beebe had some complicated business dealings and in 1843 took their differences to court.

BLANKENSHIP, [WOODSON] and FAMILY. They were poor whites from South Carolina. Woodson, the father, worked briefly in the sawmill, but drank heavily and fed his family chiefly on fish and game. In 1845 Woodson was listed for tax delinquency amounting to twenty-nine cents. BENSON (BENCE), the oldest boy, six years the senior of Sam

Bowen's Addition, and as early as 1839 he operated a tobacco warehouse in the town and was appointed the first tobacco inspector. In 1840 his brick house on the levee between Hill and Bird Streets also served as a warehouse. His primary occupation appears to have been as a fire-insurance agent. In Notebook 35 (1902) Clemens listed several sons—"Will, Sam, Bart, John Bowen"; the daughters were ELIZA and MARY. Mary, a childhood sweetheart of the author, became the wife of lawyer Moses P. Green. WILL (1836–1893), probably Sam Clemens's best boyhood friend, shared many of his adventures. He was one of the models for the character Tom Sawyer. In the spring of 1844, during a measles epidemic, Sam climbed into bed with Will to get the disease. Both, with others, rolled a big stone down Holliday's Hill and thereby did much damage. (See *Innocents Abroad*, chapter 58, and a passage discarded from *Life on the Mississippi*, chapter 53.) Both played Robin Hood games and together bedeviled Jimmy Finn, a town drunkard. The author often recalled the adventure with "the minister's baptizing robe," (e.g., Notebook 35 [1902], TS pp. 17, 18). The Reverend Barton Warren Stone, an eminent Kentucky preacher, was visiting Captain Sam, his son-in-law; Will and Sam, interrupted in a card game, hastily hid the deck in the sleeve of the divine's baptizing robe. During a baptism, a fine hand of cards floated out upon the water. In the course of the subsequent floggings, one of the boys said, "I don't see how he could help going out on a hand like that." Will, like his father before him, became a riverman: Sam Clemens used Will's name as a reference when he was persuading Horace Bixby to take him on as an apprentice. Bowen in 1857 married Mary Cunningham, daughter of a Hannibal doctor. He left the river in 1868 and about 1870 moved to St. Louis, where he formed the insurance agency of Bowen & Andrews. The author heard about him during his trip on the river in 1882. Mrs. Bowen died in 1873. Will married again in 1876 and about 1880 moved to Texas to carry on the work of the agency there. He died in Texas in 1893. Over a period of thirty years, he and Clemens exchanged letters. (See *Mark Twain's Letters to Will Bowen*, ed. Theodore Hornberger. Austin, 1941.) Bowen visited the author at least once in the East. SAM[UEL ADAMS] Bowen, Jr., also was on the river. Sam was in the Confederate company with which Clemens served briefly in 1861. In 1867 Clemens asked Will to rebuke Sam for not calling when the author and Sam were in St. Louis at the same time. In an entry dated 21 April 1882 in Roswell Phelps's Secretarial Notebook (16a) a pilot is quoted as saying that "Sam Bowen died of yellow fever in 1878." This and a later note, TS p. 42, indicate that Bowen was buried at the head of Island 65 in the Mississippi. The author tells the story about Sam and the rich baker's daughter—differing in several details—in *Life on the Mississippi,* chapter 49, and in his *Autobiography,* II, 185–186. Carondelet, Missouri (scene of the marriage), was a small village on the Mississippi near St. Louis. In Notebook 16, TS p. 27, on 8 May 1882 Clemens wrote, "The histories of Will Bowen, Sam, and Capt. McCune and Mrs. B. make human life appear a grisly and hideous sarcasm." On p. 35, he recalled joining the "Confederate army" with Sam. BART[ON STONE] Bowen, another boyhood playmate of the author, was the third Bowen boy to go on the river. Clemens mentions him kindly in letters to Will dated 7 June 1867 and 25 January 1868.

BRADY, JENNY. A schoolmate of Sam Clemens, she was the sister of his chum Norval "Gull" Brady.

BREED, DANA [F.] The son of Quaker parents, he was born in Concord, New Hampshire, in 1823. He attended Brown University and in 1842 went to Hannibal. He clerked until 1850, then with Thomas K. Collins opened a store which became the leading dry-goods store in Hannibal; it was operated by the partners until 1875. In that year, Breed bought his partner's interest. He sold out in 1878, but continued as a salesman. In 1851, he married Miss Elizabeth Foreman of Maryland, who bore him seven sons. When Clemens's mother died in 1890, Breed was one of those who met the author at his train and acted as a pallbearer in the burial services.

BRIGGS, [WILLIAM] and FAMILY. William Briggs had three sons, William junior, Carey, and John, and a daughter, ARTEMISSA. The daughter, somewhat less than two years older than Sam Clemens, was one of his first loves. She rebuffed him and married William Marsh (not Richmond, as the author recalled in "Villagers" and in his *Autobiography*) a few months before Sam left Hannibal. Twain mentions her, along with several other people of the town, in Notebook 35 (1902). JOHN, a year and a half younger than Sam, was a playmate, the prototype of Joe Harper in *Tom Sawyer.* He and Sam saw the widow in the Welshman's house on Holliday's Hill shoot the California emigrant. (*MTA,* I, 132–133, the typescript of which contains the note, "Used in —'Huck Finn,' I think.") A fragment which was written as late as 1902 (DV20a in MTP) concerns a young Negro slave who took the blame for some "shameful" act which John had committed and, to John's horror, as a punishment was sold down the river. Clemens saw John in Hannibal during the 1902 visit, five years before John's death. Notebook 35 (1902), TS p. 13 has, "Draw a fine character of John Briggs. Good and true and brave, and robbed orchards tore down the stable stole the skiff." William Briggs and his son BILL were among the Hannibal citizens who went to California in 1850.

BUCHANAN, JOSEPH [SYLVESTER] and FAMILY. They were active in Hannibal printing and journalism. "Big Joe," formerly a steamboat engineer, assisted Jonathan Angevine, proprietor, in running the *Commercial Advertiser,* the town's first newspaper, when it was founded in 1837. He was associated with it and other newspapers until 1850. In that year, he and his brother ROBERT joined the rush to California, leaving "LITTLE JOE" (as devil), and Sam Raymond in charge of the Hannibal *Journal.* Robert Buchanan left the family piano for Pamela Clemens's use in teaching her "scholars." In 1851 Orion acquired the newspaper and, it may be, the services of young Bob. Mark Twain's notation in DV71, probably intended for his *Autobiography,* reads, "The printing office—that was the darling place—Buchanan Journal (2 offices). . . ." Notebook 32a (1897), TS p. 60, has, "Ed, Joe, Charley and Big Joe Buchanan." Since Notebook 35 (1902), TS p. 2, has "Ed Buchanan plays Roman soldier in tin armor in St. Louis," Ed may have been the pathetic frustrated thespian about whom Twain writes in chapter 51 of *Life on the Mississippi.* I have found no trace of 'GYLE Buchanan.

CARPENTER, JUDGE, and FAMILY. These are Judge John Marshall Clemens (1798–1847) and his family, with their names but not their initials changed. JOANNA Carpenter was Jane Lampton Clemens (1803–1890). OSCAR was Orion, born as the author says in Jamestown, Tennessee, in 1825, apprenticed to a St. Louis printer at seventeen, destined to die in December 1897, shortly after "Villagers" was written. The manuscript ends as Twain launches upon a comic account of his eccentric brother, such as he wrote often, e.g., in "Autobiography of a Damned Fool" (*S&B,* ed. Franklin Rogers, pp. 134–164). M. was Margaret (1830–1839). BURTON was Benjamin (1832–1842). In a sketch concerning his mother written in 1890 Twain recalled an early vivid memory of kneeling with her by the side of his dead brother ("Jane Lampton Clemens" pp. 43.17–44.3 in this volume). In DV71, TS p. 5,

Twain wrote, cryptically, "Dead brother Ben. My treachery to him." Notebook 35 (1902), TS p. 21, has: "I saw Ben in shroud." HARTLEY was Henry (1838–1858), the prototype of Sid Sawyer; Twain tells of his death in a steamboat explosion in *Life on the Mississippi,* chapter 20. SIMON was Samuel, the author (1835–1910). PRISCELLA was Pamela (1827–1904), the model for Tom Sawyer's Cousin Mary. The author makes her a year older than she was when she married. Judge Clemens was a righteous, stern, undemonstrative man, proud of his aristocratic ancestry. He was married in Adair County, Kentucky, as the author says, in 1823; the bride was a month younger than twenty. The story of Jane's previous engagement to the young medical student (Richard Barrett, rather than Dr. Ray) was a family tradition. There is some evidence for its truth, but because Jane first told it in 1886 when her memory was faulty, it is subject to doubt. The note, *"The autopsy,"* refers to a terrifying experience young Sam Clemens had, of which no explicit record has been left: through a keyhole he watched Dr. Meredith perform a postmortem upon the judge. The "HAN" to whom the author refers was his brother, Pleasants Hannibal Clemens, who lived for only a few months. CARPENTER's SLAVE. This would be Jenny, who moved with the Clemenses from Tennessee to Florida and later to Hannibal. She was a nurse for the Clemens children.

COLLINS, T. K. [THOMAS] and [HENRY W.] Thomas K. Collins, born in 1822, went to Hannibal in 1840 when he began to clerk in his brother's store. In 1850, he and Dana F. Breed in partnership established a dry-goods store. Henry W. Collins, a brother, settled in Hannibal in 1832 or 1833 and by 1837 was established as a merchant on Main Street. In 1842, he took John Marshall Clemens's I.O.U. for $290.55.

COONTZ, BEN[TON E.] The son of storekeeper Rezin E. and Mary E. Holliday Coontz. His parents moved from Virginia to Florida, Missouri, in 1836, to Ralls County in 1842, and to Hannibal in 1843 or 1844. Though three years younger than Sam, he was a playmate. At twelve, Ben was apprenticed to a rope-maker; later he worked as a woodchopper. Between 1854 and 1856 he was a partner in a store in Cincinnati, Missouri; in 1855, at seventeen, he was also appointed postmaster there. In 1856 he graduated from Bacon College, Ohio. For two years, 1856 to 1858, he was a cub pilot. When he left the river, he became a partner in a grocery store. Later he was a leather-dealer, a steamboat agent, and a salesman for the Hannibal Printing Company, and held political office, as well. He was at the railroad station when Clemens arrived in 1890 to attend burial services for Jane Lampton Clemens. There is no record of his having sent a son to West Point, but his son Robert E. Coontz (1864–1935) was an admiral and for a time Commander-in-Chief of the United States Fleet. In chaper 56 of *Life on the Mississippi* Twain tells of babbling in his sleep about a tramp who burned to death in the calaboose and Henry's subsequent conclusion that Ben was responsible. The episode had been germinal to a scene in *Tom Sawyer.* In working notes for the "Schoolhouse Hill" version of "The Mysterious Stranger," Ben's name is interlined with the words, "fool—½ idiot."

CROSS [WILLIAM O.] An Irishman, Cross operated a common school on the public square facing Center Street. It was one of several schools which Sam Clemens attended. Cross was said to be the only person in Hannibal who knew French. The school and Cross both figure in the "Schoolhouse Hill" version of "The Mysterious Stranger."

DAVIS FAMILY. One of Hannibal's Davises was a partner of Shoot (q.v.) in a livery stable; another operated a ferryboat on the Mississippi.

DAWSON, [J. D.] He was a teacher with fourteen years of experience when he opened his school in Hannibal in 1847. Sam Clemens attended the school and depicted it in both *The Adventures of Tom Sawyer* and the play based upon the book, as Dobbins's school.

DRAPER, JUDGE [ZACHARIAH G.] Judge Draper was born in South Carolina in 1793. In 1833 he was one of Hannibal's fifty inhabitants. In 1837, he was active in petitioning for the incorporation of Hannibal as a town. He was an ardent Whig who over the years held various offices, among them a judgeship in the county court and a membership in the state legislature. He married Eleanor Briggs; their daughter Sarah was born in 1845 and died in 1852. He was an intimate of John Marshall Clemens. With Clemens in 1841 he served on a jury which convicted a group of abolitionists; also with Clemens in 1846 he helped found the Hannibal and St. Joseph Railroad and the Hannibal Library Institute. When Clemens ran for the office of Clerk of the Circuit Court, the judge endorsed him. Draper died "without issue" in 1856.

ELGIN, COL. [WILLIAM C.] Operator of the City Hotel in Hannibal, Colonel Elgin was a friend of John Marshall Clemens. On one occasion he was shot at by McDonald, who mistook him for Clemens. As

Colonel Elder, he figures in "Tom Sawyer's Conspiracy." He died of cholera in 1851.

FIELD, KATE. Born in St. Louis in 1838 and baptized Mary Katherine Keemle Field, she was a prominent journalist and lecturer until her death in 1896.

FIFE, DR. [MATTHEW] He was associated as editor or proprietor with Hannibal papers—the *Pacific Monitor,* the Hannibal *Journal and Price Current,* and the Hannibal *Journal and Native American.* When the *Journal* was acquired by Orion Clemens, Samuel L. Clemens set type for it. In Notebook 32a (1897) Mark Twain recalled that Dr. Fife pulled Jane Clemens's teeth.

FOREMAN, JIM. I have no information beyond Clemens's statement to Mrs. Laura Hawkins Frazer (ca. summer, 1902) that "Jim Foreman is in one of the books, but you have not spotted him." In the same letter Clemens added, "I saw Jim Foreman before I took the train for Hannibal" (TS in MTP).

GARTH, DAVID [J.], and JOHN, [SR. and JR.] David J. Garth in 1905 was "a New York capitalist, now or late president of the Mechanics National Bank there." He married the sister of Dr. Hugh Meredith. D. J. Garth & Co. in the 1850's was the leading packer of tobacco in Hannibal. Clemens's letter of 6 February 1870 recalled to Will Bowen how the pair attended David Garth's Sunday-school class and stole leaf tobacco from him on weekdays. John H. Garth, Sr., moved from Rockbridge County, Virginia, to Hannibal in 1844 and there engaged in the tobacco business. JOHN Garth, Jr., was born in 1837 in Virginia and moved to Hannibal with his parents in 1844. He was a boyhood friend of Sam Clemens. He graduated from the University of Missouri and then joined his father in the tobacco business. In 1862 or 1863 he went to New York, where he carried on the same business for eight or nine years. Returning to Hannibal, he engaged in several enterprises— banking, the lumber trade, manufacturing—and became a leading citizen. The John H. Garth Memorial Library was named after him. In 1860, he had married pretty Helen Kercheval (q.v.), another childhood friend of Clemens; they were hosts to Clemens when he visited Hannibal in 1882. Garth died in 1899. The author mentioned John Garth affectionately in a letter to Mrs. Will Bowen, written from London on 6 June 1900.

GLOVER [SAMUEL T.] He was indeed a "famous lawyer" in St. Louis, but it seems improbable that the people of Hannibal would ever have so misjudged his merit. Born in Mercer County, Kentucky, in 1813, Glover practiced law in that state for several years before moving to Palmyra, the county seat of Marion County, Missouri, which was twelve miles from Hannibal. He was admitted to the Missouri bar in 1837, and there is evidence that he and his law partner, John T. Campbell, represented Hannibal residents in several land cases. Clemens's reference to his subordinate relationship to T. K. Collins, who was his junior in years and a clerk in a dry-goods store, is therefore inexplicable. Glover moved to St. Louis in 1849, where he continued to practice law, and in 1852 Orion's newspaper reported his nomination by the Whigs for the state attorney-generalship. His prestige and the influence of his firm are attested to by the fact that he had been the counsel in thirty-five cases before the U.S. Supreme Court when he died in 1884. Twain may have learned of Glover's success during his Mississippi tour in 1882; in chapter 53 of *Life on the Mississippi* the narrator converses with a Hannibal townsman who insists that "a stupid ass," a former resident of Hannibal, had become "the first lawyer in the state of Missouri" because the people of St. Louis never learned what a dunce he was. If Glover was the inspiration for this anecdote, Twain's fictionization is evident; the "perfect chucklehead" discussed in *Life on the Mississippi* was a man whom the townspeople had "known from the very cradle." It was later said, however (*Encyclopedia of the History of Missouri,* ed. Howard L. Conrad [New York, 1901], III, 66) that Glover in life was defeated twice when running for the office of U.S. senator, principally because "he was not a 'mixer,' as the phrase is; was often absent-minded, and sometimes was forgetful of faces or names."

GREEN, LAWYER [MOSES P.], a Hannibal lawyer, later city attorney, mayor, and member of the Missouri State Convention of 1861, figures in Clemens's 1855 notebook. A page-long entry in ink addressed to Orion Clemens and signed "M. P. Green," gives him information about disposing of some property. Sam Clemens elsewhere in the same notebook reminds himself to ask Green a question.

H., MRS. Mrs. Elizabeth Horr (q.v.).

HANNICKS, JOHN. He was listed in the 1850 census as a Negro, born in Virginia, aged forty. Orion Clemens's *Western Union* on 10 July 1851 identified him as a drayman. Mark Twain referred to him in chapter 4 of *Life on the Mississippi* as "a negro drayman, famous for his quick eye

and prodigious voice, [who] lifts up the cry, 'S-t-e-a-m-boat a-comin'!' "
which roused the sleepy village. In Notebook 22 (1887–1888), TS p.
43, the author wrote, "John Hanicks' laugh" and "John Hanicks' Giving
his 'experience!' " In Notebook 35 (1902), reminiscing of various Hannibal figures, the humorist jotted down Hannicks's name.

HARDY, DICK. No information.

HAWKINS FAMILY. This was an extensive clan, apparently, in Hannibal. In November 1846 a benefit supper for Hannibal's poor folk was
held in Hawkins's Saloon. In May 1847 two visitors presented nightly
demonstrations of "Human Magnetism" there. The group includes two
—JEFF and SOPHIA—concerning whom no information has been discovered. BEN may have been Benjamin M. Hawkins, who served as a
Second Lieutenant in the Mexican War in 1846. He was listed among
the migrants to California in a newspaper of 1849 and was the Hannibal marshal in 1852, 1853, and 1855. In 1856 he was elected county
sheriff on the Know Nothing ticket. 'LIGE [ELIJAH, SR.] was the father
of ELIJAH, JR., and LAURA. Twain's intention of making further use of
'Lige is evidenced by the appearance of his name in the margin of the
"Tupperville-Dobbsville" manuscript. JAMESON F. Hawkins formed
part of the Hannibal emigration to the California Gold Rush. He was
an operator of Hannibal's ferryboat and husband of the sister of Major
General Gustavus W. Smith of the Confederate Army. He was the
uncle of LAURA (more accurately, Annie Laurie Hawkins). Laura, born
in Georgetown, Kentucky, in 1837, moved to Hannibal as a child and
for a time lived across the street from the Clemenses. She was Sam's
schoolmate and childhood sweetheart, and he frequently had dates with
her when he was a printer's apprentice. During her teens, she attended
Rensselaer Academy in Rensselaer, Missouri. In 1858 she married Dr.
James W. Frazer. The author was wrong in believing her dead in 1897.
In Hannibal in 1902 he dined with her, and in 1908 he entertained her
in Redding, Connecticut. She died in 1928. Mark Twain gave her
name to a character in *The Gilded Age* and portrayed her as Becky
Thatcher in *Tom Sawyer,* as Bessie Thatcher in *Huckleberry Finn,* and
again as Becky in the "Schoolhouse Hill" (Hannibal) "Mysterious
Stranger."

HAYWARD, MR. and MRS. Not identified.

HICKS, URBAN E. He was a Hannibal printer, eight years Sam's senior. Orion's Hannibal *Journal and Western Union* for 27 March 1851

told of a villager who had paid ten dollars to hear Jenny Lind sing in St. Louis and felt the experience was worth every cent. In the autumn of 1848 Hicks and another printer, Pet McMurry (q.v.), actively supported the Cadets of Temperance and composed a letter of thanks to the young ladies of Hannibal for the gift of a Bible to the organization. When a mesmerist came to town, Hicks allowed himself to be hypnotized; Sam pretended to be, and outdid Hicks in faked feats of telepathy. Two entries in Notebook 32a, probably written in Weggis in 1897, recall the incident (TS pp. 56, 58); so do several entries in Notebook 35 (1902). Twain recounted the story in his autobiographical dictation (*MTE*, pp. 118–125).

HOL[L]IDAY, MRS. RICHARD. A Virginian (née McDonald), she proudly traced her ancestry back to a British general of the Revolutionary War period. Her husband, Captain Richard T. Holliday, owned the finest mansion in town. In 1844 he went bankrupt. He served an unexpired term as justice of the peace concurrently with John Marshall Clemens. He went to California during the Gold Rush and died there. When Sam was a pilot, Mrs. Holliday, who often traveled on the river, urged him to visit Madame Caprell, a famous fortuneteller in New Orleans. Sam recorded a visit to Madame Caprell in a letter of 6 February 1861. Mark Twain portrayed Mrs. Holliday as the Widow Douglas in *Tom Sawyer, Huckleberry Finn,* and "Hellfire Hotchkiss." Notebook 17 (1883–1884), TS p. 20, has "Mrs. Holliday with 40 diseases and expected 4th husband and fortune-tellers." The Holliday house burned in 1894. Purportedly Mrs. Holliday died in an insane asylum.

HONEYMAN, LAVINIA [D.], LETITIA, and SAM. They were the children of Sam Honeyman, a contractor and, for a time, a road overseer. Lavinia was born in 1836; in 1853 she delivered a flowery valedictory speech in the school operated by Misses Smith and Patrick. Letitia was three years Lavinia's junior. Sam was one of the Clemenses' playmates.

HORR, MRS. [ELIZABETH] and LIZZIE. Elizabeth Horr, the wife of the village cooper, Benjamin Horr, kept a dame's school on Main Street. She received twenty-five cents per week for each pupil. In the mid-1840's her daughter Lizzie helped by teaching the upper grades. Sam was one of her pupils.

HUNTER, ELLA, a native of Virginia, was the second wife of Dr. James A. H. Lampton (q.v.), a half-brother of Jane Clemens. Although she was a strong-minded woman, she was a favorite of her great-niece, Annie Moffett Webster.

HURST. No information.

HYDE, DICK and ED. Richard married in 1849. No other information has been found about these rowdy brothers, although Mark Twain frequently recalled the two men. In "Hellfire Hotchkiss" (1897) the brothers appear as Hal and Shad Stover and are attacked by Hellfire, who clouts them with a baseball bat. In revenge they spread untrue rumors about the tomboy's morality. In Notebook 35 (1902) the author twice made notes about them and their attack upon their uncle.

HYDE, ELIZA. She married Robert Graham on 27 April 1848.

JACKSON. No information.

JONES, ROBERTA. Clemens recalled her tragic trick several times—in chapter 53 of *Life on the Mississippi*, in three entries in Notebook 32a (1897), and in two entries in Notebook 35 (1905). In *Life on the Mississippi*, a townsman is said to have told Mark Twain that Roberta's victim spent thirty-six years in the asylum and died there. Huck tells the story in "Doughface."

JOSEPHINE [PENN?]. No information.

KERCHEVAL, OLD [WILLIAM F.] and HELEN. They were the village tailor and his daughter. Before 1851 he was in partnership with Green. Later, he sold books, shoes, and ready-made clothing. Mark Twain recorded in his *Autobiography* that Kercheval's slave woman and his apprentice both saved him from drowning on separate occasions during Clemens's boyhood. Helen Kercheval, a childhood playmate of the author, married John Garth, Jr. (q.v.). APPRENTICE OF KERCHEVAL has not been identified.

KRIBBEN, BILL. In a letter to his mother and sister from San Francisco, 20 January 1865, Clemens asks that an enclosed *Territorial Enterprise* sketch by him be given to Zeb Leavenworth or Bill Kribben, secretary of the Pilots' Association. In *Life on the Mississippi* Clemens said that the association failed after an officer in St. Louis "walked off with every dollar of the ample fund." In Roswell Phelps's secretarial notebook of 1882 Bill Kribben is identified as a steamboat man on the river when Clemens was, and two entries (TS pp. 7, 42) indicate that after his death from yellow fever in 1878 Kribben was buried at Island 68 in Arkansas.

LAKENAN, LAWYER [R. F.] He was born in Winchester, Virginia, in 1820. His father died when the boy was six weeks old, and his widowed mother took the family to Fairfax County, Virginia. He was admitted to the bar in 1844 and moved to Hannibal in 1845. He and Orion were speakers at the Fourth of July celebration in 1847. Lakenan helped found the Hannibal and St. Joseph Railroad and for several years was a director and later was its general attorney. Except for 1861 to 1866, when he lived in neighboring Shelby County, he spent the rest of his life in Hannibal. He held several political offices, and his law practice thrived; he became Hannibal's richest citizen. His first wife, whom he married on 8 January 1850, died the following December. He married Mary Moss (q.v.), eleven years his junior, in 1854. When he died in 1883 he was survived by his widow and six children. Mark Twain told the story of his marriage to Mary Moss, with some variations, in a passage dictated in 1906 and published in his *Autobiography*, II, 181–182.

LAMPTON, JIM [DR. JAMES A. H.], and KATE. Dr. Lampton, the half-brother of Jane Clemens, was about the age of her older children, and he associated with them. As a youth, he lived near Florida, Missouri, and in 1839, when he was still a minor, he loaned John Marshall Clemens $747.13. At eighteen, he married; his wife died the next year. He became a physician and set up practice in St. Louis, where, in 1849, he married Ella Hunter. The couple visited the Clemenses in Hannibal in 1850. He became an agent in New London, Missouri, for Orion Clemens's newspaper. Notebook 4 (1866) has "Jim Lampton & the dead man in Dr. McDowell's College" (TS p. 20). Kate Lampton, born in 1856, was the daughter of Dr. Lampton. Clemens attempted to find her work as a typist in 1883 (*MTBM*, pp. 213–214).

LEAGUE, BILL. League was a playfellow of Sam Clemens. In September 1851, he and a partner established the Hannibal *Messenger*. After his partner retired, League published the paper, first as a tri-weekly, then as a daily. It was League who bought Orion's daily *Hannibal Journal* in 1853. In a letter to Will Bowen from Buffalo dated 6

February 1870, Clemens wrote: "What eternities have swung their hoary cycles . . . since we taught that one-legged nigger, Higgins, to offend Bill League's dignity by hailing him in public with his exasperating 'Hello, League!' "

LEVERING, CLINT, and BROTHER. These sons of Franklin and Alice Levering were boyhood friends of Sam Clemens. On 13 August 1847, swimming in the Mississippi with a group of boys, ten-year-old Clint drowned. Sam Clemens, aged twelve, a shocked witness, remembered the incident for years. He wrote about it in *Life on the Mississippi* and "The Mysterious Stranger." Clint's brother, Aaron R. Levering, was born in Clark County, Missouri, in 1839 and was brought by the family to Hannibal in 1841. With Clemens, Aaron joined the Cadets of Temperance from which both later withdrew. At thirteen, Aaron began working in a hardware store; it was the beginning of an upward climb. Before he was twenty-one, he had his own hardware store, and by the time he ended his association with this store in 1871, he had prospered as a banker. He married Judge Gilchrist Porter's daughter. For more than thirteen years he served as a public-school director and superintendent of the Baptist Sunday school.

LOCKWOOD, LUCY. No information.

McCORMICK, WALES. He was a printer's apprentice with Clemens. In the "No. 44" version of "The Mysterious Stranger," Mark Twain modeled after him a character named "Doangivadam." A huge, handsome, reckless, and gay youth, the older boy delighted young Clemens. On a lecture tour in 1885 Clemens reported to Livy that he had seen McCormick in Quincy, Illinois. The author wrote "Wales McCormick the apprentice," in Notebook 35 (1902), TS p. 22. He told about him at length (in Notebook 22 (1887) TS pp. 3–4 and in his *Autobiography*, II, 276–282), recalling Wales's setting up a sermon by the famed Alexander Campbell and changing "Great God!" to "Great Scott!" and "Father, Son and Holy Ghost" to "Father, Son and Caesar's Ghost," abbreviating the Savior's name to "J. C." and then when rebuked enlarging it to "Jesus H. Christ."

MacDONALD, [McDONALD, ANGUS] An early solid citizen of Hannibal, he was a member of the town's advisory board in 1836, the owner of land along the Palmyra Road, and a Confederate brigadier general. He was the brother of Mrs. Richard T. Holliday (q.v.).

MacDONALD [McDONALD?] R. I. Holcombe, the historian of Marion County, verifies the claim that he was a carpenter and tells the story about his fight much as Mark Twain does. Holcombe adds one detail—that "McDonald was trying to make Schnieter [as he spells the name] shoot himself with his own pistol." Perhaps this is the William McDonald described in the 1850 Hannibal census as a "cooper, aged 35." It has not been possible to identify a McDONALD who was "the desperado (plasterer)."

McDOWELL, YOUNG DR. JOHN. He was the son of Joseph Nash McDowell, a doctor who founded (in 1840) and taught in a St. Louis medical school and owned McDowell's Cave near Hannibal (Mc-Dougal's Cave in *Tom Sawyer*). The young doctor stated that his father's cruelty caused the Lamptons to adopt him. Notebook 4 (1866), TS p. 20, has: "Jim Lampton and the dead man in Dr. McDowell's College." Annie Webster backed Twain's statement about the doctor and Ella Lampton and her daughter Kate. In St. Louis in 1861 Dr. McDowell treated Orion Clemens's little daughter, Jennie. Notes for "Schoolhouse Hill," the Hannibal version of "The Mysterious Stranger," deal with Dr. Terry, a fictional name for McDowell, Senior, "great surgeon/contempt for human race/rough, but at bottom kind."

McMANUS, [JIMMY] Apparently he was a fellow boatman, since the humorist wrote of him in Notebook 16 (1882) when recalling other boatmen. The entry on TS p. 12 appears to be relevant to the note in "Villagers": "McManus (Jimmy) robbed me of brass watch chain, and $20—and robbed old Calhoun of underclothes."

McMURRY, PET [T. P.] He was a journeyman printer in Ament's shop when Sam Clemens was an apprentice there. He joined Sam and another apprentice, Wales McCormick (q.v.), in pranks. With another young printer, Urban Hicks (q.v.), in the autumn of 1848 he wrote a letter thanking the young ladies of Hannibal for the gift of a handsome Bible to the Sons of Temperance. In 1853 he married a girl from Louisville, Kentucky. Clemens told Livy in a letter of 23 January 1885 of meeting Pet in Quincy, Illinois, and contrasted the bewhiskered old man with the swaggering Hannibal youth. The humorist's Notebook 32a (1897), TS p. 60, cryptically recalls a prank: "Drinking Pet's bottle of medicine and re-filling it." Clemens recalled him again by name in a notebook entry of 1902 (Notebook 35, TS p. 22).

MEREDITH, DR. [HUGH] and FAMILY. Dr. Hugh Meredith was a Pennsylvanian, born in 1806, who for a time shipped before the mast. He was practicing in Florida, Missouri, however, when the Clemens family was there and moved to Hannibal when they did. In Florida he joined John Marshall Clemens in planning improvements for the town—the navigation company, the railroad, and the academy. In 1842, Clemens recalled long after in his *Autobiography*, the doctor saved Sam's life when the boy was seven. A man with literary interests, in 1843 the doctor helped Judge Clemens found the Hannibal Library Institute. One of the author's most disturbing memories was of seeing the doctor perform a postmortem on the boy's father in 1847. In 1849 the doctor and a son, Charles, joined the Gold Rush to California; they soon returned, no richer. Orion had him edit the *Journal* after Meredith returned to Hannibal and while Orion briefly went to Tennessee in connection with the settlement of his father's estate. When the doctor died in 1864, Clemens evidently said something unkind about him in a letter to his mother; Jane Clemens protested in a reply. Mark Twain's Notebook 32a (1897), TS p. 61, has "Dr. Meredith—hoarse deep voice." The doctor is mentioned in *Autobiography*, I, 108; II, 272–274; and in a portion removed from the manuscript (DV355). The doctor's son, CHARLES Meredith, so Clemens recalled, once saved Sam from drowning in Bear Creek. He learned the printing trade with Orion Clemens. JOHN Meredith was a member of the Cadets of Temperance with Sam Clemens. Sam recalled him pleasantly in his *Autobiography*, II, 185. In an 1897 notebook entry (32a, TS p. 59) and elsewhere Clemens recalled Orion's misadventure when he climbed into bed with two spinster sisters of the doctor. A detailed account is in the *Autobiography*, II, 272–274.

MOFFETT, WILL[IAM A.] Born in Virginia in 1816, Moffett later moved to Florida, Missouri, where he worked in a grocery store. When Florida failed to flourish and the Panic of 1837 affected business, he moved to Hannibal. Later he moved to St. Louis, where he did well in the mercantile and commission business. During a visit to Kentucky, he again met Pamela Clemens (see Priscilla Carpenter), formerly a Florida and Hannibal neighbor. After a swift courtship, he married her on 20 September 1851. Moffett is said to have loaned Sam Clemens $100 in 1857 so that Sam might make an initial payment for his apprenticeship in river piloting. During his years on the river, Clemens stayed in the Moffett home whenever he was in St. Louis. Moffett died in 1865.

Moss, Russell [W.] and Family. Russell Moss began business on the Hannibal levee in 1849 in the pork packing firm of Samuel & Moss. The firm, at one time said to be the second largest of its kind in the United States, employed a hundred men and often packed 30,000 head of hogs in a season. When the establishment was burned in 1852, the estimated loss included 14,000 pounds of bacon. That same year Moss represented Marion County in the Missouri General Assembly and served on a committee of six citizens whose duty it was to keep Hannibal alert concerning the issue of the Hannibal and St. Joseph Railroad. In his most prosperous days, Moss was one of the richest men in Hannibal. Neil Moss, a son, attended Yale and was badly treated when he returned to Hannibal. Some of his experiences were assigned to the false Tom Driscoll in *Pudd'nhead Wilson*, who returned to Dawson's Landing after attending Yale and adopting Eastern dress and Eastern ways. Mary Moss married R. F. Lakenan (q.v.) in 1854, and they had six children. A passage dictated in 1906 and included in the *Autobiography*, II, 181–182, tells the story of her marriage with some variations from that in "Villagers," omitting any mention of the sleigh ride. It adds that the author met Mary in Missouri in 1902 when he went there to receive his LL.D. from the university. Clemens said that Mary was still beautiful "although she has grandchildren." Notebook 35 (1902) TS p. 21, reads, "Ray Moss and Neil, Mary."

N., Miss. Mary Ann Newcomb (q.v.).

Nash, Old Abner [O.], and Family. Abner Nash moved from Lynchburg, Virginia, to Maysville, Kentucky, remained there a year, and in 1831 moved to Hannibal, where he opened one of the town's first general stores. In 1832 he became one of the founding members of the First Presbyterian Church. He held several local offices, among them that of postmaster. In 1844 he went bankrupt; *The Adventures of Tom Sawyer* mentions "the aged and needy postmaster, who had seen better days." Married twice, he died in 1859. Mary Nash had a reputation for wildness before her marriage in 1851 to John Hubbard of Frytown (not to Sam Raymond, as Clemens believed). She figures in "Hellfire Hotchkiss" and in some notes for "Tom Sawyer's Conspiracy." Her younger sister, Ellen, became deaf and dumb. Thomas S. Nash, who was the same age as Sam Clemens, was a playmate and also a member of the Cadets of Temperance. As the author recalls in his *Autobiography*, II, 97–99, in the winter of 1848/49 Sam and Tom went skating on the Mississippi, heard the ice breaking, and raced for the shore. Sam reached safe ground, but Tom fell through the ice. The aftermath was a series of diseases, among them scarlet fever, which left him deaf and dumb. He was sent to the asylum at Jacksonville, Illinois, where he was taught to talk. On a visit to Hannibal in 1885 Clemens made the unexplained entry (Notebook 18, TS p. 21): "Tom Nash's confidential remark." In notes for the "St. Petersburg Fragment," the earliest version of "The Mysterious Stranger," a character called Crazy Fields is said to have lost both his wife and his child after they contracted smallpox from a stranger taken into their home. Another entry concerns the results of Mrs. Nash's kindness to a homeless child: her children get scarlet fever, three die, and two become deaf. Twain tells of seeing Tom in 1902. Notebook 35 (1902) has three notations concerning him (TS pp. 13, 18, 21). That on p. 13 is cryptic: "Tom Nash—the great night of the breaking up of the ice. Tom blows up with powder-horn—scarlet fever, deaf and dumb." He is mentioned by name in a note for the "St. Petersburg Fragment" of "The Mysterious Stranger."

NEWCOMB, MISS MARY ANN. Miss Newcomb emigrated from Virginia to teach in Florida, Missouri. Shortly before the Clemens family, she moved to Hannibal to teach. She took some meals with the Clemenses as a paying guest and was one of the author's teachers; in 1902, he said that "she compelled me to learn to read." Annually the students in her school had a May Day party with dances around the maypole, declamations, band music, and a picnic. In 1852 she married John Davies, "the Welshman" who owned a Hannibal bookstore. Clemens, in a letter to Will Bowen from Buffalo dated 6 February 1870, recalled "a rebellion" which the author and Will "got up" against her. She was pictured in "Autobiography of a Damned Fool" (published in *Mark Twain's Satires & Burlesques*) as a thin spinster, devoutly pious; she contributed details to the portrait of Miss Watson in *Huckleberry Finn*; Notebook 32a (1897) suggested that she and other teachers be introduced in some story; and she appeared in the "Schoolhouse Hill" version of "The Mysterious Stranger."

OUSELEY, [OWSLEY, WILLIAM] A haughty, dandified migrant from Kentucky and a well-to-do storekeeper, in January 1845 he shot and killed a farmer, Sam Smarr (q.v.), on the corner of Hill and Main, a few yards from the Clemens house. John Marshall Clemens, as justice of the peace, earned a fee of $1.81 for administering oaths to twenty-nine witnesses and a fee of $13.50 for writing out depositions totaling 13,500 words for the case. Sam Clemens, aged nine, was greatly impressed by the incident, and he frequently recalled it—in a letter to Will Bowen dated 6 February 1870, in *Huckleberry Finn* (in Sherburn's shooting of Boggs), and in his *Autobiography*, I, 131. The aftermath was not as Mark Twain described it. The jury at Palmyra acquitted Owsley on 14 March 1846. He was still in business in Hannibal seven years later.

PAVEY. Pavey operated Pavey's Hotel in Hannibal. On one occasion Jane Clemens scolded him for mistreating his daughter; thereafter he respected Jane. (See *MTA*, I, 118, and "Jane Lampton Clemens." Chapter 31 of *Roughing It* has a scene based upon the happening. Fragmentary autobiographical notes, DV 243, have: "The Paveys. Aunt P. [i.e., the fictional Aunt Polly, whose prototype was Jane Clemens] protects a daughter. 'Pigtail done!' " The meaning of the phrase is unknown. Notebook 22 (1887–1888), TS p. 37, has: "Old Pavey's negro preacher chopping wood back of the tavern: 'Make yo' callin' and election sure brethren and sistern.' " Notebook 32b (1897) refers to "the tavern gang—at Pavey's." Notebook 35 (1902), TS p. 21, has "Becky Pavey and Pole. 'Pig-tail done' tavern. Bladder-time. Weeds. Offal given away at porkhouse." POLE (NAPOLEON PAVEY) was listed in St. Louis directories for 1855 and 1857 as a steamboat engineer, "Second Class." Clemens boarded with a Mrs. Pavey during his 1855 stay in St. Louis.

PEAKE, DR. [WILLIAM HUMPHREY] A Virginian, he was one of the few intimates of John Marshall Clemens in Hannibal. Long after knee breeches, buckle shoes, and the pigtail had gone out of fashion, the doctor still wore them. Mark Twain frequently recalled an episode involving Peake, which he wrote about for his *Autobiography* in 1903: pretending to be hypnotized by a visiting mesmerist, young Sam Clemens converted the dubious Dr. Peake by reciting details in the old man's past which the doctor did not remember the boy had heard him reveal (*MTE*, pp. 124–128). Peake figures in the "Schoolhouse Hill" version of "The Mysterious Stranger" as Dr. Wheelright, "the stately old First-Family Virginian and imposing Thinker of the village."

PITTS, OLD [JAMES P.] and FAMILY. James Pitts, a native of Maryland, moved to Hannibal in 1836 and worked as a saddler there. He figures in *Huckleberry Finn* and *Life on the Mississippi* as an enthusiastic greeter of steamboats. His son, WILLIAM R. Pitts, born in Berlin, Maryland, in 1832, at fourteen was apprenticed in the harness-maker's and saddler's trade. By working overtime, he was enabled to end his apprenticeship three years early, at eighteen. He engaged in harness-making in the Hannibal firm of Jordan & Pitts. In 1853 he married Miss A. D. Combs, who bore him ten children. He bought his partner's interest in the firm in 1878. In a letter from Buffalo dated 6 February 1870 to Will Bowen, Clemens recalls their lying in wait for Bill in order to "whale him" and reports that he saw him "two or three years ago." Notes for "Tom Sawyer's Conspiracy" (about 1897) indicate that Mark Twain thought of using Bill as the model for a character.

POMEROY, BENTON and Co. No information.

PRENDERGAST. No information.

QUARLES, JIM [JAMES A.] A first cousin of Clemens, Jim was one of the eight children of John Quarles. In 1848 he moved from Florida to Hannibal and, using three thousand dollars supplied by his father, started a firm advertised in the Hannibal *Journal* for 19 October 1848: "Geo. W. Webb & Jas. A. Quarles, Copper, Tin and Sheet Iron Manufactory, just opened for business." There is some evidence that the author's account of Quarles's marriage to a minor was inaccurate.

R., SAM. Samuel Raymond (q.v.).

RALLS, COL. [JOHN] He was a veteran of the Mexican War. In Ralls County in 1861 he swore in as private soldiers the members of the company to which Clemens belonged, although he was not empowered to give the officers commissions. Mark Twain tells of the incident in "The Private History of a Campaign That Failed."

RATCLIFFES (more properly the RADCLIFFS). They moved from Maryland to Hannibal in 1837, when Dr. James Radcliff became one of the town's three physicians. The doctor sat on the first municipal board of health. The census of 1840 indicated that he had one small son and two other sons in their teens. The census of 1850 indicated that none of his sons lived with him. In the "Schoolhouse Hill" version of "The Mysterious Stranger," Crazy Meadows (called Crazy Fields in some notes) is copied after one of the boys; a marginal note reads: "Crazy's history and misfortunes and his family and lost boy—Ratcliff."

The homicidal boy also figures in "Clairvoyant." I have found no details concerning Mrs. Ratcliff or the son who became a physician.

RAY, YOUNG DR., according to Clemens family tradition, actually was a young medical student named Richard Ferrel Barrett. In his letter to Howells dated 19 May 1886 the author told this story using Barrett's name and identifying him as a medical student.

RAYMOND, SAM[UEL], became the senior editor of the Hannibal *Journal* when the older Buchanans went west in 1850. That same year he married not Mary Nash but Miss Helen Elizabeth Holmes of Hannibal. About 1852 he was on the editorial staff of the Hannibal *Messenger*. A puzzling entry in Notebook 32a (1897) TS p. 58 has: "The new fire Co—Raymond, whose real name was Buchanan." Raymond figures as Captain Sam Rumford in "Tom Sawyer's Conspiracy." A note for "Tom Sawyer's Conspiracy" reads: "Fire Marshal Sam Raymond (envied because said to be illegitimate) Rumford."

REAGAN, JIMMY. In a letter to Mrs. Laura Hawkins Frazer, probably written in the summer of 1902, Mark Twain indicated that "the 'new boy' [it may well be in *Tom Sawyer*] was Jim Reagan—just from St. Louis." A text of the letter was published in the Hannibal *Evening Courier-Post*, 6 March 1935. In "Boy's Manuscript" (1870) Billy Rogers refers to him, evidently, as "Jim riley which I will lick every time I ketch him and have done so already."

RICE, REV. MR. No information.

RICHMOND, LETITITIA [Letitia?] Possibly the daughter of stonemason Richmond; her father was the first Sunday-school teacher of Sam Clemens at the Methodist church. I find no evidence that she married Dana Breed.

ROBARDS, CAPTAIN [ARCHIBALD SAMPSON] and FAMILY. The father of the family was born in Mercer County, Kentucky, in 1797, the son of a native of Virginia. He won his military title in the Kentucky militia. In 1832 he married Amanda Carpenter. In 1843 he moved to Hannibal with his family and his slaves. He held a number of civic positions, among them the mayorship of the town. In 1849 he took a company of fifteen to California at his own expense. On his return he prospered as a flour miller (his product won a first premium in the New York Crystal Palace Exposition in 1851), and he became one of the wealthiest men in the town. He was an elder in the First Christian Church and also a city councilman. He died in 1862. GEORGE Robards, his oldest son, several years older than Sam Clemens, was the only student of Latin in Dawson's school in the author's time there. He was the sweetheart of Mary Moss (q.v.). He went to California with his father and returned to Hannibal where he died in 1878. Twain told about him and his family at some length in *Autobiography,* II, 179–184, and gave Henry Bascom some of his traits in the "Schoolhouse Hill" version of "The Mysterious Stranger." CLAY (Henry Clay Robards) probably was a second son: Twain's Notebook 35 (1902), TS p. 21, has: "George, Clay, John Robards, Jane and Sally Robards." JOHN L. Robards was born in Lincoln County, Kentucky, in 1838 or 1839; he moved to Hannibal with his family; and he went west with his father's party. He attended the University of Missouri and later studied law in Kentucky. He married Sara Helm in 1861; they had three children. He was practicing law in 1861 when he and Clemens enlisted in the Marion Rangers. In 1876, at the author's request, he oversaw the transfer of the bodies of John Marshall and Henry Clemens from the old Baptist cemetery to the new Mount Olivet Cemetery. In 1890 he attended the burial services for Jane Lampton Clemens in Hannibal. John adopted the practice of capitalizing the *b* in his name; Mark Twain represented him as Dunlap, who called himself "d'Un Lap" in the "Private History of a Campaign That Failed." An entry in Notebook 35 (1902), TS p. 21 indicates that John's wife, Sally Robards, was the woman whom the author saw in India and who revealed that years before she had seen him as a boy prancing around nude: "Sally Robards—pretty. Describe her now in her youth and again in 50 ys after when she reveals herself." See also the *Autobiography,* I, 129–130.

RUTTER, DICK. Probably he was a printer with young Sam Clemens in Hannibal, since his name is juxtaposed with those of other youthful printers of that era. I have found no record of him.

SCHNEIDER. Probably he was the Charlie Schnieter referred to in *History of Marion County, Missouri,* p. 914: "while [John Marshall Clemens was serving as] justice of the peace Charlie Schnieter and a carpenter named McDonald got into a scuffle on the sidewalk in front of Mr. Clemens's office. . . . Clemens commanded the peace, and not being obeyed he struck McDonald on the forehead with a stonemason's mallet."

SELMES, OLD T. R., [TILDEN R] He was the leading merchant of Hannibal who ran the Wild-Cat Store which in 1849 advertised goods "manufactured expressly for the western and California markets." In 1852 as mayor of Hannibal Selmes headed a party which went down the river to invite Lajos Kossuth to visit the town. In 1853 he enlarged a three-story building, Benton Hall, named after his second wife. For many years the hall was the scene of festivals and social activities. In the 1860's one of Hannibal's ferryboats was named the "T. R. Selmes." I have found no details concerning Selmes's daughter. A note for "Tom Sawyer's Conspiracy" is "Old Selmes (English)."

SEXTON, MRS. and MARGARET. They were boarders with Jane Clemens in 1844, and Margaret, at least, was a friend of the family into the 1860's. The author sent a message to Margaret via Mrs. Clemens and Pamela Moffett from Carson City, 8 February 1862, and a picture of himself for her from Virginia City on 16 February 1863.

SHOOT [WILLIAM] and FAMILY. They were joint owners and operators of the Shoot & Davis Livery Stable which burned in March 1852. On 9 May 1853 he became the owner of Brady House (renamed the Monroe House) which he operated in conjunction with Shoot, Jordan, & Davis Livery Stable. His wife, whom he married when she was thirteen, was Arzelia Penn. The roster of the Cadets of Temperance in 1849 contained the name, John A. Shoot, possibly a son.

SMAR[R, SAMUEL] This farmer in the 1840's lived near Hannibal and came into town periodically on drinking sprees. During one of his visits, he shouted insults at William Owsley (q.v.), who, he believed, had cheated several of his friends. On a subsequent visit he again shouted accusations against Owsley outside the latter's store. A few days later, on 24 January 1845, Owsley shot him with a pistol. John Marshall Clemens took the depositions of the witnesses. Mark Twain based the shooting of Boggs by Colonel Sherburn in *Huckleberry Finn* upon the incident.

SOUTHARD, LOT. No information.

STEVENS, OLD [T. B.], DICK and ED[MUND] T. B. Stevens advertised as a jeweler in the Hannibal *Journal* in 1851. Ed was a contemporary of Sam Clemens who figured in a rebellion of the pupils against Miss Newcomb and, at another time, led an insurrection which ended with the destruction of Dick Hardy's stable. He was a corporal in the Marion Rangers; the author recalls him in Notebook 16 (1882), TS p. 35, his *Autobiography*, II, 219, and "Private History of a Campaign That Failed." The author had two notes on him in Notebook 35 (1902). One merely mentions his name; the other reads, "First whipping—Ed Stevens. Sheepskin." In a letter to J. H. Stevens of 28 August 1901 Clemens says that he and Ed were warm friends. I have found no information about Dick Stevens, but the author mentions him, Ed, a brother John, and a sister Jenny in a letter to Pamela dated 2 April 1887.

STOUT, IRA. A speculator in Missouri land, Stout in 1837 built a row of buildings on the northwest corner of Hill and Main in Hannibal. In one of several real-estate transactions with Stout, John Marshall Clemens bought this property and occupied one structure as a hotel—the Virginia House. Dixon Wecter received from Judge Clark of the Missouri Supreme Court this interpretation of the financial transaction which Mark Twain has recorded: "John Marshall Clemens, as surety, was held responsible for the debts of Stout, who took bankruptcy. The judgment in bankruptcy relieved Stout of his debts." Wecter thinks that the author may have confused an assignment under state law for federal action, but no records have been found in either the state or the federal courts. Wecter characterized Stout as a "dead beat" who became involved "in a web of litigation" with various other Hannibal residents.

STRIKER, THE BLACKSMITH and LITTLE MARGARET. No information.

STRONG, MRS. No information. She probably was one of the Penn girls, since her history is told along with theirs.

TORREY, MISS. One of Sam Clemens's teachers in Hannibal. A letter to Will Bowen, dated 6 February 1870, from Buffalo recalls how the author and other students "got up a rebellion against Miss Newcomb . . . to force her to let us all go over to Miss Torry's side of the schoolroom. . . ." She is mentioned with other teachers in an entry in Notebook 32a (1897).

TUCKER, REV. JOSHUA [P.] From 1840 to 1846 he was the pastor of the Presbyterian church in Hannibal. The church was organized in

1832; the building was erected on North Fourth Street in 1839. All the Clemenses except the judge became members of the church about 1843. The author attended Sunday school in the basement and from the age of ten or eleven listened to sermons on the first floor.

USTICK, [THOMAS W.] He is listed in Morrison's *St. Louis Directory for 1852* as "book and job printer, ne cor Locust and Second, ups."

WOLFE, JIM. Sam Clemens's fellow apprentice printer, Jim Wolfe boarded with the Clemens family. He was the butt of many jokes played by Sam and other young printers until he gave Sam a bloody nose. The author's recollection was that he told his first oral humorous story about Jim Wolfe and the cats. He wrote it out and published it in 1867 and recalled it frequently—four times in Notebook 32a (1897) and twice in Notebook 35 (1902). He told another story about Wolfe's acute shyness in his autobiography (*MTE*, pp. 136–142). The earlier notebook also has (TS p. 60): "Jim Wolf and the wasps. They were put in the bed to see if they would turn to butterflies as Nigger Jim said. (Then they were forgotten?)" This, as Mark Twain noted elsewhere, was an idea for inclusion in a new book about Huck Finn; it was never used. Wolfe was pictured as Nicodemus Dodge in *A Tramp Abroad*. He attended Orion Clemens's funeral in December 1897.

Unnamed Villagers

GRAVESTONE-CUTTER'S DAUGHTER. Not identified. David Dean, James R. Garnett, and P. J. Saul had marble works in Hannibal, but nothing has been found about their families. In his *Autobiography*, II, 214, the author recalls a stonemason, Richmond, who was his Sunday-school teacher.

HANGED NIGGER. This was probably "Glascock's Ben," who, according to Holcombe's *History of Marion County*, on 30 October 1849 murdered a white boy, aged ten, then raped and murdered the boy's sister, aged twelve. After he was convicted, he confessed his guilt. His hanging at Palmyra on 11 January 1850 was the first legal execution in Marion County. Thousands gathered to witness the event. In Notebook 32a (20 June 1897 to 24 July 1897), TS p. 57, the author recalls the story in some detail: "Negro smuggled from Va in featherbed when lynchers were after him. In Mo he raped a girl of 13 and killed her and her brother in the woods and before being hanged confessed to many rapes of white married women who kept it quiet partly from fear of him and partly to escape the scandal."

THE MINISTER. He was the Reverend Barton W. Stone, grandfather of Will Bowen (q.v.) and a noted Campbellite preacher. He stayed with the Bowen family when in Hannibal and died in their home in 1844.

PRES[BYTERIAN] PREACHER. From 1840 to 1846 this was the Reverend Joshua T. Tucker (q.v.). For two years, and hence when John Marshall Clemens died, the church was served by supply pastors. In 1848 the Reverend Joseph L. Bennett was elected pastor; he served until Sam Clemens left Hannibal.

RICH BAKER's DAUGHTER. The purported mistress, then wife, of Sam Bowen, has not been identified. Elsewhere Mark Twain reminisces about baker Koeneman's daughter; but she married Dr. C. Spiegel of Palmyra in 1852. In another recounting of this story, the girl is a German brewer's daughter, and in another instance a ward of a rich, old, childless foreigner.

SHOWY STRANGER. Unidentified.

STABBED CALIFORNIA IMMIGRANT. The author told Albert Bigelow Paine that as a boy "He saw a young emigrant stabbed with a bowie-knife by a drunken comrade, and noted the spurt of life-blood that followed . . ." (*MTB*, p. 47). In some autobiographical notes written on cross-barred paper, Clemens recalled: "All emigrants went through there. One stabbed to death—saw him. Saw the corpse in my father's office."

STRANGER. The one who married Eliza Hyde in 1848 was Robert Graham, concerning whom I have found no other information.

TWO YOUNG SAILORS. Not identified. But Mark Twain (Notebook 33 [1900], TS p. 6) evidently had them in mind when he wrote: "Huck tells of those heros the 2 Irish youths who painted ships on Godwin's walls and ran away. They told sea adventures which made all the boys sick with envy and resolve to run away and go to sea . . ."

APPENDIX B

Dates of Composition

Villagers of 1840–3

THE FRAGMENTARY manuscript in the Mark Twain Papers with the above title is thirty-four pages long. Pages 1 through 7 are ruled, tan paper, $5\frac{5}{16}$ inches by $8\frac{5}{16}$ inches; pages 8 through 34 are cross-barred paper of the same dimensions.

Paine says that while in Weggis, Switzerland, Twain wrote a "half-finished manuscript about Tom and Huck" and another uncompleted manuscript "with the burning title of 'Hell-Fire Hotchkiss.'"[1] The author himself recorded the fact that the story about Hotchkiss was started on 4 August 1897,[2] part-way through his stay in Weggis, from 18 July to 27 August of that year. Parts of both "Tom Sawyer's Conspiracy" (Paine's "half-finished manuscript") and "Hellfire Hotchkiss" were written on cross-barred paper precisely like that used for "Villagers," and a portion of "Hellfire Hotchkiss" was written on the ruled, tan paper also used in "Villagers." John S. Tuckey, who has made an exhaustive study of papers used in manuscripts of the Weggis period, characterizes the cross-barred paper as a sort "which Twain used extensively at Weggis and perhaps there only."[3] Moreover, portions of

---

[1] *MTB*, p. 1045.
[2] Notebook 32b, TS p. 24, MTP.
[3] *MTSatan*, pp. 32, 86.

the author's *Autobiography* that Paine believes were written in this period also utilize the cross-barred paper, and these recall several men, women, and children who figure in "Villagers." [4] For these reasons, this fragment has been dated 1897.

Jane Lampton Clemens

In the second paragraph of this biographical essay Mark Twain indicates that, according to his calculation, the death of his brother Benjamin "dates back forty-seven years." Since Benjamin died on 12 May 1842, the calculation (if accurate) would place the writing of this piece in 1889. However, in stating Ben's, Jane's, and his own age at the time, Twain was a year or more off: Ben died when he was not ten, but nine; the author was not eight, but six; and Jane not forty, but thirty-eight. Instead of being forty-seven years in the past, the event would seem to have occurred forty-eight or forty-nine years before, placing the time of composition in 1890 or 1891.

The first paragraph shows that the sketch was begun after Jane's death, which took place on 27 October 1890. When Paine first published a portion of the essay in *Harper's Magazine* (CXLIV [February 1922], 277–280), he dated it 1890–1891. Paper and handwriting also confirm this dating.

Tupperville-Dobbsville

Mark Twain used Crystal Lake Mills paper such as that in "Tupperville-Dobbsville" in at least thirty-six letters between 1876 and 1880 and in a number of working notes and manuscripts between the summer of 1877 and mid-June 1880. Twain wrote in violet ink of the sort that he used when in Hartford and in Europe between late November 1876 and mid-June 1880, but not thereafter for several years. As the note introducing the passage indicates, details such as those in the passage occur often in writings of the period from 1873 to 1880. It seems probable that "Tupperville-Dobbsville" was written in the late 1870's when the author was in Hartford.

---

[4] *MTA*, I, 81–115.

Clairvoyant

Except for the not very helpful fact that Mark Twain wrote about "Mental Telegraphy" between 1878 and 1907 and about the clairvoyant powers of young Satan between 1897 and 1908, there is no external evidence that can be used to date this fragment.

Internal evidence, though slightly more helpful, does not make precise dating possible. In the upper right corner of the first two manuscript pages, Paine has written "80's," and Paine often proved to be correct when he dated Mark Twain's manuscripts. The paper is Keystone Linen, used by the author (as I notice in discussing the date of the *Indians* manuscript) between 1883 and 1889. It is written in pencil, which the author used frequently in manuscripts of 1883 and 1884 and less frequently thereafter. Hence it seems likely that the fragment was written in one of those two years.

A Human Bloodhound

Paine labeled this fragment "90's." Three notebooks contain suggestions for a story with its subject matter (TS 20, p. 10, in 1885 or 1886, TS 21, p. 7, in 1886 or 1887, and TS 32a, pp. 37 and 45, in June or July 1897). The manner of writing and the materials are the same as "Indiantown," and at one point the author thought of inserting this fragment or a rewritten version of it in "Indiantown." In *WWD* (p. 151) John S. Tuckey assigns "Indiantown" to 1899; and "A Human Bloodhound" probably was written during that year also.

Huck Finn and Tom Sawyer among the Indians

In the final paragraphs of *Adventures of Huckleberry Finn*, written in 1883, Tom Sawyer proposes that he, Jim, and Huck go West for "howling adventures amongst the Injuns," and Huck talks of a plan to "light out for the Territory." In "Huck Finn and Tom Sawyer among the Indians," Mark Twain started to write the narrative thus forecast, one he never completed. Albert Bigelow Paine's biography places the writing of the fragment in 1889.[1] Ordinarily Paine's dating of manuscripts is quite reliable, since he discussed it with Mark Twain,

---

[1] *MTB*, pp. 899, 1680.

who was usually dependable on this, and since Paine also checked on the author's memory. Paper of the sort on which the fragment was written was used as late as 4 August 1889.[2] Moreover, the incomplete story was preserved not only in manuscript but also in galley proof set on the Paige typesetting machine,[3] in which the author invested huge sums between 1880 and 1895; and there is some evidence that these proofs date back to 1888 or 1889.[4]

Nevertheless, a plausible guess is that Mark Twain wrote most or all of the surviving manuscript in 1884.[5] The fact that the fragment was set on the Paige machine is not decisive, since the machine could have been used as early as 1885 or as late as 1889, to set earlier writings.[6] Although the paper used for the manuscript was used as late as 1889, it was also used during the six years preceding 1889, notably in parts of "Tom Sawyer: A Play," written in 1883 and 1884, and in an account of the author's visits to a dentist in 1884. The manuscript is written in pencil, and an incomplete but fairly extensive survey of manuscripts and letters for the period indicates that although the author ordinarily used a pencil in 1884, between 1885 and 1889 he customarily used ink.[7] Twain recorded his plan to write the book on 6 July 1884 in a letter asking his business manager, Webster, to send him books to use as sources, and on 17 July he indicated that Webster need not send any more books.[8] On 15 July he told his friend Howells that between visits

---

[2] The paper is Keystone Linen. A letter from Clemens to F. G. Whitmore, written on this date, is in MTP.

[3] *MTB*, p. 899.

[4] Type and paper of the sort used in the "Indians" galley proof were also used in galley proof of "The American Press," a speech which Clemens intended to deliver at a Chicago banquet in September 1888, and in a brief passage dated 5 January 1889 by Clemens. Both of these are in MTP.

[5] This guess discounts the author's statement in a letter of 1 September 1884 that he has not "a paragraph to show for my 3-months' working-season" (*MTBus*, p. 274). He may well have decided in the summer of 1884 that the fragment—or even a much better piece—was worthless (he had so characterized the opening chapters of *Huckleberry Finn* at the end of the summer when he wrote them).

[6] The machine was working in 1885, but since it needed adjustments it was built anew, not to become operative again until December 1888. It was working in January, February, August, September, and October and perhaps in other months of 1889 (*MTBus*, pp. 307–308, 339, 391; *MTN*, pp. 205, 206, 209; *MTB*, pp. 907–910; *MTL*, pp. 499, 506–508, 515–518, 521–522).

[7] The survey was confined to letters and manuscripts in MTP.

[8] *MTBus*, pp. 264–265, 270. His wording in the first letter suggests that the book was not beyond the planning stage: "I mean to take Huck Finn out there [on the Plains and in the Mountains]."

to a dentist "I work at a new story (Huck Finn and Tom Sawyer among the Indians 40 or 50 years ago)." [9] Composing at a speed which he often achieved, he could have written that portion of the story that survives in holograph pages and galley proofs—some 240 of his usual manuscript pages—in ten or twelve days. The manuscript offers no evidence that he wrote the fragment in more than one spurt, and the scarcity of corrections in the galleys may indicate that when he gave his incomplete story to the typesetter for a practice run on the Paige machine, he had decided not to go on writing it.[10] He makes no identifiable mention of the fragment after the summer of 1884.

Doughface

As the introductory note for "Doughface" indicates, Mark Twain mentions this incident three times in his 1897 notebook entries concerning "Tom Sawyer's Conspiracy" and twice in entries made in 1902 dealing with a projected "fifty years after" story about Tom and Huck and their gang. Although it seems probable therefore that "Doughface" was written in one of these years, the story, as presented by Huck, is highly self-contained, and there is no internal evidence that the author intended it to be part of a longer work. There is no completely satisfactory external evidence upon which to base a preference either for 1897 or for 1902 as the date of composition. Paper similar to that used in "Doughface" appears to have been used by Mark Twain only after 1900, but the nondescript quality of the papers involved makes this similarity alone an insufficient justification for placing "Doughface" in 1902. In the absence of further evidence, the precise date of composition cannot be determined, and 1897 and 1902 remain likely possibilities.

---

[9] *MTHL*, II, 496. The phrase about the time of the story would be repeated in a letter of 24 July asking Webster to change the title page of *Adventures of Huckleberry Finn* to read " 'Time, forty to fifty years ago,' instead of 'Time, forty years ago' " (*MTBus*, p. 271). A possibility is that this was urged because the sequel contains details which the author knew it would be awkward to assign to 1844—Brace's prophecy about the start of the exodus to Oregon and the assertion that lucifer matches were a new invention.

[10] Galleys 3, 4, and 5 contain six corrections of typographical errors; here and in the other galleys many typographical errors are uncorrected.

Tom Sawyer's Gang Plans a Naval Battle

This fragment was written on paper similar to paper which Mark Twain apparently used only after 1900. However, the lack of distinguishing characteristics in the paper and the absence of any other evidence make it unwise to eliminate the possibility that the piece was composed before 1900. Mark Twain's desire to write a sea story, particularly one that would burlesque the misuse of sea terms, was so nearly omnipresent that, in the absence of more definite evidence, the precise date of composition of this narrative cannot be determined.

Tom Sawyer's Conspiracy

Evidently Mark Twain began to write "Tom Sawyer's Conspiracy" when he was in Weggis during the summer of 1897.[1] A notebook entry of 1884, one of November 1896, and several entries in a notebook kept between 2 June and 24 July 1897 show him thinking about details of the plot, but they do not indicate that he was writing.[2] Paper of several of the early manuscript pages, though, is the kind he used in Weggis, and quite possibly only there, during a stay between 18 July and 26 September 1897;[3] Paine dated an envelope containing part of the manuscript, 1897;[4] and the datable draft of a letter on the back of p. 91 of the manuscript indicates that the author had written about a third of the manuscript which survives—about 12,000 words of it—by late August or early September 1897.[5]

---

[1] Two retrospective references to "Tom Sawyer, Detective" place the later story after August and September 1896, when the detective novel was published. Between October 1896 and May 1897 the author had been writing *Following the Equator* (*MTL*, p. 623; *MTB*, p. 1681).

[2] *IE*, pp. 195–196; Notebooks 31 and 32a, MTP.

[3] Concerning the paper, see *MTSatan*, p. 86. For the beginning and the conclusion of the stay in Weggis, see *MTN*, pp. 331, 339.

[4] Paine labeled the envelope containing Part I, "Vienna, 1898–9," and that containing Part II, " '97." A page reference, "p. 19–20," on the " '97" envelope suggests that the contents of the envelopes may have been switched. In *MTB*, p. 1045, Paine speaks of "a bulky, half-finished manuscript about Tom and Huck, most of which was doubtless written" in Weggis during this summer.

[5] The drafted note offered *Harper's Monthly* permission to print a poem, "In Memoriam," written on 18 August 1897 (*MTN*, p. 336). Since the poem appeared in the issue of the magazine for November, the letter must have been sent by the indicated date.

On 29 September 1897 the Clemenses moved into the Hotel Metropole in Vienna, to stay until late in the spring of 1898.[6] Mark Twain must have continued to work on the story there, since some working notes which list characters and locales in the order of their appearance through p. 114 of the manuscript are on a paper distinctive of this place and period.

Metropole stationery was used in additional working notes which outline events recounted on pp. 115–232 of the manuscript. But since this section is on a new type of paper—Joynson Superfine—the likelihood is that it was written after the Clemenses left the Metropole. Just when, is hard to say: evidence supports guesses that it was in 1898, 1899, or 1900 and perhaps in all three. Paine has labeled an envelope containing part of the manuscript "Vienna, 1898–9,"[7] and after a summer in Kaltenleutgeben the author was in Vienna again, this time at Hotel Krantz, from 20 September 1898 to 22 May 1899. During this period, so Paine says, intermittently "he worked on several unfinished longer tales"; and on the back of a discarded p. 181 is an unrelated bit of writing which Paine assigns to 1899.[8] Clemens used Joynson Superfine paper in letters written in London between October 1899 and 6 October 1900, and in New York between 15 October and the end of 1900.[9] Writing from London on 31 July 1900, he may have referred to "Tom Sawyer's Conspiracy" in a letter to R. W. Gilder: "I am 25,000 words deep in a story which I began a long while ago (in Vienna, I think) and I mean to finish it now."[10] There is some evidence that the author made numerous revisions in this part of the story, which may have thrown him off schedule.[11] Final pages of the manuscript are on Schoellerpost paper, which he used in letters in 1900 but not, I believe, in 1901 or 1902.

---

[6] *MTN*, pp. 339, 360.

[7] As I have indicated, this now contains Part I, but my hypothesis is that originally it contained Part II.

[8] *MTB*, pp. 1072–1084, 1682. The passage occurs early in *Christian Science*.

[9] For details about this period, see *MTB*, pp. 1111–1141. Reasons for ending the survey with 1900 follow.

[10] The letter is quoted in part in *Catalogue of Charles Romm Collection Sale* (New York: American Art Association, 1921). *MTSatan*, p. 49, which suggests that the letter refers to a manuscript of "The Mysterious Stranger," may be correct.

[11] A page of working notes on Joynson's Superfine paper suggests changes on pp. 115–232, and the discarded p. 181 contains matter which turns up several pages later in the final manuscript.

In 1902 Mark Twain returned to the manuscript: the verso of p. 86 contains the discarded initial page of a sketch which he wrote during the first months of that year.[12] The reason probably is indicated in a 1902 notebook entry: "Make this *brief*: Tom's selling Huck as a nigger. See the discarded Conspiracy."[13] The note indicates that (1) Twain intended to lift one detail from the fragment for inclusion in a story he was planning about his boyish heroes,[14] and (2) he had made up his mind to abandon the nearly completed narrative about Tom's conspiracy.

Tom Sawyer: A Play in Four Acts

Paine believed that "about 1872" Mark Twain began to write the story of Tom Sawyer, not as a novel but as a play.[1] This may be, but, as Bernard DeVoto has argued, Paine's belief is based upon evidence so scanty as to make it unconvincing.[2] Rodman Gilder wrote in 1944 that "*Tom Sawyer* was begun by Mark Twain as a drama in 1872 and copyrighted as such three years later. . . ."[3] Probably Gilder too trustfully accepted Paine's guess about the first version, but he was right about this copyright date. "TOM SAWYER. / A Drama. / By Mark Twain—(Samuel L. Clemens)" was copyrighted in Washington on 21 July 1875.[4]

Since this copyright was procured by submitting a one-page synopsis rather than a completed script, one cannot say with assurance how far the author proceeded with the play. The synopsis, I believe, reads as if it were written before any of the play. A letter dated 14 August 1876, however, suggests that by that date Twain had finished at least a part of

---

[12] The discarded page was from "Five Boons of Life," published in July 1902 (*MTB*, p. 1683).

[13] Notebook 35, TS p. 20, MTP.

[14] *MTHL*, II, p. 748.

[1] *MTB*, facing p. 510.

[2] Only one page has survived (see Appendix C), and there is no evidence that it was written before the novel. And Paine did not know that, with Billy Rogers as his hero, Mark Twain initially told much of Tom's story as early as 1870 in "Boy's Manuscript" (*MTW*, pp. 4–5).

[3] "Mark Twain Detested the Theatre," *Theatre Arts*, XXVIII (February 1944), 111.

[4] Copyright record #7621. The synopsis is included in the headnote to the play in this book.

the drama. The same letter shows that he had decided that he himself could not satisfactorily dramatize the story.[5]

Nevertheless, he tried again. Rodman Gilder also noted that a second copyright on a dramatization of *Tom Sawyer* was obtained by Clemens in 1884, a fact verified by the U.S. Copyright Office. "TOM SAWYER. / A Play in 4 Acts / by / S. L. Clemens (Mark Twain)" was entered in Washington on 1 February 1884, again on the basis of a synopsis rather than a script.[6]

Paine believed that the version of the play completed in 1884 was destroyed,[7] but the close correspondence of the 1884 synopsis with the play which has survived in the Mark Twain Papers discredits this belief. The first three acts of the surviving version are in holograph, and all four acts are in typescript (except for one lengthy handwritten replacement for a canceled part of the typescript). The initial thirty-three pages of the holograph version appear to have been salvaged from the 1875/76 version, because they are on paper often used during those years but evidently not used after mid-June 1880.[8] A classroom scene (mentioned in the letter to Conway of August 1876), or possibly a revision of it, occurs in Act III. The parts of the manuscript written after August 1876[9] pretty clearly were written early in 1884. Paine reported that a version of the play was composed "within the space of a few weeks";[10] Clemens boasted to Howells on 13 February 1884 that in four weeks he had written all of the play *Tom Sawyer* plus two and a

---

[5] Clemens to Eustace Conway, son of the author's British agent, Moncure D. Conway. A copy is in MTP.

[6] Gilder, p. 111. A photostatic copy shows that the entry is a portion of a galley proof that has been torn off part way through the summary of Act III. The entire synopsis, however, survives in holograph in the MTP (see Appendix C).

[7] *MTL*, II, 439.

[8] This paper, which has an embossed design containing the letters "P & P," is discussed in my article "When Was *Huckleberry Finn* Written?" *American Literature*, XXX (March 1958), 7–8.

[9] Clemens included pages from a printing of the Toronto edition of *Tom Sawyer*, revised to conform to dramatic usage; this pirated edition had appeared on the American market by the early part of November 1876. Clemens also incorporated a dialogue from a part of *Huckleberry Finn* written during the summer of 1876 (Huck's discussion of Tom's robber gang and of his own experiment with the lamp). The excerpt from *Huck* later was discarded from the play.

[10] *MTB*, p. 764. However, Paine places the writing in 1883 (*MTB*, p. 1679), and Twain may at least have done some preliminary work during that year.

half acts of another drama;[11] and in a letter to his old friend Mrs. Fairbanks he placed its completion precisely on 29 January 1884.[12] Evidence afforded by the writing materials supports these indications of the time of composition;[13] and an entry in a notebook, some time shortly after 21 December 1883, contains Aunt Polly's speech at the end of Act III and a version of a speech by Tom Sawyer which closely resembles a speech in Act IV.[14] Augustin Daly read the play *Tom Sawyer* early in 1884 and rejected it in a letter dated 27 February.[15] There is no evidence that the author worked on it after that date.

---

[11] *MTHL*, II, 471. Although *Tom Sawyer* is not specified in the letter, other references clearly identify it. The second play was *The Prince and the Pauper*.

[12] *MTF*, p. 256. A letter to Webster (28 January 1884) had predicted that the play would be finished a day earlier (*MTBus*, p. 233).

[13] With the exception of the first thirty-three pages, Mark Twain wrote the holograph version in pencil on Keystone Linen paper. He also used these materials in letters and manuscripts written between May 1883 and the summer of 1884. He used the same materials in a series of working notes and in an insert replacing pages 42 through 47 of the typed manuscript.

[14] Notebook 17, TS p. 31 (MTP), has some of Aunt Polly's exact words, and then almost the same phrasing as Tom's speech on finding the searchers in the cave (see Appendix C).

[15] *MTBus*, pp. 236–237.

APPENDIX C

Mark Twain's Working Notes and Related Matter

MARK TWAIN's working notes and other matter related to the manuscripts in this volume are translated into type here as faithfully as possible. Although the author's holograph ampersand has been expanded, instances of misspelling and faulty punctuation have not been corrected. Cancellations are preserved and marked by angle brackets, thus ⟨ ⟩; editorial explanation is enclosed by square brackets, [ ].

Orion Clemens's sketch of Jane Lampton Clemens is included in the appendix because Twain probably drew on it for background when writing his own biographical impressions of their mother. Also included in this section are the only surviving manuscript page of another dramatic version of "Tom Sawyer" and the play synopsis Twain submitted to the United States Copyright Office in February 1884.

Jane Lampton Clemens

Less than a week after Jane Clemens's death, Orion was approached with an offer to write a sketch of her life for publication in western newspapers (Orion to SLC, Keokuk, 1 November 1890, MTP). In a telegram which is now missing, Clemens suppressed the project. Replying to a letter which followed the "dispatch to halt," Orion wrote from Keokuk on 13 November that he was "glad" Clemens had decided to write a "magazine article" about their mother (MTP). A six-page fragment of Orion's biographical sketch, presumably sent to his brother for approval early in November 1890, survives in MTP and is printed here: A single page of manuscript by Mark Twain, rehearsing the Clemens family history and probably written just prior to "Jane Lampton Clemens," follows Orion's sketch.

Orion's Sketch

Jane Clemens died at Keokuk, Iowa, at the residence of her son, Orion Clemens, October 27th, 1890. She was buried at Hannibal, Missouri, between her husband and her son Henry, who was killed in the explosion of the steamer Pennsylvania, near Memphis, Tennessee, in 1858.

She was born in Columbia, Kentucky, June 18, 1803. Her father was Benjamin Lampton. He was sociable, and a good singer.

On her mother's side was her grandfather, Col. Casey, who earned honorable mention in the printed history of Kentucky, as a leader of the defenders of the pioneers against the Indians. He was a member of the Constitutional Convention of that state. His wife, Jane Casey, was a member of the Montgomery family, who also have received honorable mention in Kentucky history; and she herself shared in the perils of Indian warfare. Though a good Baptist she never could, while she lived, endure the presence of Indians, because by savages five of her relatives were killed.

During her girlhood Jane Lampton was noted for her vivacity and her beauty. To the last she retained her rosy cheeks and fine complexion. She took part in the custom in Kentucky and Tennessee, of going on horseback from house to house during the week from Christmas to New Year. To the music of one or two violins they danced all night, slept a little, ate breakfast, and danced all day at the next house. To the last Mrs. Clemens maintained dancing to be innocent and healthful. Even in the last year of her life she liked to show a company the beautiful step and graceful movement she had learned in her youth. Until within a very few years she was so straight she almost leaned backward. Her happy flow of spirits made her a popular favorite wherever she lived.

Cyrus Walker was a young attorney, just married to a cousin of Mrs. Clemens, and was traveling on his circuit. He took his fees in cash or other articles of value as might suit the convenience of his clients. Once he was returning home with a silk dress pattern, when he heard uproarious laughter in his own house. On entering there was instant hush. After a good deal of examination and cross-examination he brought out the truth that Jane Lampton, then about 15 years of age, had been imitating his dancing. He wished to see himself as she saw him, but she refused till he offered the silk dress. She then showed him his own awkward dancing. It amused him, and she got the dress.

In 1823 she married John Marshall Clemens, and about 1825 they removed to Gainesborough, Tennessee. One day, while he was absent, practicing law on his circuit, a

Mark Twain's Sketch

⟨Y⟩My mother's maiden name was Jane Lampton; my maternal grandmother's maiden name was Margaret Casey; Margaret Casey's mother's maiden name was Montgomery.

⟨Mate⟩My paternal grandmother's maiden name was Pamelia Goggins.

The Lampton⟨'⟩s are descended from the Lambtons ⟨(⟩now Earls of Durham (see Burke's Peerage.)

The Clemenses are descended from Geoffrey Clement, one of the signers of the death warrant of Charles I. There have been no other prominent Clemenses, except Sherrard and Jere. Clemens, of Virginia.

Tom Sawyer's Conspiracy

In addition to the entries in Mark Twain's notebooks relating to "Tom Sawyer's Conspiracy," five pages of working notes survive. I have divided these into three groups (A, B and C), according to types of paper. Notes numbered here A1 and A2 are on cross-barred paper characteristic of the Weggis period. Both are written on the verso of pages discarded from the manuscript of "Hellfire Hotchkiss," another novel begun at Weggis during the summer of 1897 and never finished. Group B (notes B1 and B2) is written on stationery of the Hotel Metropole in Vienna, where the Clemens family stayed from 29 September 1897 until late in the spring of 1898. The final working note, C1, is written on the Joynson Superfine paper used for pp. 115–232 of the manuscript.

Group A
A1

Old Miss Watson
Wid. Douglas
Ben Rogers Briggs
Joe Harper Bill Bowen
The King
The Duke Bilge-bridgewater
Hair lip
The Cave
Aunt Polly
Sid
Mary
Judge Thatcher
　　Becky Thatcher.
Genl. Gaines (new town drunk-
　　ard) 60
Pete ⟨Koontz⟩ Kruger, German
　　blacksmith
Col. Elgin (Elder)
Col. Ayres Hare
Sheriff Ben Hawkins (Haskin) and Capt. Militia
Fire Marshal Sam Raymond (envied because said to be
　　illegitimate) Rumford
Tan Yard. Cold spring. Pork house
　　Slaughter-house swamp and point
　　Coon creek
Steam ferry.
Jackson's Island. Glaucus Point.
　　Superstitions.
　　Hookerville (Saverton) bluffs.
　　undertaker, Jake Trumbull

Jim
Cardiff Hill
Hanted House on
Crawfish branch
in Catfish Hollow.
Shiloh church Pres.
Old Ship of Zion
Ed Stevens⟨—⟩(Jimmy Steel)
Bill Pitts (Jake Fitch)
Capt. Bowen (Capt. Harper)
Tom Nash (deaf and dumb) Jack
　　Benton
old Benton (postmaster)
Mary Benton (wild)
Admiral Grimes
　　Keelboatman
⟨Brick⟩ Buck Fisher (with Gaines.

A2

Measles
Harvey Wilks
Miss Mary Jane
Oliver Benton, postmaster and undertaker and ⟨editor⟩

Buck Fisher and Genl Haines.

Orion (Plunkett) frantic editor
Duke (jour print)
King (mish., preacher etc.)
Hair-lip (Joanna)⎫
Susan   ⎬
Miss Mary Jane ⎭   (sand)
Justice of Peace (Claghorn)
Old Selmes (English)
Constable Jake (Flacker) detective.
Huck disguised as negro.
One-legged Higgins (Bradish's nigger)
Arrest the camp-meeting
Baxter, foreman
Abe Wallace the sexton
Mrs. Lawson, lawyer's wife

Group B
B1

Bat Bradish
Hookerville (Saverton)
Catfish Hollow
Crawfish ⟨Creek⟩ Branch
Hanted house
Aunt Polly
Sid—Mary
⟨Jimmy Finn⟩⟨
Genl. Gaines
Widow Douglas
Uncle Fletcher (Quarles)
Capt. Harper (Bowen)
Joe Harper   Bill
Jack   Sam   Mrs. Lawson, lawyer's wife
Baxter, foreman of printg office, Mason, etc
Paxton, deacon.   Claghorn, Justice peace
Christiandum   Capt. Haskins (Hawkins)
Slater's alley   Capt. Sam Rumford (Raymond)
Oliver Benton P.M. and under- Judge Thatcher
    taker   Becky Thatcher
Plunket the editor
Jake Flacker, detective

Col. Elder, Provo Marshal
Pete Kruger, Germ blacksmith
Abe Wallace, sexton

B2

Flacker takes clews.

King is broken leg, and hiding—fell over in the dark.

T. watches the place—⟨rem⟩ it is half a mile away—stamps out or ⟨scrap [page torn]⟩ dusts over the first footprints. Sees Duke finishing dragging him to hanted house. Creeps there through high weeds of deserted garden, ⟨sees he has⟩—too dark to see anything, but hears low voices and moans—"my leg's broken."

Will watch the place every night and judges they will leave in a boat on a dark one—which they do, in a skiff and go to the cave, T. following silently in canoe.

[Page cut off.]

Group C
C1

The strangers seen belong to Murrel's gang.

Their purpose is to murder and rob Bat, who keeps money in his lonely cabin. Tom overhears them before he slips off his disguise. He discovers himself—saves Bat—they carry him off to the cave.

Bat alarms town with news his nigger saved him but was carried off. Tom is missed. Great alarm.

But first, the reward-bill is postofficed and Tom goes to hanted house and Huck betrays his presence to Bat who captures him to get the $100 reward.

"But now you know it got to be *serious*—Providence changed the program."

The King and the Duke come along selling Demosthenes's pebble. But King precedes, offering reward—it has been lost (not stolen).

"Tom Sawyer: A Play"

Section I

Twenty-six pages of working notes and one notebook entry may be classified into five groups on the basis of their content and relationship to the composition of the play, though the grouping is not the author's, but mine.

Group A

This group consists of three pages now in the Edward Doheny Library, St. John's Seminary, Camarillo, California. A1 outlines some of the action summarized in paragraph 2 of the synopsis of the play which was entered in the copyright office, Washington, D.C., 21 July 1875 (see pp. 244–245): it must have been a continuation of a synopsis of an early act since Twain labeled it "2." A2 outlines action to be included in Act IV and A3 that of Act V. After writing A3 the author may well have noticed that he was planning too long a play, since so far his outline had covered only about half of the events covered in the synopsis.

A1
2

eye and can't—talks. Spelling, Geography etc. Nap. Cat. When row over, ⟨fragments dis⟩ says sch. is dismissed presently—will see their fathers. Discovers fragments. Tom catches it. Dismissed. Tom goes— will not look at Amy. Gracie comes breathless—has just remembered about cake. Amy flies to catch Tom. and can't. ⟨Curtain⟩

Return of Joe—then Tom—then the Red-handed. All plans made. Curtain.

A2
⟨3d⟩ 4th Act.

⟨Pirate talk and plans⟩
⟨Aunt Polly and⟩
Near A.P.'s house. ⟨Amy and Gracie; wailing.⟩ Citizens talk. Tom's jacket found and given to A P   Name date of funeral. and how dragged river. Various opinions.

Amy and Gracie wailing. Ben and others. Bid each other good-night. Miss Fletcher, perhaps.

Scene 2d—Aunt Polly's. Mrs. Harper, Sid and Mary. All in mourning. Tom steals in and eavesdrops. By and by exit Mrs. Harper, Sid and M. Old lady examines contents of sacred drawer. This is his ⟨jacket.⟩ or cap. Prays. (He done his level best.) Letter from Amy. Tom ⟨kisses shoe) watches her fall asleep. Talks about how he got there (3 *strikes*) Must hurry back before caught. Remembers letter—reads it. Kisses her shoe. ⟨Writes no⟩ Is going to write note—hears noise—drops pencil and ⟨Exit⟩. Finds hunk of molasses candy—rolls it up in letter.

A3
5th Act.

Curtain discovers funeral well along. Three coffins. Make it a love-feast. Brethren asked to speak. 3 do. Preacher concludes. General burst of weeping. The boys crawl from under pews—preacher staring—everybody faces around—the ragged piratically dressed chaps come forward. General rejoicing. Everybody forgives. The 3 take back their compliments. Ain't anybody goin' to be glad Red's back? Yes, *I* will! Amy steals to Tom's side—Gracie to Joe's and as concourse breaks up they name the day. *Curtain.*

(*Mem.*—In planning, the boys are going to discard their caps for plumed paper ones—wear tin swords, turn their coats, get flashy sashes, false horse-pistols etc., and it is in this preposterous gear that they appear.)

Group B

Mark Twain made the notes classified here as Group B to indicate passages in the novel *Tom Sawyer* which might provide scenes for his dramatization, citing pages in the Toronto edition or an edition with the same pagination. The first three of these, in MTP, are on paper such as that used in the 1884 holograph of the play (Keystone Linen); and, like the text of the manuscript, they are in pencil. Originals of the last two have disappeared, but their partial texts (which have been used here) appeared on pp. 65 and 9, respectively, of *A1911.*

B1

Previous reference to Hoss's death and body-snatchers. [Inserted in the left margin at the top of the page.]

In act 1 insert boy's fight. | Die village.

Tom's Gang formed and discussed.
learn to smoke in graveyard.

Act 2.

Graveyard.—95

Bring dead cat and talk about it. The tragedy. Boys ⟨remain⟩ *return* and talk 104.

---

brass knob returned—113. [i.e., p. 112]

114

People accusing Muff in gravyard.

<table>
<tr><td></td><td>3d act</td><td>been there 2 days</td></tr>
<tr><td><u>On the island.</u></td><td></td><td>Put in Robin Hood.</td></tr>
</table>

2 of them pray.
The pirates wish they had a Bible—or may be they've got one.

152

Must come in.
bottom 153 [1]
Tom returns and tells what he saw at home.

B2

Graveyard—95.   They go there *Monday* night.
Doodle-bug—88.
Robin Hood fight—89
School (go sit with girls—70.
The tick—(school)—77.
Tom's love scene—before school-blackboard. 71–78

71—Amy sees him with Becky—is huffy, and takes up with Alfred for spite.
(It can come in, all right, at school—and in a huff—has a hateful passage with Amy afterwards—saves Amy the whipping, which makes him fall in love with her again.

---

[1] The reference is to the conversation which Tom overhears after sneaking home from Jackson's Island in chapter 15. Aunt Polly enlarges upon the fact that Tom "warn't *bad*, so to say—only mischeevous."

Dead cat—good.—64–9 (all good graveyard stuff.
Graveyard bright moonlight.

Add on 78 (Do you love rats?) after 71 [2]—before school takes in
76—the *tick* is *in* school. OVER [On the back of this page is the
matter of the note numbered C5.]

B3
199

School scene—spelling, reading, bzz—bzz—buzz of study. Classes
reciting.

232—also 241

This in the graveyard or on island before murder—they've come to dig
for treasure.

328

Wind up with it? [3]

B4

89—Robin Hood—after cat and warts . . . 92—Sits down on a nettle
after shooting his last arrow—close R H with that . . . Next, they
discuss Tom Sawyers Gang—See "Huck Fin."

B5

Pirate. in place of R H—135 [4] . . . In cave, Tom and Huck not
lost—got provisions—while girls eat tell 'em they know the way out.
Then people come;

Group C

Like Group B, these notes are in pencil on Keystone Linen, the paper of the manuscript of the 1884 version of the play. C1 summarizes the

---

[2] Tom asks Becky the question during the course of a conversation on p. 78.
The note suggests that this dialogue be placed after the one on p. 71 about Tom's
drawings.
[3] The author evidently considered the possibility of ending the play with the
party described in chapter 34, which begins on p. 328.
[4] On p. 135, Tom, Huck, and Joe Harper begin a discussion of the pleasures of
being a pirate.

settings of all four acts; C2 sketches the action of each act. C3–C5 summarize Acts I through III. C6 and C7 evidently provide an early plan for Act IV; C8 through C10 evidently provide a later plan. All these except C4 are in MTP; C4 (partially quoted on p. 17 of *A1911*) is in the Yale University Library.

C1

4th act in the cave—a surprise party for Tom and Huck.

Resume.

1

in front of house

2

in graveyard

3

in school house.

---

a. School scene: b. trial.

4

in cave.

C2
1st

girl-talk.
whitewash. Tom flogs Temple.

⟨1⟩2*d*.

Boys see Muff sneak back to get knife, while crowd there—arrested, (Injun Joe follows him to keep an eye on him and see that he don't peach,)—he is carried off to jail.

3d

Ends with (Tom's flogging ends one act.
One act to close with Tom's testimony in court and flight or manacling of Injun Joe. and Muff's gratitude.

Tom—Huck I can't stand it (struggling).
Huck—O, Tom *don't* ruin us!
(Hold court in school-house with black-boards around.)

C3

1.

1.   The girls.   *Jim.*

_____

2. The old lady. and Mary. "You Tom!"

_____

3. Tom and Temple. Fight.
   Aunt P. Sid, Mary. Bring the whitewash.
   Tom alone, whitewashing. Enter and exit *Jim.*
   Sublets whitewashing to Ben Rogers.
   Exit rogers very weary; enter another boy and takes contract. Wants orders; "Well, whitewash the trees and the barrel." Tom, Huck and Joe Harper discuss a robber association. Another and another boy apply. Tom sends and borrows brushes of the neighbors—sends back to woodshed for more whitewash. Finally has a dozen boys at it, whitewashing sidewalks. Man drags practicable black calf across—whitewash the calf. Aunt Polly finds em w[hitewash]ing the *house.* Tableau. Curtain.

C4

Potter and Dr.
   ″   objects to job
quarrel
fight
Potter knocked down with Tom's shovl
Joe rushes in and stabs Dr.
Potter insensible
Joe will bury Dr in Tom's hole and will
make Potter think *he* is accessory
Finds treasure—goes and hide it.
—returns and finds P up.
No use to bury body, for Potter
thinks *he* did it.
When boys leave, they carry
their tools with them and will **never tell.**

_____

Somewhere previously it is said
Joe lives in the cave.

C5

Becky asks if Tom is going to the picknick and cave ⟨?⟩ ⟨next week?⟩ to-morrow. Yes.

Enter Alfred and Amy—they flirt, Amy being angry to see Tom with Becky and he not having answered her note, though some days have gone by.

Amy sees Alfred ink Tom's book—resolves she will keep mum about it.

Exit all but Amy—looks at teacher's book—Tom slips in, to tell her ⟨if⟩ she has deeply wronged him by sending no cake and taking up with Alfred, and will always hate her and *never* forgive her—"I *do* love her best of all, but I know this is the way they do in the books"— sees her tear teacher's book. see 196–197.[5]

General school scene.

Tick. "*I* done it!" ⟨Solus. That warnt any slouch⟩

C6
1

⟨3⟩4*th Act.*
⟨Schoolhouse. (No, between that and Court—a front scene.)⟩ [6]

Huck and Tom. ⟨They⟩ Tom has learned that Joe lives in the cave. Been wanting ⟨f⟩ to find out where he uses, so they can get that money. Got to give it up, now—won't venture into the cave ⟨while *he*⟩ if *that* is the case. [A single line drawn through the paragraph.]

(That's the way they do in *books*).
(*frequent.*)

In cave, they talk of having learned that 2 weeks after Joe's escape his apparent body found in river. This is a new *part* of the cave. They have

[5] In the Toronto edition this scene begins not on p. 196 but on p. 197.
[6] The parenthetical note indicates a plan to insert a scene in front of the curtain between the school scene and the courtroom scene in Act III.

provisions, and been in there 2 or 3 days. Are in bitter distress, for they have been *lost* for last 24 hours. Tom has one bit of crust left. Despondent. Find a hole—uncover it [7]—sound it with fish-line—no bottom. Can't escape *that* way. (Exit.)

Enter Amy and Becky. Famished, and worn out. 1 inch of candle. Embrace and get ready to die, but fall asleep—candle out. "The candles are *gone!*"

Enter Joe, with bag. Has seen distant flash

C7 [8]

of candles—⟨heard noises⟩ horrible joy—will kill the boys—begins to sneak on them [9]—will flee the cave. Sets down bag—goes skulking and listening. Tom and Huck shout—Joe darts away—they glimpse him just as he goes down hole. Coming back, find his money. Examine—it is all there. *Now* (Huck says it) no use—we're lost. Leave it where 'tis. Got to die here. Discover girls asleep.

Wake them—joy—gives 'em the crust. Encourages them—*he*'ll get them out. ["Aside—" written in the margin at this point.]

Learns of the pic-nic. *Two days?* All right, then, cave been full of people ever since, searching, of course. Hear distant noises. Less go and see. (Exit.

Enter crowd. Affecting remarks of Aunt Polly, Widow Douglas, parents etc over the dead children—down some hole in the dark. ⟨(Exit to search)⟩

(All kneel in silent prayer—children appear—'sh!—creep stealthily up and ⟨lay hands⟩ steal arms about necks—tableau and kisses.

"Somebody got to be glad to see Huck!"

Widow—*I* am—and he shall by [be] my *son* (Jones has told her, 10 minutes before when all given up for dead. (Money now exhibited.

(Back.) Crowd winding about with torches, pretty scene.

C8
1

	Huck Tom
They catch bats—or try to.	
Heard of Joe's death.	—one short piece of candle.

---

[7] Twain has written "rotten boards" above "uncover it."

[8] Note C7 is written on the back of C6.

[9] Although the eleven words beginning with "horrible" are written as an insert, probably intended to appear here, the author has not used a caret indicating where they are to be placed.

Huck and Tom—lost and hungry
Talk. "Good! here's plenty candles!"
Find hole—covered with paper boards.
Sound it with fish-line—can't get into lower story *that* way.
(They don't find candles   *Exit.*

Amy and Becky.

Hungry and worn. "Candles gone!" They don't remember just where
they left them. Talk about Tom and Temple. Despair. Cry. Pray. Go to
sleep. (meaning to die, but overcome. Candle goes out.

Enter Joe.

Scared. Has heard noises. Will fly the cave. Will return in a year or two
and settle with Tom and Huck. Hears distant voices—sees light—badly
scared. Drops bag and flies.

Exit.

Enter Tom and Huck

Find bag. "No use, now—got to starve." Tom says "No." Examine—
money all there. Discover girls asleep.

C9

Wake them. Talk. *We'll* save you. Gives them his crust and some bats.
⟨You been here so⟩ People hunting them *sure*—"we'll be found—don't
you wory. May be a week, cave is so big—but don't you worry.

Devilish face of Joe peers out—will hive those boys—steals behind
boys. Girls see him and scream. Boys jump up and stand paralyzed.
Then they jump for the rock and the dodging begins for life and death,
the girls looking on. (Maybe Tom trips him.) *"Now,* Huck. They fly
—Joe pursues, the girls scream. Boys lose their hats near the hole. Cross
the bridge. Joe⟨s⟩ crashes through. Boys return and examine. They hear
nothing—he is dead. ⟨Rejoin⟩ Call the girls, to hunt their way out.
Exit.
Crowd come winding in. ⟨Huck[?]⟩ ⟨"Come here!"⟩

C10

They talk their despar. Jones reveals that it was Huck saved the
Widow. A loiterer discovers the hats. Takes off his own reverently. In

reverent voice "Come here!" They gather and cry on each other, examining broken bridge. Then come down front and kneel silently.

Tom discovers them. 'Sh! Now do as I tell you⟨.⟩ (then whispers the *girls* only.) All tip-toe down. Girls disappear and take their stations— Huck disappears. Ap's *cowhide*

O, you *darling* I'm so glad to get you back again! (Embrace). Cowhides him—embrace again and so on.

Mary and Ben Rogers go wandering back and discover the hats, with a scream.

Group D

Written in pencil on paper of the sort used in surviving pages of Groups B and C, these notes start with remarks on the casting of the play, then outline dialogue and action for use in Act IV as it was finally written. In the upper left corner of D1 the author wrote "S. L. Clemens Hotel Brunswick." The hotel was one in which he frequently stopped when in New York.

D1
1

Tom Sawyer

The principal girls in this play can as well be full grown; (and fat or lean) and merely *dressed* as children. The burlesque will do no harm.

Jim can be burlesqued also—a negro boy 6 feet high or 6 feet through.

It is only Huck and Tom that must not be burlesqued.

If Mr. Lewis and Miss Rehan ⟨would have⟩ had the parts of Tom and Huck, the rest ⟨no⟩ would be undifficult.

D2
2

⟨It's ⟨Becky's⟩ Temple's⟩ pic-nic, so of course Tom not invited. It goes Saturday morning, T and Huck go mid-night Friday. Tom knew of the picnic, but cared nothing about it. He and H heard of Joe's death Friday ⟨evening⟩ evening, and left *immediately*. ⟨T⟩ Huck told A P *nothing*. She *hopes* it will turn out he *was* with the pic nic, notwithstanding the unlost ones say he *wasn't*.⟩

⟨Discovers the boys—war-whoop.

Injun Joe with knife—chases them—they dodge round and round a big rock—keep up the hide and seek for some time—then Tom and Huck—"*Now* Huck!" make⟨s⟩ a break toward the fatal passage, Joe following at full speed ⟨—Tom wheels and throws himself down⟩— they jump the hole, Joe goes *into* it with a death-yell.

D3
3

The boys go into cave with picknickers, but immediately desert, ⟨and are⟩—*all* break up into parties, as usual. Amy and Becky are supposed to be with Tom—⟨but they got lost in a hide and whoop game.⟩ and not missed from the 30 children—supposed to have gone home with the Harpers.

All 4 expected to be found *dead* together.

Hole covered with *paper* boards. Boys too light, but Joe breaks through.

⟨Cowhide—I wish I'd *never* used it.⟩ Brought along to humiliate myself—I will *bury* it with him for a testimony against me.

Tom's hat found—mashed candle—"Well, you can depend upon it they were all together. They give up and go away to weep and pray.

D4
4

Tom discovers the weeping crowd. "Look! Now 'sh! not a word—⟨follow me⟩." ⟨They ⟨slip a-⟩ tip-toe down—creeping on hands and *feet*.⟩ Wait—and watch me ⟨let me tell you each what to do—whispers— they disappear—and when I holler you *come* ⟨a⟩!

Tip-toes down—lies down behind A P—stretches out—A P gradually notices it—reaches for it, picks it up, applies her glasses to the shoe— ⟨springs⟩ "You *Tom!*"—springs up.

⟨He g⟩ ⟨O,⟩ you've got your Tom, but O, my poor lost Amy—

Tom—Look behind you!
(Amy steps out with a candle.
O my poor lost Becky—
(*She* appears)
Look behind you!

D5
5

Presently Huck appears meekly. Nobody notices.
Tom—Aunty, *somebody's* got to be glad to see Huck.
Widow goes for him.

_____

Tom, I've spent over two dollars, hunting for your worthless carcase.
Tom—Allow me. ($5)
A.P. Bites it—rings it on the floor. Where'd you get so much money?
O never mind
(Money sack must be long enough to hold a corpse)
Sid—And I will buy him (a) some new clothes and some—

D6
6

Tom. You will? *You*'ll buy him some new clothes? You idiot, he's *rich!*
Sid.—Huck Finn rich! O, I *like* that!
T. Well I'll *show* you. (Going.) (Bringing back the sack.) Huck Finn's able to buy you and *sell* you, just as often as he wants to.—Yes, and I can do the *same.* (Emptying sack) Look at *that,* now!
A.P. What on *earth?* Tom, whose money is that?

D7
7

T—Half of it's Hucks, half of it's *mine.*
A P Where *did* you ever get it?
T. It isn't a *short* story, but it's a *good* one. We'll *tell* you, when we get home.
⟨H⟩ A.P. ⟨I⟩ Thought you went down that hole.
T. Somebody did.
A P. Who?

T. Injun Joe!

A P How'd you know?

T *We heard* him smash through—right *behind* us.

D8
8

A.P. Howd you come to be in front of him?

T. Why he was *chasing* us!

A P. *My!* (Pause) Poor cretur—so he's lost his *life!* I wouldn't had it happen for the *world!*

⟨A⟩ *Tom.* (seriously) No, not *now* of course—but at the *time* we felt's though we could spare him.

A P. Shut your *head!* None of your impudence!

Group E

This entry in one of Mark Twain's notebooks (TS 17, p. 31), written shortly after 21 December 1883, closely resembles speeches by Aunt Polly and Tom in Acts III and IV, respectively.

E1

I'll be bound *you'd* be mixed up in it, what*ever* it was!

———————

'Sh! *There* they are! Lost, and sick and discouraged—pleading for help. Huck, what did I *tell* you—what did I tell you? Its the most ⟨miraculous⟩ extraordinary triumph I've ever achieved in my *life*—and yet I believed from the *start* I could do it. I've found this whole gang! ⟨Huc[?]⟩ (Pause)—(Impressively). Huck, we'll be *heroes* for this. It'll be in the papers—maybe in *books*. 'Sh! now do as I *tell* you—we'll work off a *surprise* on them.

A. P. Been trapsing around this hole 2 days and nights, most, hunting for you trash.

Section II

A

The only surviving page of another dramatic version of "Tom Sawyer" was numbered "2" by Mark Twain (MTP).

2

Act 1.

Scene 1.

A village cottage, with back door looking into garden. A closet and the ordinary furniture. Old lady of 50, cheaply and neatly dressed. Wears spectacles—knitting.

Aunt Winny. (the old lady)—Tom! (No answer.) Том! (No answer.) What's gone with that boy, I wonder? You

B

The following synopsis was submitted to the U.S. Copyright Office on 1 February 1884 to secure copyright number "P 2377." The portion which survives in the files of the office ends with the words "Amy pries," part way into Act III, at which point the galley proof on which it was printed has been torn off. Since, except for some punctuation, this exactly corresponds to the same part of a summary in holograph in the MTP, I assume that the rest of it did. The present text reproduces the galley proof in the copyright office, with the missing portion supplied from the holograph.

TOM SAWYER.

A Play in 4 Acts

BY

S. L. CLEMENS (MARK TWAIN).

SYNOPSIS.

Act I. Amy Lawrence and another girl. Love-token left. Jim gets it.

Aunt Polly and the fire-crackers.

The sorrowful lover: "Rats and worms are for the gay and happy." The fight with the St. Louis boy. Aunt Polly ends it. Shirt-collar sewed with the wrong thread. Tom must work.

Ben Rogers buys a chance to whitewash a while. Tom makes preparation for the other boys; sends Jim to collect more whitewash and brushes. Huck Finn and the two armies arrive and buy chances to whitewash. (Interview between Potter, Robinson, and Injun Joe.) Re-enter the armies, properly equipped, and proceed to whitewash everything whitewashable in the neighborhood. Tom (*aside—counting his gains*) "I've broke the crowd." Aunt Polly appears at the door: "Well, for the land's sake!" (Tableau —Curtain.)

Act II. A graveyard, by moonlight. Tom and Huck come, to dig for treasure. Hear voices, and jump out of their excavation and hide, Murder of the young doctor. Injun Joe unearths the boys' treasure, and carries it off. The boys agree to keep silent about the murder.

Act III. Country school-house. Alfred Temple inks Tom's book; discovered at it by Amy. Tom and Becky—courtship by apples and pictures. Engagement. The rupture. Amy pries into Dobbins's desk; breaks whisky bottle; Tom the only witness. School takes in. Tom magnanimously resolves to not tell on Amy. Teacher announces result of Muff's trial. Then, classes in ⟨ma⟩ arithmetic, declamation, spelling, etc. "Who inked your book?—Doesn't know; gets thrashed. "Who broke this bottle?—answer, Thomas Sawyer." "I cannot tell a lie—it was Alfred Temple." The said Alfred becomes whaled. Gratitude of Amy.

(*Front Scene.*) Huck plays mumbly-peg. Aunt Polly's pious mistake about it. Tom and Huck, conversation. "Well, good-bye to that money—we shan't ever find it."

(*Court-Room.* The black cap put on. Sentence of death being pronounced upon Muff. "Wait!—I was there, and I saw the killing done." Tom rapidly describes it; and closes with—"It was bright moonlight, and I saw the man as plain as I see him now—and there he stands!" Injun Joe plunges through the crowd and the window, and escapes. Aunt Polly: "Well, I'll be bound *you'd* be mixed up in it, *whatever* it was!" (Tableau—Curtain.)

Act IV. In the Cave. Tom and Huck. "No, we're not LOST, *either;* because we know where we are: we're in the cave." They conclude that the general public have started to hunt for them and got lost themselves. They will hunt for the general public—and rescue them. Find a well, covered over with rotten boards. Jump over it. Sound it: "4,000 feet deep." Exit.

Amy and Becky. Lost. Weary—fall asleep. Enter and exit Injun Joe. Re-enter Tom and Huck; discover the girls. "What are you doing *here?*—are *you* lost?" Starving—gives them a crust.

Enter Injun Joe with the money. Scream. Race for life. The boys jump the well, Injun Joe fares not likewise. Exit the boys and girls.

Enter the public, with torches. The hole found, and the boys' hats by it. "The children are dead!" A solemn time. Discovered by Tom, who puts up a dramatic surprise on ⟨?these⟩ his aunt Polly, who sees his dramatic surprise, and goes him one better.

TABLEAU. CURTAIN.

TEXTUAL
APPARATUS

Editorial Principles

EVERY EFFORT has been made to preserve Mark Twain's words—his "substantives"—and his "accidentals"—his spelling, punctuation, word-division, and capitalization—in the ten works reproduced in this volume. Spelling has not been corrected except where, as with his habitual misspelling "sieze," no nineteenth-century authority for a Clemens spelling can be found. Mark Twain was meticulous about his punctuation; it has been left as written except where it is obviously inadequate or in error. For instance, where he interlined a number of song titles in "Villagers" with periods or with no punctuation at all, necessary semicolons have been added.

Similarly, no attempt has been made to impose consistency upon Mark Twain's accidentals unless he showed a demonstrable preference for one form. Thus "dog fight" in "Tupperville-Dobbsville" has been emended to conform to the more usual "dog-fight" used one sentence later because it appears that the unhyphenated form was a lapse rather than a conscious selection on the author's part. But inconsistent references to the "bad god" or "Bad God" in "Huck and Tom among the Indians" have been allowed to stand because it is clear that Mark Twain had not made up his mind about the status of the god. To alter his usage would be to obscure his indecision. When Mark Twain appeared to be indifferent about equally acceptable usages, as in the alternative spellings "recognize" and "recognise," these forms have been allowed to stand unchanged.

Silent revisions have been kept to a minimum. However, manuscript forms peculiar to the written page have not been transferred to the printed page. Ampersands have been expanded to "and," "&c." to "etc." Parentheses and square brackets have both been rendered as parentheses, and superscript letters and figures have been lowered to the line. Eccentricities of Mark Twain's handwriting have not been noted. The lines of various length and number with which he divided his manuscripts into sections have been dropped, as have instructions such as "over." Chapter headings have been silently standardized: periods following chapter numbers have been dropped; chapter numbers have been supplied where the author left a blank; and "Chapter" has replaced Mark Twain's "Chap.," "CHAP" or "CHAPTER." Except for these silent changes, all departures from the copy-text have been listed in a table of emendations.

The textual apparatus consists of the following:

Textual Commentary: Whenever a text presents unusual features which require some modification of the general editorial principles set forth above, its features are described in the textual commentary, and the editorial principles followed are noted.

Emendations of the Copy-Texts: The emended reading as it appears in the text is given first, followed by a square bracket and the rejected copy-text reading. The emendations for the first nine works all originate with the editor. The list for "Tom Sawyer: A Play" includes editorial corrections of the typescript plus revisions and corrections drawn from the manuscript. When the manuscript is the source for the emendation, the bracket is followed by the notation "MS" and a semicolon. Asterisked readings are discussed in the textual notes.

Textual Notes: The textual notes comment on vexed readings, emendations or refusals to emend which require explanations, and special characteristics of the text such as repagination.

Alterations in the Copy-Texts: The variety of works included in this volume makes it impossible to treat Mark Twain's alterations in the copy-texts in a uniform fashion. In some cases his revisions are so trivial or the works themselves so fragmentary that a full listing is superfluous. To tabulate every revision in the Tom Sawyer play manuscript and typescript would require as much space as the text itself. In three instances, the revisions have been described and only cancellations of major importance have been printed in full. The works treated in this fashion are "Clairvoyant," "Tom Sawyer's Gang Plans a Naval Battle," and "Tom Sawyer: A Play."

All alterations in the manuscripts of the other works are included in full. The only exceptions are unrecoverable cancellations and essential corrections which Mark Twain made as he wrote or reread his work. These latter fall into six categories: (1) letters or words which have been mended, traced over, or canceled and rewritten for clarity; (2) false starts and slips of the pen; (3) corrected eye skips; (4) mended or corrected misspellings; (5) words or phrases which have been inadvertently repeated, then canceled; and (6) inadvertent additions of letters or punctuation which have been subsequently canceled, for instance, an incorrect "they" or "then" altered to "the" or superfluous quotation marks canceled at the end of a narrative passage.

"Above" in the description means "interlined" and "over" means "in the same space." The presence of a caret is always noted. Square brackets signify one or more illegible letters; letters within square brackets are conjectural.

Word-Division: When a possible compound is hyphenated at the end of a line in the copy-text, it is reproduced in this volume according to the author's usual practice. His practice is determined by other examples or by parallels within the manuscript when possible, or by the practice of other works of the period when it is not. The word-division tables list the words as they appear in this text.

Textual Commentary

Villagers of 1840–3

IN TWO instances the editorial practices followed in printing "Villagers" depart slightly from the procedures followed throughout this volume. Where Clemens misspells proper names which he spells correctly elsewhere in this manuscript, such as the variant "Peak" for "Peake" (p. 37.16), the spelling has been corrected. If, however, there is no other evidence in the manuscript that Clemens remembered the correct spelling, for instance when he wrote "Ouseley" (p. 36.1) though he certainly referred to "Owsley," the manuscript spelling has been retained. The historically correct spelling is then supplied in Appendix A.

Clemens's frequent practice of writing "St L" for St. Louis and "St P" for St. Petersburg has also been allowed to stand. "St" has been rendered with or without a period as the author wrote it.

Albert Bigelow Paine penciled three corrections into the manuscript. He interlined "Clemens" above "Carpenter" (p. 38.28); changed the year "1838" to "1839" (p. 39.1); and added a necessary "be" to Clemens's sentence (p. 38.20). This last change has been incorporated into the text as an emendation. The former two have been ignored.

Jane Lampton Clemens

The copy-text for "Jane Lampton Clemens" is a thirty-five-page holograph manuscript in MTP. Pagination and other physical evidence in the manuscript suggest that Mark Twain composed it in two major stages. He evidently wrote and revised his first version on manuscript pages numbered consecutively 1 through 17 (although the manuscript lacks a page numbered 5). Then he added two long, separately paginated insertions, revising or shifting his original pages further to integrate the new material.

Mark Twain revised the initial 17-page version at paragraphs 5 and 7 of the present text. Paragraph 5 originally moved directly from the discussion of Jane Lampton Clemens's "eloquence" to a description of her "wit." Then Mark Twain canceled the first line on MS p. 8 ("but gentle, pitying, persuasive, appealing;") and restored it at the bottom of MS p. 7 (p. 45.12), reserving the description of wit on MS p. 8 for incorporation later in the essay. The page was eventually renumbered 14, to follow the description of Jane Clemens's dancing. As a result of the two long insertions, it was moved, with the preceding manuscript page, still further from its original position and appears in this text as part of paragraph 20, between "playful duels of wit" and "pause, then this" (p. 52.9–20).

After withdrawing p. 8 from the manuscript, Mark Twain wrote four manuscript pages, completing paragraph 5 and supplying additional examples of his mother's compassion and eloquence in paragraphs 6 and 7. However, at the end of paragraph 7 Mark Twain was unsure about how to proceed, and three separate versions of the paragraph survive in MTP.

In the present text the conclusion ("rat to be restrained of its liberty") stands at the beginning of the first long insertion added in the second stage of composition. Before settling on this conclusion, Mark Twain wrote a partially filled MS p. 11 which read: "rat to be restrained of its liberty. She would have made trouble enough for Noah if she had been there." Then, before continuing the 17-page sequence, he discarded (but did not cancel) this page, substituting on a fresh page a passage which introduced slaves as still another object of his mother's compassion. It began:

> rat to be restrained of its liberty. Consider, then, what of pain it must have cost her to have to live for sixty years with human slaves always present to her eyes—for she spent all those years in Kentucky and Missouri.

The paragraph continued with the story of Sandy, which appears in the present text as paragraphs 13 (from "For a time") and 14. Mark Twain completed the 17-page version by writing the long paragraph on his mother's "sunshiny disposition," restoring the renumbered p. 8, and continuing through three additional manuscript pages the paragraph on her wit and the concluding paragraph about her marriage.

Evidently still dissatisfied with paragraph 7 and its description of Jane Clemens's attitude toward slavery, Mark Twain expanded the 17-page sequence by adding two digressive insertions—the first immediately before and the second immediately after the paragraphs on Sandy. The first insertion of eleven pages begins "rat to be restrained of its liberty" (concluding paragraph 7 for the third and last time) and goes on to contradict the second version of the paragraph. In order to preserve the story of Sandy, which was written on the same page as the second conclusion to paragraph 7, Mark Twain folded back the top of the manuscript page and renumbered the bottom half "11-A" to follow page 11 of the insertion.

Finally, Mark Twain began the second insertion, numbering its pages consecutively 13-1 through 13-5. This sequence appears as the present paragraphs 16 through 19. But before completing this second insertion, Mark Twain added a paragraph (paragraph 15) on a partially filled manuscript page, which he again numbered 13-1. He folded MS p. 13 to indicate that the additional pages were to intervene between the end of the Sandy anecdote above the fold and "She was of a sunshiny disposition," now paragraph 20, below it.

A briefer version of "Jane Lampton Clemens" was published previously by Albert Bigelow Paine in his edition of *Mark Twain's Autobiography* (I, 115–125). On the back of MS page 13-5, Paine wrote: "An unfinished sketch of M.T's Mother"; and on partially filled MS page 11 (the first discarded version of paragraph 7, discussed above), he wrote: "Article on Jane Clemens. Jervis Langdon has part of this. These sheets were found later—." "Later" seems to mean "after a part of this was published," since Paine's version does not include paragraphs 13 through 15 of the present text and ends part way through paragraph 16 with the word "everywhere." Paine was evidently confused by the separate pagination of the insertions, and probably did not have all 35 pages of manuscript. Although this version is more complete than Paine's version, and although it has no apparent hiatus, some pages may still be missing.

A Human Bloodhound

Some time after he had completed the twenty-seven manuscript pages of "A Human Bloodhound" and had passed MS p. 46 of "Indiantown,"

Mark Twain decided to transfer Harbison's sense of smell to Orrin Lloyd Godkin of "Indiantown." He redrafted a portion of the "Human Bloodhound" manuscript on five manuscript pages, numbered 46A–46E. (These pages are printed after "A Human Bloodhound" in this volume.) Then he borrowed eight pages from the original "Human Bloodhound" manuscript, renumbering them and making a number of substantive changes in order to integrate them into "Indiantown."

Since Mark Twain used the same ink throughout the writing and rewriting of "A Human Bloodhound," it is frequently impossible to tell which of his alterations were made when he wrote the story and which were a part of the process of revamping the tale for inclusion in "Indiantown." Where he changed "Harbison" to "Godkin" his intentions are clear. But where he interlined "until the listener was tired— which would happen" (p. 73.35) above the canceled "until you were tired; you would tire" there is no way of knowing when the revision took place. Since almost all the interlineations in the manuscript are on the borrowed pages, one may conjecture that they were intended for "Indiantown," but the manuscript offers no other evidence to confirm this supposition. The name "Harbison" has, therefore, been restored throughout, but in all other cases the latest reading has been adopted. Revisions have been reported in the table of "Alterations in the Copy-Texts," and textual notes discuss those which may in fact have been meant for "Indiantown."

Huck Finn and Tom Sawyer among the Indians

The authorities which have been considered in establishing the copy-text of "Huck Finn and Tom Sawyer among the Indians" are Mark Twain's holograph manuscript and twenty-six single-column galley proofs set by the Paige typesetter.

The major part of the manuscript, consisting of 218 pages, is in the Detroit Public Library, and that manuscript, supplemented by three additional pages in the Mark Twain Memorial in Hartford, is the principal copy-text. Twenty-one pages are missing from Mark Twain's manuscript, however, and here the Paige typesetter galley proof has necessarily become the copy-text.

The Detroit-Hartford manuscript has been collated with the galley proof. The collation reveals that the type was set directly from the manuscript; all variants may be confidently assigned to the printer. The usual printer's corruptions and typographical errors in the portions of the galley proof used as copy-text have been silently emended. For example: "roghest" has been emended to "roughest," and "vlley" has been emended to "valley." The Paige typesetter apparently did not have italic type, so none of the material from the galley proof is italicized although portions of the text might have appeared in italics in the manuscript.

Tom Sawyer: A Play

Two authoritative texts exist for the first three acts of "Tom Sawyer: A Play"—a holograph manuscript and a typescript of the manuscript with extensive holograph revisions and corrections. The fourth act survives only in a professionally typed fair copy, probably prepared from a now-missing revised typescript.

Each of the three acts which survive in manuscript is separately paginated, with a number of short insertions and renumbered pages supplied at later stages of composition. Act I incorporates 33 manuscript pages from the 1876 version of the play (see Appendix B). Mark Twain wrote these pages in black ink on paper embossed "P & P" in the upper left corner. When he inserted them in the 1884 manuscript of the play, he retained their pagination (1 through 33), but revised them extensively in pencil. He made several brief cancellations and one three-manuscript-page deletion; he also added several passages of dialogue on the versos and made various changes in wording. A brief hiatus in the manuscript occurs between pp. 266.20 and 267.13; the typescript is the only text for this passage, although it seems likely that the 1876 pages were its original source.

The first entrance of Aunt Polly (p. 267.14) marks the beginning of the 1884 version. This portion of the manuscript is written (with minor exceptions mentioned below) on cream-colored, laid paper from a Keystone Linen pad. Mark Twain wrote so rapidly, in fact, that most of the pages are still held in their original order by the adhesive of the writing tablet. There are, however, several minor insertions throughout the manuscript.

Act II begins with a brief 7-page manuscript sequence, followed by a series of revised pages from the Toronto edition of *The Adventures of Tom Sawyer*. Mark Twain canceled long passages from these pages, supplied stage directions and speech designations, and added or deleted words, condensing the original narrative. The past tense used in the original narration was inadvertently preserved by this process, but this text has not been emended to eliminate the incongruity. After inserting these revised pages, Mark Twain wrote a 9-page sequence (MS pages 35–43) which was copied directly from the as yet unpublished *Adventures of Huckleberry Finn* (1885, pp. 31–33). At some later point, he returned and withdrew these pages, substituting new MS pages 35 and 36 and noting at the bottom of 36: "Run to page 45" and "9 pages knocked out." The remainder of Act II is continuously paginated from 45 through 59.

Mark Twain began Act III with an 11-page manuscript sequence, after which he again inserted revised pages from *The Adventures of Tom Sawyer*. He apparently finished the first scene of Act III, running to 35 manuscript pages, before going back and inserting a long passage dealing with the school exercises. The last scene of Act III (the courthouse scene) has a separate pagination and was written before the present "front scene" (Scene 2), which survives only in the typescript.

Two typewriters were employed in transcribing the first three acts of the play. Neither was equipped to underline words, and one had no means for making an exclamation point. Mark Twain did not use the manuscript when he revised the typescript. Thus, in addition to several long cuts, one insertion of three typescript pages, and the numerous substantive revisions and corrections which he made on the typescript, Mark Twain had to supply his marks of emphasis anew. He had to rehear the speeches, and in doing so he often changed the underlining and pointing of the manuscript. A further consequence of revising the typescript without reference to the manuscript was that a great many of the typist's misreadings, corruptions, and sophistications of the manuscript survived the author's scrutiny.

Thus, the present text rests on divided authority. In order to preserve Mark Twain's typescript revisions and the new texture of emphasis, the typescript has been chosen as copy-text. It has been collated with the manuscript; and where variants in substantives or accidentals (other than italics and exclamation points) have been introduced by the typist, the manuscript reading has been preferred. The typist's obvious typographical errors, such as "muching" for manuscript "munching" (p. 260.34) and "somebode" for manuscript "somebody" (p. 269.26), have been silently corrected where Mark Twain's usage in the manuscript is correct. Editorial corrections are noted only when both the manuscript and the typescript are in error. All other rejected typescript readings are included in the table of emendations. When Mark Twain underlined only a portion of a word and it is unclear how much of the word he wished to appear in italics, the manuscript has also been consulted. One typewriter (type *B*) printed only upper-case letters; and in this case capitalization has been determined by the manuscript. In one instance Mark Twain canceled nine typescript pages and substituted ten freshly written manuscript pages which are the sole authority for the passage. Various other brief passages, including one three-page insertion, rest entirely on the typescript.

In some cases, Mark Twain's revisions were occasioned by a typing error. Working without the manuscript, he was unable to restore the manuscript reading; instead he revised on the basis of the corrupted reading and produced a passage that differed from the manuscript and from the faulty transcription. For instance, at p. 275.28, the manuscript reads, "let on that you *like* it?"; but the typist typed "let on like that?" The revision, incorporated in the present edition, is "let on you *like* it?" Similarly, where Mark Twain wrote "a new St. Louis boy that's come to town" the typist transcribed the phrase as "a St. Louis boy that's come to town," and the author revised to "that St. *Louis* boy that's come to town" (p. 298.1). At p. 297.24 the typist supplied the word "nice" to the manuscript reading *"ever* so jolly"; Mark Twain inserted "and" so that the present text incorporates the typist's language as *"ever* so nice and jolly." At times, the repunctuation of the typescript is also based on the altered rhythms or language introduced into a speech by the typist's departure from the manuscript; the addition of italics can have the effect of incorporating a typing error into the text. For example, at p. 264.3 the manuscript reads "now own right up"; the typist dropped "right"; Mark Twain in effect replaced the omitted word by underlining "up," producing the present reading "now own *up.*" The decision to emend or to leave standing such readings of the typescript has called for an individual judgment in each case.

Mark Twain's stage directions present a different sort of editorial problem. His italicizing, paragraphing, and use of parentheses are erratic and inconsistent. So many portions of the stage directions were interlined in the manuscript with new parentheses and punctuation that the typist was frequently unable to render them as written. While the original form has been carefully considered, the stage directions have been silently standardized. All of them appear in italics, and all but those which head scenes are surrounded by parentheses. Confusing internal parentheses have been eliminated, and punctuation has been altered where the original hindered comprehension.

Mark Twain's underlining has required one further typographic convention. He underlined to indicate variations of oral emphasis to the actor. Words underlined once have been rendered in italics; words underlined twice have been rendered in small capital letters, except for the pronoun "I" which appears in a bold italic; words underlined three times have been reproduced in full capitals.

The sole authority for Act IV is a typescript which appears to have been professionally prepared as an acting copy. Here, the typist normalized stage directions and centered them and the speaker's names on the page. They have been rearranged to conform to the practice of the first three acts.

Emendations in the Copy-Texts

THE EMENDED reading as it appears in the text is given first, followed by a square bracket and the rejected copy-text reading. When emendations for "Tom Sawyer: A Play" are drawn from the manuscript, the bracket is followed by the notation "MS" and a semicolon. Asterisked readings are discussed in the textual notes. Line references do not include titles or chapter headings.

Villagers of 1840–3

29.3   Dawson's] Dawsons

30.34   desperado] desparado

32.14   The baker] The Baker *See "Alterations in the Copy-Texts"*

33.16   auburn] aburn

34.18   *Cloak*] (*Cloak*

*34.24–26   Last Rose of Summer;] Last Rose of Summer.
            for the . . . bride;] for the . . . bride
            Gaily the Troubador;] Gaily the Troubador.

34.30   River.] River

35.17	exigent] exigeant
35.29	belt.] best.
37.1–2	blocks and blocks and blocks] blocks and blocks and block
37.16	Dr. Peake] Dr. Peak
37.24	protégé] protegè
38.20	would be found] would found ("be" *interlined with a caret in pencil in MS by ABP.*)
40.1	about her neck] about his neck

Jane Lampton Clemens

45.3	single] single,
49.16	there] There *See "Alterations in the Copy-Texts"*

Tupperville-Dobbsville

56.20	dog-fight] dog fight

Clairvoyant

63.27	yard where] yard was
65.4	looked at me] looked me
65.29	there with the] there will the

A Human Bloodhound

70.9	weirdness] wierdness
70.20	there."] there?"
73.27	myriad] miriad *Also emended at* 73.29
75.19	mothers] mother's
78.4	hours ago."] hours ago.

Huck Finn and Tom Sawyer among the Indians

*93.9	much lazying] much lazing
93.26	anyway.] anyway?
95.22	war paint] war-paint *Also emended at* 106.6, 115.24
96.5	camp fire] camp-fire
98.23	After a while] After while
*101.18–19	shading . . . hand] shading . . . eyes
106.35	Flaxy,] Flaxy,; *See "Alterations in the Copy-Texts"*
109.3	"Tom, where] "Tom, Where *See "Alterations in the Copy-Texts"*
111.17	Peggy?"] Peggy."
112.11	thing—if] thing— —if *See "Alterations in the Copy-Texts"*
112.16	and he darted] and He darted *See "Alterations in the Copy-Texts"*
113.9	examining them] examing them
113.13	Sioux] Sioux/Dacotah [*twice*]
115.16	didn't kill the nigger] didn't the nigger
115.27	war dance] war-dance
116.27	Millses'] Mills's
118.4	to do it] to it
121.9	a while] awhile
123.32	then—"] then—
*132.5	whizzing by!!] whizzing by.!! *See "Alterations in the Copy-Texts"*
132.34	along, this] along; this
*135.30	clear weather] clear water
135.31	'heap water coming,'] "heap water coming,"

136.1   high ground.] high ground."

139.26   "A war] A war

Doughface

143.5   warn't] warnt

Tom Sawyer's Conspiracy

165.17   it's] its *Also emended at* 204.4

165.21   any glory in] any in

167.18   What's] Whats

169.28   t'other] tother *Also emended at* 187.28

173.3   And what] And What *See "Alterations in the Copy-Texts"*

176.21   licence] license

181.29   its] it's

181.34   Well, that] Well, That

188.4   he had no] he no

189.15   it. There's] it; There's *See "Alterations in the Copy-Texts"*

189.19   Speak out] Speak Out *See "Alterations in the Copy-Texts"*

189.23   says—] say—

191.10   necessary] nessary

200.1   town] Town

201.5   Branch] branch *Also emended at* 201.16

201.9   ablishonists] ablishonits

201.13   dusk we come] dusk come

201.17   and meet up] and me up

204.9	solemn, and] solemn, and and *See "Alterations in the Copy-Texts"*
204.13	if he had] if had
205.35	turn him in in] turn in in
210.14	down-stream] downstream
212.36	it's him] its him
214.9	tadpole?"] tadpole? *See "Alterations in the Copy-Texts"*
215.1	stumbled] stumbed
215.18	want's] want's,
215.20	Marse] Mase
218.29	was not] was
221.3	foc'sle] foc'sl *Also emended at* 221.14
225.4	Why, blame] Why, Blame *See "Alterations in the Copy-Texts"*
226.7	mustn't] must'nt
226.31	them—including] them.—including
227.14	agoing] a going
228.9	"don't] don't
230.29	t'other] 'tother
234.9	reckon.] reckon."
235.17	if they] if we
235.26	hadn't been] had been
237.26	Widow] widow
237.30	judge] Judge
237.31	made a speech] made speech
240.18	"he's] he's
241.19	principles] principals

Tom Sawyer: A Play

258.15	tell.—] MS; tell.
259.2	tell you,] tell, you,
259.15	you—you!—so] MS; you—you.—so
259.23	it's] its
259.27–28	spiteful and ugly and disagreeable] MS; spiteful **and** disagreeable
259.28	*be,*] MS; *be*
259.29	did—] MS; did,
259.30	shouldn't] MS; shan't
260.2	*did.*] *did*
260.4	*welcome.*—] MS; *welcome.*
260.20	a *behaved*] MS; *behaved*
261.2	you,] MS; you
261.3	*can't I,*] MS; *can't* I
261.5	Yes,] MS; Yes
261.7	that,] MS; that
261.12	*caught* you!—] MS; *caught* you!
261.19	loved] Loved
262.22	Grace] MS; Gracie
262.31	kinds] MS; kind
262.31–32	know—] MS; know;
263.3	Gracie,] MS; Gracie
263.3	come] MS; coming
263.4	boy from St.] boy from St
263.5	From St.] MS; From St
263.15	*gloves,*] MS; *gloves*

263.16   *co*llars;] MS; *co*llars, too;

263.18   *hate* him!] MS; *hate* him?

263.23   plaguey] plaguy

263.35   Ah!] MS; Aha!

264.16   *night.—*] MS; *night.*

264.20   door-knob] MS; door knob

264.23   always away off] MS; always way off

264.28   thing,] MS; thing

264.32   time?] MS; time.

264.36   *chicken*-thieves] MS; *chicken* thieves

265.6   ever, *ever*] MS; ever *ever*

265.18   half a mind] MS; half a mine

265.19   Yah-yah-yah!] MS; Yah—yah—yah!

265.22   *Tom* he choice,] MS; *Tom* de choice

265.23   er] MS; or

265.23   *prar*-meeting] MS; *prar*-meetin'

265.25   *lots* o'] MS; *lots* of

265.30   ketch] MS; catch

265.35   reck'n] MS; reckon *Also emended at* 274.27

266.1   dat-away] MS; dat way

266.7   outen her.—] MS; 'outen her.

266.8   *All* boys is] MS; *All* boys has

266.9   *'mount*] MS; *mount*

266.13   'I'] MS; I

266.15   nowhah.—] MS; nowhah.

266.18   *axe.—*] MS; *axe.*

266.33	de *head—*he] de *head.*—he
267.6	o'] 'o
267.18	T-o-m] MS; To-o-m
267.21	*peering*] MS; *peeking*
267.23	aunty] MS; Aunty
267.24	Why,] MS; Why
267.35	think to look which way] MS; think about which way
268.2	*larn*] MS; *learn*
269.6–7	(*in gaudy . . . string.*] MS; (*on white pine stilts, glides in stealthily dragging a dead rat on a string.*
269.13	pocket,] MS; pocket
269.18	I wonder] MS; Wonder
269.27	*jaws in*] MS; *jaws on*
270.11	be it so:] MS; be it so;
270.32	Yes,] MS; Yes
271.12	*will, if*] MS; *will if*
272.8	*nothing*] MS; *anything*
272.9	*Contemptuous snort*] MS; *Snorts contemptuously*
272.10	*snort*] MS; *snorts*
272.27	it's his aunt *Polly*] MS; it's aunt *Polly*
273.7	O, *Tom!*] MS; O *Tom!*
273.15	yourself?] MS; yourself
273.19	suppose. Tom] MS; suppose, Tom
273.20	*seizes*] *siezes*
273.22	I'd got] MS; I got
273.30	Well,] MS; Well
273.31	won't] MS; wouldn't

273.33   *Reflectively*] MS; *Reflecting*

274.4   *the others*] MS; *and others*

274.6   oh, *please*] MS; oh *please*

274.12   and I] MS; and I've

274.20   *with tin pail*] MS; *with the pail*

275.19   Why,] MS; Why

276.15   *Reflecting—then reluctantly.*] MS; *Reluctantly reflecting—then*

276.18   *mighty*] MS; *very*

276.29   *privately, in*] MS; *privately and in*

276.30   15] MS; fifteen

276.31   No!—] MS; No,—

277.2   neighbors'] MS; neighbor's

277.27   bet you I] MS; bet I

278.7   *corn-cob*] MS; *a corn-cob*

278.9   *blue or yellow*] MS; *blue and yellow*

278.14   *orders,*] MS; *order*

278.16   Don't go] MS; Don't you go

278.25   gim *me*] MS; give *me* Also emended at 279.29

278.29   Tom,] MS; Tom

278.30   'fore] MS; before

278.34   boys,] MS; boys

279.1   *soldiers—*] MS; *soldiers*

279.4   *right;*] MS; *right:*

279.7   agoing] MS; going

279.12   *Joe Harper.*] MS; *Joe.*

279.30   *can't*, Huck.] MS; *can't* Huck,

279.32	it,] MS; it
280.16	Yes.] MS; Yes
280.17	best—each] best each
280.20	ago—] MS; ago,
280.32	*old*] MS; *ole*
280.34	*Huck's*] MS; *and wearing Huck's*
281.9	*contemplating*] MS; *contemplates*
282.6	*somebody,*] MS; *somebody*
282.17	be] MS; been
282.22	I'll] MS; I
282.28–29	tell me, Huck.] tell, me, Huck.
283.14	Lemme] MS; 'Lemme
283.17	*give?*] MS; *give.*
283.19	slaughter-house] MS; slaughter house
283.29	*No, I hain't*] MS; *No I hain't*
284.14	a *got*] MS; *got*
284.15	layin'] MS; laying
284.19	it,] MS; it
284.19	we're] MS; we've
284.28	a tick down] MS; down a tick
285.1	*bit*] MS; *piece*
285.1	*unrolled*] MS; *examined*
285.8	*enclosed*] MS; *inclosed*
285.9	per'aps] MS; perhaps
285.16	the end of a limb] MS; the limb
285.20	sup'rintendents] MS; superintendents

285.28   by-and-by] MS; by and by *Also emended at* 297.8

286.2   or on an island] MS; or an island

286.3   dead-limb trees] MS; dead limb-trees

286.28   Hop your] MS; Hop, your

287.5   S'pose] MS; Suppose

287.5   dead limb tree] MS; dead limb

287.18   ain't any] MS; ain't no

287.23   necktie,] MS; neck-tie

287.31   *I'm*] MS; *I* am

287.33   you better] MS; you'd better

287.35   ain't] MS; isn't

288.1   some time] MS; sometime

288.5   Consound] MS; Confound

288.7   Where you] MS; Where are you

288.17   Why] MS; Why,

288.23   so. I] MS; so I

288.24   afeared] MS; afraid

288.31   they do, I've] MS; they do. I've

288.36   *Don't*, Tom!] MS; *Don't* Tom!

289.1   Huck, I] MS; Huck I

289.6   amongst] amonst

290.27   sh] 'sh *Also emended at* 321.8 *and* 321.13

292.3   got here ahead] MS; got ahead

292.6–7   spelling-book] MS; spelling book

292.13   *book in spite*] MS; *book spite*

292.14–15   I—would] MS; I would

292.19	you'll] MS; you will *Also emended at* 293.21
293.22	*a very*] MS; *a bit very*
293.33	*black-board*] MS; *blackboard Also emended at* 293.35
293.36	6] MS; *siv*
294.9	Oh,] MS; O, will
294.12–13	go. What's your *name? (They sit down again.)*] MS; go—(They sit down again) What's your *name?*
294.14	what's *yours?*] MS; what *yours?*
294.16	by—here] MS; by, here
295.9	deed and deed and *double*] MS; deed and *double*
295.11	No, I] MS; No I
295.13–14	*her small hand*] MS; *her hand*
295.14	*pretending*] MS; *pretended*
295.15	*hand*] MS; *hands*
295.17	Oh, you] MS; Oh you
295.17–18	*(And she . . . nevertheless.*] MS; *not in* TS
295.27	I've got some] MS; I've gots some
295.35	grow] MS; crow
296.27	*hesitating*] MS; *hesitated*
296.35	*Now,* Becky] MS; *Now* Becky
297.2–3	*the desks and benches*] MS; *the benches*
297.6	Don't you be] MS; Don't be
297.7	PLEASE,] MS; PLEASE
297.10–12	*Amy . . . hear her.*] *follows* "and said" *in MS and* TS
297.17	to ever] MS; ever to
297.24	Oh it's] MS; Oh, it's
297.25–26	*(The big . . . confused.)*] MS; *not in* TS

297.28   (*The child . . . said:*)] MS; *not in* TS

298.1   St.] St

298.2   town—and] MS; town.—and

298.35   mean, if] MS; mean if

299.1   Hateful, hateful,] MS; Hateful, hateful

299.3   *gazing*] MS; *gazes*

299.8   Dobbins, but] MS; Dobbins; but

299.9   do just the] MS; do the

299.10   does—ask] MS; does.—ask

299.22   *40*] MS; *forty*

299.27   *stare*] MS; *start*

300.2   *hand*] MS; *hands*

300.26   *again.*] MS; *places.*

300.37   Gee—*whillikins!*] MS; Gee*whillikins!*

301.14   a whole] MS; the whole

301.15   *seat!*—] MS; *seat!*

301.17   *multitude?*—] MS; *multitude?*

301.24   *tense,* and refers] MS; *tense,* refers

301.31   Persons] MS; Person

301.35–36 poor show *out*] poor *out*

302.1   *There!*—Ah, mine] MS; *There!*—mine

302.2   *genius,*] MS; *genius*

302.6   over and over and *over* again,] MS; over and *over* again

302.10   *poor poor fellow*] MS; *poor fellow*

302.12–13 tums four're *twelve,*] MS; tums four are *twelve,*

302.13   six're] MS; six are

302.14	eight're] MS; eight are
302.15	fifty-*four*] MS; fifty *four*
302.16	tums . . . tums] MS; times . . . times *Also emended at* 302.17 *and* 302.18
302.20	D.] MS; R.
303.3	Please, mayn't] MS; Please sir, mayn't
303.14	*attention,* now] MS; *attention* now
303.23	*gestures*] MS; *features*
303.29	*spelt*] MS; *spelled Also emended at* 304.11, 304.12, 304.13 (*twice*), *and* 304.14
304.1	cat—] MS; cat,
304.21	*won't:*] MS; *won't;*
305.12	(*Solemnly . . . impressively*)] MS; (*Solemnly*)
305.17	*slowly up*] MS; *up slowly*
305.20	this] MS; that
305.32	*shoulders*] MS; *shoulder*
305.33	*his ear*] MS; *her ear*
306.22	Huck. You'd] Huck. you'd
306.25	yes'm] yesm *Also emended at* 324.14
307.16	ha'nted] hanted
307.20	it's] its
308.17	previously] MS; previous
309.15–16	why sentence of death] MS; why death
309.18	*hand*] MS; *hands*
309.26–27	*or a damned*] MS; *or damned*
309.29	August,] MS; August
310.6	*bushes,*] MS; *bushes*

310.6   towards] MS; toward

310.7   *sleeve,*] MS; *sleeve*

310.13   *rise to*] MS; *rise and to*

310.18   *Seize*] *Sieze*

311.1   *comes*] *come*

311.5   ain't] aint *Also emended at* 311.29, 311.30, 311.34, 312.3, 312.4, *and* 312.16

311.25   thirty-five] thirty five

312.5   you] You

312.19   how] How

312.22   *passages.*] *passages*

312.36   Tom,] Tom

313.1   *won't—where*] *won't* where

315.15   deed and deed] deed and dead

315.24   Becky,] Becky

315.28   you are] You are

317.1   come] Come

317.36   *yourself.*] *yourself*

318.26   *feint*] *faint*

320.24   *shan't*] *shant*

320.30   *here.*] *here*

322.24   *place.*] *place*

323.8   *longer.*] *longer,*

323.22   *what?*] *What?*

323.24   *Dead?*] *Dead.?*

Textual Notes

Villagers of 1840–3

34.24–26   Last Rose . . . Bright Alforata.] The number of interlineations and the erratic punctuation in this passage indicate that the old songs flooded his memory and he wrote
them down in haste.

Jane Lampton Clemens

44.22   She was the] MS p. 6 begins here, following immediately
upon MS p. 4. Twain appears to have erred in his pagination, although it is possible that some matter is missing.

45.12   but gentle, pitying, persuasive, appealing; and] These
words (except "and") were originally written at the top
of MS p. 8, later renumbered 14. Clemens canceled
them there, then squeezed them in at the foot of MS p. 7.
See textual commentary.

45.12   so genuine] Twain replaced old p. 8 with a page numbered 7, which begins here. He then proceeded (in the
first 17-page version) with pages numbered consecutively through 12. But before inserting p. 14 (renumbered from p. 8), Twain mended old numbers 7

through 12 to new numbers 8 through 13, thus making the manuscript consecutive from p. 6 through p. 17. He did not correct the skip from p. 4 to p. 6, however. It is possible that the renumbering was required in order to incorporate a separate sequence of pages, but it seems most likely that Twain simply erred in his original pagination of this 6-page sequence.

46.22   rat to be restrained of its liberty] Here begins the first long insertion discussed in the textual commentary.

50.3   incident in point.] The first long insertion ends here. It is followed by the remainder of the page which Twain folded back and renumbered "11-A" to follow the last page of the insertion. MS p. 11-A (originally p. 12) is followed immediately by MS p. 13, which extends as far as "stop singing.'" (50.14–15) where it is interrupted by the second long insertion.

50.10   away from] At this point Paine inserted a penciled addition (not printed in *MTA,* I, 125): "his home. When it sings it shows maybe he is not remembering. When he's still I'm afraid he is thinking, and I cant bear it."

50.14–15   stop singing."] Twain originally began a paragraph, "Well, he didn't stop" but canceled it before continuing with the present paragraph 20 ("She was of a sunshiny disposition"). The second long insertion begins here.

52.2   nearer my grade.] The second insertion ends here, and the transition to the next paragraph is made rather awkward by the digression.

A Human Bloodhound

73.11–21   any advantage . . . of earth,] Although Mark Twain renumbered the manuscript page to which this passage corresponds, he apparently never successfully integrated it into the Godkin fragment and later canceled the new number.

73.21   grass, water, bees] The "Human Bloodhound" pages renumbered to follow the pages written for "Indiantown" begin here.

73.33–34   always pretending to do it by sight.] This clause, interlined in the manuscript, is one of those revisions which Mark Twain may have made when he excerpted the "Human Bloodhound" manuscript for "Indiantown." (See the textual commentary.) Harbison—whose peculiar powers were known to the townspeople—has less motive for concealing his gift than Godkin—who was to reveal it only on his deathbed. Several other interlineations in the borrowed pages emphasize this ruse.

73.34–35   until . . . happen] By interlining these phrases above the canceled "until you were tired; you would tire," Mark Twain shifted from direct address to the reader to impersonal discourse. This suggests that the change may have been made to bring the story in line with the third-person narrative of "Indiantown."

74.12   His sense of smell] See "Alterations in the Copy-Texts" and the textual note to 73.34–35, above.

74.30–31   All . . . pretended.] See "Alterations in the Copy-Texts" and the textual note to 73.33–34.

74.32   with Harbison.] In the manuscript "Harbison." is canceled and "him." interlined with a caret. The change was almost certainly made for "Indiantown," and the original reading has been restored.

75.3   discriminating sight] See "Alterations in the Copy-Texts" and the textual note to 73.33–34.

75.5   knew the track] See "Alterations in the Copy-Texts" and the textual note to 73.33–34.

75.14   and tracked] "Godkin" is interlined with a caret before "tracked" in the manuscript. Rather than emend to "Harbison" the original reading has been restored.

Huck Finn and Tom Sawyer among the Indians

92.4–10   Tom . . . other book.] Supplied from the galley
                 proof; replaces MS p. 2.

93.7–10   Tom he . . . no] Supplied from the galley proof; re-
                 places missing MS p. 5.

93.9   much lazying] The galley proof, which is copy-text
                 at this point, reads "lazing" here and "lazying" in the
                 following line. Either reading could be attributed to
                 compositor's error because the galley proof abounds
                 both in dropped letters and unconscious normaliza-
                 tions of Huck's dialect. The word does not occur again
                 in the "Indians" manuscript. In other works, however,
                 Mark Twain wrote "lazying" in parallel situations.

93.10–99.10   choice . . . anything] These pages were originally MS
                 pp. 2–33. They were subsequently renumbered as MS
                 pp. 6–37. Apparently Mark Twain revised the open-
                 ing segment of the manuscript, but the exact nature
                 of the alteration remains uncertain because MS p. 5
                 (presumably the original MS p. 1) and MS p. 2
                 (presumably added to the MS as part of the revision)
                 are missing.

101.18–19   shading . . . hand] The manuscript reads "shading
                 her eyes with her eyes." The galley proof corrects this
                 obvious slip. Although there can be no certainty that
                 Mark Twain didn't intend to have Peggy shade her
                 eyes with her bonnet, for example, or with an arm,
                 the galley proof reading has been accepted as at least
                 equally probable and satisfactory. Later, Peggy is seen
                 "looking out over the country with her hand over her
                 eyes" (105.22).

103.3–105.7   a little . . . when he was gone.] This passage cor-
                 responds to MS pp. 57-a to 57-k, inserted by Mark
                 Twain.
                 come] In the few instances where it was difficult to
                 distinguish between Mark Twain's "came" and "come,"

the latter has been preferred as being more consistent with his dialect usage.

117.20–30 Well . . . him] This paragraph follows canceled "a sweat, now, but he wasn't, and I was powerful glad." at the top of present MS p. 117. The cancellation is not continuous with canceled MS pp. 117–119 (see "Alterations in the Copy-Texts"). Apparently Twain had reached MS p. 121 when he discarded MS p. 120, canceled "a sweat . . . glad." which had followed it at the top of MS p. 121, and mended the page number from 121 to 120. The latter number was further revised to 117 after Mark Twain canceled the original MS pp. 117–119.

129.9 leave] This word is part of an interlineation. The handwriting is unusually cramped, which makes it difficult to determine whether Mark Twain wrote "have" or "leave." The latter has been accepted here because it seems more colloquially accurate.

132.5 come—and next . . . whizzing by!!] The exclamation points originally appeared after "come." Twain interlined "—and . . . whizzing by." with a caret. Although the placement of the caret is somewhat ambiguous, it is probable that Twain wanted the exclamations to follow "by," and the period was inadvertently added.

133.2–16 any wheres . . . such a] Supplied from the galley proof; replaces missing MS pp. 192–193.

133.19 beat them] Clemens's *h*'s are often indistinguishable from his *b*'s. The galley proof reads "heat them," a phrase which implies stimulation, but the context makes it clear that the liquor has an incapacitating effect on the horse thieves and thus can be more logically said to be beating them.

134.9–25 Brace says . . . wall] Supplied from the galley proof; replaces missing MS pp. 198–199.

134.34–135.5   "Out . . . glad] Supplied from the galley proof; re-
                  places missing MS p. 201.

135.30   clear weather] The manuscript reads "clear water," but
                  Huck's and Brace's earlier discussion about the rela-
                  tionship between clouds and a water-spout (134.13–
                  20) indicates that it is indeed clarity of weather, not
                  water, that is at issue here. Brace's description of the
                  Indians' rare ability to sense a coming water-spout
                  paraphrases chapter 30 of *Roughing It:* "They [the
                  Indians] said, 'By'm-by, heap water!' and by the help
                  of signs made us understand that in their opinion a
                  flood was coming. The weather was perfectly
                  clear. . ." The galley proof also changes "water" to
                  "weather," and in this instance all external and in-
                  ternal evidence indicates that the compositor's cor-
                  rection was a fortunate one.

136.19–26   We left . . . men, wo-] Supplied from the galley
                  proof; replaces missing MS p. 209.

137.10–138.17   print . . . man that was] Supplied from the galley
                  proof; replaces missing MS pp. 213–219.

137.12–15   I don't . . . track again,] The Carnegie Book Shop
                  Catalogue 241 (February, 1960, p. 6, item 79) offered
                  for sale MS p. 213, one of the pages still missing from
                  the "Indians" manuscript and gave the following ver-
                  sion of these lines: " '. . . I don't understand it. I'm
                  afraid there's a general trouble broke out between the
                  whites & Injubs; & if thats so, I've got to go mighty
                  cautious from this time out.' He looks at the track
                  again, . . ."

138.32–140.3   got it . . . examined] Supplied from the galley proof;
                  replaces missing MS pp. 222–227.

Tom Sawyer's Conspiracy

163.1–165.19   Well . . . in it,] The first six pages of the manuscript
                  are written on cross-barred paper.

| 164.20 | it don't *go*] On one of the envelopes containing the manuscript, Albert Bigelow Paine noted that "Conspiracy" was "not convincing—not humorous and not interesting—Should be destroyed." Before abandoning the fragment, however, Paine had made two revisions, with the obvious purpose of preparing the work for publication. He canceled *"go"* and interlined "happen" in pencil, repeating the revision two paragraphs later. |

| 165.19 | I'll say] Beginning on p. 7 of the manuscript and continuing through p. 101, the paper is ruled. |

| 166.21–25 | It shows . . . nigger.] Olivia Clemens demurred. On a separate sheet of cross-barred paper interleaved between pp. 9 and 10 of the manuscript, she noted the passage and wrote: "a little too elegant for dear old Huck." |

| 190.15 | got mine yet.] At this point (MS p. 85) Twain added a directive note: *"Private, to compositor.* Use battered type, and mix in italics, wrong font, and so on, with turned letters, up-ended ones, etc., mis-spellings, and all the various aids to a phenomenally bad proof. SLC." |

| 190.16 | COMPOSITION] Tom's exercise in typesetting fills MS p. 86. On the verso of the manuscript page Twain wrote an early draft of the beginning of the story "Five Boons of Life," published in July 1902. |

| 192.4 | this on it.] On the recto of MS p. 91, which follows this passage, Twain drew the bill and instructed the printer: *"(Make reverse fac-simile)."* He repeated the instructions for the "protection-paper" on MS p. 108 (198). In both instances, his actual drawings are reproduced according to his instructions. |

On the verso of MS p. 91 (192) Twain wrote the draft of a letter to *Harper's Monthly,* offering permission to print a poem composed on 18 August 1897. See Appendix B.

196.8   was a horn] On MS p. 102, the narrative resumes on
                       cross-barred paper.

200.24   So Everything] Beginning with chapter 5 on MS p.
                       115, the manuscript continues on Joynson Superfine
                       paper.

200.24   So Everything] In the upper left corner of MS p. 115,
                       on which this chapter begins, Twain wrote a note to
                       himself in pencil: "Stuck up the bill Sat. night."

204.34–205.22   I asked . . . "Tom!"] Immediately preceding "I asked"
                       at the bottom of MS p. 130, Twain canceled "All of
                       a sudden I thought of something—'Tom!'" He then
                       inserted three manuscript pages numbered 130A to
                       130C and at the end of p. 130C restored the canceled
                       passage.

208.28–212.31   It warn't . . . says—] This lengthy passage corre-
                       sponds to thirteen manuscript pages, numbered 141A
                       to 141M, which Twain inserted between pp. 141 and
                       142. MS p. 141 may itself be an added page, replac-
                       ing a discarded and now missing p. 141. MS p. 142
                       begins with a canceled sentence fragment (see "Altera-
                       tions in the Copy-Texts"), which may be either a
                       rather awkward continuation of "'whilst Tom exam-
                       ined around amongst the clews" or the surviving
                       remnant of an older plot in which the boys return to
                       town on foot instead of floating back in a skiff.

224.16–17   tell me how."] The cancellation (see "Alterations in
                       the Copy-Texts") following this paragraph on MS p.
                       179 suggests that Mark Twain began to rework his
                       story here. The cancellation breaks off in mid-sentence,
                       and the pages which follow evidently replaced a dis-
                       carded sequence of undetermined length. One dis-
                       carded page, numbered 181, survives because Mark
                       Twain used the verso to write a portion of *Christian
                       Science*. It is printed below. MS p. 187 "know what to
                       say . . . care; I knowed" (226.11–19) was renumbered
                       from p. 182 and was also part of the earlier sequence.
                       The discarded p. 181 reads:

be along down pretty soon and run him off again and
ship him over to England, and then he would be safe.
The widow Douglas told me so, herself.

Besides, if we found the men whilst they was gone
South for the papers, and Jim got cleared, we could
start him for England anyway and beat the game.

It was two chances to save Jim, and the chance of
getting hold of the men wasn't hardly any chance at
all. Everything was dead against it. It looked good to
me, and I told them to count me in, and said I would
swear to the nigger-auction.

Then the Duke asked me what I was doing on the
boat, and I didn't

The page was replaced by a partially filled MS p. 186.

231.12   We was over] At the top of MS p. 206, above the
          chapter heading, Twain wrote in pencil, "funeral of
          Bat."

239.8   Captain Sam] In the interval between setting the
          manuscript aside and returning to it, Twain might
          have forgotten the Captain's surname, Rumford. At
          this point in the manuscript he left a space, possibly
          intending to insert the surname later.

240.12   murderers talk,] Beginning on p. 233, the final nine
          pages of the manuscript are written on Schoellerpost
          paper.

Tom Sawyer: A Play

259.6–8   Who did . . . heart?] Twain originally canceled a
          similar passage in the manuscript, but noted on the
          typescript: "(Something left out here, about her
          brother sliding on cellar door and sticking a splinter
          in his heart.)" He then wrote the present passage on
          the verso of TS p. 2, apparently reconstructing the can-
          celed matter from memory.

260.15–16 (*A. is interested.*)] Typewriter B began its first stint
          here, part way through MS p. 7.

265.31–32 (*Making ghastly efforts*] Typewriter A began its sec-
          ond stint here, at the top of the verso of MS p. 32.

266.20–267.13   Dah's ole . . . (*Exit both.*)] The manuscript for this
                 passage has not survived; the TS is the sole authority.

267.15   *Aunt Polly and Mary.*] Here begins the portion of the
                 manuscript written on Keystone linen in 1884.

277.8–12   *Business . . . exertion*] This passage inserted in the
                 manuscript on page numbered 75½.

278.1–15   (*Rolling . . . around.*)] This passage inserted in the
                 manuscript on page numbered 78-A.

278.25   *Joe.* (*Dismounting*] Typewriter B began its second
                 stint here, beginning at the top of MS p. 80.

278.35–279.15   particular job . . . *countermarch all*] This passage is
                 inserted on MS pp. 81-A and 81-B. The remainder
                 of the stage direction immediately following this pas-
                 sage was probably written on a now-missing MS p.
                 81-C. The typescript is the only authority for the pas-
                 sage from 279.15 (*"about"*) through 279.18 ("lead-
                 ers.")

281.1–9   *Tom.* Come, . . . *laboring armies*] This passage in-
                 serted in the manuscript on p. 89-A.

281.21   A Graveyard] on the first manuscript page of Act II,
                 Mark Twain wrote and canceled: "In first act, make
                 Dr. appoint *Saturday* night for body-snatching."

281.21   A Graveyard] Typewriter A began its third stint at
                 the beginning of Act II.

283.14   Lemme] MS p. 8 begins here. From this point through
                 285.8 (*percussion-cap box.*) the manuscript consists
                 of revised pages from the Toronto edition of *The Ad-
                 ventures of Tom Sawyer,* pp. 63–69.

284.20   (*Huck gets out*] Typewriter B began its third stint
                 here, at the bottom of MS p. 12.

285.9–11   T. Well . . . dig?] This passage inserted in the manu-
                 script on p. 15.

285.12   *T. Oh,*] MS p. 16 begins here. From this point through 289.1 ("a *bit*") the manuscript consists of revised pages from *Tom Sawyer*, pp. 232–240. Mark Twain originally included pp. 241 and 242 as well, but the matter on these pages was canceled in the typescript.

289.1–291.8   *—sh! . . . do!*] The authority for this passage is a 12-page manuscript sequence inserted into the typescript to replace ten canceled typescript pages. The typescript pages drew on *Adventures of Huckleberry Finn,* and Mark Twain noted in the margin of canceled TS p. 46: "(Might a trifle of this be preserved and thrust in back yonder before they talk of the skull speaking?)" Typewriter A began its fourth stint on now-canceled typescript page 44, half way through MS p. 29. The lines immediately following, *"Muff . . . off."* (291.9–11) survive on the typescript only.

292.1   Village Schoolhouse] Typewriter B began its fourth stint here, at the beginning of MS p. 1.

294.8–298.13   *T. It's easy . . . cries.*] This section is comprised of revised pages from *The Adventures of Tom Sawyer.* Tom's speech (297.35 through 298.5) has been written out on a separate sheet and inserted between the leaves from *Tom Sawyer.* Mark Twain used portions of pages 72–73, 78–83 of the book.

299.5–19   *Tom. . . . do!*] This passage is also based on a revised page (200) from *Tom Sawyer.*

300.6–11   *(After . . . children.)*] This stage direction was inserted in the manuscript on a page numbered 27½. Mark Twain had originally noted on the verso of MS p. 10: "(before Master raps to order.) / Spit-balls— / blow-guns— / pop-guns / pins in benches— / fly-catching. / swapping unsight unseen." After the stage direction at 300.11–12, Mark Twain noted in the manuscript: "(Shall we insert *tick* episode in Chapter 7?)"

300.12   *Dobbins.* First] Here begins a long section (ending at
              304.19) which was inserted in the manuscript on pages
              numbered "28-1A" through "15-A." Before writing
              and inserting this passage, Mark Twain noted on MS
              p. 28:

                                    Insert:
                   1. Lesson in multiplication table.
                   2. Please, may I go out?
                   3. Declamations.
                   4. Whose turn to go for water?
                   5. Lesson in spelling—the whole school—spelling
              down. Tom mis-spells a word—declares it's spelt so in
              his book—is required to get and *bring* his book. The
              ink discovered.

306.1   (*A front scene*] At the top of a manuscript page headed
              "Act. III-continued" Mark Twain noted:

                   Here insert a brief front scene between Tom &
                   Huck, who speak of impossibility of finding where the
                   money is hid—so they give it up. And they can't resist
                   the horrid fascination of the court—they've attended
                   the trial all along, and *wish* they could keep away now
                   it is such a strain to hold in, and they don't/can't sleep,
                   these nights.
                   (Meantime the schoolroom is turned into a court-
                   house.)

              All of Scene 2 survives only in a typescript insert
              headed A–C. Typewriter A began its fifth and final
              stint at the beginning of Scene 2, starting in the mid-
              dle of TS p. 67.

310.30   *SCENE:*] Here begins the professionally typed fair
              copy prepared as script. No manuscript survives for
              this act.

Alterations in the Copy-Texts

Villagers of 1840–3

28.2   *Wife,* Joanna.] *interlined with a caret.*

28.4   Dr. Meredith] *originally* 'Drs', *the* 's' *wiped out and the period added.*

28.9   Lawyer] *the* 'L' *written over wiped-out* 'D'.

29.3   not much] *follows canceled* 'a'.

29.24   the mates] *follows canceled* 'her'.

30.1   Lucy Lockwood] *follows canceled period.*

30.14   Worked] *follows canceled* 'Became'.

31.20   Little Joe] 'L' *written over* 'J'.

32.6   *Mary.*] *written over wiped-out* 'Eli'.

32.12   He died in Texas. Family.] *squeezed in.*

32.13   Slept with] *interlined with a caret above canceled* 'Married'.

32.14   The baker] 'The' *appears to be added at the end of the line before; the* 'B' *in MS* 'Baker' *not reduced to* 'b'.

32.28–29   —serenader] *interlined with a caret.*

33.13   But one college-man.] *interlined with a caret.*

33.16   Pet] *follows canceled* 'B'.

34.9   didn't] *follows canceled* 'then'.

34.9   succeed] 'ed' *written over* 'ss'.

34.15   talked] *interlined with a caret.*

34.15   N-Yorliuns] *originally* 'N. Yorlyuns'; *the* 'y' *canceled and* 'i' *substituted.*

34.22   Boz] *follows canceled dash; the* 'B' *written over* 'D'.

34.22–23   Pirates . . . society.] *interlined with a caret.*

34.24–25   Last Rose of Summer.] *interlined above* 'The Last Link'.

34.25–26   for . . . bride] *squeezed in.*

34.26–27   Gaily . . . Alforata.] *squeezed in.*

35.12   it] *originally* 'its'; *the* 's' *canceled.*

36.18–19   brought Helen Kercheval] *originally* 'brought Helen to'; 'to' *written over first by the beginning loop of a capital letter, possibly* 'G', *and then by the* 'K' *of* 'Kercheval'.

36.24   cursed] *written over what may be wiped-out* 'ab' [*i.e.* 'abused'] *or* 'al' [*i.e.* 'always'].

36.29   modest] *interlined above* 'the'.

37.5   Masons] 'M' *mended from* 'm'.

38.15   before] *follows canceled* 'and [   ]'.

38.20   year] *interlined with a caret above canceled* 'fortnight'.

38.20   the family] *interlined with a caret above canceled* 'his mother's'.

38.21   spring lock] 'spr' *written over wiped-out* 'the [   ]'.

38.30   neighboring town] *follows canceled* 'ball in'.

38.35   M. born . . . 10.] *interlined above* 'Small storekeeper'.

39.6   benefit] *followed by canceled quotation mark.*

40.12   commission] *the 'c' written over 'p'.*

40.13   1865] *mended from '1866'.*

Jane Lampton Clemens

43.5   I knew her] *follows canceled* 'In many ways she proved herself a forceful character; in continuing to live for nearly half a century after the physicians had placed her under sentence of death'.

43.11–12   Technically . . . sort.] *added on verso with instructions to turn over, inserted with a caret before canceled* 'For I think her character had interesting features, whereas this cannot be claimed for her career.'; 'was' *interlined with a caret above previously canceled* 'had', *then canceled.*

43.14   my mental] *follows canceled* 'I must'.

43.15   first] *follows canceled* 'earliest'.

43.16   of early date] *interlined with a caret.*

44.1–2   a very strong impression] *originally* 'so strong an impression'; 'a very' *interlined with a caret above canceled* 'so'; 'an' *canceled.*

44.2–3   holds . . . memorable.] *interlined above canceled* 'has held its place unimpaired in my memory until now.'

44.7–8   is this] *follows canceled* 'was this'.

44.9–10   she felt a strong interest] *interlined with a caret above canceled* 'took'.

44.10   everything and everybody in it.] *squeezed in at foot of page following canceled* 'all its concerns.'

44.16   and an] *interlined with a caret above canceled* 'and a clear'.

44.16   formidable] *interlined with a caret above canceled* 'tough'.

44.17   vanquish] *interlined with a caret above canceled* 'kill.'

44.21   in the] *follows canceled* 'in even the'.

44.27   sure enough,] *follows canceled* 'the'.

44.31   Satan was just] 'S' *possibly written over canceled* '&'.

45.2–3   a single] *interlined with a caret; followed by a misplaced comma. See "Emendations of the Copy-Texts."*

45.12   but gentle . . . appealing; and] *added later at the bottom of the page.*

45.13   simply] *interlined with a caret above canceled* 'beautifully'.

45.13   many] *interlined with a caret replacing canceled* 'a hundred'; 'hundred' *interlined with a caret above previously canceled* 'thousand'.

45.14   have] *interlined with a caret.*

45.18   in our village] *interlined with a caret.*

45.19   chasing his] 'his' *written over wiped-out* 'a'.

45.27   the man's] 'the' *interlined with a caret above canceled* 'that'.

45.28   asked] 'a' *written over wiped-out* 'g'.

45.34   she walked] *originally* 'I saw her walk'; 'I saw her' *canceled;* 'she' *and* 'ed' *interlined with carets.*

45.35   surprised] *originally* 'surprise and amuse'; 'and amuse' *canceled;* 'd' *interlined with a caret.*

46.1   persuasive] *interlined with a caret above canceled* 'moving'.

46.2   tripped] *interlined with a caret above canceled* 'surprised'.

46.3   also into] *interlined with a caret.*

46.4   —a promise that he] *interlined with a caret above canceled* '—that'.

46.18   including] 'in' *written over wiped-out* 'to'.

46.21	was out of the question] *interlined with a caret.*
46.21	my mother] *follows canceled* 'why,'.
46.33	with] 'w' *written over* 'o'.
46.36	States] 'S' *mended from* 's'.
47.6	and also] *follows canceled* 'and d'.
47.7–8	the Lambtons] *follows canceled* 'her ancestors the Lambtons'.
47.8	family] *interlined with a caret above canceled* 'same'.
47.9	that they] *interlined with a caret above canceled* 'and'.
47.11	—cautiously,] *follows canceled* 'that'.
47.15	an entail] 'an' *written over wiped-out* 'enta'.
47.16	do it,] *comma mended from semicolon.*
47.19	own] *interlined with a caret.*
47.35	a painful] *follows canceled* 'an'.
48.2	Lambton] 'b' *interlined with a caret above canceled* 'p'.
48.3	or so] *interlined with a caret.*
48.4	fraud,] *interlined with a caret above canceled* 'sham,'.
48.11	—a second . . . his,—] *interlined with a caret.*
48.20	sometimes] 'so' *written over wiped-out* 'of'.
48.30	animals.] *follows canceled* 'cattle'.
48.30	wish I] *follows canceled* 'used to'.
48.33	with it] 'it' *interlined with a caret above canceled* 'the institution'.
49.7	be daily] 'be' *interlined with a caret.*
49.8	Manifestly] *follows canceled* 'It is'.
49.8	can accomplish] 'can' *apparently added to the end of the line.*
49.14	meek] *apparently added to the end of the line.*

49.16   However, there] 'However,' *interlined with a caret;* 'T'
               of MS 'There' *not reduced to* 't'.

49.17–18   the mild] *interlined with a caret.*

49.20   separate and] *interlined with a caret.*

49.24   and commonplace] *interlined with a caret.*

49.26   once,] *follows canceled* 'in'.

49.31   He] 'H' *written over wiped-out* 'T'.

49.32   bought and conveyed] *follows canceled* 'glided about by
               night, tempting straightened masters with the chink of
               his unholy coin'; 'glided' *preceded by unrecoverable can-
               celed word.*

49.36   nothing would] *follows canceled* 'he was'.

50.3   incident] *interlined with a caret above canceled* 'in-
               stance'.

50.3   For a time] *follows canceled* 'Once' *on discarded portion
               of the manuscript.*

50.10   she is] 'she' *interlined with a caret above canceled* 'her
               master'.

50.14   and always] 'and' *interlined with a caret.*

50.15 *   singing."] *followed by canceled paragraph* 'Well, he
               didn't stop'.

50.17   own personal] 'own' *apparently added at end of line.*

50.20   trial,] *comma replaces a canceled semicolon.*

50.21–22   she pleaded hard—] *interlined with a caret above can-
               celed* 'the woman pleaded'.

51.13   at that.] *followed by canceled quotation marks.*

51.21   was] *interlined with a caret above canceled* 'had'.

51.22 $50] *follows canceled* '$250.'

51.26   exile] *follows canceled* 'separation'.

51.31	years.] *follows canceled* 'years and the blessed destruction of'.
51.33	I being] *originally* 'for I was'; 'I being' *interlined with a caret.*
52.1	ever ready] *follows what appears to be canceled* 'was'.
52.8	fond of] *originally* 'fonder'; 'of' *written over wiped-out* 'er'.
52.11	to be] *interlined with a caret above canceled* 'was'.
52.25	gone by;] *interlined with a caret above canceled* 'ago;'.
52.27	and her] 'her' *interlined with a caret.*
52.32	disordered fancy] *interlined with a caret.*

Tupperville-Dobbsville

55.3	some few] 'few' *interlined with a caret.*
55.8	building] *originally* 'build-/ing'; 'build-' *followed by canceled* 'ing projected a corner over the water'; 'ing' *restored at the beginning of the next line.*
55.9	for the next] *follows canceled* 'till'.
55.12	Twice] *follows canceled* 'Every'.
56.10	main floors] *follows canceled* 'first'.
57.10	superior] *follows canceled* 'the average'.
57.11	will be easily perceived] *follows canceled* 'was'; 'will' *interlined with a caret;* 'perceived' *follows canceled* 'seen'.
57.12	rudeness,] *follows canceled* 'nakedness,'.

Clairvoyant

This list of alterations in the manuscript includes those which emphasize or change language, dialect, tone, or characterization and those which seem to indicate a shift of direction. Other alterations have not been recorded.

61.4   excited] *interlined with a caret above canceled* 'drew'.

61.4   curiosity] *follows canceled* 'attention'.

61.5   place;] *follows canceled* 'hamlet;'.

61.14   cooked . . . ate,] *interlined with a caret; the comma preceding added.*

61.15–16   seen . . . hours.] *follows canceled* 'very often'; 'oftener . . . hours.' *interlined with a caret following a canceled period.*

61.20–62.1   and . . . anywhere] *interlined with a caret.*

62.3   everybody.] *followed by canceled* '; and yet nobody'; *the period added.*

62.9   wish to.] *followed by canceled paragraph* 'Two other things about this man had been noticed and remarked upon. One was,'.

62.18   while] *interlined with a caret.*

62.19   plausible] *follows canceled* 'very'.

63.8   believed] *followed by canceled* 'I was'.

63.16   out of his seat] *interlined with a caret above canceled* 'to his feet'.

63.26   felt foolish enough; I] *interlined above canceled* 'and'; 'and' *restored at the end of the line above.*

65.34   searched] *follows canceled* 'soon app'.

66.11   face] *follows canceled* 'eye'.

A Human Bloodhound

69.4   always] *originally* 'almost'; 'ways' *written over wiped-out* 'most'.

69.7   with me,] *followed by canceled* 'I being'.

69.13   Corpse] 'C' *written over* 'c'.

69.15   although] 'a' *written over* '&'.

70.4	his breadth] *follows canceled* 'the'.
70.7	birthmark] *originally* 'birthmarks'; *the* 's' *canceled*.
70.9	effect] *follows canceled* 'result'.
70.29	The children] *follows canceled* 'Then followed'.
71.5–6	but it . . . him to] 'it . . . to' *interlined with a caret above canceled* 'but he would not'; 'but' *added to the end of the preceding line*.
71.6	exhibitions of it] *followed by a wiped-out period*.
71.19	Corpse] 'C' *written over* 'c'.
71.36	room in] *follows canceled* 'of,'; *the comma wiped out*.
72.9	will you search] *follows canceled* '—between the ticks, I think; will you take it out, deacon, or must I?" '
72.21–22	name all] *follows canceled* 'tell you'.
72.24	Black] *interlined with a caret above canceled* 'So and so'.
72.25	made by Mr.] *follows canceled* 'of Mr.'
72.28	the scent-spectres] 'the' *interlined with a caret following canceled* 'his'.
72.30	like crowding] *follows canceled* 'like being'.
73.22–23	strenuous] *interlined with a caret above canceled* 'powerful'.
73.24	projected] *interlined with a caret above canceled* 'sent'.
73.32	by his nose] *interlined with a caret*.
73.33–34	—always . . . sight.] *interlined with a caret above canceled* 'That is,'; *the period preceding canceled*; 'He' *following mended from* 'he'.
73.34–35	until . . . happen] *interlined with a caret above canceled* 'until you were tired; you would tire'.
73.36	of course,] *interlined with a caret*.
74.2	fleas, nor] *interlined with a caret*.

74.12   His sense] 'His' *interlined with a caret following canceled* 'You perceive that his'.

74.19   miraculous,] *the comma mended from a period.*

74.28–29   easily following] *follows canceled* 'without' *and canceled* 'protected against mishap'.

74.30–31   All . . . pretended.] *squeezed in.*

74.36   the whole circuit] *follows canceled* 'a'.

75.2   frightened] *follows canceled* 'badly'.

75.3   discriminating sight.] *interlined with a caret above canceled* 'gift.'

75.3   had *seen*] *interlined with a caret above canceled* 'saw'.

75.5   track] *interlined with a caret above canceled* 'scent'.

75.6   small] *interlined with a caret above canceled* 'new'.

75.11   thoughtless . . . has] *squeezed in at foot of page following canceled* 'stupid you are—he's got'.

75.13   swiftly] *interlined with a caret.*

75.19   with him,] *interlined with a caret.*

75.23   nose.] *follows canceled* 'smell.'

75.36   paper] *interlined with a caret.*

76.2–3   he had concealed] *follows canceled* 'it'.

76.32   bush,] *the comma mended from a period.*

77.6   no one] *follows canceled* 'he'.

77.21   said] *the* 's' *written over a wiped-out* 'p'.

77.24   otherwise] *interlined with a caret above canceled* 'or'.

78.24   visible] *followed by canceled* 'in the dark'.

Huck Finn and Tom Sawyer among the Indians

92.1   book] *follows canceled* 'big'.

92.11	Well then,] *follows canceled 'There warn't no use for it.' This cancellation appears at the top of MS p. 3. Since MS p. 2 is missing it is impossible to determine whether or not this is the complete cancellation.*
92.13	about] *follows canceled* 'aunt'.
92.16	two months] *interlined with a caret above canceled* 'so'.
93.2	little] *interlined with a caret.*
93.5	Well,] 'Wel' *written over* 'Bla' *and what appears to be the beginning of an* 'm'.
93.11–12	rousted . . . and] *interlined with a caret.*
93.13	and cut] *interlined with a caret following what seems to be canceled* 'and slide out' *or* 'and shin out'; *the manuscript is badly blurred at this point.*
93.14	hemp farm,] *interlined with a caret above canceled* 'plantation,'.
93.15	me and Jim] *follows canceled* 'Jim'.
93.21	k'n] *interlined with caret following canceled* 'kin' *at end of line before.*
93.21	ain'] *a final* 't' *canceled.*
93.23	need] *interlined with a caret.*
93.24	f'r] *interlined with a caret above canceled* 'for'.
93.32	ketches] *the* 'es' *squeezed in.*
93.33	him] *followed by a canceled comma.*
94.15	had] *the* 'd' *written over an* 's'.
94.16	person] *followed by a canceled comma.*
94.17	it] *followed by a canceled comma.*
94.18	budge] *followed by a canceled comma.*
94.26	a white] *follows canceled* 'an'.
94.29	time] *followed by a canceled comma.*

94.30   out] *followed by a canceled comma.*

94.31   but] *follows canceled* 'and you know it;'.

95.10   santering] *originally* 'sauntering', *the* 'u' *canceled.*

95.12   shucks for] *interlined with a caret above canceled* 'any-
             thing for'.

95.14   an Injun] *interlined with a caret above canceled* 'a white
             man'.

95.14   splinters] *follows canceled* 'slivers'.

95.20   flour] *follows canceled* 'flower'.

95.20–21   they can see him.] *interlined with a caret above canceled*
             'another person could do it with a brickbat.'

95.21   and fiery, and eloquent,] *interlined with a caret.*

95.22   and war paint,] *interlined with a caret.*

95.35   if he] *follows canceled* 'he'.

96.5   smell] *interlined with a caret above canceled* 'color'.

96.8   supernatural] *interlined with a caret above canceled*
             'gorgeous'.

96.9–12   the Injuns . . . strong."] *added on verso of MS page with
             instructions to turn over;* 'Amongst' *squeezed in at end
             of line on recto.*

96.13   so] *written over* 'he'.

96.16   Dem's . . . Jim!] *interlined with a caret.*

96.17   rotten] *interlined with a caret above canceled* 'powful'.

96.17   'e] *follows canceled* 'he'.

96.18   to study] *follows canceled* 'fer'.

96.23   behind] *follows canceled* 'if'.

96.23   I was.] *followed by canceled working notes for Chapter 2*
             'Outfit—preparations—escape from windows and door.
             Pack mule—lear[n]ed of Mexican. '

97.2	took] *squeezed in at end of line to replace* 'captured' *canceled at beginning of the following line.*
97.5	could a] 'a' *interlined with a caret above canceled* 'have'.
97.7	ornery house] *followed by a canceled comma.*
97.8–9	that . . . farm, and] *interlined with a caret above canceled* 'on the river and'.
97.10	and blankets,] *interlined with a caret.*
97.11	and fish hooks,] *interlined with a caret.*
97.12	and pipes and tobacco,] *interlined with a caret.*
97.16	farm] *interlined with a caret following canceled* 'plantation'.
97.19	fifteen] *follows canceled* 'the river'.
97.19	further] *interlined with a caret.*
97.20	five] *interlined with a caret above canceled* 'four'.
97.20	and saddles,] *interlined with a caret.*
97.23	in the State of Missouri,] *interlined with a caret above canceled* 'in that part of Arkansas,'.
97.25	months or so,] *interlined with a caret above canceled* 'weeks,'.
97.25–26	longer than that, I reckon,] *interlined with a caret above canceled* 'a month,'.
98.8	wrote a] 'a' *interlined with a caret above canceled* 'some'.
98.8	letter] *final* 's' *canceled.*
98.8	to . . . Polly] 'to aunt Polly' *interlined with a caret; then* 'his' *interlined with a separate caret.*
98.9	telling her] *interlined with a caret following canceled* '[2 illegible words] aunt Polly, and uncle Silas and aunt Sally, bidding them'.
98.11	her] *interlined with a caret following canceled* 'them'.

98.11   was] 'were' *mended to* 'wase' *then canceled and* 'was' *interlined with a caret.*

98.14   letter] *a final* 's' *canceled.*

98.19   started west.] *followed by canceled paragraph*

     'We didn't know where the Injuns was, but Tom said he knowed they warn't north or east or south, and so it stood to reason they'd got to be west, there warn't no other place for them. What he meant was, he didn't know just what particular place they was located in, nor how far off.'; 'north or east or south,' *follows a canceled* 'wes'; 'it stood to reason' *interlined with a caret.*

98.28   slept] *mended from* 'sleep'.

98.28   Three more] *interlined with a caret above canceled* 'two'.

98.29   way,] 'w' *written over a* 'd'.

98.32   daylight.] *followed by canceled* ', and keep'; *the period added.*

98.34   and at] *follows canceled* 'which was a disappointment, of course,'.

99.2   girl'] *follows canceled* 'strapping'.

99.3   Peggy . . . old.] 'Peggy.' *Interlined with a caret following canceled* 'Sal'; *the period subsequently mended to a comma and* 'and her little sister Flaxy, seven year old.' *added to the interlineation.*

99.4   Missouri,] *interlined with a caret above canceled* 'Arkansas,'.

99.9   good-naturedest] 'est' *written over* 'nes'.

99.9   folks] *interlined with a caret following an illegible one word cancellation.*

99.10   hardly] *follows canceled* '—specially about Injuns, till Tom told them,'.

99.10–11 —I mean . . . "learning."] *interlined with a caret; the original period after* 'hardly' *inadvertently not canceled.* See "Emendations in the Copy-Texts."

99.21   the brothers] *originally* 'they'; 'brothers' *interlined with a caret above canceled* 'y'.

99.24   ever] *originally* 'ever'; *the italics canceled.*

100.7   or a pistol,] *interlined with a caret.*

100.10   cave in] *interlined with a caret above canceled* 'knock'.

100.11   any] *follows canceled* 'off'.

100.12   through your hat] *interlined with a caret.*

100.17   comfortable] 'c' *written over an ampersand.*

100.23   down] *follows canceled* 'right'.

100.27   about a couple of weeks] *interlined with a caret below canceled interlined* 'some time'.

100.27   left the] *follows canceled* 'crossed the Missouri river and'.

100.28   was ever so far away] *interlined with a caret above canceled* 'got considerable way'.

100.28–29   we struck . . . and went] *interlined with a caret above canceled* 'and had just g[one]'; *the last word badly smeared.*

100.30–32   sun-down . . . glad] *MT originally wrote and canceled* 'sun-down, we struck the first Injuns we had run across yet. Tom was powerful glad to see them.' *on the verso of the manuscript page. He substituted the present language on the other side of the page following his revision of 100.28–29 above.*

101.2   Big] *interlined with a caret above canceled* 'Good'.

101.7–8   and here . . . around] *interlined with a caret above canceled* 'and not any more'.

101.10   most of them] *interlined with a caret above canceled* 'they'.

101.11   he would] *follows canceled* 'he judged'.

101.11   and rest] *follows canceled* 'about 2 weeks'.

101.11   the animals.] *followed by canceled* 'and fleshen them up a little.'; *the period added.*

101.13–14   her cheeks] *follows canceled* 'I see her eye lit up,'.

101.15   she never] *follows canceled* 'and I see her glance over kind of grateful at the old man, but'.

101.18   grass-waves] *follows canceled* 'low'.

101.26   as near . . . make out;] *interlined with a caret.*

101.28   boy,] *followed by canceled* '; k[in]d'; *manuscript smeared at this point. Canceled word too short to be* 'knowed' *which is used several times later in sentence; the comma added.*

102.3   upwards of] *interlined with a caret above canceled* 'more than'.

102.3–5   She said we . . . horses needed to.] *added on verso of page with instructions to turn over.*

102.6   Injuns,] *interlined with a caret above canceled* 'Indians,'.

102.6   spry] *follows canceled* 'five'.

102.7   tolerable] *interlined with a caret.*

102.12   I mean] *follows canceled* 'they'.

102.27   from] *follows canceled* 'of'.

102.30   named Hog Face] *interlined with a caret.*

103.2   and always said] *follows canceled* 'and sa'.

103.3   She showed me] *squeezed in.*

103.3–105.7   a little . . . when he was gone.] 11 inserted pages bracketed by instructions for insertion and for return to sequence.

103.5   and . . . her.] *squeezed in; the period after* 'for' *mended to a comma.*

103.6   "Who . . . you?"] 'Who' *mended from* 'What'; 'did give it to you?" ' *follows canceled* 'is it for," '.

103.14 mightn't] *follows canceled* 'mustnt'; *cancellation badly smeared, no apostrophe visible.*

103.17 "Goodness . . . and for why?"] 'I says,' *follows cancelled* 'sakes," ' *comma and quotations after* 'Goodness' *added;* ' "and for why?" ' *follows canceled* ' "and did you ask'.

103.25 said,] *follows canceled* 'quit trying to get me to promise'.

103.34 style] *interlined with a caret above canceled* 'way'.

104.2 sheath] *follows canceled* 'bucks'.

104.10 day,] *follows canceled* 'did'.

104.23 when he did] 'he' *interlined with a caret after canceled* 'they'.

104.32 maybe] *interlined with a caret.*

105.10 so,] *follows canceled* 'he made them understand it, and they was willing, and so it was all settled.'

105.15 and Jim] *interlined with a caret.*

105.21–22 with Flaxy,] *interlined with a caret.*

105.27–31 Man-afraid-of-his-mother-in-law . . . stuck to it.] *added on verso of page with instructions to turn over.*

105.32 The Injuns talked] *marked with a paragraph sign following insertion of 105.27–31 above.*

106.1 of a half] 'a' *interlined with a caret.*

106.2 the boys] *originally* 'they'; 'boys' *follows canceled* 'y'.

106.2–3 Hog Face in] *interlined with a caret following canceled* 'the other Injun in' *at bottom of previous page.*

106.5–8 They . . . time.] *added on verso of MS page with instructions to turn over;* '—all . . . gun—' *interlined with a caret.*

106.9 talking.] *followed by canceled* 'and the sun going'; *the period mended from a comma.*

106.17 or two] *interlined with a caret.*

106.28 the other] *follows canceled* 'all'.

106.30   he] *interlined with a caret following canceled* 'they'.

106.35   all of them] *interlined with a caret.*

106.35   and Jim and Flaxy,] *interlined with a caret; the semicolon after* 'her' *inadvertently left standing. See* "Emendations of the Copy-Texts."

107.7   at first,] *interlined with a caret.*

107.11   up as] *written over* 'as'.

107.18   set] *written over* 'sat'.

107.22   twenty-five] *the first* 't' *written over an* 's'.

107.24   knives] *interlined with a caret above canceled* 'guns'.

108.10   but] *follows canceled* 'But you knowed that before; I needn't to told you;' *the semicolon after* 'dead' *mended from a period.*

108.27   or anybody] *interlined with a caret.*

109.3   "Tom, where] 'Tom,' *interlined with a caret;* 'W' *of MS* 'where' *not reduced to* 'w'.

109.5   He give me] 'He' *interlined with a caret above canceled* 'Tom'.

109.12   We] *follows canceled paragraph* 'When night was coming on'; *paragraph mark inserted before* 'We'.

109.12   camp fire] 'c' *written over an* 'n'.

109.12   down] *interlined with a caret.*

109.21   sucked] 'u' *written over what appears to be an* 'o'.

109.26–27   or Injuns, or both,] *interlined with a caret above a canceled comma.*

110.8   blowout,] *interlined with a caret.*

110.13   as] *interlined with a caret.*

110.23–24   the air is so clear] *interlined with a caret; the comma after* 'there' *added.*

110.25   make] 'm' *written over an* 's'.

110.33   three] *interlined with a caret after canceled* 'two'.

111.4   minute] *follows canceled* 'second'.

111.15   of] *interlined with a caret.*

111.31–32   my poor little] *follows canceled* 'but'; 'little' *interlined with a caret.*

112.1   strangle] *interlined with a caret above canceled* 'throttle'.

112.11   thing—] *interlined with a caret above canceled* 'child," '; *the dash inadvertently repeats the dash before* 'if'. *See* "Emendations of the Copy-Texts."

112.16   He see . . . and] *interlined with a caret;* 'H' *of* 'he darted' *not reduced to* 'h'. *See* "Emendations of the Copy-Texts."

112.19   considerable] *interlined with a caret.*

112.19   entirely] *follows canceled* 'al'.

112.34   how] 'h' *written over a* 'w'.

112.36   and Flaxy] *interlined with a caret.*

113.11   was laying] *originally* 'way'; *the final* 's' *of* 'was' *squeezed in before canceled* 'y'.

113.19   he was coming] 'was' *interlined with a caret;* 'coming' *mended from* 'come,'.

113.32   lived.] *followed by canceled* 'I wished she hadn't ever parted with it; but of course it warn't no use to grieve about that now, so I forced it out of my mind, and wouldn't let myself think about it any more.'

114.2   me and] *interlined with a caret.*

114.2   told] *follows canceled* 'and me'.

114.12–13   with] *follows canceled* 'to ask'.

114.15   war path.] *originally* 'war-path'; *the hyphen canceled.*

114.15   It] *follows canceled* 'And I wonder'.

114.21   —there's] *follows canceled '!—'; the exclamation point reinstated after 'thing'.*

114.23   days,] *the comma follows a canceled semicolon.*

114.23   because] *followed by canceled '*, like enough it ain't'.*

114.24   job in,] *the comma mended from a period.*

115.12   and Flaxy] *interlined with a caret.*

115.21   by and by] *followed by a canceled comma.*

115.25   before] *interlined with a caret.*

115.34   and we . . . anyway.] *interlined with a caret; comma after 'it' added but the original period inadvertently left standing.*

116.4   a white man] *follows canceled 'an'.*

116.4   He] *follows canceled 'Th'.*

116.7   as soon] *follows canceled 'to'.*

116.8   again.] *followed by canceled closing quotation marks.*

116.10–12   So . . . him.] *added on verso with instructions to turn over; 'guessed' interlined with a caret above canceled 'was'.*

116.16   and cachéd] *follows canceled 'and the'.*

116.16   —that is,] *follows canceled '—hid'.*

116.16   buried] *follows canceled 'hid'.*

116.18   Me and Tom] *follows canceled 'The trail didn't follow any path or road, but went through the grass pretty straight across the country.'*

116.20   on the ground] *follows canceled 'out'.*

116.33–   He seemed . . . she wouldn't.] *added on verso with*
117.12   *instructions to turn over and to proceed to following page.*

116.33   seemed] *follows canceled 'ain't'.*

117.1–2   No hurry . . . by and by.] *interlined with a caret.*

117.18   or fifty] *interlined with a caret.*

117.18   that day,] *interlined with a caret apparently written over a comma.*

117.19   camp.] *followed by canceled paragraphs beginning on last line of MS p. 116 and continuing through canceled MS pp. 117–119* 'After supper I got Tom out to one side and says:

"He don't say anything about Flaxy. Ain't it your idea that he's chasing after these Indians only so as to find Peggy's body and bury it?"

"Certainly," he says.

"Well, then," I says, "what's next?"

"I've been thinking about that. He'll strike for Oregon, where his farm is, I reckon."

"That's my notion, too. Then what are going to do?"

"Why, get him to go along with us till we find out where Jim is, and then let us have a couple of the mules and we can shift for ourselves."

"It's good as far as it goes, Tom; but suppose he *don't* find her body?"

"Well, I never thought of that—he's been so certain. And I hope he *won't* find it. That will be the best of all, of course—for Peggy and for us, too; because then he will keep right on with us."

I never said anything more, but that wasn't the way I was looking at it. Whenever we struck the Injun's first camp, he would be expecting to find the remains there, and I judged he was going to be mistaken about that. What then? Why, then he will think he has overlooked that body along the road, somewheres, and as sure as guns he'll turn back and hunt for it for a year; and we wouldn't want to desert him in his trouble, and he wouldn't want us to; and so there we'd be—up a stump; for I warn't going to tell him about the dirk, I'd die first.'

'He . . . Flaxy.' *interlined with a caret;* 'only' *inter-*

lined with a caret preceding 'so far'; 'go along' *follows canceled* 'let us have'. *See "Textual Notes".*

117.20   Well,] *follows canceled* 'a sweat, now, but he wasn't, and I was powerful glad.'

117.21   away] *follows canceled* 'or more'.

117.35   with] *followed by a canceled comma.*

118.8   three] *follows canceled* 'all'.

118.14   anybody said.] *followed by canceled* 'I didn't have anything to be ashamed of, and so I warn't ashamed.'; *and by canceled instruction to turn over.*

118.15   After] *follows canceled paragraph* 'Well, in the morning we reckoned he would talk Oregon trail, but he never said anything about it. He just took up this same old Injun trail, and moved right along. We let him alone, judging he would tell us his plans when he got ready.' *In* 'we reckoned', 'we' *interlined with a caret above canceled* 'I'; 'CHAP. 6' *squeezed in and centered.*

118.20   careful,] *follows canceled* 'mighty'.

119.5   thirty] 't' *written over* 'd'.

119.12   a hundred yards off,] *interlined with a caret.*

119.16   says:] *follows illegible short cancellation and canceled* 'said we better wait a minute and let him die first'.

119.20   When] *follows canceled* 'as long as you live.'; *the period after* 'it' *added.*

119.20   I don't] 'I' *followed by canceled* ''ve known better than to'; 'don't' *interlined with a caret following cancellation.*

119.22   Tom a look,] *followed by canceled* 'It was'; *the comma mended from a period.*

119.23   is] *originally* 'is'; *the italics canceled.*

120.8–16 We . . . ones.] 'We . . . glad,' *squeezed in on recto;* 'for his . . . ones.' *added on verso with instructions to turn over;* 'glad,' *follows canceled* 'very'.

120.13   Grounds] 'G' *mended from* 'g'.

120.23   but] *interlined with a caret.*

120.25   or] *follows canceled* 'nor'.

120.30   for them,] *interlined with a caret written over a comma.*

121.1   his] *squeezed in at end of line.*

121.9   Brace] *follows canceled dash.*

121.13   keep] *follows canceled* '[ ] it'.

121.19   a body] *follows canceled* 'it'.

121.25   vowing to] *interlined with a caret.*

121.25   allow] *originally* 'allowing'; *the* 'ing' *canceled.*

122.8   and the pack mule] *interlined with a caret.*

122.11   After a while] *interlined with a caret.*

122.20   answer up again;] 'up' *followed by a canceled comma.*

122.24   When we] 'Chap. 7.' *interlined with a caret and centered above.*

123.3   "Huck,] *follows canceled paragraph* ' "Great Scott, you don't'.

123.5   But I didn't.] *interlined with a caret.*

123.13   chance."] *follows canceled* 'little'.

123.20   I says:] *follows canceled* 'I warnt'; *no apostrophe visible.*

123.26   a greeny] *interlined with a caret above canceled* 'he'.

123.27   Loses] *follows canceled* 'In'; 'L' *written over an* 'a'.

124.9   He didn't . . . he says:] 'He didn't say . . . but' *squeezed in above canceled paragraph* 'He looked a good deal worried, and started to say first one encouraging thing and then another, but didn't finish, and at'; 'at last he says:' *follows cancellation;* 'at' *interlined with a caret.*

124.11   If] *follows canceled opening quotation marks.*

124.17   But] *follows canceled* 'But the sun come up at last, and'; 'But' *written over an ampersand.*

124.18   patches] *follows canceled* 'hunks and'.

124.19   and took . . . with him,] *interlined with a caret.*

124.21   around camp] 'camp' *written over* 'in'.

124.26   mile] *originally* 'miles'; *the* 's' *canceled.*

124.28   time] 't' *mended from* 'd'.

124.29   an] *interlined with a caret above canceled* 'a half an'.

125.7   hands] *follows canceled* 'face'.

125.8–9   and all swelled up] *interlined with a caret.*

125.13–14 very . . . steel-trap.] *interlined with a caret above canceled* 'like a skeleton—'.

125.18   then tried] 'then' *interlined with a caret.*

125.19   struggling] *followed by a canceled comma.*

125.20   pitiful] *interlined with a caret at end of line, replacing what seems to be canceled* 'piteous' *at beginning of following line.*

125.26   spoonfuls] *originally* 'spoonsful'.

125.28   hid it;] *follows canceled* 'put it'.

125.29   half an hour] 'an' *interlined with a caret.*

126.4   once] *mended from* 'one'.

126.13   about] *interlined with a caret.*

126.17   had pulled] *follows canceled* 'was loose from'.

126.21   but I dasn't] *follows canceled* 'beca'; *the* 'a' *half-formed.*

126.21   go] *interlined with a caret.*

126.29   before . . . home] *interlined with a caret.*

127.9   yet,] *interlined with a caret which cancels the original comma.*

127.9   breathe] *followed by a canceled exclamation point.*

127.11   he hadn't sloped] *interlined with a caret.*

127.12   the tent] 'the' *interlined with a caret above canceled* 'my'.

127.25   around] *followed by a canceled comma.*

127.28   comes one of them] *interlined with a caret.*

127.33   his relics] *interlined with a caret above canceled* 'this dead man'.

128.4   or more] *interlined with a caret.*

128.19   bearing to the right,] *interlined with a caret.*

128.20   must be] *interlined with a caret above canceled* 'was'.

128.20   on a short-cut] *interlined with a caret.*

128.21   I misjudged] *follows canceled* 'they didn't'.

128.22–23 because . . . fog.] 'because . . . comes' *interlined with a caret on recto;* 'from, in a fog.' *added on verso with instructions to turn over.*

128.26   wish the fog] 'the' *interlined with a caret above canceled* 'that'.

128.32   my] *squeezed in at end of line.*

128.33   ever] *the first* 'e' *written over what appears to be a* 'w'.

129.2   it might] *follows canceled* 'it would'.

129.8–9   and stuck . . . track] *interlined with a caret.*

129.23   We was . . . now.] *interlined with a caret.*

129.30   late] *follows canceled* 'in the'.

129.30   flattish] *interlined with a caret.*

129.30–31 small trees] *follows canceled* 'trees'.

130.2–3   a nearly . . . swale] *interlined with a caret.*

130.7–8   and a bucket,] *interlined with a caret.*

130.10   new-made] *interlined with a caret.*

130.11	twenty] *follows canceled* 'a'.
130.11	there was] *follows canceled* 'they was'.
130.15	easy] *interlined with a caret.*
130.16–17	up and] *interlined with a caret.*
130.17	here] *interlined with a caret.*
130.25	and I told] 'a' *of* 'and' *mended from* 'A'; *the semicolon following* 'camped' *mended from a period.*
130.27	traveling] *follows canceled* 'g'.
130.30	Sis,] *followed by a canceled dash.*
130.35	one of] *interlined with a caret.*
130.35	somewheres."] *follows canceled* 'onc'.
130.36	"Seen him?] *followed by canceled closing quotation marks.*
131.3	poor] *interlined with a caret.*
131.8	I says] *follows canceled* 'So'.
131.12	sure as] *interlined with a caret.*
131.16	from] *follows canceled* 'so's'.
131.34	and sung] *follows canceled* 'which'.
132.5	—and next . . . by] *interlined with a caret; the period following* 'by' *inadvertently added. See* "Emendations of the Copy-Texts."
132.10	Brace reined] 'Brace' *interlined with a caret above canceled* 'he'.
132.10	horse] *followed by a canceled comma.*
132.10	him] *interlined with a caret above canceled* 'the fellow'.
132.17	allowed] *interlined with a caret above canceled* 'didn't seem to' *and canceled* 'said we'.
132.20	and the men's . . . things] *interlined with a caret.*

132.21	our animals.] *interlined with a caret above canceled* 'ours'.
132.24–25	and no sign . . . fire] *interlined with a caret; the comma added following* 'anything'.
132.26	them for the] *interlined with a caret above canceled* 'the'.
132.26	the night,] *follows canceled* 'the gang for'.
132.26	animals] *follows canceled* 'horses'.
132.34	and he took . . . guns.] *added on verso with instructions to turn over; the semicolon after* 'to' *mended from a period.*
132.35	fresh] *interlined with a caret above canceled* 'new'.
133.1	cautious] *followed by a canceled comma.*
133.20	then] *interlined with a caret.*
133.33	to him] *follows canceled* 'at'.
133.36	broke] *follows canceled* 'was ready to break camp'.
134.7	You could] *follows canceled* 'The star'.
134.7	stretch] *follows canceled* 'w' *and what appears to be beginning of* 'a'.
134.26	and nearly . . . down,] 'and' *added at end of line;* 'nearly . . . down,' *interlined with a caret at beginning of following line.*
134.29	up . . . under] *interlined with a caret above canceled* 'out, and under'.
135.5	danger.] *followed by canceled paragraph* 'Our h'.
135.6	little low] *interlined with a caret.*
135.9	long, gradual slope,] *interlined with a caret above canceled* 'hill,'.
135.9	it come] *follows canceled* 'for as much as a half an hour, or more'.
135.25–26	on account . . . Flaxy,] *interlined with a caret.*

135.28   others,] *follows canceled* 'Injuns, bu'.

136.2–3   a water-spout] *follows canceled* 'an'.

136.18   hour.] *followed by canceled paragraph* 'We left, then,
                and traveled along the edge of the high ground'; 'high'
                follows canceled 'g'. *Since MS p. 209 is missing, it is
                impossible to determine whether this is the complete can-
                cellation.*

137.1   ragged] *interlined with a caret.*

137.4   I hid] *follows canceled* 'But if this rag'.

137.6   and] *follows canceled* 'and five steps off I found an'; 'an'
                doubtful.

137.7   and Tom] *follows canceled* 'and when we got to'.

138.29   too,] *interlined with a caret; the comma added following*
                'it'.

Doughface

143.2   hymn-book for,] *interlined with a caret above canceled*
                'Bible for, which I had took for an old debt'.

143.6   and I] *follows canceled* 'but'.

143.7   thing] *followed by canceled* 'made out of pasteboard'.

143.19   She never] *follows canceled paragraph* 'She never
                laughed any more after that'.

143.20–144.1   done what . . . had] *originally* 'done it if she had'; 'done
                what she' *interlined with a caret;* 'it' *mended to* 'if'; *the
                second* 'if' *canceled.*

144.14   like] *the* 'l' *written over an ampersand following a can-
                celed comma.*

Tom Sawyer's Gang Plans a Naval Battle

Out of 22 alterations in the manuscript, 11 are listed here as being of
special interest to the reader, dealing with emphasis or change of dialect,

tone and characterization. Apparent shifts of plot direction are also included.

147.12   gorjious] *interlined with a caret above canceled* 'tremen-
          juous'.

147.17   a-chipping] 'a-' *interlined with a caret.*

148.1   fifty-gun frigate,] *interlined with a caret above canceled*
          'sixty-gun brig,'.

148.5–6   on . . . Captain Hardy] *follows canceled* 'Captain
          Hardy'.

148.11   and aggravated,] *interlined with a caret.*

148.17   always] *interlined with a caret.*

148.20   he would] *follows canceled* 'it was all a picnic'.

149.15   and was] *interlined with a caret above canceled* 'such
          being'.

149.21   he] *written over* 'a'.

149.24   Van Wagner] *interlined with a caret above canceled*
          'Dick Fisher'.

150.10   whilst] *originally* 'while'; 'st' *written over* 'e'.

Tom Sawyer's Conspiracy

163.2   up on Cardiff Hill] *interlined with a caret.*

163.7   and hoops] *interlined with a caret.*

163.10   everybody] *follows canceled* 'the'.

163.13   schoolboys] *followed by canceled* 'was'.

163.15   river] *written over wiped-out* 'wa'.

163.17–18 dismal and ornery and uncomfortable] 'dreary and dismal
          and uncom-' *interlined with a caret above canceled*
          'uncom-'; *then* 'dreary and' *canceled and* 'and ornery' *in-
          terlined with a caret above* 'dismal'.

163.20–164.1 took the dug-out and] *interlined with a caret.*

164.3–4   to do] *interlined with a caret.*

164.7   lazy] *followed by canceled* 'fool'.

164.8   use] *interlined with a caret above canceled* 'sense'.

164.11   en he] 'en' *written over wiped-out* 'and'.

164.12   dat Prov'dence]' 'd' *written over wiped-out* 'i'.

164.27   keep] *follows canceled* 'plan out'.

164.29   ain'] *originally* 'ain't'; *the* 't' *canceled.*

164.32   as many] *followed by canceled* 'plans'.

164.33   Prov'dence . . . fust,] *interlined with a caret above canceled* 'dey ain' no harm in dat,'.

164.35   shovin' ahead en] *interlined with a caret.*

164.36   ain't] *follows canceled* 'don't allow." '

165.1   satisfactry] *interlined with a caret above canceled* 'comfortable'.

165.2   out at] 'at' *interlined with a caret above canceled* 'of'.

165.5   just] *interlined with a caret.*

165.5   buzz,] *interlined with a caret above canceled* 'gay'.

165.7   good] *follows canceled* 'mighty'.

165.10   biggest,] *followed by canceled* 'and noblest,'.

165.13   danger] *followed by a canceled comma.*

165.17–18   a person] *follows canceled* 'me'.

165.23   very] *interlined with a caret above canceled* 'awful'.

166.3   knowed] *originally* 'know'd'; 'ed' *written over wiped-out* ''d'.

166.6   'low] *interlined with a caret above canceled* 'have'.

166.17   and ontrustful,] *interlined with a caret.*

166.23   it] *followed by a canceled comma.*

166.24   biggest] *followed by canceled* 'kind of a'.

166.28   I think, was] *follows canceled* 'was,'.

166.29   That] *interlined with a caret following canceled* 'It'.

166.31   all] *interlined with a caret.*

167.1   sight.] *followed by canceled* 'Pork he would do without, if crowded, muskets he would do without, but musicians he would have'.

167.1   civil] *interlined with a caret.*

167.4–5   gets all] *follows canceled* 'gets the'.

167.5   that war] *interlined with a caret above what appears to be canceled* 'it'.

167.6   in the . . . yet] *canceled then reinscribed above the cancellation.*

167.7   Yes,] *followed by canceled* 'sir'.

167.12   place] *interlined with a caret above canceled* 'spot'.

167.22   What's a] *originally* 'What is a'; ''s a' *interlined with a caret following canceled* 'is a'.

168.2   over.] *interlined with a caret above canceled* 'done'.

168.6–7   found out . . . had] *interlined with a caret above canceled* 'says "b'George there's'; *an exclamation point and closing quotation marks canceled following* 'revolution'.

168.7   but] *interlined with a caret following canceled* 'which showed that'.

168.14   you] *interlined with a caret.*

168.25   for me.] 'me' *interlined with a caret following canceled* 'Jim'.

168.25   ole cuss] *followed by canceled* 'I ever struck'.

168.27   duke] *follows canceled* 'Duke'.

168.28	kings."] *originally* 'kings, you hear *me."'*; *the comma mended to a period; the quotation marks added and* 'you hear *me." ' canceled.*
168.35	likely] *follows canceled* 'mighty'.
168.35	oneasy] *originally* 'uneasy'; 'o' *written over* 'u'.
168.36	resk] *originally* 'risk'; 'e' *mended from* 'i'.
168.36	pulled] *interlined with a caret above canceled* 'jist braced up and pulled'.
169.1	and. . . . of] *interlined with a caret above canceled* 'That busted up'; *the comma after* 'Jim' *mended from a period.*
169.3	but ever since,] *interlined with a caret above canceled* 'but all these years'.
169.6–7	wages . . . rent.] *interlined above canceled* 'wages, and when you catch them paying the rent, you let me know.'
169.32	let it go] *follows canceled* 'had to'.
170.2	solid] *interlined with a caret above canceled* 'real'.
170.18	That] *follows canceled quotation marks.*
171.15	bent] *interlined with a caret above canceled* 'propped'.
171.18	conspiracy was] *followed by canceled* 'all right and'.
171.22	he] *interlined with a caret above canceled* 'Tom'.
171.23	It was] *followed by canceled* 'just'.
171.24	We knowed that for] *interlined with a caret above canceled* 'For'.
171.24	past] *interlined with a caret.*
171.25	strangers] *follows canceled* 'abli'.
171.29	yet,] *interlined with a caret above a canceled comma.*
172.7	paterollers, and] *followed by canceled* 'arm'.

172.13	terrible state] *interlined with a caret above canceled* 'most awful sweat'.
172.17	said] *interlined with a caret following canceled* 'allowed that'.
172.17	randyvoozes] *follows canceled* 'what he called'.
172.21	hanted] *originally* 'haunted'; *the* 'u' *canceled*.
172.22	lonesome] *interlined with a caret above canceled* 'lonely'.
172.32	hide] *the* 'i' *written over a wiped-out* 'o'.
172.33	on] *written over wiped-out* 'be'.
172.33	beat] *interlined with a caret following canceled* 'live against'.
172.35	would] *interlined with a caret.*
173.3	And] *interlined with a caret following canceled quotations marks;* 'W' *of MS* 'What' *not reduced to* 'w'. *See* "Emendations of the Copy-Texts."
173.5–6	give myself away.] *originally* 'commit myself.'; 'give' *interlined with a caret above canceled* 'commit'; 'away.' *interlined with a caret above a canceled period.*
173.6–7	to, either.] *originally* 'going to commit himself either.'; 'commit himself' *canceled; the comma following* 'to' *added.*
173.32	up] *interlined with a caret.*
173.36	conspiracy] *the first* 'c' *written over* 's'.
174.21	to propagate immortality?] *interlined with a caret above canceled* 'a Sunday school?'
174.36	cert'nly] ''n' *written over wiped-out* 'a'.
175.3	would] *the* 'u' *written over* 'r'.
175.15	take] *interlined with a caret above canceled* 'get'.
175.17–18	or trade in niggers,] *interlined with a caret.*

175.19   licence,] *followed by canceled* 'or they would fine you,
                and if you didn't pay it they'.

175.20   conspiracy, and] *followed by canceled* 'it'.

175.21   becuz it] *follows canceled* 'because it'.

175.21–22   the gover'ment.] *interlined with a caret above a can-
                celed period.*

175.25   en] *written over a wiped-out* 'and'.

175.31   our new] *interlined with a caret above canceled* 'this
                elegant'.

175.35   for] *interlined with a caret.*

175.36   becuz] *follows canceled* 'knowing'.

176.6   wisdom] 'wisdom' *canceled and* 'ingeniousness' *interlined
                above with a caret; then* 'ingeniousness' *canceled and*
                'wisdom' *interlined with a caret.*

176.10   catched] *interlined with a caret above canceled* 'took'.

176.11   no matter,] *interlined with a caret.*

176.15   thinking] *follows canceled* 'remind'.

176.17   thought of it] *followed by canceled* 'and we'.

176.25   full] *follows canceled* 'very'.

176.29–30   sell Tom] *followed by canceled* 'to'.

176.31   swindling.] *interlined with a caret above canceled* 'cheat-
                ing.'

176.34   was not] *originally* 'wasn't'; 'not' *interlined with a caret
                above canceled* 'n't'.

176.35   Sunday school] *interlined with a caret above canceled*
                'prayer meeting'.

177.1   handbills] 'hand' *interlined with a caret.*

177.8   but he] *followed by canceled* 'snickered, and'.

177.10	we would,] *interlined with a caret above a canceled comma.*
177.18	up garret,] *interlined with a caret above canceled* 'in his room,'.
177.20–21	except . . . satisfied,] *interlined with a caret.*
178.2	he] *follows canceled* 'we'.
178.10	home] *followed by canceled* 'and [ ]'.
178.11	satisfied] satis-/fied; 'fied' *reinscribed following canceled* 'fied and went to sleep.'
178.12	Tom's] *interlined with a caret.*
178.13	Tom warn't . . . but] *interlined with a caret.*
178.20	Tom] *written over wiped-out* 'to p'.
178.27–28	and some . . . grease,] *interlined with a caret.*
178.29	a] *written over wiped-out* 'I'.
178.30	could by] *follows canceled* 'could' *and doubtful* 'by'.
178.34	it wasn't any use] *interlined with a caret following canceled* 'we never dreamed of'.
178.35	she wouldn't;] *originally* 'we knowed she wouldn't do it,'; 'we knowed she' *and* 'do it,' *canceled; then* 'she' *interlined with a caret and the following semicolon added.*
178.35	got] *follows canceled* 'we'.
179.6	too,] *interlined with a caret.*
179.9	mysterious] *followed by canceled* 'and'.
179.18	mysterious] *as before, followed by canceled* 'and'.
179.22	right, and everybody] *follows canceled* 'the way it's been ordered from the beginning of time.'
179.24	basket] *follows canceled* 'basket and hid it in the woodshed'.

179.25   Jim's] *follows canceled* 'the'.

179.29   up garret,] *interlined with a caret preceding canceled*
              'where we had hid them in the woodshed'.

180.7   a hundred and] *interlined with a caret.*

180.9   up garret] *interlined with a caret above canceled* 'there'.

180.14   tired] *follows canceled* 'young, and'.

180.23   and thrashing] *interlined with a caret.*

180.25–26   die down] *follows canceled* 'come in'.

180.26–27   and then wheeze,] *interlined with a caret.*

180.35   wished] 'ed' *interlined with a caret following canceled*
              'did'.

181.1   one of] *interlined with a caret.*

181.2   L,] *followed by canceled* 'and I [?] jumped down into
              the garden and started.'

181.31   money] *follows canceled* 'price as'.

182.6   of packing-straw] 'of pack' *written over wiped-out* 'of
              straw'.

182.7   when it lightened,] *interlined with a caret.*

182.9   thunder might] 'might' *interlined with a caret above can-
              celed* 'would'.

182.10   might go] *follows canceled* 'would likely'.

182.20   Widow] *the* 'W' *written over* 'w'.

182.25   it,] *the comma replaces a canceled semicolon.*

182.26–27   he only] 'he' *interlined with a caret above canceled* 'but'.

182.27   done it] *interlined with a caret.*

182.27   in his mouth.] *interlined with a caret above a canceled
              period.*

182.29   out] *interlined with a caret.*

182.30	Providence] *follows canceled* 'the'.
182.31	as far . . . got.] *interlined with a caret above a canceled period and canceled* '(as far as we had got.'
183.2	when] *mended from* 'where'.
183.9	Fletcher's] *follows canceled* 'Fetch'.
183.9	thirty] *interlined with a caret following canceled* 'about thirty'.
183.20	herself] *interlined with a caret.*
183.29	Tom?"] *followed by canceled paragraph* ' "So Sid's'.
184.10	"Die,] *the comma replaces a canceled question mark.*
184.15	I would.] *followed by canceled* 'He wanted'.
184.17	Sid's] *originally* 'Sid was'; ' 's things' *interlined with a caret.*
184.17–18	when he said . . . us,] *interlined with a caret; the* 's' *in* 'said' *written over wiped-out* 'h'.
184.18	as fast as] *follows canceled* 'now,'.
184.28	all puzzled . . . up, and] *interlined with a caret above canceled* 'clean astonished, and'.
184.30	judged he] *interlined with a caret.*
184.31	vividest] *interlined with a caret above canceled* 'plainest'.
184.34	awe anybody] *followed by a canceled comma.*
185.1	from this . . . and] *interlined with a caret following canceled* 'and'.
185.10	she] *interlined with a caret.*
185.20	with the] *follows canceled* 'at the'.
186.6	me] *follows canceled* 'us'.
186.17	her.] *followed by canceled* 'run the business.'; *the period added.*
186.19	kind] *followed by canceled* 's'.

186.19   waiting] *follows canceled* 'and'.

186.20   and bleeds] 'and' *interlined with a caret above canceled* 'but'.

186.22–23   and so gets] 'so' *interlined with a caret.*

186.25   off] *followed by canceled* 'on'.

186.28   let] *follows canceled* 'and didn't'.

187.3   and got very bad,] *interlined with a caret.*

187.3   then] *followed by canceled* 'he'.

187.8   him, and cried] *follows canceled* 'him, and kissed'.

187.13   pet] *follows canceled* 'dear'.

187.14   but he couldn't,] *interlined with a caret.*

187.16   he took] 'he' *interlined with a caret.*

187.21   cry] *interlined with a caret above canceled* 'sorry'.

187.23–24   and aunt Polly crying,] *interlined with a caret.*

187.27–28   begun . . . t'other one] 'begun . . . down,' *interlined with a caret;* 'went . . . one' *added at foot of manuscript page.*

187.29–30   though . . . true] *interlined with a caret.*

188.7   she'd] *follows canceled* 'learn'.

188.9   to us] *interlined with a caret.*

188.10   we wish] 'we' *interlined with a caret.*

188.23   agoing] *originally* 'going,'; *the* 'a' *added and the comma canceled.*

189.1   of Rebecca] *follows canceled* 'of Rebbe'.

189.15   it;] *followed by canceled* 'he *shan't* die.' See "Emendations of the Copy-Texts."

189.15–16   and the mould's busted.] *interlined with a caret above canceled* 'The town can't spare him.'; *the comma after* 'Sawyer' *mended from a period.*

189.19   Speak out,"] *originally* 'Out with it," '; 'Speak' *interlined with a caret;* 'with it," ' *canceled and the comma and quotation marks after* 'Out' *added;* 'O' *of manuscript* 'Out' *not reduced to* 'o'. *See* "Emendations of the Copy-Texts."

189.26   In about a minute] *interlined with a caret.*

189.29   fetch] *follows canceled* 'go'.

189.32   place;] *followed by canceled superscript numeral* '1'.

190.11–12   can prove] *interlined with a caret above canceled* ' 've got documents for'.

190.12   what] *the* 't' *written over wiped-out* 'n'.

190.12   saying] *originally* 'a-saying'; 'a-' *canceled.*

190.21   buchstaben] *originally* 'Buchstabung'; 'ung' *canceled and* 'en' *added.*

190.32   setting it up] 'it' *interlined with a caret.*

191.4   fell] *interlined with a caret above canceled* 'dropped in'.

191.6   word] *originally* 'words'; *the* 's' *canceled.*

191.9   judging] *follows canceled* 'thinking'.

191.20   over] *followed by a canceled comma.*

191.21   solid useful] *interlined with a caret.*

193.11   up type] *follows canceled* 'up that'.

194.4–5   emblumatics] *originally* 'emblematics'; *the* 'u' *interlined with a caret above the canceled* 'e'.

194.16   asleep,] *followed by canceled* 'on the corner'.

194.28   window] *followed by a canceled comma.*

195.2   town] *followed by canceled* 'Saturday night'.

195.5   Flacker,] *followed by canceled* 'been here'.

195.28–29   you can't . . . And] *interlined with a caret above canceled quotation marks and canceled* 'And'; *the semicolon preceding mended from a period.*

195.34   Colonel Elder said] *follows canceled* 'But around'.

196.1   abandund] *interlined with a caret.*

196.4   night] *originally* 'nights'; *the* 's' *canceled.*

196.11   uncertainty] *follows canceled* 'blamed'.

196.12   and maybe . . . too,] *interlined with a caret.*

196.19   firelock] *originally* 'forelock'; *the* 'i' *written over the* 'o'.

196.25   iron] *the* 'i' *written over* 'r'.

196.26   Elder,] *interlined with a caret above canceled* 'Elgin,'.

196.27–28   war and] *followed by canceled* 'fit'.

196.28   the battle of] *interlined with a caret.*

196.34   all that.] *followed by canceled* 'and he shut down on anybody going around late, nights, without a pass.'; *the period following* 'that' *replaces what appears to be a canceled semicolon.*

196.34   up,] *interlined with a caret at the end of the line above canceled* 'up, feeling better'.

197.1   seem so] *originally* '. . . seem to me so.'; 'so.' *canceled following* 'me' *and interlined with a caret above* 'seem'; *the period added.*

197.3   "How] *originally* ' "We hain't got any passes; how'; ' "We . . . passes;' *canceled;* 'H' *written over* 'h' *and quotation marks added.*

197.3–4   Won't . . . us?] *interlined with a caret.*

197.6   going to be] *interlined with a caret.*

197.6   than ever, now."] *followed by canceled* 'We can get around, but other people are shut off." '; *the quotation marks following* 'now' *added.*

197.7   "How?"] 'Ho' *written over wiped-out* 'Th'.

197.8   "They'll"] 'll' *written over* 've'.

197.18   passes,] *follows canceled* 'the'.

197.18	for us . . . right.] *added; the comma following* 'passes' *mended from a period.*
197.22	a-rumbling] *interlined with a caret above canceled* 'a-fluttering'.
197.24	a-screaming] 'screaming' *interlined with a caret above canceled* 'tooting'.
197.33	Mary] *followed by canceled* 'ain't'.
198.2	wasn't] *originally* 'warn't'; *the* 's' *written over* 'r'.
199.14	noble] *interlined with a caret following canceled* 'gorjus'.
199.35–200.1	And we . . . back.] *added to verso of manuscript page with instructions to turn over.*
199.36	asleep] *interlined with a caret.*
200.12	up] *followed by canceled* 'with'.
200.24	went] *interlined with a caret above canceled* 'slid'.
200.27	me and Tom] *interlined with a caret above canceled* 'we'.
201.3	escape and] *followed by canceled* 'wash up and'.
201.5	Branch, and] *followed by canceled* 't'.
201.9	fire] *follows canceled* 'give'.
201.10	things] 'thi' *written over wiped-out* 'up'.
201.22	got] *follows canceled* 'laid his hand on'.
201.30	nigger] *followed by* 'man' *interlined with a caret then canceled.*
201.35	road] *followed by canceled* 'and w'.
202.6	him] *interlined with a caret above canceled* 'me'.
202.20	yonder] *originally* 'to'; *the* 'y' *written over* 't'.
202.36	chained,] *interlined with a caret.*
203.13	this way and that,] *originally followed by* 'like a'; 'like' *canceled; the* 'e' *of* 'examining' *written over the* 'a'.
204.6	design] *follows canceled* 'move'.

204.7   Huck, but we] *follows canceled* '; but Huck we' *and canceled* 'Huck, we only'.

204.8   for the best] 'for' *interlined with a caret.*

204.9   solemn,] *originally* 'solemn, and awful, and'; 'awful,' *canceled;* 'and' *inadvertently left standing. See "Emendations of the Copy-Texts."*

204.21   get] *the* 'g' *written over wiped-out* 'l'.

204.34   with it.] *followed by canceled* 'all of a sudden I thought of something—' *and paragraph* ' "Tom!" '; *the cancellation is reinstated on an inserted manuscript page* (205.21–22).

205.19   two weeks] *originally* 'a week'; 'two' *interlined with a caret above canceled* 'a'; *the* 's' *added to* 'week'.

206.1   Sawyer?"] *originally* 'Sawyer," I says'; 'I says' *canceled and the question mark written over the comma.*

206.2   you'll see.] *followed by canceled quotation marks.*

206.3   ask you that.] *followed by canceled* 'There's two frauds ain't there? One's got the two hundred dollars, and tother's yonder playing nigger.'

206.11   says, as] 'as' *interlined with a caret.*

206.19   weeks, but] 'but' *interlined with a caret following canceled* '; and'; *the comma added.*

206.19   glory] *followed by canceled quotation marks.*

206.21   ruther] *interlined with a caret above canceled* 'almost'.

206.25   he can't get] 'he' *interlined with a caret above canceled* 'they'.

206.36   meat.] *originally* 'meat?'; *the question mark canceled and the period added.*

207.28   When] *the* 'W' *written over what appears to be* 'T'.

208.4–6   then he . . . Bat's] *interlined with a caret above and following canceled* 'then we struck out and got to Bat's'; 'Bat's' *in interlineation followed by canceled* 'just'.

208.19   me.] *originally* 'me to'; 'to' *canceled and the period added.*

208.28   clews.] *followed by canceled* 'to be studying. One of his mysteries, I reckoned, that warn't ripe yet, so I let it alone. We slackened up, and it felt good; we had been worked pretty hard, when you come to look at it.'; *the period added.*

208.32   reckoned.] *followed by canceled* ' ; he would know it again'; *the period added.*

209.4   "They don't] *follows canceled paragraph* ' "They hadn't'.

209.16   half-dry mud] *follows canceled* 'damp sand'.

209.19   a dragging] *interlined with a caret above canceled* 'a toe'.

209.29   best way] 'way' *interlined with a caret.*

209.32   at it all] *followed by canceled* 'around. What is there'.

209.34   doctor.] *originally followed by quotation marks and paragraphs* ' "Tom, he dasn't go to town." ' *and* ' "What's the reason he dasn't?'; *the quotation marks and both paragraphs canceled; then* 'They don't know there's anything for them to be afraid of.' *added then canceled.*

210.5   "In] *written over wiped-out* 'W'.

210.6   they stole] *follows canceled* 'they stole, for Cap Haines ain't lending'.

210.12–13 I reckon] *interlined with a caret.*

210.15   five hours] *follows canceled* 'their best show.'

210.35–36 and change . . . clothes] *interlined with a caret.*

211.1   got a] *originally* 'pal's disguised,'; 'got a' *interlined with a caret and* 'd' *of* 'disguised' *canceled; the comma added after* 'disguise'.

211.5   Well . . . washing] *added following canceled quotation marks and above canceled paragraph* 'Well, when we had gone along down about a half a mile and was back of the hanted house, right there we struck the trail'.

211.9   gone] *follows canceled* 'got'.

211.13   like we was] *follows canceled* 'the same'.

211.30   took . . . compass and] *interlined with a caret.*

211.32   quiet] *interlined with a caret.*

212.3   through] *follows canceled* 'under'.

212.20   got] *originally* 'gone'; *the* 't' *written over wiped-out* 'ne'.

212.21   roosters] *follows canceled* 'chi'.

212.22   have it hatched] *follows canceled* 'hatch'.

212.27   saying] *follows canceled* 'muttering'.

212.28   good] *interlined with a caret.*

212.30–31   By and by Tom says—] *added to foot of inserted MS p. 141M;* 'By and by Tom got done thinking, and says—' *canceled on MS p. 142 following.*

213.8   starts in in] *the second* 'in' *interlined with a caret.*

213.9   village,] *interlined with a caret above canceled* 'town,'.

213.11   believe] *originally* 'believed'; *the* 'd' *wiped out.*

213.16   lay still] *interlined with a caret above canceled* 'jog along'.

213.17   town] *followed by a canceled comma.*

213.17   went ashore] *interlined with a caret above canceled* 'coming along'.

213.17   Cold] 'C' *written over wiped-out* 'c'.

213.28   a dime] *follows canceled* 'a quarter'.

214.5   idiot—] *the dash cancels a period.*

214.9   you tadpole?] *interlined with a caret above canceled* '? —ain't I here?" '; *the comma preceding added; quotation marks following* 'tadpole' *inadvertently omitted. See* "Emendations of the Copy-Texts."

214.13   for us all] *interlined with a caret.*

214.14   catfish] *originally* 'cat-fish'; *the hyphen canceled and the space closed.*

215.4   old Cap.] *follows canceled* 'old Genl'.

215.7   anyway.] *followed by a canceled dash.*

215.11   says,] *followed by a canceled dash.*

215.13   how] *originally* 'hows'; *the* 's' *canceled.*

215.20   What's] ' 's' *squeezed in.*

215.24   good,] *the comma replaces a canceled semicolon.*

216.11   old . . . come] *interlined with a caret following canceled* 'that the widow Douglas come'.

216.12   river and] 'and' *interlined with a caret above canceled* 'that time'.

216.14   her] *interlined with a caret above canceled* 'the widow,'.

217.11   nuther,] *the* 'u' *appears to be mended from* 'ei'.

217.23   me and Tom] *follows canceled* 'Tom and me'.

217.30   'tend the] *interlined with a caret above canceled* 'shirk the'.

217.30   be on hand] *follows canceled* 'not'.

218.26   an hour after] *interlined with a caret.*

218.28   and still] *interlined with a caret.*

218.32   he'll] 'he' *written over wiped-out* 'they'.

219.2   only hadn't] *follows canceled* 'had'.

219.20   made it] *follows canceled* 'the next minute'.

219.21   took any] *follows canceled* 'paid any'.

219.22   harricane] *the first* 'a' *written over a* 'u'.

219.22–23   to watch for the canoe,] *interlined with a caret above canceled* 'and talked two hours till we got to that town and went ashore,'.

220.4   I wish] *follows canceled* 'Lordy,'.

220.12   true] *follows canceled* 'shape'.

220.19   desprate] *originally* 'desperate'; *the* 'e' *canceled.*

220.19   would square] *follows what appears to be canceled* 'didn't'.

220.23   told him] *followed by canceled* 'a lie. I told him I heard a canoe'.

220.24   becuz] *the* 'uz' *written over wiped-out* 'aus'.

220.33   in a canoe] *interlined with a caret.*

221.1   we'll catch up] *follows canceled* 'we might'.

222.10   King's] *follows canceled* 'du'; *the* 'K' *of* 'King's' *written over* 'k'.

222.31   "It's] *originally* 'It was'; 'was' *canceled and the* ' 's' *added.*

222.36   running] *follows what appears to be a canceled period.*

223.3   really] *interlined with a caret.*

223.14   "No. And besides] *follows canceled paragraphs* ' "You bet they haint!" ' *and* ' "How do you know?" '

223.14   there'd] *originally* 'there was'; 'was' *canceled and the* ' 'd' *added.*

223.19   one of these days.] *follows canceled* 'some d'.

223.23   Everybody] *follows canceled* 'I'.

224.4   Jim's] *interlined with a caret above canceled* 'our'.

224.4–10   for we've . . . trail] *added to verso of manuscript page with instruction to turn over.*

224.5   requisition] *originally* 'requision'; 'tion' *written over* 'on'.

224.5   for Jim] *interlined with a caret.*

224.14   It's] *originally* 'It rests'; 'rests' *canceled and* ' 's' *added.*

224.18   "It's easy] *follows canceled paragraph* ' "It's like this. Suppose Jim warn't a free nigger, but a slave. A slave in Louisiana, where the'.

224.18	down yonder] *follows canceled ' 'way'.*
224.20	helping] *originally* 'helpin' '; *the apostrophe canceled and the* 'g' *added.*
224.21	rights] *followed by a canceled comma.*
224.22	discovery,] *followed by canceled* 'for'.
224.29	"Not by] *follows canceled paragraph* ' "No, I don't. Becuz Jim never done it.'; 'I don't' *interlined with a caret.*
225.4	"Shucks!] *follows canceled paragraph* ' "Der'.
225.4	Why,] *interlined with a caret; the* 'B' *of MS* 'Blame' *not reduced to* 'b'. *See* "Emendations of the Copy-Texts."
225.6	order of] *follows canceled* 'oder of'.
226.5	he sees us] *follows canceled* 'he sees us and finds we are sheriffs and hears what we've come for—it'll have a good effect.'; 'and finds . . . for' *in the cancellation interlined with a caret.*
226.9	let on to] *interlined with a caret.*
226.10	idea.] *followed by canceled* 'You can keep up your heart, you needn't be afraid, now. Jim ain't ever coming to trial at all. We'll be back and snake him out of jail and rush him South before that.'
226.11	so I] *interlined with a caret above canceled* 'and'.
226.17	reckoned] *follows canceled* 'wouldn't peach on me.'
226.21	chased] *follows canceled* 'slo'.
226.23	whispers] *follows canceled* 'says'.
226.27	die.] *followed by canceled quotation marks.*
227.4	and of course] *follows canceled* 'and the fire doors was open'.
227.6	freight.] *followed by canceled* 'and swinging the stages down.'; *the period added following* 'freight'.
227.9	raft] *followed by canceled* 'on it and'.
227.10–11	with our . . . water] *interlined with a caret.*

227.17   tell anybody] *follows canceled* 'let on'.

227.17–18   and nearly . . . gay;] *interlined with a caret above canceled* 'splendid,'.

227.19   good] *follows canceled* 'lovely'.

227.23   Shackspur's] *follows canceled* 'Shakspe'.

228.6–7   down there,] *interlined with a caret above canceled* 'somewheres,'.

228.9   breaking in,] *followed by canceled* ' "why, it's nearly bound to happen, I didn't think of it—'.

228.13   for the] *originally* 'for them'; *the 'm' wiped out.*

228.13–14   a couple of days] *interlined with a caret.*

228.16   prime] *interlined with a caret.*

228.30   couldn't tell] *follows canceled* 'say'.

229.14   about a couple] *follows canceled* 'a'.

229.25   did he,] *followed by a canceled question mark and canceled quotation marks; the comma after 'he' added.*

229.30   a listening] 'a' *interlined with a caret above canceled* 'and'.

229.33   foolishness] *originally* 'foolishess'; 'ness' *written over wiped-out 'ess'.*

229.36   Gang—] *followed by what appears to be canceled* 'he'.

230.1   clos'ter] *interlined with a caret above canceled* 'nearer'.

230.11   cal'lated] *follows canceled* 'for'.

230.18   common] *interlined with a caret.*

231.1   across] *followed by canceled* 'and see'.

231.9   becuz Tom] *follows canceled* 'becuz she knowed'.

231.16   run tallow] *follows canceled* 'run tallow into them from the candle and made a thin mould'; *this cancellation followed by canceled* 'drawed them on a'.

231.17   leaf] *follows canceled* 'paper'.

231.20   heel,] *interlined with a caret above canceled* 'one,'.

231.21   do us . . . reckoned,] *interlined with a caret.*

231.25   so then I] 's' *of* 'so' *written over wiped-out* 'I'.

231.28   place] *followed by* 'there' *interlined with a caret then canceled.*

232.16   pow-wow] *interlined with a caret above canceled* 'row'.

232.22   jumps up,] *followed by canceled* 'and says—'.

232.28   ain't it so?] *followed by canceled question marks.*

232.33   about it, then.] *followed by canceled quotation marks.*

233.11   "No] *followed by a canceled comma.*

233.12   "Yes] *followed by a canceled comma.*

233.13   ain't. If] 'ain't' *followed by canceled quotation marks.*

233.33   and said so.] *followed by canceled quotation marks.*

234.1   pulled it in] *follows canceled* 'pulled it in'.

234.11   told him] *followed by* 'he warn't going to be hung' *interlined with a caret then canceled.*

234.30   and in the morning] *interlined with a caret following canceled* 'and took them down to the wharf in the morning and left them on the freight pile, and'; 'and took . . . in the' *canceled first and* 'and in the' *interlined with a caret above* 'morning'; *then the remainder canceled.*

234.31   eight] *interlined with a caret above canceled* 'five'.

234.32   get no information] 'get' *mended from* 'git'.

235.1   to say no,] *followed by canceled* 'plenty'.

235.3   Jim was] 'was' *interlined with a caret.*

235.11   disappointed] *originally* 'disapp'inted'; *the apostrophe canceled and* 'o' *squeezed in.*

235.21   calaboose,] *the comma replaces a canceled exclamation point.*

236.9   pretended] *followed by canceled* 'to be'.

236.15   couldn't] *follows canceled* 'was'.

236.18   showed he] *originally* 'showed he h'; 'h' *canceled and replaced by* 'was'; *then* 'was' *canceled.*

236.20   sorry for us.] *follows canceled* 'sorry about us.'

236.25   nudge] *follows canceled* 'sing out, to'.

237.1   she watched] *follows canceled* ' 'stead'.

238.4   made a speech and] *interlined with a caret.*

238.7   I was sorry] *follows what appears to be canceled* 'we'.

239.8   'most] *follows canceled* 'ha'.

239.15   Jim come down] *follows canceled* 'we'.

239.21   more] 'm' *written over* 'f'.

239.21   too, and Mr.] *follows canceled* 'too; but at'.

239.29   "Why] *originally* ' "What'; 't' *canceled and* 'y' *written over* 'a'.

240.10   tracks] *followed by canceled* 'and'.

240.15–16   and a lot of] *follows canceled* 'and some of the' *and canceled* 'but the others didn't'.

240.20–21   now and then] *interlined with a caret.*

240.28   yell] *followed by a canceled comma.*

240.36   'have it] *follows canceled* ' 'if you hadn't made me believe your leg was broke,'.

241.4   in such] *the* 'i' *of* 'in' *written over* 's'.

241.18   How was] *follows canceled* 'There ain't'.

241.18   them] *followed by a canceled comma.*

241.26   fooling] *follows canceled* 'play'.

242.1   George,] *followed by what appears to be canceled* 'in'.

242.9   Well, you] *follows canceled quotation marks.*

242.12   astonished] 'a' *written over* '&'.

242.20   He] *follows canceled quotation marks.*

242.26   Tom] 'T' *written over quotation marks.*

Tom Sawyer: A Play

The alterations in the Tom Sawyer play manuscript and typescript are too extensive to print in full. Only those changes which show a shift in plot direction or language or are of great length or importance are summarized here.

Act I. Mark Twain made extensive pencil revisions on the thirty-three pages of manuscript which he preserved from the 1876 version of the play. He changed Gracie's last name from Harper to Miller and expanded the description of the girls' period costumes. (Later he cut much of this description in the typescript.) After *"pull up garters"* he added *"no, re-tie them,"* producing the contradictory stage direction which appears in the present text (258.5).

He canceled a shorter version of the girls' quarrel and wrote a longer version of the scene (259.22–31) on the verso of a manuscript page. Their language was also revised: "Much I care about your old cat" became "I don't care anything about your old kittens" (259.17); "I'd druther die" was replaced by "I'd rather go without happiness all my days" (259.32); "dirty my *hands*" became "soil my *hands*" (260.5), "awful rich," "ever so rich" (263.9), and so on. A concession to the taste of Northern theater audiences is probably reflected in the change from "the Bloody Avengers had jay-bird heels like niggers" to "the Bloody Avengers were *chicken*-thieves" (264.35–36).

Four manuscript pages introducing Becky Thatcher as a new girl in town were excised in pencil. Amy's love note and Jim's attempts to digest it were added at the same time. Mark Twain must have been satisfied with the extent of his revisions in manuscript, for he made very few further changes on the typescript.

The remainder of Act I, written in 1886, shows very little manuscript revision until the entrance of the two armies (278.6). What revision there is, shows Mark Twain moving from simple narration toward more detailed dramatization. Aunt Polly's first entrance *"flying out at the door, fire crackers tied to a long string behind her"* (267.15–16) originally read simply *"appearing in the door."* Tom's search for the cake was set forth in a single stage direction, *"hunts for the cake doesn't find it"* before Mark Twain incorporated it into Tom's long entrance speech. In several interlineations and an addition to the verso of a manuscript page, Tom accumulates loot from the boys. An arresting revision is the change which eliminated the name of Huck Finn's Hannibal prototype: "Tom Blankenship doesn't know anything" to "Tom *Hooker* doesn't know anything" (269.11).

Mark Twain canceled the entrance of Joe Harper (originally called Jake Thompson) and added the entrance of the armies on an inserted manuscript page. He worked over the nature and description of their paraphernalia considerably, canceling references to kites and wagons; giving one boy a corncob pipe in an interlineation, then adding as another afterthought that the pipe-smoker was an officer; and changing Joe Harper's stilts to crutches. Tom's harangue to the troops is added on three inserted manuscript pages. Mark Twain also took great pains with the whitewashing scene which concludes the act, rewriting his stage directions and adding Tom's speech beginning "Come! Pay in advance" (281.1) on an inserted page.

In the typescript, Mark Twain added still more detail to Aunt Polly's entrance "(*or the popping of them heard before she appears*)" and cut a part of Tom's self-pitying soliloquy. He added "each . . . direction" and "or very soon after" (280.17–19) to the doctor's instructions to Muff Potter and Injun Joe.

Act II. Revisions in the first set of manuscript pages and the first group of pages from *The Adventures of Tom Sawyer* are slight. The reference to Murrell's gang (282.2) was added on the verso of a manuscript page. Huck's intervention originally saved the widow from being robbed; "murdered" was interlined later (282.4). Mark Twain originally intended to include from the novel more dialogue about the spunk water cure and Pap Finn's witching and revised the book's pages accordingly before canceling the passages.

With the second insertion of *Tom Sawyer* pages, Mark Twain began a process—continued in subsequent insertions—of altering dialect forms to standard English. He eliminated "ain't" at 285.14, 286.16, 286.20 and 287.31; changed "but mostly" to "sometimes" (285.15); "lays" to "lies" (285.27); and "was" to "were" (286.25). He followed this practice with still more vigor on the pages which he revised and later canceled.

Revisions on the typescript to this point (289.2) are minimal. Mark Twain deleted references to Jackson's Island and the haunted house as likely places for treasure-hunting and eliminated a passage where Huck suggests that the Widow will claim treasure found on her land and Tom boasts that she can't take it away from them.

With the exception of two brief passages which he preserved from the typescript, Mark Twain completely rewrote the remainder of Act II, substituting 12 manuscript pages for 10 canceled typescript pages. On the discarded typescript pages, Tom describes the robber band he plans to create when the boys strike it rich. The discussion is copied from chapter 2 of the not-yet-published *Adventures of Huckleberry Finn* with only slight verbal changes. It is introduced by a passage in which the boys decide to rest and talk a bit. The conversation ends when the boys hear what they think are devils coming to carry off Hoss Williams's body. Muff Potter enters, followed by the doctor, who begins quarreling with Muff.

Mark Twain preserved from the typescript the fight between Muff and the doctor and the stage direction for the murder with which the act now ends. He deleted the remaining typescript pages in which Injun Joe finds the gold in the hole the boys had dug, the boys try to abscond with the money, Injun Joe discovers that Muff is alive and claims that Muff killed the doctor, and the boys vow to keep secret what they have seen.

The manuscript for these discarded pages also shows signs of struggle. Originally Mark Twain concluded the discussion of the robber band with a retrospective account of the attack on the Sunday-school picnic, taken from *Adventures of Huckleberry Finn*. Subsequently he replaced these nine manuscript pages with two pages in which Tom berates Huck for suggesting that the band go marauding on Sundays so that the boys can continue to fight wars on Saturdays.

The manuscript pages on which the final version of the graveyard scene is written, however, contain only three or four minor revisions.

Act III. The manuscript for this act also shows few alterations. Mark Twain continued to expand his stage directions with minor additions: *"roguishly"* (292.6); *"and opens"* (292.5); *"goes with a heroic swagger"* (299.20); and *"in dresses of 40 years ago"* (299.22). He also continued to move away from dialect, changing "was" to "were" (295.31 and

296.4), "shucks" to "a *circumstance*" (295.34), "*licked*" to "*whipped*" (299.6) or "*thrashed*" (299.12), and so on.

He revised the pages from *Tom Sawyer* by reversing the original plot: Becky leaves in a huff when she discovers that Tom has been engaged before, while Tom stays and "*apparently cries*" (298.11–13). The stage directions which show Dobbins preoccupied by Muff Potter's fate were systematically added. "*That poor poor fellow*" (302.10); "*Ah, poor Potter*" (303.1); "*absently, from time to time*" (303.23–24); and finally, "(*To himself*) *'Who could ever have dreamed of his killing any one!*' " (303.25–26) all were interlined in the manuscript.

Mark Twain also carefully adjusted the climactic point when Huck and Tom interrupt the courtroom proceedings with their story. He lengthened the judge's already pompous sentencing speech (p. 308). Huck's "Go *on* Tom!" originally interrupted the judge before he pronounced sentence, but Mark Twain added the words "are *dead*—and may God have mercy on your—" and moved Huck's exclamation.

Mark Twain also tinkered with the long, separately paginated insertion which forms the schoolhouse exercises (see textual notes), by adding on the typescript: "(Pronounce it Ge-*no*-ah.)" The chief revision of the act, however, took place in the typescript, when Mark Twain introduced the three-page insertion, the "front scene" (306.1–307.36). No manuscript survives for this section, but Mark Twain added Tom's last speech and revised Huck's by adding, "Injun Joe would break loose and *kill* us, right *there!* We mustn't let out a single *sy*llable, Tom" (307.33–36).

Since only a fair copy of Act IV survives, there is no specific evidence of revision. But the working notes (see Appendix C) indicate that there must indeed have been considerable reworking.

Word Division

1. End-of-line hyphenation in this volume

The following possible compounds are hyphenated at the ends of lines in this volume. They are listed here as they appear in Twain's manuscripts.

Villagers of 1840–3

29.16   heart-hurt
34.16   Sunday-school
37.8   Gingerbread

Tupperville-Dobbsville

56.36   deer-horns

A Human Bloodhound

75.18   tree-roots
75.28   bedroom

Huck Finn and Tom Sawyer among the Indians

95.13   death-song
98.14   nigger-quarter

119.27   race-horse
130.36   blacksmith
136.2   water-spout

Tom Sawyer's Gang Plans a Naval Battle

148.17   light-hearted

2. End-of-line hyphenation in the manuscripts

The following compounds or possible compounds are hyphenated at the ends of lines in the manuscripts. The form in which they appear in this text has been determined by other occurrences and parallels within these works and by their appearance in Twain's other works of the period.

Villagers of 1840–3

32.16   antedate

Jane Lampton Clemens

51.15   soft-hearted
51.30   homesick
52.23   carefree
52.32   gray-headed

Tupperville-Dobbsville

55.9   overhanging
56.12   sidewalks
56.15   horseback
57.5   household

Clairvoyant

66.25   note-book

A Human Bloodhound

70.7   birthmark

Huck Finn and Tom Sawyer among the Indians

95.22	buckskin
96.27	tumble-down
98.29	daytimes
100.7	horseback
101.3	which-way
105.21	grass-waves
111.28	war-whoops
115.25	war-outfit
119.1	kindest-heartedest
119.8	zig-zagging
127.29	midnight
135.20	down-hearted
137.10	shoe-print

Tom Sawyer's Conspiracy

163.6	wind-flowers
172.27	slaughterhouse
178.14	nigger-show
188.14	between-time
197.24	a-screaming
226.21	mud-clerk
227.6	fire-doors
239.10	scare-bills
240.23	cry-baby
240.31	a-growling
242.1	a-working

3. Special Cases

The following compounds or possible compounds are hyphenated at the ends of the lines in Twain's manuscripts and in this volume.

Tupperville-Dobbsville

56.35	splint-|bottom (i.e. splint-bottom)
57.3	bed-|chamber (i.e. bedchamber)

Clairvoyant

66.13   crest-|fallen (i.e. crestfallen)

Tom Sawyer: A Play

269.10   fish-|hook (i.e. fish-hook)
281.13   hard-|hearted (i.e. hard-hearted)
307.28   *half*-|breed (i.e. *half*-breed)